Brothers-in-Arms

A World War II story

Also by Jack Lewis Baillot

Brothers-in-Arms

A World War II story

Jack Lewis Baillot

Dove
Publishers

Dove Christian Publishers
P.O. Box 611
Bladensburg, MD 20710-0611
www.dovechristianpublishers.com

ISBN: 978-0-9903979-9-1

Published in the United States of America

Brothers-in-Arms is a work of fiction. Names, characters, places and incidents are the products of the author's imagination or are used fictitiously. Any resemblance to actual events, locales, or persons, living or dead, is entirely coincidental.

Book design by Raenita Wiggins

To the unknown men and women who served in WWII

So many stories from the war have never been told for one reason or another. Although my story is a work of fiction, I hope that through it, those forgotten stories might have a chance to be remembered.

Contents

Part Three
The dreams that you dare to dream

Foreword

In January 2014, I arrived at work and did something unusual. I stopped to read the newspaper. The front headlines caught my eye. It had been an oddly warm winter, and the spring-like weather had made the front page.

Weather in my hometown has always amused me. Usually in January we hit below zero temperatures and everyone passing through flees as fast as they can go. This time, the rest of America was being buried in snow while I wore my jackets and enjoyed the sunshine.

The paper had an article about how the weather had passed up a 1970 something record. I thought if I read down far enough I'd see someone shouting global warming even though they'd been shouting second ice age the year before. I forgot all about it, though, when I noticed a man sitting nearby. Since it was part of my job, I smiled at him then went back to the paper.

"You're the author, aren't you?"

I looked up in surprise. I wasn't surprised he knew me to be an author, even though no stranger at work should have known I was Jack. However, I worked with my mom, and I remembered her telling me about a man whose car wouldn't start and she'd called my dad to come and help him. I put two and two together, being that she had talked to the man, this man was he, and my mom – proud of the book you're about to read – had been telling everyone about it.

No, what surprised me was someone talking to me.

"Yes," I answered.

"You're writing about Auschwitz?"

Still not over someone talking to me, my mind went blank and I didn't understand the question, so I quickly replied with, "WWII."

He nodded, and I calmed down. We began to talk. He told me he'd visited Auschwitz and I nearly began to cry. He then told me his dad had served in Africa during WWII, he was a pilot. I almost jumped up and down. I was currently reading *A Higher Call* and Franz – the pilot in the story – was in Africa. I recognized all the places the man named.

I listened with rapt attention as the man said, "My dad never talked of the war. He only had one picture taken while he was in Italy. He was staring off into the distance and one day I asked him what he was thinking when the picture had been taken."

(The picture was taken soon after the Germans had surrendered.)

His dad told him he'd been waiting for his orders to be sent to Japan. He would have flown the front lines, and he knew he wouldn't make it home alive.

"If they hadn't dropped the atomic bomb," the man concluded, "I wouldn't have been born. I copied the picture of my dad and gave it to each of my kids so they wouldn't forget."

The story struck me hard. I'd been editing this book at the time and was again ready to give up on it. I don't pretend for one moment that my story is anything like to what the men and women who fought in WWII went through. Mine is a work of fiction. But I hope through it, the men like this man's father, might not have their stories forgotten. Even when they don't talk about it, and all they have is one picture.

Part One
Somewhere over the rainbow

One
A friendship forged over sisters

1944

There were many times in the next few years when Japhet Buchanan wished he could escape his world and flee to another one like Dorothy in The Wizard of Oz. He wanted to slip away and find himself in a place where the biggest concerns were witches and shoes. He would even have been willing to face the flying monkeys.

He sometimes liked to pretend he was able to escape into Oz. He would close his eyes when Stein stood in front of him and yelled, demanding Japhet give up the others in the resistance. Japhet would cast himself and others as the characters and imagine how different life would be.

He would be the Cowardly Lion looking for his courage. Courage to stand up to his friend, to stand up to the world even after the world took everything from him.

Jimmy was Dorothy, pulled out of the world he had always known and thrown into one full of insanity. The idea of Jimmy being Dorothy always made Japhet smile because Jimmy would have thrown a chess piece at him if he knew Japhet cast him as Judy Garland.

Stein was the Wicked Witch of the East, out to take what he wanted and kill whoever got in his way. Sadly, he didn't die when he got wet.

The role of the Scarecrow was always filled by those who had insanity forced on them by the Nazis.

And Franz – Franz Kappel was the Tin Man. The man with no heart. The man who could coldly turn his best friend over the Nazis without batting an eye.

1931

They hadn't always been best friends. They hadn't known each other until they were eight and seven. But when they met, it was an instant bond.

It happened at church. The Buchanans were Jewish, but also born-again Christians. They didn't go to the local synagogue every week, but instead attended a nearby church fairly often. That was how they first met the Kappels.

The Kappels had one of those long, boring family histories that Japhet Buchanan had never cared about. Everyone in Germany seemed to have one, his own family included, and after hearing ten such stories he stopped listening. From what he did hear, the Kappel family had been living in Germany for over a hundred years, and the recent Kappels had been living outside of Berlin for fifty years.

There weren't many kids Japhet's age in the little church. Japhet saw Franz from time to time but for some reason never thought to talk to him. Instead, it was Mrs. Buchanan who went to talk to Mrs. Kappel one day after the service. After that the two women talked after church for a month, then Mrs. Kappel came to tea and Mr. Buchanan and Mr. Kappel began to talk. It was only a matter of time before the two mothers forced their sons into an introductory meeting.

It happened during one of the tea sessions. Mrs. Kappel brought her son over and Mrs. Buchanan told Japhet he should take him out into the backyard to play. Japhet thought the whole thing was stupid. Mothers couldn't just arrange friendships, and he knew Franz Kappel was older than he, so he didn't know why he had to play host. But Japhet wasn't one for arguing with the woman who could send him to his room without supper. He obeyed.

Franz also wasn't overly impressed with the friendship attempt, and for a while, the two boys sat on the woodpile and said nothing. That was until Japhet's older sister thrust her brown head out of her bedroom window and demanded that Japhet return her brush.

"It's your brush," Japhet retorted back. "Why would I have it?"

She'd yelled at him until she saw Franz, then she glared and yanked her head back inside. Once she was gone from sight, Franz grinned almost wickedly at Japhet.

"Did you take it?" he'd asked.

There was something in that grin. Some kind of camaraderie Japhet had never seen before in any of his other friends. He matched the evil grin.

"Yes."

The evil grin widened.

"I did that to one of my sisters last week."

One of. That stuck in Japhet's mind faster than eggs stuck to a hot pan.

"You have more than one sister?" he asked.

Franz laughed scornfully. "I have five older sisters," he muttered.

Japhet felt instant sympathy.

"I'm sorry. I have only three older sisters."

And that was the start of it. Because boys know something mothers might not ever understand. Nothing creates a friendship faster than finding a fellow sufferer in a household of all girls and no boys.

***

1933

The fire snapped and devoured a log as Franz stared at the page laid down in front of him. The words on the page danced in front of his eyes. He knew if he blinked they would clear, but he didn't feel like it. Across from him, Japhet had his homework book closed already. He had his sketchbook open and was drawing.

Franz refrained from smashing his head down on his open history book. It was December. One more week of school before the Christmas holiday. Franz had to remind himself of this, over and over. He could make it.

Of course, making it would have been easier if Japhet didn't get through his homework so fast, or so easily. The two of them always got together after school to work in the Buchanan kitchen, and Japhet always finished an hour before Franz. Then he would "doodle" with his left hand, even though he was right-handed. It was almost aggravating since his so-called doodles probably could have been sent to an art museum.

"You could at least pretend to care about my agony," Franz finally grumbled.

Japhet didn't look up from the landscape his pencil flew over. Trees and a rolling hill were starting to take life.

"I could," he replied, "but then I'd have to tutor you again. And you're an annoying student."

"Am not." Franz spun his pencil around on the table. "You're a know-it-all teacher."

"I pay attention in class."

A bird joined the trees. The bird was so lifelike it could have flown off the page. Franz considered shooting his pencil at Japhet.

"No one likes a bragger," Franz muttered just as Mrs. Buchanan walked into the kitchen. When she saw them at the table, she placed her hands on her hips and frowned.

"What are you two doing in here? There's fresh snow on the ground. Why aren't you outside?"

"Franz is too slow with his homework," Japhet complained.

Walking over, Mrs. Buchanan studied his history page over his shoulder. She smelled like firewood and fresh bread. She was a short woman, plump, with bony arms. Franz knew they were bony. He'd once startled her when he'd barged into the kitchen and she'd caught him in the stomach with her elbow.

"History," Mrs. Buchanan said. She shook her head. "It's almost the school break. You two need to go outside for a bit and get into a snowball fight or something. The snow is perfect for snowballs."

When Franz looked at Japhet, his eyes were twinkling. They both knew how important it was to get outside while the snow could be formed into snowballs. If they waited too long, it would start to melt and then all they'd have would be slush. Besides, when an adult said they ought to have a snowball fight it was impossible to say no. Franz slammed his book closed, Japhet laid his pencil on his sketchbook, and they raced to the door. They tried to pass through the kitchen door at the same time, crashed into each other, and fell into the living room where Mr. Buchanan was just coming in the front door. He removed his hat and stared down at them.

"I'm so glad to see my son racing to see me," he teased. "There's a mob of boys outside, by the way." As he spoke, Mrs. Buchanan came out of the kitchen, stepped over the boys, and went to kiss her husband.

"I just ran into Gert," Mr. Buchanan said, speaking of their neighbor across the street, after he'd returned her kiss. Franz only half listened as he wiggled out from under Japhet's leg and ignored his glare.

They snatched up their coats as Mrs. Buchanan did the proper thing and asked how the neighbors were doing. Japhet grabbed one of the Franz's gloves, dropped it on the floor, and pinned it under his foot.

"Great. The baby has finally stopped howling," Mr. Buchanan continued. Husband and wife ignored the boys as Franz shoved his shoulder against Japhet's chest. The younger boy didn't budge.

"Did they find out what's been wrong?"

Franz lived a block from the Buchanans but, like everyone else in the little village, he knew Mr. Leitz—Gert to the adults—and his wife had just had a baby boy who had been howling non-stop since he'd been born. No one could make the baby happy, and he kept neighbors and his parents awake. Right now, though, babies hovered in the back of his mind. He shoved his shoulder harder against Japhet, who braced his feet and grinned.

"The baby couldn't figure out how to eat."

Japhet and Franz stopped their struggle and Japhet squinted at his dad. "How can a baby not know how to eat?" he asked.

"It happens more often than you'd think," Mrs. Buchanan answered. "A baby is fed by a tube while in the womb. Then one day it comes out into the cold world and it isn't fed anymore and has to eat on its own. And no one is there to give it instructions."

Japhet grinned and dug his elbow into Franz's side.

"Bet you needed instructions since I wasn't around yet to help you out."

Franz pounced on him and knocked him to the floor as Mr. and Mrs. Buchanan continued their baby conversation.

"Gert said we can come over and see the baby now. You have to come with me so it won't be strange that I'm over there."

It wasn't easy holding Japhet down. He was smaller and skinnier than Franz and could squirm away. He wiggled like a fish and slithered across the floor. Franz jumped up and threw himself on top of him again, pinning him by the couch. They both banged loudly onto the floor, but Japhet's parents said nothing.

"You need more babies in your life," Mrs. Buchanan said.

"Yes, you should give me more. Then I wouldn't have to make excuses to go over and hold the neighbor's."

Franz heard lips smacking, a sound he'd gotten used to. Mr. and Mrs. Buchanan always seemed to be kissing.

"I'd gladly give you more kids, but then we might have another son."

Japhet snatched a cushion off the couch, somehow twisted around under Franz, and beamed him in the face with it. Franz stumbled back and looked for something with which to retaliate when he realized he was now being talked about.

"What's so bad about another son?" Mr. Buchanan had asked.

"Well, Japhet is this bad with a part time brother. Can you imagine him with a full-time one?"

Their hair standing on end from the wrestling match, Japhet and Franz both looked up. Mr. Buchanan's eyes had gone wide.

"What?" he exclaimed. "You mean Franz isn't my son?" He glanced down at Franz. "Why are you always over here then, eating my food?"

"Because I'm so amazing and he hopes to pick up on it."

Franz spun around with a retort to counter Japhet's teasing but instead got a face full of cushion.

Mr. Buchanan picked up Franz's glove and tossed it to him. "I guess you'll have to keep coming over then," he said with a wink.

"Funny." Franz tried to swallow his grin, but like always he failed. Instead he got to his feet, yanked on his coat, and dashed out the door before Japhet could hurl the cushion at his head.

Two
Snowball fight

1933

The first snowball fight of Christmas break always proved to be the best. Franz and Japhet held it in the Kappel's front yard since it was bigger than the Buchanan's.

Mrs. Kappel kept the water in her teapot hot so the boys could have hot chocolate when they came inside. Mr. Kappel helped them build their first fort. After that, they would pile more snow on it to fortify it as needed.

The moment they were let out of school on the last day, Franz and Japhet would dart out the door and meet up in the schoolyard. They would then race each other to the Kappel's front yard.

Franz always won the races. Japhet did his best. He pushed himself until his lungs burned, but his short legs refused to allow him to pass Franz. He always made up coming in second by jumping on Franz's back the moment he stopped.

Snow started to fall by the time Franz and Japhet reached the front yard. The fort was already built—they and Mr. Kappel had worked on it the night before. The moment they reached it, Franz and Japhet dove behind it and began rolling snowballs while keeping an eye out for the other boys. They took turns, one keeping watch while the other rolled.

"Are they coming yet?" Japhet hissed after half an hour had passed. Their pile had grown to a good size, but he was concerned. None of the other boys had ever been this late before.

"I'd have told you if they were," Franz retorted. "I'm not sleeping up here."

Picking up one of the smaller snowballs, Japhet threw it at Franz's back. Franz turned and jumped on him and they rolled back and forth in the snow, their grunts interrupted only by their laughter.

Japhet was getting the upper hand, which rarely happened since he was smaller than Franz, when a shout alerted them that they were no longer alone. Before they could get back behind their fortress, a snowball whizzed at them and got Franz in the head. Japhet snorted with laughter as he snatched up snowballs to return fire.

"I got one of them!" Japhet's friend, Amell, shouted. Amell was his neighbor, the one with the new howling baby brother.

"Duck!" another boy, Gilbert, yelled. He hit the ground behind a neighbor's car but wasn't fast enough. Japhet got his leg as he dove for cover.

Franz now at his side, Japhet picked up two snowballs and hurled them at Amell, who took longer to duck in an attempt to hit Franz before he got behind the fortress. Amell's snowballs flew harmlessly over Franz's head while one Franz threw found a mark. It smacked Amell full on the face and Japhet grinned with glee when he saw snow drop down his collar.

"How's your face?" Japhet asked Franz before he stuck his head up and hit the stunned Amell in the chest.

"Not fair!" Amell accused. He dropped to his knees and rubbed at his face. "I'm blind!"

"War isn't fair!" Japhet shouted. He glanced at Franz, who nodded. With a war cry both leaped up and charged Amell, hurling snowballs as fast as they could.

From behind the car, Gilbert whimpered and said something which sounded like surrender. Japhet ignored his pleas, ran past Amell, and pummeled Gilbert as he tried to wiggle away under the car.

The massacre was swift but merciless. Franz and Japhet never took prisoners and didn't let up until both Amell and Gilbert begged for mercy.

Grinning, Japhet sat down on the sidewalk and watched as Amell pulled off his coat and beat snow out of it.

"Your shirt is wet," Japhet said.

"You think you're so good at this," Amell complained. He brushed snow out of his hair and Japhet howled with laughter when it dripped down his shirt.

"You wouldn't be laughing so hard if this were a game of hide-and-seek tag and not a snowball fight," Gilbert grumbled. He had his glasses off. He kept rubbing them on his shirt to get the snow off but just smeared it.

Franz sat beside Japhet and said little, though Japhet had long since gotten used to his silence. Franz talked to Japhet but never said much to the other boys. Japhet didn't care, it made his friendship with Franz feel different than with Amell and Gilbert – closer somehow.

"I've been getting better," Japhet told Amell. Not only could he not outrun Franz but he couldn't outrun the other boys either. Amell was a year older, so not being able to outrun him didn't matter as much. Gilbert was a year younger and another matter. His mom considered him a genius, Japhet figured there might be some truth in that. Gilbert was the youngest one in Japhet's grade and he knew more than Japhet ever planned on learning. He spent all his time reading and was slightly pudgy, which only made it worse that he could outrun Japhet.

"Sure you have," Amell mocked.

Lifting his head, Franz glared at Amell and then exchanged glances with Japhet. They both grinned at each other.

"Don't believe me?" Japhet asked.

"Does it look like we do?" Gilbert asked. He put his glasses back on and water dripped down the lenses.

"You look scared to me," Franz said.

"We're not scared!" Amell shouted. He got to his feet and scowled. Japhet grinned just to annoy him.

"Fine." He got up too, Franz scrambling up beside him. "Prove it."

Then, before Amell had time to react, Franz reached around Japhet, slapped Amell's arm, and took off.

"You're it!"

"Try to find us and catch us!" Japhet added as he also turned and ran. Gilbert followed suit, stumbling off in the other direction, leaving Amell standing alone in the cold.

Japhet found an empty trashcan that didn't smell of dying bananas and someone's leftover dinner. He heaved himself inside, pulled on the lid, and slowed his breathing, not moving a muscle. Franz had taught him all his hiding tricks.

"If you can't outrun them find another way to beat them."

And he had. All through the summer he and Franz had perfected his hiding skills. Now Japhet bit his lip to keep from smiling as Amell ran past his hiding place. Once, twice, three times. It started to get cold and Japhet had to fight to keep his teeth them from chattering. "Buchanan!" he heard Amell shout once or twice before his voice faded off down the street. Japhet could have laughed.

Finally, Amell's voice was joined by Gilbert's, a sign that Gilbert had been found. More time passed. The chill got worse. Icy fingers came up Japhet's backside and climbed his spine. He still refused to move.

"When I get my hands on him I'm going to strangle him!" Amell snapped once, then his stomping feet faded.

"Where is he Franz?" were the next words to reach inside Japhet's trashcan. The question came from Gilbert. By then his fingers were little icicles.

"I don't know," Franz murmured.

Amell snorted in anger. "You do so, Kappel. Tell us! Before we all turn to snowmen ourselves."

"You give up?" Franz kept his voice level, but there was a note of triumph in it.

"Yes, sure. I can't feel my toes. Just find him for us so we can go inside. My dad will kill me if I leave him out here all night."

Franz laughed and Japhet closed his eyes as the lid came off the trashcan. Cold air hit his head and he lifted his face, opened his eyes, and looked up to find Franz grinning down at him.

"I think you won," Franz said.

Three
Hanukkah

1933

"I'm supposed to invite you to Hanukkah."

Franz looked up from the pile of wood and nails. He had locked himself in his dad's back shed, even though it wasn't really locked since the lock had long since broken off. It had something to do with Franz and Japhet trying to see if they could kick doors in, though nothing had ever been proven.

"What?"

Japhet stood in the doorway and somehow he'd gotten a hold of Franz's hammer. He held it out to him.

"Hadi said I had to come over and invite you and your family to celebrate the last day of Hanukkah with us." Japhet leaned in the doorway and frowned at his boots.

Hadi was one of the middle Buchanan girls. Her full name was Hadassah, but Franz could only remember one time she'd ever been called that. She and Kirsten, who was Franz's 19-year-old sister, were close. Probably because they had boyfriends with whom they liked to spend almost every waking moment.

"We always come over on the last day of Hanukkah." Franz, now armed with his hammer, began nailing boards into place.

He spoke between the banging. "Why is she inviting us now?"

"Something to do with Ross," Japhet said. Ross was Hadi's boyfriend. "I guess he's coming over and she said it should be more formal. Or something. I didn't really listen."

"If it's so formal why is she making you ask us over? Why doesn't she do it? Or have Kirsten ask us?" Franz didn't expect an answer. He had sisters. He knew half of what they thought up wasn't meant to make sense.

"I don't know. Just make sure you come, okay? I don't want to spend the whole day alone with Ross. I need you there for moral support."

Holding nails in his teeth, Franz turned from his hammering. He raised his eyebrows and Japhet grinned. Franz pulled the nails from between his lips.

"Maybe I don't want to come over now that I know Ross is there."

"If Kirsten hears he'll be there then she's going to bring Hardy. So you'd better come or I'm going to climb in your window at midnight and bury you in snow. And you know I'll do it."

Since Japhet had done it before, Franz didn't doubt one word. He shrugged and returned to his catapult. Japhet entered the shed and helped him by holding boards into place for him.

Franz had come up with the catapult design and idea. His talent didn't lie in drawing so he made up for it in other areas. Usually, they involved pulling pranks on Amell and Gilbert. He planned to set the catapult up behind the fortress and get Amell and Gilbert on the last day of the Christmas break.

They worked on it until Mrs. Kappel called them into dinner. Franz didn't know if Japhet had originally planned on staying to eat, but he didn't say anything as his friend sat at the table.

Not that it mattered. Both boys often ate at each other's houses.

If they didn't show up at their own home for dinner, their parents knew where they were.

"How's the catapult?" Mr. Kappel asked as Japhet and Franz claimed their seats.

"Good. I think we'll have it done by the end of the week," Franz answered.

Kirsten shook her head as Mr. Kappel grinned.

"This is one reason Hardy doesn't like to come over, Dad. And you encourage it."

Mr. Kappel's grin turned evil.

"You're my girl, Kirsten. If Hardy is as interested in you as he claims, he will brave anything the boys throw at him. This is my way of testing him, to see if he's worthy of you."

Sighing, Kirsten tugged on a strain of blond hair. Franz settled back into his seat and beamed at his sister. Thankfully she had gotten too old to fling peas at him.

Japhet had taken a few bites of food before he seemed to remember his invitation.

"Mr. and Mrs. Kappel," he said, ripping his eyes from his plate, "my sister is being weird. She wanted me to invite all of you to Hanukkah. I told her you always come, but she told me to ask. I think it has something to do with Ross."

Franz saw his dad's eyes shine, but he held back any laughter. He glanced slyly at Kirsten but said nothing. She didn't notice the look, which disappointed Franz. He liked it when her face turned as red as an apple.

"Is your mom cooking?" Mr. Kappel asked Japhet.

"Wilhelm!" Franz's mom rebuked. "You're going to make the boy think the only reason we go over is for Sarah's cooking!"

"That *is* the only reason I go over," Mr. Kappel teased.

"I'm telling her you said that," Mrs. Kappel warned.

"I'm not scared."

"You will be when Josef finds out you are trying to horde all his wife's cooking."

"Traitor," Mr. Kappel said into his peas.

The rest of the meal passed with Kirsten, Bea, Elsa, Gabi, and Sophia trying to decide what they would wear to the Hanukkah gathering and Franz and Japhet kicking each other under the table. When the meal was over and Japhet started for home Mr. Kappel made sure to remind him they'd be over for the celebration, and Franz made him promise to come back the next day to help finish the catapult.

"I want to get Hardy tomorrow night; we can test it out on him."

Japhet grinned. "I'll be here then."

Four
Standing up

1934

Ten was a special age. When Franz turned ten, he'd been given permission to go alone to the field a mile outside of town — not that he ever went alone. Japhet always went with him. They just no longer had the need to beg their sisters to take them. Ten was an age which meant more freedom. Except Japhet had school the day of his birthday.

"It's not fair," he grumbled as he and Franz walked down the middle of the road together. It always made them feel like they were walking on the edge of danger even though there were few cars in town. "Last year my birthday was on Sunday."

"It's because the days are always changing," Franz pointed out, trying his rarely used big brother tone. He swung his books in an arch, almost hitting Japhet with them. "But it isn't going to be so bad. I'm coming to spend the night again. And Ruth said she will make your cake. Besides, I had to go to school on my birthday."

Ruth was Japhet's fourteen-year-old sister and the youngest out of the three girls. She excelled at baking even if her big sister skills needed work.

"You owe me this birthday," Japhet said.

"I owe you?" Franz stopped swinging his books. "For what?"

"For my last birthday. Remember? Last year you came up with the idea to prank our sisters, and I got grounded for it. I had to spend the whole day inside."

"You're just whining," Franz said. "I spent all day with you while you were imprisoned and you know it. Even though I'd already served my punishment."

Japhet laughed gleefully. "You had to polish all of your sisters' shoes and do their laundry. For a week."

"And cook dinner on Kirsten's night so Hardy could take her to a restaurant. If anything, you got off easy." Franz smacked Japhet lightly on the back of the head.

Such gestures always called for war. Japhet shoved Franz and took off running down the snowy street, the cold winter air stinging his lungs. Franz gave chase and they dashed into the school yard and made it to the lawn before Franz tackled Japhet to the ground. Books went flying and the boys rolled over and over each other. When they came to a stop, they were covered in snow and there was a hole in Franz's pants leg.

"I'm dead," he said.

"Good. Serves you right, tackling me on my birthday." Japhet sat up and reached for his hat, which had gotten knocked off his head. As he brushed snow out of his hair and tried to keep it from going down his back, some of the other boys walked past him and Franz. Looking up, Japhet smiled at them, not sure if it surprised him anymore when the other boys didn't return it. Something strange had been going on with Amell, Gilbert, and the others for the past few months. Japhet had given up trying to find out what.

"Franz, what are you doing?" Gilbert stopped and looked

down at them. Japhet shifted his seat when he felt the snow beginning to melt and seep into his pants. He peered up at Gilbert.

That was another thing Japhet had started to notice. Whenever the other boys were around now, which wasn't often, they spoke to Franz instead of him. At first it had been funny, watching Franz glare and sputter for sentences. Now it was annoying.

Franz stopped making half-hearted grabs for his scattered books.

"I'm sitting in the snow, idiot. What does it look like?"

With his new thrust into the social world, Franz's temper had made an appearance. Japhet made a snowball and threw it at Gilbert, but the boy just ducked and kept his eyes on Franz.

"No." A couple of other boys joined Gilbert. "What are you doing with him?" Gilbert pointed right at Japhet.

"Him?" Franz stared at Japhet in confusion and Japhet stared right back. Japhet racked his mind in a sudden panic, trying to remember if Franz had talked him into pulling a prank on Gilbert, which would have ended looking like Japhet had done it. He couldn't remember anything. They'd only seen Gilbert once that summer.

"I'm sitting in the snow with him. And he has a name."

"But—" One of the seven-year-old boys stared in horror as if Japhet had suddenly grown fangs.

"But he's a Jew!" Amell suddenly joined the group and the conversation.

"Duh," Franz muttered. "Everyone knows he's a Jew. Everyone has always known he's a Jew. You've always known he's a Jew."

Japhet's face reddened. He had never really considered his heritage. He had been born and raised in Germany, just like all the other boys. He was a Jew, but that didn't make him all that different from everyone else. His parents were Christian and only celebrated some of the Jewish holidays to remember their past. Japhet couldn't understand why, all of the sudden, being called a Jew made him uncomfortable.

"But you shouldn't be...playing...with a Jew," Gilbert said slowly.

"What?" Franz got to his feet and glared, his temper running shorter with each second. "Why not? He's my best friend! Besides, you play with him all the time."

"I don't anymore!" Gilbert yelped.

"It doesn't matter what we used to do," Amell cut in. He held his head high, using his height advantage over Franz. "He's a Jew!"

Japhet didn't know how to react to the argument and kept his seat in the snow as Franz clenched his hands into fists.

"Stop saying that!" he shouted. "It doesn't matter if he's a Jew or not! It has never mattered and it never will!"

Amell stepped closer to Franz. "It does matter! He's a stinking Jew and he shouldn't even be allowed here! He's so stupid he shouldn't even try going to school! He can't learn anything!"

Stunned, Japhet didn't know how to react. He'd never once dreamed Amell would say anything like that about him. Japhet's head felt like it was spinning and he couldn't make sense of what was happening.

Unexpectedly, Franz's fist slammed into Amell's stomach. The boy doubled over and Franz kicked him in the shin, then jumped on him and knocked him to the ground where he punched him again.

"You take it back!" Franz shouted as he let his fists fly.

Gilbert, gasping in horror, grabbed one of Franz's arms and tried to pull him off Amell, but Franz wouldn't budge.

"Take it back!" he yelled.

Japhet heard his friend's angry shouts. He heard girls screaming and calling for the teachers. He heard Gilbert's words of reason and Amell's grunts of pain, but it all sounded far away and muffled. The only thing he heard sharply was the sneering taunt of Jew as it rang loudly in his head.

***

Franz and Japhet sat outside the principal's office. Franz's lip bled slowly from a lucky swing Amell had gotten in. The cut hurt, but he didn't care, because it was the only blow Amell had been able to land – and the other boy, doubled over and gasping for air, had two black eyes and had to be helped off the school lawn. That would teach him to insult Japhet.

Inside the office, Franz could hear a murmur of voices. His parents and Japhet's had been called in. That had been over an hour ago, and during that time Japhet had not once uttered a sound. He sat stiffly in his chair and stared at the opposite wall. He looked as if someone had taken his world and turned it on its head. The vacant look frightened Franz.

"I've never liked Amell. That's why I put those ants in his desk last semester." Franz tried to break the silence. Japhet didn't as much as blink.

"Tomorrow I think I will put a tack on his seat. You have one I can borrow, don't you?"

Even then Japhet didn't respond. Franz was about to poke him when the office door opened and the Kappels and Buchanans emerged. They said nothing, but Mrs. Buchanan held out her hand to Japhet and Mrs. Kappel motioned for Franz to follow her. The two boys did as they were instructed, but as they left Franz noticed the principal frowning at them and he knew things were never going to be the same.

Not a word was said until they had all left the building, then Mr. Kappel demanded to know what had happened.

"I beat up Amell," Franz explained, trying to sound sorrier about it than he actually was.

"You beat him up?" Mr. Buchanan asked. Franz didn't know why he sounded surprised.

"Yes, and I'm not really sorry I did." Franz could still see Amell's sneer and it made his blood boil.

Stinking Jew. What did Amell know? He was stupid, and he'd been held back a year in school.

Mr. Kappel stopped walking and faced his son. "And Japhet. Where was Japhet when this happened?"

"By me. Well, not really. He was sitting." Franz didn't understand why it should matter where Japhet had been. Japhet didn't get into fights.

"He didn't beat up Amell?" Mr. Buchanan asked. He looked at his son.

"No." Franz frowned deeply and answered since Japhet was still quiet. "I beat Amell up, by myself."

"Why?" Mrs. Kappel asked gently.

"He called Japhet a stinking Jew," Franz explained. "So I punched him. You can punish me for it, but I'm not sorry."

Mr. Kappel sighed and ran both hands through his neatly combed hair. When he lowered his arms, a small smile played on his lips.

"You shouldn't beat your fellow schoolboys up," he said in his fatherly tone, "but to be honest, I don't really feel like punishing you. You stood up for your friend. Soon, we might all have to decide how far we'll go to do that." He glanced swiftly at Mr. Buchanan as he spoke.

"What do you mean?" Franz's stomach tied into a knot. He wasn't getting in trouble, and his father sounded worried. Something wasn't right.

Mr. Buchanan placed one hand on his shoulder and one on Japhet's. He smiled.

"Don't worry about it right now. Come on. Let's get you two home and cleaned up. We have a birthday to celebrate."

***

Franz sat up and glared over the top of the bed, but he couldn't see Japhet on the other side of it. Leaving his warm blanket, he rolled onto the bed and dangled his head down the other side.

"You're not asleep so wake up!" he hissed. He poked Japhet's ear, the only thing visible above his blanket.

Japhet ignored him so Franz retaliated and snatched his pillow. Japhet's head hit the floor and he came up fighting. Franz smacked him with the pillow, momentarily stunning him. There was something satisfying about knocking his best friend slightly senseless on his tenth birthday.

Sitting up on the bed, Franz crossed his legs, pulled the pillow to his chest, and smiled over the top of it. He kept that position until Japhet recovered enough to hurl himself at Franz. They crashed backward, off the bed, legs and arms flailing as they tried to keep from hitting the floor. The attempt ended with them landing in a thunderous crash.

Both of them laid still and listened. Franz knew they had just made enough noise to wake the dead, but he hoped they hadn't been loud enough to wake anyone in the house. He counted to ten, but when no sounds came, he turned his head and saw Japhet grinning at him.

"That was an unfair fight," Japhet said, "I was almost asleep.

You can't hit an unarmed man."

"It's only ten o'clock, and it's your birthday. You can't just go to sleep like that," Franz rebuked. "And you would have been armed and prepared if you'd been awake."

Japhet looked away and Franz knew he had begun thinking about school again. He refused to let Japhet sulk on what was left of his birthday and shoved the pillow into his chest.

"Come on, we can't go to sleep yet. Besides, I didn't have a chance to give you my present."

Tossing the pillow away, Japhet twisted his night shirt around so it wasn't strangling him.

"What present?" He leaned forward.

"The one...from me. I already said that. I didn't think you wanted it..."

Japhet reached for the discarded pillow, but Franz kicked it even farther from his reach.

"Of course I want it," Japhet said.

With the pillow safely out of the way, Franz pulled a package out from under the bed. He had hidden it there when he'd come up to change into his night clothes. He'd been waiting for the perfect moment to give it.

Japhet accepted the box and Franz sat back and grinned as he watched Japhet eagerly tear into the paper. When he had it all pulled back, Japhet sat back and stared, then lifted his large eyes and stared at Franz. Franz felt a spike of pleasure and his grin turned smug.

"You...where...how...?"

Franz clasped both hands over his mouth so he wouldn't risk bringing down the wrath of the sleepy Buchanan girls as he laughed.

"I've been saving up for it. Do you like it?" he asked after a few moments.

"I...it's the best present I've ever gotten!"

Japhet held the knife up in the moonlight so he could get a better look as his eyes gleamed. He turned it over and over, examining the black handle and the shiny, sharp blade.

"Your dad and mine helped me pick it out. They said it would last you for the rest of your life. It even has a sheath."

Pulling the black leather sheath out from the paper, Japhet beamed a grin at Franz.

"Thank you," he said in that almost mushy way that made Franz's face turn red. "It's perfect! But you know what this means, don't you?"

"What?"

"This means I have the upper hand when we play war."

Franz reached for the pillow. "I'm older, and taller. You'll never have the upper hand. I'll always be able to catch you."

Five
The world begins to change

1935

Snow covered the ground, at least three inches thick. Outside Japhet's bedroom window, he watched Mr. Leitz and Amell as they tried to free their brand new Opel Olympia from a snow bank. Two years ago, Japhet would have gone out and helped, but that was before he'd been labeled a Jew. No one wanted help from a Jew anymore.

Japhet turned back to his history book. Normally, history was a subject that held his rapt attention but this morning his thoughts kept wandering. The night before he'd overheard his parents talking. The conversation replayed through his mind, over and over, even though he tried to force it out.

"They cut my hours," Mr. Buchanan had said.

This was followed by silence, then Mrs. Buchanan's gentle, "We knew it was going to happen sooner or later. At least you still have a job. Aaron lost his."

"I know I should be grateful," Mr. Buchanan murmured, "God has been taking care of us. There are others worse off than we are. But, everything about this is wrong! Japhet and Ruth being forced to leave school, me losing hours at work and being forced to turn over my gun, you not being allowed into the shoe—"

"Hush," Mrs. Buchanan whispered. "I told you not to worry about the shoe incident."

"Things are so much worse in Berlin," Mr. Buchanan whispered back. "How long before it really begins to affect us? They've already stamped our papers with a J. They're labeling Jews, keeping an eye on them."

"All we can do is pray," Mrs. Buchanan reminded him. "Pray, and stick together."

Pray and stick together. Isn't that what families did? When one of them got kicked out of school, the other followed. When hours were taken from a job schedule families learned to do without sugar and other non-necessities. And life went on.

But for how much longer?

Giving up on history, Japhet grabbed his sketchbook. He'd finally decided that he wanted to start taking art seriously, maybe even pursuing it as a career when he got older. That wasn't why he'd started drawing more. It helped when he began to remember the stories he'd heard about families being dragged off and never seen again. Stories about people fleeing Germany, of people who vanished into the night.

Smack!

Something splattered against Japhet's window and he jumped, falling backward out of his chair. One of the chair's arms dug into his rib cage and he rubbed his side as he picked himself up and tried to look around the snowball covering the middle of his window. He wasn't surprised to see Franz standing in the yard, his hat askew, a snowball in one hand, and a grin on his face.

"Goodness!" Mrs. Buchanan gasped from downstairs. "Please don't tell me that was another bird!"

"I keep telling you, Mom...we need to stop washing the

windows so much then that wouldn't happen," Ruth said from the kitchen. It was her favorite spot to do school since she could sit by the oven. Japhet preferred the quiet of his room – when it was quiet.

"It wasn't a bird!" Japhet called down as he shoved his window open after frowning at his sketch book. His picture of a deer now had a jagged line through it. "It was just Franz!"

"Just Franz?" Franz retorted, catching the last part as the window jerked free of the ice which held it to the window sill. "Since when did I become 'Just Franz'? I'm almost another member of your family!"

Japhet leaned on the frame, not caring when cold snow seeped into his sleeves. "That's when you became 'Just Franz'," he said. "Like Ruth is 'Just Ruth.' And you ruined my drawing. I hope you're happy."

"I beg your pardon?"

Ruth, wearing socks, had managed to sneak up behind him without making a sound. It was one of her more annoying talents, in a long list of annoying older sister talents.

Before Japhet could say anything to her, she was at the window. She scowled down at Franz.

"What are you doing out there, throwing snowballs at our windows?" she scolded. "Why aren't you in school?"

"It was canceled since half of the teachers couldn't get there because of the snow on the roads," Franz explained. He tried to look pensive for the snowball.

"Well, Japhet still has school," Ruth reported, tilting her nose high in the air, "so why don't you go home and let him study?"

"Study?" Somehow Mrs. Buchanan had joined them, also without making a sound. "With this much snow on the ground? I don't think school should be allowed on days like this." She smiled and held Japhet's gloves up. "Besides, Franz is out there all alone. And, knowing him, he will probably stand there until you go out. You had better hurry."

Japhet could have kissed his mom, but he was eleven. Instead, he accepted his gloves, smiled smugly at Ruth, and dashed down the stairs where he stopped long enough to pull on his boots, coat, hat, and gloves – then he was out the door, snatching up snow, and hurling it at Franz's head.

Franz ducked, barely avoiding being hit in the eye, and released the snowball he had been holding. Japhet saw it coming for him and dived into a snow bank. He rolled over and ended up sprawled out on his back. Franz walked over and looked down at him.

"Does this mean war?" he demanded, his arms crossed over his chest.

Japhet didn't answer. Instead he swept his legs to the side, knocking Franz's legs out from under him. His friend went down hard, his arms flailing as he tried to catch himself. As soon as he was down, Japhet fought to get to his feet, crawling until he was out of the deeper snow, then running into the road. Once there he spun around, grabbed a handful of snow, and rolled it into a ball. Franz rolled out of the snow bank and sprawled out on what used to be the walkway but was now just a smaller pile of snow.

"So, war it is," Franz yelled as he got to his feet.

Grinning, Japhet threw his perfectly made snowball, hitting Franz in the back of the head, then laughed and ran away as Franz spun and came after him. They dashed down the street, breath rising in puffy clouds in the cold air. Japhet could hear Franz closing the distance behind him and knew it wouldn't be long before he caught up. Franz was still faster, even though Japhet did all he could to beat him in races. Sometimes he even resorted to cheating but always failed.

Even so he kept trying. Japhet wasn't going to give up without a fight.

Japhet took a road that led to one of the open fields. He darted right into the deep piles of snow and pushed through even when the wet cold tried to pull his boots off and slow him down. There was a hill in front of him — one he and Franz liked to roll down in the summer — and Japhet charged up the side of it. By then his breath was coming in desperate gasps. His lungs burned from cold and lack of air, but he kept going. Franz would shove him head first into the snow if he caught him and that was his motivation to keep pushing.

At the top of the hill, Japhet risked a glance over his shoulder and saw - with not enough time to avoid it - a snowball flying for his head. He ducked, but it still smacked him, right in the face. Stunned, he stopped running and Franz threw himself forward. He wrapped his arms around Japhet's legs and both lost their balance and crashed down the other side of the hill.

They rolled over each other and down, snow filling their coats and boots. Japhet lost one of his gloves and he was certain at one point he got Franz's boot in his teeth. Then it was over, and both lay on their backs - cold, wet, panting, and laughing.

"Who won?" Japhet asked when he was breathing normally again.

Without warning, Franz pulled Japhet's knife from its sheath. Japhet always wore it, strapped to his belt.

Sitting up, Franz knelt over him and pointed the knife at his throat as he grinned.

"I won," he declared.

Six
Unfair fight

1936

Japhet sat at the table and drew. Lead from his pencil smeared the side of his left hand, showing how long he'd been working on the picture. Already it had more detail than any of his other pictures. Franz stared in amazement at the individual blades of grass and each feather on the bird's back. Normally such a picture would have made him proud of his friend's talent, now it just made him sad.

The worse things got, the more Japhet drew. He'd pulled back and hardly spoke to anyone now, not that there were many who spoke to him. All of the other Jews in the village had fled, and everyone else pretended the Buchanans didn't exist. Whenever Franz and Japhet went out, only Franz was addressed in conversations. Even with school out for the summer Japhet kept reading text books and never left the house unless Franz went with him.

Franz hated it. He hated the way Amell spoke about Japhet in school, and he hated the way Gilbert went out of his way to avoid walking past the Buchanan house. Franz had spent most of the school year perfecting his catapult. When he had Gilbert in his sights, he'd shot three shovel loads of snow on him. He'd howled with laughter while Gilbert crawled through the snow, looking for his glasses. Franz then talked Japhet into helping him fling mud the next time Gilbert was in range.

"I'm bored," Franz complained. He had to force himself to stop thinking about revenge on Gilbert.

"Good for you." Japhet didn't look up as he added realistic clouds to his sky. Franz thought they had more detail than real clouds.

"You're drawing is making me sick. One person shouldn't be that talented."

"That's what I keep saying," Mr. Buchanan said. He stood on a kitchen chair, patching up a hole in the ceiling. He'd become an almost permanent figure around the house since losing even more hours at work. Just the night before he and Franz's dad had gotten into an argument.

"They're only working you two days a week now?" Mr. Kappel had shouted when Mr. Buchanan told him the news while they were in the back yard making homemade ice cream. "Those weasels! Who do they think they are?"

"I can see where Franz gets his temper," Mr. Buchanan had laughed.

Curious, Japhet and Franz had gone to the window and looked out, watching the whole exchange.

"This isn't funny, Josef! They can't just go and cut all your hours at work just because you're a Jew!" Mr. Kappel's face was red and his eyes bulged.

"It is funny! You should see your face!"

"Stop laughing and help me shoot them."

"That won't fix the world, Wilhelm," Mr. Buchanan said. He continued laughing.

"No, but it'll make me feel better." Mr. Kappel suddenly got serious. "Promise me if you need anything you'll let me know?"

"God will provide for us," Mr. Buchanan said, equally serious.

"I know, but He also gave you friends to help you out when things get bad. Please, Josef. Promise."

"I promise," Mr. Buchanan had said.

After that, Franz and Japhet had stopped listening. Now, as Mr. Buchanan whistled and re-plastered the ceiling, Franz wondered if anything would ever bother him.

"You have talent, you just use all yours in other areas," Japhet said, reminding Franz that he'd been whining seconds before.

"Yes, I do." Franz grinned as he again thought of Gilbert's scramble through the snow. "But really, I'm bored. Let's go and get ice cream."

"Go and get ice cream," Mr. Buchanan agreed. "If you use up all your talent in one afternoon, you won't get a job later in life and I'll have to continue supporting you even when you're forty and forget how to shave."

"I won't forget how to shave," Japhet said, but he closed his sketchbook. "Don't let Ruth see my bird. She insulted the last one and called it a chicken."

"I'll guard it with my life," Mr. Buchanan promised. "Now get out of here. I'm tired of seeing Franz, his face is giving me a headache."

"Gee, thanks, Mr. Buchanan." Franz shoved back his chair, caught Mr. Buchanan's quick wink, and pulled Japhet to his feet.

"Anytime. Eat an extra scoop for me."

Franz got Japhet to race him out the door and they ran down the street. By the time they reached the ice cream shop, Franz well in the lead, they were both out of breath; Japhet more so. He'd lost some weight over the winter and hadn't gained it back.

He'd been sick for most of the winter, but Franz didn't think all of Japhet's weight loss had to do with the illness.

"Milkshake or cone?" Franz asked as they started up the walkway to the little shop.

Japhet shoved his hands in his pockets. "Shake of course. Cones aren't patriotic."

"What would you care about patriotism?"

Franz had noticed the other boys coming up the sidewalk, but he'd made a point to ignore them. They, apparently, didn't want to be ignored.

"What do you care about Germany? You're a Jew, not a German!" It was Amell who spoke, as he started up the walkway after them. Franz stopped and turned to face him, putting himself between Japhet and the other boys.

"He was born and raised in Germany," Franz spat, "and his family has been here longer than yours. Yours immigrated from France years ago! He's more pure blood German than you are!"

Japhet laid a hand on Franz's arm, but he didn't want to heed the warning.

"He's a Jew!" Amell snapped.

Franz had long since gotten tired of that insult.

"I'm pretty sure he'd rather be a Jew than a sniveling coward who gets beat up all the time." Over the last couple of years, Franz had gotten pretty good at his own insults.

Passersby stopped as the boys' voices rose. Most of them stared at Japhet and Franz could feel his awkwardness. Franz started to see red.

"Just leave us alone, Amell." He fought to control his temper. "We just want some ice cream."

"Go and get some then." Amell crossed his arms over his chest. "Just make sure the Jew stays outside. And I would be more careful if I was you. No one is taking kindly to Jew lovers."

Reason snapped. Even Japhet's restraining hold on his sleeve wasn't enough to stop Franz. He charged Amell, satisfied when the other boy yelped and his face went white. Even then, Franz didn't stop. He swung hard and fast and his fist sank into Amell's stomach. There was a satisfying *wooph* as the air was knocked out of Amell's lungs.

Amell doubled over and wheezed. Franz stood over him, smiling as he watched the other boy struggle to breathe. He was so busy feeling proud of himself that he didn't see the punch which caught the side of his head. Dazed, Franz fell to the pavement and felt blood trickle down his temple and cheek. He blinked, saw stars, and blinked a few more times. Turning his head, Franz saw someone coming for him and was able to push himself away just in time.

Stumbling to his feet, he faced one of the older schoolboys who was bigger than Amell. He glared at Franz and Franz tried to glare back even though the stars weren't leaving him alone.

"So it's true," the other boy said, "you are a Jew lover! You're the one who visits Jews all the time, aren't you?"

Franz ignored him, rubbed his eyes, and curled his hands into fists. Bigger or not, he would teach this boy to hit him when he wasn't looking. He launched himself again, swinging and kicking, and was easily knocked aside by a backhand to the face. Franz hit the pavement hard and lay still, staring up at the spinning sky above him.

"Had enough?" The older boy stood over him and sneered down. Franz wished he had Japhet's knife, he would show this boy! A second later he forgot all about knives when he heard a cry of pain.

Sitting up so fast his head spun, Franz stared in horror as two boys grabbed Japhet's arms and held him upright as another punched him twice in the stomach.

"Leave him alone!" Franz jumped to his feet, but the other boy grabbed him and held him back. Franz fought, but the boy had too strong of a grip and didn't even seem aware of Franz's kicks.

The boy punched Japhet in the stomach again, then another in the head. The other two boys laughed and let him go. Japhet fell hard, laying on his side. He stirred and one of the boys drew his foot back and kicked him hard. Japhet groaned and lay still. Fear, unlike any Franz had felt before, tore through him and he pulled free of the other boy's hold and ran to Japhet's side, ignoring the blood which rolled into his left eye and blurred his vision. He knelt down as the older boy stood over them.

"Don't forget this," the boy said as Franz rolled Japhet onto his back. Japhet grasped his side and closed his eyes. "Jews and their friends are no longer welcome here – do you really want to be considered the friend of a Jew?"

Franz looked up through the blood and his own blinding anger and gave one last look of defiance.

"I'd rather be his friend than the friend of a bully," he snapped.

Without warning the bigger boy kicked him in the side, then turned and walked off as Franz crumpled and tried to remember how to breathe.

The owner of the ice cream shop left the building long enough to tell Franz Japhet was no longer welcome anywhere close to the store as he only caused trouble. If he had been able to breathe, Franz would have said something, but as it was, he could only kneel and gather in small puffs of air. As soon as the man left, Franz turned his attention back to Japhet and tried to help him sit up.

Wincing, Japhet bit his lower lip and kept his eyes closed. His breathing was ragged and slow and he tenderly kept one hand on his side as Franz got him upright.

"Can you stand?" Franz asked, wishing his voice didn't squeak and reveal just how frightened he was. All he could think about was the last part of the winter when Japhet was so sick and close to dying. He still didn't have all his strength back and Franz feared something might be wrong from the way Japhet kept panting.

"You're bleeding," Japhet said. He lifted his head and squinted in pain.

"Doesn't matter. Are you okay?" Franz demanded.

"My side hurts, but I'll live."

Franz didn't feel much better but said nothing. He carefully eased Japhet out of his bent over stance, but the moment he stood straight Japhet gasped and bent back over. Franz held him upright, pulling his arm over his shoulders.

"Here, lean on me," he instructed.

Japhet didn't protest and put most of his weight on Franz. Ignoring the pain throbbing through his own body, Franz bore Japhet upright and together, slowly and painfully, they limped to the Buchanan house.

Mrs. Buchanan was outside when they stumbled down the road. She was pulling weeds out of her garden when she saw them. She jumped up when she saw them, yelled for Mr. Buchanan, then ran down the road to meet the two boys before they reached the house.

"What happened?" she demanded. She took Japhet's weight on her own shoulders and allowed Franz the chance to place his hands on his knees and breathe in small amounts of air.

"A fight," Franz panted as the front door slammed open. He

heard Mr. Buchanan say something and Ruth scream. He hadn't thought they looked that bad.

"Ruth!" her father scolded as he hurried into the road and helped Franz straighten. Then, much like Franz had helped Japhet, Mr. Buchanan half carried him into the house. Both boys were taken to the kitchen and eased into chairs while Mrs. Buchanan told Ruth to get water and bandages.

"What happened?" Mr. Buchanan asked as Mrs. Buchanan helped her son out of his shirt. Japhet yelled when he had to move his arms and Franz winced.

"It wasn't his fault," Franz said as Mr. Buchanan examined the cut above his eye. "I got mad at Amell and attacked him. Then some older boys attacked us. They beat him up and I couldn't help him." The same helpless feeling he'd had on the sidewalk returned. Franz wasn't sure what burned his blood more, anger or shame over the fact he'd been unable to do anything.

Mr. and Mrs. Buchanan exchanged a grown up look over Franz's head, then Mrs. Buchanan laid a motherly hand on the boy's shoulder.

"Let's get you cleaned up before we send you home or your mother will worry," she said gently.

Seven
Flying monkeys

1939

War had finally come. The whispered rumors and the fearful glances that passed between people were real now. Japhet had listened in while his father and Mr. Kappel talked about it a week after Hitler announced the war.

"England and France have declared war on us," Mr. Buchanan had said. "They said it was because we invaded Poland."

"It has more to do with the Treaty of Versailles. Everyone knows that. I don't know why they're trying to pretend it isn't," Mr. Kappel replied, shaking his head and sighing.

Japhet had read about the treaty. It had been written up after the Great War and said Germany should accept the blame for causing the war. The German government had to pay $6.6 billion for damages, give up some of their land, and most of their army. The country was plunged into poverty and many said it was through the work of Adolf Hitler alone that they had pulled out of poverty and were becoming a proud country once again.

Before, Japhet hadn't really cared. It was in the past; it wasn't affecting his life as far as he could tell. The government could deal with their own problems. But since getting banished from school he started to realize the past was changing his life and choices made then were shaping his future. He had to become involved because he wasn't going to stand back and let the world decide what to do with him. He wanted a say in the matter, though he didn't know how to go about it.

The older he got, the more time Japhet spent alone. It had gotten worse after the boys had broken his rib outside the ice cream shop. Now he would hide in his bedroom, too scared to leave the house unless someone went with him. Japhet preferred that someone to be Franz, though he sometimes caught himself wondering how long Franz would stay when all his other friends had long since left him.

Other things had changed as well. Leah had moved out of the house. She lived with Bea and Elsa, Franz's next two oldest sisters. They worked in a little factory in Munich and seemed happy from their letters. Japhet still worried. He worried about Hadi and Ross – now married – who had gotten a house close to Berlin. He worried about Kirsten and Hardy, who were expecting their first child. He worried about Gabi and Sophia since they visited Kirsten and her Jewish husband often. Sophia was even considering moving in for a while after the baby was born to help out.

More than any of them, though, more than himself and his family, Japhet worried about Franz. Franz was getting angrier and more rash. All anyone had to do was mention the word Jew and he flew into a rage. His grades were slipping and he usually left school with a new bruise. Japhet had lost count how many black eyes he'd ended up with in the past year.

"You're never going to get a girl to like you if you keep looking like a raccoon," he'd told him one day as Franz sat at the Buchanan kitchen table, holding a package of frozen peas to his eye.

"No girl will date me, black eyes or not" Franz had muttered. At sixteen, Franz was becoming handsome. His blond hair had a wave to it, his blue eyes were intense, and his arms muscled. He was the opposite of Japhet, who had gotten so thin his ribs stuck out through his shirt. It wasn't that he was starving; he just found he had little appetite these days. Food turned his stomach and now his cheeks were hollow and pale with lack of food and worry. He could see why girls avoided him, even if it wasn't just over the fact he was a Jew and now had to wear the Star of David on his jacket or shirt whenever he went out. But Franz, if things had been different, should have had the local girls falling at his feet.

"Franz." Mrs. Buchanan had looked up from where she was scrubbing the life out of the kitchen oven. "If you're not careful you're going to get into real trouble one of these days."

"I don't care," Franz had said. "I will stop fighting them when they stop insulting my best friend."

And Mrs. Buchanan had smiled, but had to hide it because she was a mom and moms weren't supposed to encourage fighting.

A horn honked and brought Japhet back to the present. He looked out the window. Mr. Leitz pulled out in his now-not-so-new Opel. Japhet stared until the car disappeared from sight. Amell had been in the passenger seat, wearing his Hitler Youth uniform.

Japhet dropped his head to his school book and closed his eyes. His head pounded. The ache beat against his temples and refused to go away. Japhet knew he shouldn't be worrying; he should be praying like his dad and mom did. Their faith hadn't been shaken, even as things slowly got worse. They still trusted that God could work all of this out, and even if He didn't, it was all according to His plan.

Japhet wanted to ask why. He wanted to yell. What purpose could all of this have? The star he was forced to wear, the anger in Berlin that had slowly spread to the village, the constant worry for his friends and family. War coming. How could the world falling apart be something God wanted or was allowing to happen? What would it accomplish in the end?

While these thoughts tumbled through his mind, Japhet remembered what had happened last year and a cold chill went down his back. They called it the Night of Broken Glass. Japhet had heard it being talked about while shopping with his mom. It started when a Jewish teen assassinated a German official.

On November 9th, 1938 an unplanned attack took place, though everyone questioned just how unplanned it was. Synagogues were burned, Jewish businesses destroyed, and Jewish homes, hospitals, and schools were looted while the police and fire department did nothing. A lot of Jewish men – so many Japhet had never heard the exact count though it was in the thousands – were rounded up and taken away. Their crime? They were Jews.

Women were also arrested and sent to jail, and Germans were only allowed to open their businesses if they agreed not to serve Jews. Japhet feared the Nazis would soon show up in his village, break into his home and drag his family off.

"I knew it!"

Japhet sat upright so fast he knocked his book to the floor. It landed with a loud thump. He spun around to find Franz standing in the doorway of his bedroom. Franz grinned and looked pleased with himself.

"You really have to stop doing that," Japhet complained as he picked up his book and set it back on the desk. For a moment he thought Franz was a Nazi soldier ready to drag him off. His heart fought to slow back to normal.

"All that studying is making you jumpy," Franz said. He laughed and threw himself on Japhet's bed. Japhet was pleased to see no black eye.

"It is not," Japhet retorted. He considered throwing his book at Franz but changed his mind. He didn't want to be the one to give him a new black eye. "It's making me smarter, unlike you."

"You've been studying so long you fell asleep," Franz said, rubbing his scar. He'd been pleased with the scar. He'd gotten after the fight outside the ice cream shop.

Pushing himself up, Franz snatched Japhet's book and examined the cover as he asked, "What are you studying this time? More of the Brothers Grimm?"

"No," Japhet retorted. He had given up on fairy tales after he'd heard about the Night of Broken Glass. "And I wasn't asleep."

"You were asleep," Franz said, then wrinkled his nose. "You're learning English? The American language?"

Japhet snatched his book back, opened it to the last page he had been on, and laid it back on his desk. He shrugged.

"I thought it would be interesting."

"Is it?" Franz looked doubtful.

"Not really," Japhet admitted, a little reluctantly. Franz always said that someday soon Japhet was going to find one subject he couldn't master. Japhet feared he finally had and would have to put up with a lot of "I told you so" from Franz.

Franz's eyes lit up. "Really?" he asked slyly.

"It's a stupid language," Japhet muttered with a sigh as he glared at the book. "It doesn't make sense."

"So you haven't learned anything from it?" Franz asked hopefully. He swung his feet over the bed and thumped them on the floor, grinning.

"No, I've learned some of it."

"Really?" Franz didn't believe him, Japhet could hear it in his tone. He glanced up from the book and squinted, then recited – as best he could – a sentence in English.

"The dog eats the rodent."

Franz hurriedly looked out the window, then pretended he hadn't. Japhet understood. A lot of books were being burned and having a book that taught English in his bedroom was dangerous. If caught, Japhet could be one of the people who vanished and got sent who knew where. Japhet wasn't sure he cared. He couldn't stand up to the Nazis; he was just one kid. But he could defy them and do the things they told him he couldn't.

"You're right, it does sound like a stupid language. But I forgot I came over for a reason."

"It wasn't to mock my book?" Japhet asked.

"Not this time. Mr. Astor was able to get one last movie."

Mr. Astor ran the little theater in town. He used to play American films, mostly Westerns, which he personally did subtitles for in German. Japhet and Franz liked to go and watch them, but lately Mr. Astor hadn't been able to get many movies, not unless they were German made. That meant no more Westerns.

"How did he get it?" Japhet asked excitedly.

"He told me not to ask. And he said it was the last one he is going to be able to do. He also said it's getting too risky and he can't let us in after this one. He's taking a chance letting us watch this one, but he said we could sneak in the back door like last time as long as we make sure no one sees us going in."

Japhet did not want to go. He didn't want to cause trouble for Mr. Astor, but he knew the older man would be disappointed if he didn't show up, especially if he had gone through all the work to get one final American movie and translate it for Japhet and Franz.

"When are we going?" he asked, fingering the hilt of his knife for courage.

"Tomorrow night."

"And what movie is it?"

"A popular one in America. The Wizard of Oz."

Japhet didn't wear his star. Instead, he wore a baggy suit, a crooked tie – he hadn't learned how to tie his own ties and usually got Franz to help – and a hat. He looked like a gangster out of the American history book he'd been reading. Franz would have laughed, except he recognized the suit. It was the same one Japhet had worn to Hadi and Ross' wedding and it should have been too small for him by this time. It shouldn't have hung on him as if it belonged to his father.

Franz tried to hide his aggravation. He knew his friend was barely eating. Since learning of the Night of Broken Glass, he had been forced to watch Japhet waste away to nothing. He was just skin and bones now and there were usually dark rings under his eyes from lack of sleep. He was shallow and fading away. The only reason he hadn't completely given up, Franz felt, was because Japhet knew Franz wasn't going to let him. Franz made a point to visit the Buchanan house for dinners and stare until Japhet ate.

For the time being Franz tried to forget it. Tonight he planned on making Japhet laugh and forget about having to wear stars and thinking the only way he could stand up to the Nazis was by learning English. Tonight they were going to stand up to the Nazis together and watch an American-made movie with an actress named Judy Garland.

"I guess she's popular in America," Franz said as he and Japhet walked down the quiet, dark streets.

Mr. and Mrs. Buchanan almost hadn't let Japhet go. It was dangerous being out after dark, even in their quiet village. If Japhet were caught, he could get worse than a beating. It had taken all of Franz's charm to get Japhet's parents to consent.

"I'll be at his side the whole time. And the theater isn't far from your house. We will go straight there and back. Promise. And I won't let him out of my sight. I'll bring him back in one piece."

"There and back," Mr. Buchanan had instructed.

"I heard she's a real beauty, and she has a great voice," Franz now said.

"Who told you that?" Japhet asked.

"Mr. Astor."

"Oh, I believe it then."

Franz rolled his eyes and pretended to be offended, but Japhet didn't show any remorse.

"You believe Mr. Astor over me?" Franz asked.

"Of course. Mr. Astor wasn't the one who told me John Wayne was a real life cowboy who lived all of the adventures in his movies."

Shrugging, Franz stopped outside the theater's back door.

"How was I to know?" he said. "I thought the camera people just followed him around so they would be able to catch everything he did-"

"Oh give it up." Japhet playfully shoved him. "I haven't believed that since I was twelve."

Franz shoved back, then tapped on the door. Mr. Astor was there in a heartbeat and he led them into the empty theater They were now the only ones he let see his American movies; it was too risky to allow anyone else. Someone else might turn him in.

"Get some popcorn," he ordered the two of them, "and find a seat. Make sure you're comfortable, you won't want to miss this one! Especially Judy Garland!"

Life is full of embarrassing moments. One time Japhet and Franz had tried to scare Kirsten and Hardy and instead caught them kissing on the front porch. Catching someone kissing was awkward enough without that someone being one's sister. But if there were ever a point when Franz looked back on his life and was asked to pick his most embarrassing moment it would have been the night he saw The Wizard of Oz and hid behind the seats with his best friend because they were scared of the flying monkeys.

Judy Garland was just as pretty as Mr. Astor promised, maybe even more so. She had a dazzling smile, great hair, and cute eyes – everything Franz had heard American girls were supposed to be.

The plot of the movie wasn't too bad either; a girl getting sucked into another world and fighting to get back home. The sparkly shoes were a little weird, but it didn't matter because Judy Garland looked great in them.

Franz enjoyed the whole thing right until the creepy, flying monkeys came onto the screen. Franz and Japhet ducked at the same time and Franz knew neither would be able to pick on the other.

As they left the theater later on, surprised at the movie's ending, they stopped outside the door and looked at each other for a minute without speaking. Then they made a pact.

"Let's keep the monkeys to ourselves," Japhet said.

Franz held out his hand and they shook on it.

"Never a word," Franz promised.

That wasn't the only thing they kept secret about that night. Japhet went to the Kappel's to spend the night, and he and Franz stayed up late, staring into the shadows, jumping at every little sound – convinced monkeys were ready to fly out at them and eat them.

Some things had to be kept secret.

Eight
Saving the baby

1939

Hardy and Kirsten had a son. Mr. Kappel never looked more proud in all the years Japhet had known him. He came bursting in the Buchanan house an hour after he received the news and hugged Mr. Buchanan. When he released him, he was grinning from ear-to-ear.

"I'm a grandfather!"

"What did she have?" Mr. Buchanan demanded, nearly jumping up and down himself.

"Didn't you hear me?" Mr. Kappel held tightly to Mr. Buchanan's arms. "I said I'm a grandfather! She had a boy!"

"What's his name?" Mr. Buchanan asked as Japhet poked his head through the top banister railing to watch them.

"I forgot to ask," Mr. Kappel admitted.

"When was he born? Is he healthy?"

"I forgot to ask how he was," Mr. Kappel said. He shrugged. "But he was born an hour ago. We're going to see him now. Want to come?"

Japhet could tell his dad wanted to go. He had been hoping for his own grandchild and still tried to hold babies whenever he got the chance. But he refrained himself.

"We'll all go and visit tomorrow or something. You should get to see him first."

"Right," Mr. Kappel was already at the door but Mr. Buchanan stopped him.

"Do me a favor," he called, "and find out his name."

His name was Roderick and he wasn't completely healthy. In fact, he was a sickly little baby and the doctors told Kirsten and Hardy he wouldn't live the week out and they should leave him at the hospital. Hardy had heard stories, though; whispered rumors of deformed and sickly babies dying in the hospitals. He said he would rather take his son home and look after him himself.

The week passed with husband and wife keeping constant watch over their son. Sophia moved in with them and lived in their spare bedroom. She did all the house cleaning and cooking for her sister so she could devote all her time to little Roderick.

After a week, Roderick showed improvements, though he didn't escape the near death experience without complications. Hardy and Kirsten were certain he was blind in one eye, but they loved him nonetheless.

The second week of Roderick's entrance into the world, Japhet, his parents and Ruth went to see the new baby. Franz went with them and they took Mr. Kappel's car.

Hardy met them at the door, beaming as he led them to the warm living room. Kirsten sat in a rocking chair cradling her son and she looked up and smiled. Sophia perched on the window sill, attempting to darn a sock. She was doing a horrible job, if her quiet yelps when she stabbed her fingers were any indication. Japhet decided not to laugh at her, especially when Ruth frowned at him then went and sat down on the floor beside her friend.

"Mr. and Mrs. Buchanan!" Kirsten exclaimed when they entered the little room. "I'm so glad you came even though it's snowing!"

"Your dad loaned us his car," Mr. Buchanan said. He tiptoed over and looked down at Roderick. "We wouldn't have missed a chance to see him for the world!"

"Oh!" Mrs. Buchanan was at her husband's side in the time it took Japhet to blink. She cooed at the baby. "He's beautiful!"

Franz nudged Japhet in the ribs, then frowned. He did that a lot, almost as if he were still surprised and displeased over how thin Japhet had gotten.

"Poor kid," he whispered, "getting called beautiful."

Japhet grinned as Kirsten held her son up, asking if Mr. or Mrs. Buchanan would like to hold him. Mr. Buchanan eagerly, and gently, took the little bundle as Hardy appeared with cups of coffee.

"Franz, Japhet, come and sit," he said. He pointed to the couch.

Sophia wrinkled her nose at them, then sank to the floor to sit beside Ruth. Japhet returned the favor as he sat beside Franz and accepted one of the coffee cups. An hour passed. Kirsten and Mrs. Buchanan chatted happily while Mr. and Mrs. Buchanan kept taking baby Roderick from each other. Every once in a while Ruth would take a turn holding the baby. Japhet and Franz talked quietly together, whispering flying monkeys when they didn't think anyone could hear them. Sophia continued to stab the needle into her sock and Japhet admired her persistence.

The pleasant evening had just turned drowsy when someone knocked on the door. Hardy lifted his head with a strange look in his eyes, though he stood calmly. Nodding to his company to show they could continue visiting, he walked to the front door and opened it.

Japhet couldn't see him from the living room, but he could hear murmuring voices. He glanced at Franz to see if he had caught any of the words. The voices, though low, sounded angry and insistent. And they were steadily getting louder. Even Mr. Buchanan, who held Roderick again, started to notice.

"I'm sorry," they finally heard Hardy say, his voice deep and angry though calm, "I have company and I cannot let you in at this time."

"I know this is hard for you to accept, Mr. Kantor, but it's for the best. Not only for you and your wife but for your child." The voice belonged to a woman, a reasonable woman with an annoyingly smooth voice.

"And who decides what is best for me and my family?" Hardy demanded. "He's my son, and I say he stays with me and my wife!"

"The child is going to be at a disadvantage if what we have heard is true," a man said. His deep voice seemed to shake the house. "We just want to help him."

"I've heard what happens to the babies you 'help,'" Hardy snapped. "Now get off my porch!"

Kirsten's face had gone white and her hands shook. Even Sophia was pale, her eyes large and frightened. Mr. Buchanan slowly stood up and placed Roderick back in the safety of his mother's arms. He smiled at everyone in the living room as he made his way to the hall and door.

"Stay here," he instructed.

"If we could just come in," the woman was saying.

"Is something wrong?" Mr. Buchanan asked when he joined Hardy in the hall.

"Nothing," the woman said, "we were just speaking to Mr.

Kantor. You do not need to concern yourself."

"Well, Mr. Kantor is my son-in-law, so I think I do need to concern myself." Mr. Buchanan's tone was firm. Japhet squirmed in his seat.

"Sir, please, we need to speak to Mr. Kantor alone."

Mr. Buchanan was not about to leave Hardy on his own. Japhet could hear it in his choice of words and tone of voice.

"What you need to do is leave and allow him and his wife get back to enjoying their evening."

"Not until we have the child," the man spoke.

"Just to take to the hospital. Just to make sure he's healthy and normal," the woman added quickly.

"My son is perfectly healthy and normal. And the only way you are taking him is to go around me," Hardy snapped.

"That is easily arranged, Jew!" The man's voice turned cold, and at that moment Japhet's world slowed to a crawl. He could never clearly remember what happened next as, every time he recalled it, it just came back to him in a series of pictures and sounds.

There were a shout and a gunshot in the hallway. Kirsten screamed and ran for the front door, but Mrs. Buchanan was faster and reached there first. Japhet came right behind her. In front of him he saw his father lying at the feet of a Nazi, a Nazi who held a pistol. Hardy sat on the floor, his back against the wall as if he had been shoved there, and blood was turning the front of Mr. Buchanan's shirt red. Behind him, Japhet heard Ruth scream.

Next to the man stood a woman, small and stern, her lips pressed into an angry frown. She scowled down at Mr. Buchanan. Japhet was only slightly aware of himself trying to reach his father's side, unable to move. There were firm arms wrapped around his chest, holding him back.

In front of him, his mother flew at the Nazi, her screams tearing through the house. They were cut off by another gunshot, a strangled gasp of air, and then his mother lay next to his father. And just like that, Franz no longer held Japhet back but was holding him up. He thought he heard Ruth fainting but couldn't be sure. His legs gave out and Japhet sagged against Franz as the back door slammed opened and closed.

The Nazi shoved past the two boys, Hardy, and Ruth and stormed into the house, but Sophia, Kirsten, and Roderick weren't there. Japhet didn't find out until later that Sophia had dragged her sobbing sister out into the winter evening and hid with her until the Nazi and the woman left.

Hardy somehow got to his feet and pulled the boys into the living room. He picked up Ruth and laid her on the couch. Franz sat on the floor with Japhet, who felt tears filling his eyes but not coming out. They said nothing until Hardy went to the front door and came back with his face even graver.

The Nazis had taken Mr. and Mrs. Buchanan's bodies with them.

Part Two
There's a land that I heard of

Nine
Grief

1940

It had happened three days before Christmas. Japhet didn't realize it until the next year. He was aware of little of what happened after the death of his parents and he wouldn't have made it if his grief-stricken friends hadn't taken him and Ruth in to live with them.

Franz let Japhet move into his room with him, even gave up his bed. Ruth slept in Kirsten and Bea's old room. During the weeks between Christmas and New Year's, Mr. Kappel helped Kirsten, Hardy, and Roderick escape Germany. He then helped Hadi and Ross, who were expecting their first child and didn't wish to raise the baby in the country where their parents had been coldly murdered for trying to save a baby. Sophia escaped with Kirsten and Hardy.

Japhet didn't remember much about them leaving. He didn't forget Hadi's hug or her crying on his shoulder. He would never forget Mr. Kappel promising to join them all soon; Japhet heard him say they would be a family again but he didn't see how that could happen. Their family was broken, and nothing would ever fix it.

A week after Christmas the fog which had settled over Japhet cracked and he finally cried. It happened at his parents' funeral. Since they had no bodies to bury, a ceremony was held and two markers placed in the ground. Reality sank in for Japhet. His parents weren't coming back.

Japhet broke, falling to the snow covered ground and covering his face with his hands as he sobbed. Franz sat beside him, ignoring the snow, and wrapped an arm around his shoulders. He said nothing, but Japhet didn't want to hear words. He wanted to be comforted, but not even Franz could do that.

Fear and emptiness consumed him. Over and over again he heard the word Jew like it was some kind of curse. For the first time in his life, he wondered if it might be. That was why his father had been killed. Why his mother was shot. Why he had been banished from school. Why half of his family had to leave Germany. Why Franz was always getting beaten up. Why all his friends had left him. If that wasn't some kind of curse, he didn't know what was.

Faith. Believe. God is in charge. His dad had always said things like that. When Jews fled. When Jews were killed. When Jews went missing. It was always the same. God knows what is going on, it's all in His control. But Japhet wasn't sure he believed it.

How could so much pain and suffering be part of God's will and plan? How could Hadi fleeing Germany while five months pregnant be something God wanted? The world was crumbling and Japhet was just supposed to accept that God had this all planned out. What happened to the God of love he had heard so much about?

The sobs tore the air from Japhet's lungs until he wasn't sure he would be able to breathe. He wished he could stop. He wanted to give up, but Franz's arm around his shaking shoulders reminded him he couldn't. Franz needed him, at least Japhet hoped he did.

Something cold, something that wasn't the winter air, flowed through his body and Japhet shivered. What if he really was better off dead? If he were dead, then Franz wouldn't get beaten up for being his friend. Franz's life wouldn't be in danger because he chose to spend time with a Jew. What if the Nazis came back? What if they found out about Franz? What if they shot him like they had done Japhet's parents?

The thought was unbearable and Japhet made a silent promise to make sure Franz never died for him.

Franz made it a point to walk past the now boarded up Buchanan house every day after school even though it took him out of his way. He liked to pretend he could still walk in the front door anytime he pleased. Sometimes he threw a snowball at Japhet's old window just to imagine his pale face appearing behind the glass.

After he had gotten into fights at school, he'd walk even slower past the front door so he could remember the times he'd limped into the kitchen and put frozen food over his eye. One time Mrs. Buchanan had caught him holding a package of wrapped chicken to his forehead. She'd taken it from his hands and handed him a steak.

"We're having chicken tomorrow, steak tonight," she had said.

Franz considered praying sometimes, but he didn't see the point to it now. The Buchanans were dead, prayers wouldn't bring them back. Other days he wanted to lay on his bed and sob, but he couldn't.

He had lost two people who were like parents to him, Japhet had lost real parents. There was a difference. Franz could see it in Japhet's hollow cheeks, in the dark circles under his eyes, and in the vacant look he got when he thought no one watched.

Something was happening, something Franz had trouble understanding at first. It took him a week, almost two before he realized.

Japhet was dying. His grief was killing him and Franz had to find a way to save him. He had to give him a reason to live.

He had lost two parents, he was not about to sit back and lose his brother.

Ten
Threats and a nightmare

1940

One evening everyone gathered in the living room after dinner. Mr. Kappel sprawled the length of the couch and lazily flipped through the newspaper while Mrs. Kappel worked on a cross stitch project. Gabi and Ruth had found a fashion magazine somewhere, Japhet hadn't a clue where they'd gotten it and didn't care to ask. They used it to pick a style of bridesmaid's dresses.

A man had helped Hardy, Kirsten, and the others get out. Japhet hadn't met him at the time, but Mr. Kappel told Japhet about him. The young man's name was Karl and he'd been able to obtain new papers for those getting out. He hadn't been able to get them for everyone, though. He said he could, given time.

Japhet had met Karl later on and decided he liked him. Karl wasn't much older and had a sense of humor even though he could be stern and serious at times. He and Gabi had also met, started courting, and Karl had proposed only a week before. Now all Japhet heard about were weddings, not that it bothered him too much. He liked to see Ruth smile a little.

"You gave up on English?" Franz asked.

Japhet looked up from his drawing. He had been working on

a detailed menorah. Twisting designs of leaves and roses wound up the base and to each of the nine candle holders.

"I've not given up," Japhet said. He rubbed the lead on his palm but it didn't come off, only smeared. "I just took a break."

"It defeated you, admit it." Franz jabbed him with his elbow.

"You could learn it with me," Japhet said. He almost hit Franz with a pillow but didn't feel like it.

"I like it better this way." Franz shoved blond hair back from his forehead then leaned back on his hands. "You learn it and if we ever meet an American, I'll let you translate."

Aware Mr. Kappel now watched them through half-closed eyes, Japhet settled back against the side of the couch, ignoring the sharp end which dug into his back.

"Okay. But if we ever meet Judy Garland you're on your own."

"Oh, so you two have plans to meet Judy Garland, have you?" Mr. Kappel opened his eyes all the way and pushed himself up on his elbows.

"I guess we do, now," Japhet answered. He drummedhis teeth with his pencil.

"You have to get her signature for me when you do," Mr. Kappel ordered.

"Really now?" Mrs. Kappel raised her eyebrows. "And why would you want her signature? You didn't even see the movie."

"But she's Judy Garland," Mr. Kappel replied, winking at his wife. "I could hang her signature on the wall, like a piece of art, and charge the neighbors to come and see it."

"Always with your schemes," Mrs. Kappel murmured.

"You love them and you know it. That's why you married me."

"No, I married you because you kept following me home

from work – every day. And you told me you wouldn't stop until I went on a date with you. Then when I agreed you said you would keep asking me on dates until I married you."

"You sound as if you regret it." Mr. Kappel pretended to pout. "You know you love me. My charm, my fabulous good looks – the way I can still sweep you up in my arms-"

"If you're trying to sweet talk me out of cleaning out the gutters tomorrow it isn't going to work," Mrs. Kappel interrupted him.

Winking at the boys, Mr. Kappel swung his feet to the floor and dashed over to his wife's chair. Before she could protest, he had her in his arms and was kissing her.

"Put me down!" Mrs. Kappel screeched, giggling.

Mr. Kappel just laughed, and Japhet felt a laugh bubble up inside him even as tears filled his eyes. He remembered days when his dad chased his mom around the kitchen and into the backyard where he'd always catch her and kiss her. She always chased him back into the house with a wooden spoon.

Mrs. Kappel's laughter was abruptly cut off when a glass in the kitchen shattered. Mr. Kappel set his wife on the floor and ran to see what had happened. He told everyone to stay where they were.

Japhet forgot how to breathe as he watched Mr. Kappel snatch up a pistol and disappear from the living room. He expected to hear a pistol shot at any second and his hands turned clammy.

Silence fell over the house and none of them moved until Mr. Kappel came back. He held a brick in one hand and the pistol in his other. Japhet felt light headed and closed his eyes for a moment.

"Someone broke our window?" Mrs. Kappel asked, irritated.

"Kitchen window," Mr. Kappel said. He hefted the brick in his hand, tossing it up and down.

"I will clean up the mess tomorrow," he added. "We don't have to worry about it tonight." He set the brick down and held up a piece of paper. "There was a note on it."

"What does it say?" Gabi whispered.

Sighing, Mr. Kappel unfolded it and read, "If you want to live, stop harboring Jews."

***

Japhet had a nightmare that night. Franz, from his pallet on the floor, was awakened by his cries and thrashing. Franz didn't even give himself time to wake up all the way. He jumped up, grabbed Japhet's shoulders, and shook him.

Instead of opening his eyes, Japhet kept tossing and yelling. He came close to punching Franz twice, but Franz didn't care. He shoved Japhet back into the bed, kept him down, and called out his name over and over.

"Wake up!" he begged and shook Japhet as hard as he dared. "Japhet, wake up! It's a nightmare, just wake up! It's going to be okay!"

Franz shook him again and this time Japhet responded. His eyes snapped open and he sat up, throwing his arms around Franz's neck.

"Franz!" Japhet gasped and started to cry.

Holding him tightly, Franz let Japhet cry on his shoulder. He forgot about Japhet being sixteen and nearly considered a man. At that moment, he was nothing more than a scared little boy who had seen his parents shot right in front of his eyes, who'd had his world shattered by something he couldn't change and wasn't responsible for. Right now all Japhet needed was something solid to cling to.

"It'll be okay," Franz whispered when the worse of Japhet's

tears passed. "I promise it will be okay."

Sitting back, Japhet stared at Franz. He reached up and rubbed his eyes. His shoulders still shook, but no more tears fell.

"How can you say that?" he whispered. He stared at his hands. "How can you promise that? Your parents are in danger because they took Ruth and me in."

"Do you really think they care about that, Japhet?" Franz gritted his teeth together. "You're family. You're my brother! You're like a son to them – they would do anything to help you and Ruth!"

"You might be killed for it," Japhet said. His shoulders stopped shaking and his body stiffened.

Leaning forward, Franz clasped his shoulder until Japhet looked up. He scowled, not out of anger but to get his point across.

"You're my friend. If I had to, I would die for you," he said with so much feeling he almost scared himself.

"I can't let you die for me," Japhet choked. "I don't want to see anyone else die-"

Franz shook his head, cutting him off. "You don't think I know that?" he asked, softening. "I said I would die for you if I had to. That doesn't mean I plan on dying. Japhet, you need me as much as I need you. If we are going to survive this, we have to survive it together. You can rely on me, always, to be here for you. You have to trust me on that. No matter what the world tells you, I'm never going anywhere. And we will get out of this, alive and together. Do you understand? We both have to live."

The longer Franz spoke, the more desperate he sounded, but he had to make Japhet understand how much he needed him. He had to make him realize he couldn't die. Franz would live, but he could only do so if Japhet did the same; he understood that now.

"I'm scared," Japhet admitted quietly. "I didn't...it's real now, Franz. They really mean to kill us. I can't watch them kill Ruth, or Leah, or you."

"They won't," Franz promised. "We're going to save your sisters. We are going to save mine and my parents. And then you and I, we're going to get out of Germany together. Please, Japhet. Promise me that. Promise me you'll leave with me. You have to keep fighting because I can't make it without you."

Doubt shown in Japhet's eyes and it turned Franz's blood cold. But he also saw something else. Small. Nothing more than a sliver, but there. It was the smallest hint of hope Franz had ever seen and he wanted to grasp it and never let it go.

"I will," Japhet whispered finally. "I will escape...with you. After we get everyone else out."

Eleven
Plans to enter Berlin

1940

Japhet and Franz talked over their plan until they had every detail worked out; only then did they talk to Mr. and Mrs. Kappel about it. As expected, neither took the news well.

"You want to go into Berlin?" Mr. Kappel shouted, slamming his fist down on the kitchen table.

Franz had rarely seen his dad angry, and when Mr. Kappel had gotten angry, he didn't direct it at his children. Now Franz sat back in his chair and Japhet stared down at the table cloth.

Mrs. Kappel was no better. She glared hard at Franz, directing all her anger right at him. Franz didn't mind.

"It would be the best thing right now," Franz said. He kept his tone calm and level. He understood his parents' anger. When he and Japhet had first come up with the plan he had hated it just as much – he wasn't sure he liked it even now – but after a lot of consideration it did seem like their best option.

"How?" Mrs. Kappel snapped. Her face was white, her lips drawn and tight in a deep frown. "How can you two going into Berlin be a good thing? Japhet is a Jew, Franz! He could be killed! You could be killed for being around him!"

"We know the risks, mom," Franz said. He wanted to remind her that he knew Japhet was a Jew but held his tongue.

"I don't think you do," Mr. Kappel said, his shoulders relaxing slightly. "Your mom is right, Franz. You could both be killed, or worse. You've heard the rumors about those who disappear and never come back."

Franz sat up straighter when a chill spiked up his back, but he wasn't going to be so easily deterred.

"What is to stop that happening if we stay here?" he asked quietly. "Dad, they know about us. They aren't going to stop with warnings and smashing our windows. They were going to take Roderick because he was blind in one eye. They-" a sob caught in his throat and he had to choke it down. "They killed Mr. and Mrs. Buchanan. They've beaten me up because I'm friends with Japhet, and they know he and Ruth are living with us. How much longer do you think we can hide here? Live here? It's time we all need to think about leaving. We need to hide somewhere until Karl can get us out."

"And go where?" Mr. Kappel whispered, anger draining from him. "Go to Berlin like you want? We won't be any safer there than we are here."

"We shouldn't all go," Franz agreed. "It would be too much of a risk. If Japhet and I go-"

"How is that better?" Mrs. Kappel cut in, but Mr. Kappel held his hand up.

"Let them finish," he said heavily.

Franz took his chance and explained before anyone else could interrupt, rubbing his scar as he talked.

"If Japhet and I went into Berlin we could find work there. There are jobs, we could help get money, and find ways to get all of you out of Germany. Leah, Bea, and Elsa too. Once all of you are out Japhet and I will leave. And while we are helping you get out Karl said he knows of a place you can stay. It's a farm, about ten miles from here. No one would know who you are there, and they wouldn't be able to turn you in. The family is willing to take you, Mom, Gabi, and Ruth and hide you."

"Why can't you come with us?" Mrs. Kappel demanded. "And how do you plan on getting Japhet into Berlin? There is a reason Jews have been leaving."

"We've been thinking about that. We can forge his papers like Karl did to get everyone else out. Japhet has lived in Germany his whole life; with new papers and a different name no one will know he's a Jew," Franz explained.

"Forge his papers?" Mr. Kappel shouted. Franz jumped. "That is almost worse than getting him into Berlin! If he is caught, there will be nothing we can do to save him. It's fine to forge papers to get us out, but he'll have to keep this lie up for who knows how long!"

Japhet's face reddened and he opened his mouth, but Franz was quicker.

"You can't expect him to stay here-"

"Why can't he come to the farm with us?" Mrs. Kappel asked. "That would be safer-"

"Maybe I don't want safer." Japhet broke off the argument. He continued to stare at the table cloth, but there was a quiet resolve in his voice.

"Franz wants to go into Berlin to help his family escape. He wants to save all of you. He and I can't join the war, not on this side of it. We can't fight for what Hitler is asking us to fight for, but if we do this, we can fight for all of you. We can help save you. Franz wants to help his family, and I want to do the same. Why should I not be allowed to save my sisters, just because Hitler has decided I'm worthless? Please, can't you understand? This is the only way I can see to stand up for those I love. I can't sit back and do nothing. I can't watch my sisters murdered."

Mr. Kappel lowered his head and Mrs. Kappel brushed tears from her cheeks. Franz didn't need his parents to say anything to know he and Japhet had won the argument. It didn't feel like a victory.

"You will keep him safe, right?" Mrs. Kappel whispered, looking intently at her son.

"You know I will," Franz reassured her. "I'm not going to let anything happen to him, I promise."

"We're going to protect each other," Japhet added. "We're both going to make it out of this."

Mrs. Kappel stood up and hugged Japhet, then went over and hugged Franz. Franz accepted the hug, wrapping his arms around her waist and burying his head in her shoulder.

"You have to get out," she ordered, lifting his head so he had to look her in the eyes. "Do you hear me? My boys have to make it out of Germany."

Franz could only nod. When his mother released him, his dad was there. He laid a hand on his shoulder. It was a warm, firm grip and made Franz want to give up the whole scheme. What chance did he and Japhet have if they left home? Mr. Kappel wouldn't be there to save them from whatever messes they found themselves in.

"Don't let them change you," Mr. Kappel whispered, looking from Franz to Japhet. "It was easier here, but you're going into Berlin. You will be in the middle of all the lies. Don't listen to them, and don't let them change you."

Franz nodded, though as he did he felt that it was going to be more complicated than that. They were walking into a lion's den.

A lion who was going to do everything in its power to devour them.

***

Planning was one thing, carrying the plans out another. Karl helped in securing false paperwork for Japhet. He knew of a forger who sometimes made new identifications for Jews.

"We can trust him?" Japhet asked, wishing his voice didn't crack. He couldn't forget Mr. Kappel's warning.

"Karl knows him. He's the same man who is going to help Gabi get out so I'm sure Karl would make sure he was trustworthy," Franz reassured him.

Japhet had wondered why it took so long to get fake paperwork, so Karl had explained it to him. There were only so many papers a forger could make at a time without risk of getting caught. He couldn't write up one for every Kappel and Buchanan family member without putting them in even more danger.

A week before they left, Japhet learned Franz also would be given a new identification.

"It's too risky, me going in as Franz Kappel," he explained. "I'm known as someone who helps Jews. I have to become someone different."

"We both do," Japhet said, defeated. The Nazis were getting what they wanted. They had found a way to change everyone – even Japhet and Franz – waving in front of their noses a desperate plan to save those they loved.

When Franz saw him frowning, he slapped Japhet on the back. The wind was knocked out of his lungs and Japhet wondered if there might be truth in Franz saying he needed to eat more.

"You know what we should do?" Japhet could think of plenty of things they should do. High on the list involved ice cream and a long bike ride, now that they both had bikes; unlike when they were kids and he'd been forced to ride on the handlebars while Franz insisted he wasn't going to get them killed.

"Maybe. What should we do?"

They were sitting out in the Kappel kitchen. They had made all the progress they were able to until the papers came through. The Kappels had packed the necessities they would be taking to the farm and were waiting for Karl to give the word that it was time to leave. Japhet hated waiting. Every little sound made him jump. In spite of all his doubt about God, he prayed like he had never prayed before. He figured that, if the God his parents believed in was real, He might take pity on the Jewish boy the Nazis wanted dead and save the remaining family members he had.

"We should go to America."

"Now?" Japhet realized that all Franz had to do was say the word and he would have followed him out of the kitchen, out of Germany, and to the place where Judy Garland lived. Maybe they could meet her. That thought made him blush.

"Why not? How well can you ride a bike?"

"Not well enough to ride across the ocean," Japhet admitted. A smile escaped.

"Really?" Franz feigned shock. "I thought you had more talent than that."

"I limit myself," Japhet teased, surprised it suddenly came so easily. "I already have ten times more talent than you, so I made sure there are things I couldn't do so you don't feel too bad about yourself."

"Oh, really?" Franz raised both eyebrows. He still hadn't mastered it, not like his dad, and the expression just looked comical.

"Really. Who is the one who actually read his history book? And who is learning English? And let's not forget my art."

"Reading a history book does not make you talented," Franz retorted, "it makes you a book worm. And learning English makes you stupid because you hate the language and you still insist on studying it. I refuse to talk about your drawings."

"At least I'm putting my brain to use, unlike you-"

The back door banged open. Both he and Franz jumped up and Franz grabbed his dad's pistol which was always kept on a shelf with the flour. In one fluid motion, he had it down, cocked and aimed as he hurried down the hall. Japhet ran behind him, his heart pounding in his ears as he relived the night his parents were shot.

Entering the living room, Franz stopped and leveled the pistol at the intruder. He froze just before pulling the trigger.

"Karl!" he snapped and Japhet let out his pent up breath.

"I certainly hope you know how to use that," Karl said as he pulled off his scarf and knocked snow to the floor. Karl was tall and handsome – at least Japhet figured girls would consider him handsome. He had high cheek bones, wavy blond hair, and finely arching eyebrows. He also had dimples. (Japhet didn't know this for a fact because he had never actually seen them, he'd just heard Gabi talking to Ruth about them.)

"I wouldn't be pointing it at you if I didn't know how to use it," Franz snapped. He pointed the pistol at the floor. "Why are you barging in here like that?"

"I should hope so, because if you shoot me I want it to be a clean shot. And I'm here because I brought your papers." Karl pulled off his coat, extracting papers from an inside pocket. "Is everyone else here?"

Franz snatched the files and scowled. "You couldn't knock

like a normal human being?" he asked as he pulled one or two sheets from the folder.

"No, they have all gone for a walk but they should be back soon," Japhet said, answering Karl's question and eager eyes as he looked down the hall for his girl.

"So," Franz looked up from the sheets, his face suddenly pale, "I guess this means we're going."

Karl instantly sobered. "It's not too late," he said. "You can still go to the farm and hide there until we find a way to get you out with your family."

Franz shook his head. "No. We have to do everything we can to help."

Japhet nodded in agreement and accepted the sheet that Franz held out to him. His new name, his new identification which would hopefully hide the fact he was Japhet Buchanan the Jew.

Stephen Achen. The name stared up at him, then blurred. He felt like he was giving into the Nazis, accepting their terms. They told him he couldn't be a Jew and live, so he was becoming what they wanted.

Twelve
Escape in the night

1940

Rupert Hoffmann. Franz blamed Karl for his new name. He'd gotten Japhet renamed as Stephen. Stephen was a good name. Rupert sounded like a sneeze and Hoffmann a strangled choke.

He complained, but Karl showed no sympathy.

"Just be glad Rupert isn't your real name," he said.

"I wish your name was Rupert," Franz muttered.

The subject of names dropped and final preparations were made. At the end of the week Karl said he would come back and take Ruth, Gabi, and Mr. and Mrs. Kappel to the farm. At the same time, Japhet and Franz would leave for Berlin.

As the end of the week loomed closer and closer, Franz slept less and less. For this reason, he heard more of Japhet's tossing, turning, and frightened shouts as nightmares descended on him. Soon they both had dark rings under their eyes. Mrs. Kappel noticed and did everything she could to put their minds at ease.

"God will work this out," she told them at breakfast one morning. "We have to trust Him. You two have to trust Him. You're going to kill yourselves if you keep worrying like this."

God. The same God who had allowed the Buchanans to be

shot for trying to save Roderick. The same God who would have allowed Roderick to be taken for no reason of his own. Franz only felt bitter anger when he thought about God. He wondered if he even believed in His existence. If the God his parents loved was real and allowed all of this, Franz wasn't sure he wanted to serve Him.

The day before they had to leave was the hardest. Japhet had another nightmare, even worse than the ones he'd had before. Franz awakened to him shouting and when he'd finally been able to wake him, Japhet had buried his head in his pillow and refused to speak.

Franz tried to talk to him, tried to get something out of him. His parents, he knew, were awakened by the shouting but hadn't come into the room. They had all learned, after Japhet's third nightmare, that it was better to leave him alone with Franz.

Finally, Japhet fell back asleep. Bone weary and heavy-eyed, Franz slipped down into the kitchen where he found Gabi at the table. She had made three cups of warm milk; one for her, one for Japhet, and one for Franz. She'd even found three of Ruth's cookies which had escaped dinner.

"Sit," she said, motioning her brother into one of the chairs. "Have some milk."

Too tired to talk, Franz dropped into the chair, cupped his hands around the mug of milk, and lowered his face over it, allowing the steam to roll over his cheeks. He closed his eyes and took a deep breath.

"How is he?"

Gabi's question reminded him he was not alone and he forced his head up. She wore a bathrobe over her nightgown. The robe used to fit but was now too large. Her hair flowed down her back, bouncing over her shoulders in soft curls, and somehow she was smiling.

Her question, though, pushed Franz too far. He'd been able to hold back all of his tears before. The lump which kept growing in his throat since the Buchanans' death he'd been able to swallow. He'd been able to hide his fears over going to Berlin, and he'd been able to pretend he felt like a man in control of the upcoming endeavor – not like a little boy who'd been forced out of his childhood long before he was ready.

"How do you think he is?" Franz whispered. He was angry, but not with his sister, and his words came out in a strangled whisper rather than the shout he'd been trying for.

"I'm worried about him, Gabi. Not just, worried – terrified. He doesn't sleep, he barely eats. He said he was going to make it out of this alive, with me, but I'm not sure he meant it. I think he's dying, and I don't know how to stop it. I can't just sit here and watch him die..."

Franz had never put his deepest fears into words, and he never thought he would be able to spill his emotions to one of his sisters, but it all came out in a rush and wouldn't stop. Exhaustion had taken its toll on his body, his nerves were strung too tight, and his emotions rubbed raw. He had nothing left to hide behind, the wall he had put up for Japhet was gone. He knew Gabi was seeing him for what he was, a coward who didn't have the strength to go on.

Shame filled him. He was supposed to be brave, to hold everything together, and now he couldn't.

Dropping his head to the table, Franz pulled his arms up over his face and did something he hadn't allowed himself to do before. He cried. Heart-wrenching sobs which tore through his body and ripped his heart in two.

He hated what his life had become. He hated what his country was doing to his best friend. He hated that his sister had to flee to save her son. Ha hated that nothing would ever be the same again, and he wanted to make someone pay for the pain they had caused him – for the pain they were inflicting on his family, and for the suffering they were putting Japhet through.

"Franz."

In the midst of his misery and sobbing he heard Gabi saying his name, then he felt her arms around him. He turned and threw himself into her embrace, not caring that he was supposed to be the one protecting her. Right now he needed his older sister to hold him.

Arms around each other, they eased to the floor. Franz clung to her, his head on her shoulder, and he cried like he never had before. He sobbed until he had nothing left – then he fell asleep, still locked in his sister's loving embrace.

The next morning Franz had a headache, but it was almost a relief. A weight had been lifted off his shoulders and he even managed to smile at Japhet when he stumbled down the stairs and crashed into one of the chairs.

The day wore on painfully slow. Mr. Kappel went to work and came home. Mrs. Kappel cleaned the oven and Gabi and Ruth flipped through a magazine and talked about dresses. Both knew the wedding would be a long time in coming now, but Franz figured there was something soothing in planning things in the future. It helped to believe there would be a future.

When ten o'clock came none of them could sleep, so they sat together in the living room and said nothing. There was some small peace in the knowledge they were together and Franz enjoyed it, wondering if they would ever have moments like this again.

The clock struck midnight after what felt like hours, and

Japhet jumped. He took a deep breath and smiled sheepishly, but no one said anything. Not that they had a chance. Without warning, the door leading to the backyard flew open, and Karl came in, trailing snow.

"Karl!" Gabi gasped. She jumped up and rushed to hug him, ignoring the snow covering his coat.

Karl returned her hug, then pulled back and yanked his scarf off.

"Get your things," he ordered as everyone else stood. "We have to get out of here, now!"

"What's going on?" Mr. Kappel demanded as he snatched up one of the bundles they had brought down into the living room after dinner.

"We just got word that there is a group of Nazis coming here."

Mrs. Kappel covered her mouth with her hands.

Franz knew he wasn't going to like the answer, but he couldn't stop himself from asking.

"Why?"

"To take you all away."

***

The night air stung with bitter cold. In spite of his boots, coat, gloves, hat, and scarf, Japhet shivered. He clutched one of the bundles, holding some of the Kappels necessary goods, to his chest as he hurried after Karl.

It was dark. Dark and still, as if the air were holding its breath to see if everyone would get away in time. Japhet could feel invisible eyes watching them from every inky black, mysterious house they hurried past. He almost didn't dare to breathe.

"We'll get you out of the town," Karl whispered once they had gone two blocks. "We have a car waiting a few miles out for you. Franz, Japhet, you'll have to continue on foot to Berlin. Keep off the road until you get to the city. It shouldn't take you more than a day. I know of a place you can stay tomorrow night."

Franz nodded but said nothing, so Japhet followed his example. It helped, not having to think of his own responses.

Lights cut through the darkness in front of them and they all ducked behind the nearest house. Mr. Kappel wrapped his arms around his wife and held her close while Gabi clung to Karl. None of them dared to move until the car and lights had passed. As they went, Japhet tried to pretend his shaking legs and chattering teeth were brought on by the cold and not fear.

Ruth stumbled and Karl helped her up. They kept going, for what felt like hours. Japhet didn't remember the town being this large and he didn't think they were ever going to get to the end of it. Then, just when he wasn't sure he could keep pushing himself, they reached the last house and stopped to make sure the road in front of them was empty.

"This way," Karl whispered as if the Nazis behind them could hear. He stood up and moved down the road at a steady jog. Everyone else followed. Japhet glanced over his shoulder every few seconds.

There was a small road which branched off the main one and Karl lead them down it. The woods around them were silent with heavy snow. Nothing stirred in their branches, but the further they went, the more Japhet felt like something was wrong. He slowed and scanned the trees, fearful of what he might see. All he saw, though, was blackness and strange shapes which in the daylight might have been nothing more than roots, snowdrifts, and branches.

"Keep up!" Franz hissed, slowing down long enough to grab Japhet's sleeve and pull on it, trying to get him to move.

"Something's wrong," Japhet whispered, not wanting his voice to carry in the silence. "Can't you feel it?"

"We're running away from our home in the middle of the night. Of course something is wrong," Franz hissed, but he stopped and looked around.

Japhet turned in a slow circle, and his heart dropped into his boots when he saw them, stepping out of the trees. They moved like ghosts, without a sound even as they lifted their rifles to their shoulders. Japhet forgot how to breathe, how to move, but Franz thankfully turned about the same time and didn't freeze at the sight of the Nazis taking aim at their backs.

"Off the road!" he shouted and yanked Japhet into the trees just as rifle shots shattered the heavy nighttime silence.

Japhet heard Mrs. Kappel scream, he heard Ruth's cry of either fear or pain, and he heard Karl yelling for them to duck.

Using the trees for cover, Japhet and Franz ran to catch up to where everyone else was. The cold air tried to freeze Japhet's lungs as he ducked under branches and tried not to trip over roots. Snow got into his boots, but he didn't care. All he cared about was getting to the others and finding them alive.

They found Mr. and Mrs. Kappel first. They were hiding in the trees, Mr. Kappel holding his wife up. Japhet feared the worse when he saw them, but then Mrs. Kappel broke away from her husband and rushed to hug Franz and Japhet. The moment she released them, Ruth, Gabi, and Karl found them.

Karl's face was drawn and white and he said little.

"Come," he ordered and lead them in the direction they had been heading as the sounds of heavy booted feet clomped down the road behind them.

They ran, or tried to, as silently as they could through the trees. Karl lead the way and Japhet saw him stumble more than once, but he said nothing. A few moments of running and Karl shoved aside some branches. Men stood on the other side.

Japhet jumped back and Franz drew his dad's pistol, but Karl held up his arm. He grabbed onto the tree next to him and motioned the family closer.

"Re-enforcements," he whispered. "They're with us."

"We heard shots," one of the men said, concerned. "We were coming to help."

"Nazis behind us, close," Karl explained. "Get them to the cars and get out of here while you still can." He motioned to the Kappels.

Some of the men nodded and began to lead Mr. and Mrs. Kappel and Ruth toward the road. Gabi stayed beside Karl as more men passed, back the way the Kappels had just come, their pistols ready. Japhet glanced at Franz but forgot his unspoken question when Gabi choked on a breath of air.

Snapping his head back around, Japhet saw Karl now knelt in the snow, his hand clenching his left side.

"What happened?" Gabi and the man in front of Karl demanded. Both knelt beside him but Karl waved them off.

"I was shot," he whispered, his voice too calm. Something cold passed through Japhet's chest.

"We have to get you to the car then!" the man snapped.

"No." Karl pushed his hands away. "I won't make it to the car, Warren. You take Gabi, get her to the farm, I'm relying on you. Keep her safe, she means a lot to me."

"Karl!" Gabi grabbed his arm and held on tightly. He smiled at her, patting her hand just as gunshots broke the silence.

"Not much time," he whispered, then he leaned in and kissed her. When he moved back, his smile was dim, but still there. "I love you. Don't forget that, okay?"

"You...you can't leave me!" Gabi sobbed.

"I know," Karl murmured, then he lifted his head and fixed his eyes on Warren. "Those two," he said and pointed to Japhet and Franz, "they're the two I told you about. You need to be ready to get them out when the time comes. I'm trusting you. They're like brothers to me and they have to make it out of this. Help them while they're in Berlin, any way you safely can."

"You know I will," Warren whispered, his voice choked with tears.

"I know, I had to say it, though." Karl's smile slipped as his face twisted with pain. He fixed his eyes back on Gabi, his face went pale, and there was a momentary look of panic in his eyes – just before he toppled to his side, his final breath escaping his lips.

Stunned, Japhet didn't move until Franz grabbed his arm and hauled him in the direction the Kappels and Ruth had gone.

Thirteen
Fight in the woods

1940

Warren proved himself to be a man of action. He moved with purpose, picking up Karl's body and ordering Gabi, Japhet, and Franz to follow him. He stopped near the road, set his friend's body beside a tree, and grabbed Gabi's shoulders.

Franz's sister was crying, her shoulders shaking, but Warren didn't give her time to weep.

"I'm sorry," he said and his deep voice cut through the fog Franz had fallen in. "I truly am. He was a good man. But now is not the time to weep. He wanted you out of here, and that's what I mean to do. Now go!" He turned her and pointed her toward the road. Gabi stumbled off without once looking back.

As soon as she was hurrying in the right direction, Warren turned and looked at Japhet and Franz. There was pity in his eyes.

"Karl told me what you two are doing. I admire your courage. You're going to have to hurry, though. Head deeper into the trees, away from the road for a mile, and then go north. If you keep to those directions exactly, then you will be able to find the farmhouse where Karl made plans for you to spend tomorrow night."

Franz nodded, only partly aware of what he agreed to. He was almost surprised when Warren began nudging him and Japhet in the right direction.

"Keep off the roads at all times. Stay alert. I will be in contact as soon as I can...and here." Warren pulled a pistol from his holster and handed it to Japhet. "You are both going to need to be armed. Now get out of here before the Nazis find us!"

He gave each of them an extra push, and Japhet and Franz stumbled off into the cold night. It was only when they had gone a few hundred feet that Franz realized he hadn't had a chance to say goodbye to his family.

The cold night gave way to an almost equally cold morning. Franz followed Warren's directions as best he could. It was difficult concentrating with the cold biting through his coat and with the heavy weight of Karl's death pressing down on him.

When the sun finally lightened the sky, Japhet and Franz stopped and took a moment to rest. They sat down on stumps after they brushed the snow off of them. The moment he sat, Japhet dropped his head into his hands and closed his eyes. Franz wasn't sure if he was tired or upset that he hadn't had another chance to see Ruth.

Neither spoke. Franz felt he should say something comforting, but he couldn't think of the right words. He even opened his mouth a couple times but nothing came, so he finally gave up, buried his chin in the depths of his coat, and closed his eyes. The woods were silent, but he kept listening, just in case.

"Are we doing the right thing?"

Franz wasn't sure how long he'd had his eyes closed, but he opened them when Japhet spoke. Lifting his head, he squinted at his friend.

"Going to Berlin, you mean?" he asked even though he knew

what Japhet meant.

"Maybe we should have gone to the farm with everyone else."

There was nothing Franz could say, he realized. He had the same doubts and questions and no answers for them. So, instead of even trying, he stood up and held his hand out to Japhet. Japhet stared at it a moment, then clasped his wrist, and allowed Franz to pull him to his feet. Without another word, they set off deeper into the forest, their only comfort being the fact that they were together.

They didn't stop again until around noon, and then only long enough to try and chew the hard bread they had packed for the journey. Franz had trouble swallowing but kept choking it down because every time he took a bite so did Japhet. When he had forced himself to eat as much as he felt he could stomach, he packed up the rest and they walked again.

By then the forest started to look the same. All of the trees blurred and Franz no longer believed there were different kinds of trees. They were just trees. White and brown and blocking him off from the rest of the world.

Japhet walked beside him when he could. More than once he tripped and Franz had to grab him and keep him on his feet. It got worse as the sun began to set. Franz hadn't thought it had gotten any warmer when it came up, but now that it was gone he could feel a new depth of cold seep into his bones.

"Remember when we were eight and nine?" Japhet asked as they kept pushing through the snow.

"Yes, of course, I do," Franz muttered. It was too cold to talk, his jaw clenched and he had to pry his lips apart to speak. He wanted to tell Japhet to shut up so he didn't have to try and get words out between his chattering teeth.

"And you said we should camp out in the snow. Remember?"

Somehow, Franz was able to smile in spite of his teeth clanking together. "Yes. You almost froze your toes off."

Japhet tried to glare at him.

"Why can't you ever plan these adventures in the summer?" he asked.

"Maybe you should plan the next one," Franz suggested.

"I think I will. An all day hike, in August, through the Black Forest."

It was a threat Franz knew Japhet had every intention of trying to carry out.

"You know a lot of people who go into the Black Forest never come out," he pointed out.

"Why do you think I'm taking you there?"

"Is that a threat?" Franz scowled at him or tried to. It was hard with his face freezing.

"You threatened to shove me in a lake when I couldn't swim," Japhet reminded him.

"I was just being a good big brother," Franz answered. He couldn't even remember what they had been fighting about, just him wishing there was a lake nearby.

"Well, I'm going to be a good little brother and take you hiking in the Black Forest."

"And I was going to take you to America to meet Judy Garland. I guess it just shows which of us is the better brother." Franz stopped talking when he heard something snap behind them.

He turned and tried to tell himself it was just a small animal, then told himself not to lie. In the crouching shadows, he caught sight of a Nazi uniform and a pistol aimed for Japhet. Without thinking, Franz fired, shoved Japhet into the snow, and fell beside him. Yet, even though he got his shot off first, the Nazi had time to fire before he ducked.

Pain, unlike anything Franz had ever felt before, ripped through his side, but he tried to pretend it wasn't there as Japhet rolled to his stomach and lifted his head out of the snow. He had the pistol Warren had given him clenched in his hands, his eyes wide.

"How many?" he asked.

"I only saw one, but there has to be more." Franz crawled over so he was beside Japhet. He made sure to keep his left side from his view.

Japhet lifted his head up over the bush in front of him and Franz yanked him back down.

"You're going to get your stupid head blown off!" he hissed and peered around the bush. He fought to hold his pistol steady even though his hands were starting to shake and his vision blurred. He was nauseated and unconsciousness tried to ease the pain. He had to fight it off as he aimed at one of the shadowy Nazis who moved toward him and Japhet.

"Keep your head down and only shoot when you see them," Franz instructed. "There can't be too many. We just have to try and convince them there are more than two of us."

"Easy," Japhet muttered. He stared at the other side of the bush.

Saying nothing to him, Franz fired at the Nazi. He watched as he crumpled into the snow and forced his hand to remain steady. He had never killed before, but he didn't want to sit back and let these men kill his best friend.

Japhet fired off a shot and when Franz risked a glance at him, he saw his face had gone deadly white. Franz bit his lower lip until he tasted blood. His anger toward the war and Nazis boiled his blood. Japhet shouldn't be here, he shouldn't have to kill. He was still just a kid.

Forcing his attention in front of him, Franz saw two more figures had emerged. He shot one and Japhet the other. After that seven more emerged, coming out of the woods from different positions to try and surrounded the two boys. Franz could no longer take careful aim but fired as many bullets as quickly as his shaking hand let him. Somehow, between him and Japhet, the Nazis never made it close enough to shoot either of them.

After the last shot had been fired, Franz and Japhet continued to lay in the snow, listening for other sounds of approach. Franz didn't dare think of moving until he was sure they were alone.

An hour wore by. Franz managed to press his scarf against his bleeding side without Japhet noticing, but he felt weaker as each minute passed. The cold tore through him, his side throbbed, and exhaustion tried to rob the last bit of energy he had left.

"Do you think they're gone?" Japhet finally whispered. His voice cracked.

Franz wasn't sure. He was having trouble focusing, but he pushed himself to his knees.

"Let's go," he ordered. He shoved himself to his feet, took one step, and fell over into blackness.

When Japhet was ten and Franz eleven they had decided it would be fun to climb up a pine tree and jump out. They kept going higher and higher, wanting to see just how high they could get before they lost their nerve to jump.

Franz made it the highest, but when he jumped he fell wrong and didn't get up like he had the other times. Japhet had never been more scared in his life, certain Franz had broken his neck. That moment was nothing compared to the night in the frozen woods when Franz fell over and wouldn't get up.

Japhet threw himself down beside him and shook him, an icy

cold chill snaking up his back. He forgot how to breathe when he saw the blood which covered Franz's coat. For one horrifying moment, the nightmare that haunted him most became real. Franz was dead and it was his fault.

Unsure what to do, his heart racing, Japhet touched the wound and Franz growled under his breath. Air rushed into Japhet's lungs and relief flooded through him so fast he felt dizzy. He quickly grabbed Franz's scarf and tied it over the wound in an attempt to stop the blood flow.

Wasting no time, Japhet holstered his pistol, crammed Franz's into his pocket, and rolled to his knees. Franz was not only taller than him he also weighed more, since he had not suffered the loss of appetite like Japhet had. That didn't matter at the moment, though. Japhet pulled Franz's arm over his shoulders and rose to his feet, straining himself as he lifted.

"Lean on me," he said though he wasn't sure if Franz could even hear him.

The bodies he had been staring at for the last hour – bodies which he knew were going to add to his nightmares – no longer bothered Japhet as he turned and walked in the opposite direction. Franz was no help and Japhet had to drag him through the forest, one arm wrapped around his waist and the other holding Franz's arm over his shoulders.

Warren and Karl had both said they would find help if they kept north. Japhet used the stars to direct him whenever they appeared between the clouds. He stayed alert, searching for any sign of a farmhouse.

Once or twice, as he walked, Franz moaned, the only indication Japhet had that he was still alive. He pushed on faster after each groan, determining to ignore the pain which stung his shoulders and legs. As time passed, Japhet worried he would be too late. He feared Franz would bleed to death before he found help.

The cold sapped his energy and he stumbled. His legs started to shake with exertion and with each step Japhet feared it would be his last. When he finally did smell wood smoke, he almost sat down and gave up, certain his tired mind was playing tricks on him.

Pushing aside branches, Japhet sagged against a tree and looked out into a small clearing. Warren had given him a description of the farmhouse, but Japhet blinked several times before he could accept it was the house in front of him.

"Hang on," he whispered to Franz. He pushed himself away from the tree and staggered to the house. Getting up the steps was almost impossible, and when he finally fell against the door, Japhet didn't have the energy to knock. Thankfully, there was no need to.

A moment after his body slammed into the wood, the door opened and Japhet lost his balance, falling into the house. He and Franz crashed to the floor and Japhet lifted his head, looking up into the eyes of an elderly man.

"Please," he panted, "help him."

The man didn't live alone. He was married to a plump wife who moved faster than her size should have allowed. She was also stronger than her short frame looked. She alone lifted Franz up off the floor, pulled him into the house, and laid him on her living room rug. She knelt beside him and began to remove his coat, jacket, and shirt.

Japhet pushed himself to his knees. He tried to stop his legs from shaking so he could stand. Before he had the chance, the elderly man reached down and somehow pulled Japhet to his feet. Before Japhet was aware of what was happening, the man had shoved him into a chair and stood over him, his scowl deepening the wrinkles in his face.

"What's your name?" he snapped.

Japhet's mind went blank. His head spun and he realized he knew nothing of Warren. What if he had betrayed them? What if the woman let Franz die rather than saving him?

Desperate, Japhet tried to stand, but the old man shoved him back down.

"Name!" he shouted.

All his focus on Franz, Japhet said the first thing which came to mind.

"I'm Japhet Buchanan."

The hand came out of nowhere. It connected with his cheek, snapping his head back, and Japhet saw stars.

"You idiot!" the old man shouted. "What if I was a Nazi? Do you want to end up with a bullet in your dumb head? You're no longer Japhet Buchanan! You have to get that through your thick head, do you understand? It doesn't matter what's going on around you, who is dying, who is talking to you. You have to become Stephen Achen! You have to be so convinced you are him no one will ever have need to doubt you! Your own mother could pass you on the street and call to you and you'd not answer!"

The slap stunned Japhet only momentarily. Instinct kicked in before the sting left his cheek, an instinct he didn't know he had. Shoving the man back, Japhet stood and pulled his knife from the sheath. He held it the way Franz had taught him, an inch from the old man's throat.

"Are you Nazis?" he demanded, glancing back over his shoulder at the woman.

"Put that away!" the woman ordered. "We're not Nazis. And husband, leave him be! He has been through so much already, look at him. He's nothing more than a boy."

The man's eyes did not soften, he didn't even look bothered to have a knife next to his throat. He glared at his wife and then Japhet and Japhet felt his resolve slip.

"I know that, wife," the old man snapped. "But this isn't a world for boys, this is a world for men. If he doesn't accept that now, then it might get him killed. Now put that away, boy, before I have to kill you!"

Japhet felt a mixture of anger and shame, his anger outweighing the shame. Not sheathing his knife, he turned his attention to the wife.

"My friend," he asked as she cleaned Franz's wound. "Is he all right?"

The woman looked up and frowned, showing no more welcome than her husband. "He will live. He just lost a lot of blood. He's going to be weak for a while, but he's not going to die."

He didn't near to hear more. Japhet dropped back into the chair, deciding the old man could slap him all he wanted.

Fourteen
Entering Berlin

1940

They stayed with the husband and wife through the rest of the winter. Franz healed quickly, considering he'd been shot, but then they got snowed in before they could leave. They had to wait until spring and for some of the snow to melt before they could continue.

Franz counted the weeks. They'd spent two months with the couple, and in all that time they never learned their names. The husband and wife refused to tell them, even though Japhet asked a couple times before finally giving up.

When the day came to leave, a cold spring day, the husband gave Franz and Japhet each a rusty bicycle he pulled out a shed. He wheeled them into his front yard and leaned them against a tree. Overhead, gray clouds covered the sky and the sun had to fight to get light through them. Snow lay in drifts all over the yard and sat heavy on the branches of the trees. Franz and Japhet had to fight to get the bikes onto the road.

As they shoved, Franz shouted a farewell over his shoulder but the couple didn't so much as wave.

"You can reach Berlin by nightfall if you don't stop to rest," the husband called after them.

"Watch out for Nazis," the wife cautioned.

That didn't make Franz feel any better, but he couldn't say anything because, with that warning, the couple shoved the door closed. Japhet and Franz stared at it, then looked at each other and started to walk again.

"I feel like we've been shoved out into the cold to survive on our own. Like little birds."

His bike slipped and Franz nearly fell. He caught it, leaned on it, and shoved it through a drift. "I'm not being compared to a bird, Japhet," he grunted through clenched teeth.

"You'd be a cute bird." It was the first joke Japhet had made since arriving at the cabin. Franz had hated to see him sitting and watching him, his face drawn with worry. He hated that he'd gotten himself shot and given Japhet cause to worry.

Things would be different in Berlin. Franz decided that as he had laid on the couple's spare bed. He wouldn't do something so foolish again; he'd look after Japhet the way he was supposed to.

The lights of Berlin greeted them an hour after the sunset. It had started to snow and if it wasn't for his legs pumping the bike pedals up and down Franz would have frozen hours ago.

"We'll have warm beds tonight," Franz said. He pushed the pedals down harder, bringing himself up beside Japhet. He touched his own side, holding onto the bars with one hand. The pain from the gunshot had long since vanished though it was still tender.

Japhet said nothing. He nodded but concentrated on pedaling. Half an hour later they found themselves just outside of Berlin. Once in sight of the city Japhet slowed down, then came to a complete stop. Franz stopped beside him, glancing at Japhet's white face.

"Are you okay?" he asked, though he knew the answer.

"Are...you sure about these papers?" Japhet asked. He stared down at his handlebars and his voice choked with shame.

Reaching over, Franz grabbed his shoulder and Japhet lifted his eyes and looked at him.

"I wouldn't be letting you do this unless I was certain of us making it in and out. I'm going to be right beside you the whole time. I promised and I meant it. I'm not going to let anything happen to you."

Japhet nodded twice, then pushed his pedal down and shoved off down the road. For a second or two, Franz just sat and watched him. His heart sank like a cold rock into his stomach and he hoped he hadn't just lied to his best friend.

There were two men on patrol outside the city. They stopped Franz and Japhet, though neither seemed to take much interest in his job. It didn't matter to Japhet. One look at their sharp uniforms and his hands shook as he relived the night his parents were killed.

Japhet pulled on the brakes and his bicycle slid to a stop. He dropped his feet to the ground and hoped his deadly white face wouldn't give him away. He wondered if he even looked enough like a German to pass. Could they see Jew written all over his face?

One of the guards walked up to them, smoke curling up from his cigarette. He pulled it from his lips and flicked ashes at Franz's feet.

"Kind of late to be out, isn't it?" the Nazi asked.

"A little. We were detained, because of the snow." Franz somehow managed to keep calm.

The Nazi shrugged.

"Let me see your papers," he ordered.

Franz reached inside his coat and pulled out his papers as if he had nothing to hide and really was Rupert Hoffmann. Japhet felt like his name was written in bold letters across his chest. He tried to remember everything the old man had told him.

"You have to become Stephen Achen so much that you believe it."

There was a problem with that, though. He didn't believe it. He couldn't just stop being Japhet, he didn't want to. And now the Nazis were going to see that he wasn't Stephen Achen and were going to shot him.

"Rupert Hoffmann," the Nazi murmured, holding Franz's papers up to the light spilling from a small building behind him. Laughter joined the light and poured out into the cold night air. "What brings you to Berlin?"

"My cousin and I, we lived on a farm, but our dads weren't making enough to provide for everyone in our families. We're looking for jobs."

Japhet didn't know until that moment they were passing themselves off as cousins. He figured it was one of Franz's last minute ideas, something he had come up with since Karl said they didn't look enough alike to go as brothers. Japhet wasn't sure being cousins was much better.

The Nazi scoffed, handed Franz his papers back, and moved over to Japhet. Japhet forgot how to breathe and wasn't sure he was going to be able to get his hands to work when asked for his papers. When he pulled them from his coat, it was almost as if someone moved his hands for him.

Time slowed. In the following seconds, Japhet heard the Nazi yelling for his comrades. He heard the shout of Jew. He saw Franz take a bullet in the heart and fall off his bike into the snow. Japhet felt hands grabbing him and saw them dragging him off as the snow turned blood red behind him. All of his worst fears stared him in the face – until the Nazi slapped the papers back in his hands and ended the horrible images.

"Best of luck to you," he said and waved them past. He laughed.

Japhet's legs sagged out from under him and the only thing that kept him upright was his bike. Helplessly, he followed Franz right into Berlin.

1940

It took two months for Franz and Japhet to settle in. The first month was the worst. It wasn't easy finding an apartment and took even longer to find jobs. Franz finally found one working in a factory manufacturing parts for rifles. Japhet got a position at the library.

Japhet's nightmares didn't go away as Franz had been hoping. Their apartment had two bedrooms side-by-side and at night Franz could hear Japhet restlessly thrashing around in his bed at night.

By the second month, Franz felt almost settled. As settled as he could get without his family and seeing his friend's bloodshot eyes every morning.

"How did you sleep?" Franz asked one morning.

Japhet sat at the table, his black hair sticking up in matted clumps all over his head. His face was drawn and he looked half dead.

"Fine," Japhet wearily answered.

Franz wanted to hit something, but instead he went and grabbed two eggs out of the icebox and began to boil them.

"Hmm," he murmured. He wished he had the courage to tell Japhet to open up and stop trying to hide. He wondered if it would help to tell Japhet he'd been having his own nightmares. They'd only just started, and only happened once in a great while, but they always left him feeling cold. Every single one was about a Nazi shooting Japhet in the head and Franz unable to get there on time. He'd started sleeping with his pistol under his pillow.

"Are you murdering more eggs for breakfast?" Japhet raised his head as the sound of boiling water filled the small apartment.

"Don't insult my eggs, Buchanan."

"You insulted my roasted chicken, Kappel, so I can insult your eggs all I want." Japhet's voice was dull, but Franz took any small sign of life he could get as a good sign. By the time he and Japhet left for work, he felt a little less worried about his friend.

That night they stayed up later than usual before going to bed. Half an hour after Franz laid down he could hear Japhet's bed creaking as he tossed in his sleep. As with most nightmares Franz didn't move, just lay and listened and hated the world. Minutes wore by and grated on his nerves when Japhet shouted.

Even though he'd been just drifting off, Franz jumped out of bed and grabbed his pistol. He crashed into his small dresser but kept going, out the door and into the living room. Blinking, he turned and shoved the door to Japhet's room opened. He leveled his pistol over Japhet's bed, but no one stood there.

Japhet still lay in the bed and yelled, his shouts having not yet awakened him. His blanket had become tangled around his legs, his face was as white as the sheets Franz's mother had kept on their beds back home, and his brow was wrinkled in fear. That wasn't the worst part, though.

Stumbling into the room, Franz froze when he realized what Japhet was shouting. His arms flailing, Japhet yelled Franz's name over and over again, and he sounded scared to death.

Franz set his pistol on Japhet's desk and rushed to his side. Grabbing his shoulders, Franz yanked him upright and held to him as Japhet swung his fists. He tugged the blanket free with one hand.

"Japhet!" he shouted, "it's me, it's Franz! Come on, Japhet! Wake up! It's going to be all right, but you have to wake up!"

It was a feeble promise, because the nightmares weren't just in dreams, not this time. The nightmare was all around them, closing in, ready to kill them given the chance. But Franz didn't care about that right then. All he cared about was that Japhet refused to wake.

"Franz!" Japhet nearly screamed, his face twisted with horror. Franz felt an unknown fear grip him. What was Japhet dreaming about that made him look like that?

Desperate, he shook Japhet as hard as he dared but it did no good. Finally, clenching his shoulder in one hand, Franz slapped him with his other hand. The slap worked. Japhet's eyes flew opened and he stared around his room, his face still white and tears in his eyes.

"Franz!" Japhet yelled again while trying to pull free of Franz's grip. "Franz!" He looked frantically around him, unaware of where he was and who was with him.

"I'm right here!" Franz grabbed both his shoulders. "Right here, like I promised I would always be. I'm not going anywhere, Japhet. Remember? I said I would be at your side...." He didn't know what else to say, the lump in his throat cutting him off.

Japhet blinked, stared at him, then the tears escaped. Franz pulled him forward into a crushing hug. He held him tightly, not wanting to let go. Franz had been scared of losing Japhet, but he hadn't ever realized there was a risk of Japhet losing his mind.

For one terrible moment, Franz had seen him change right before his eyes, and at that moment he wasn't Japhet but someone so broken Franz no longer recognized him.

The Nazis were going to steal his brother, in one way or another. Franz could feel it now. If they couldn't break his body, they were going to break his mind. And Franz wanted to stop that from happening, but all he could do was hold Japhet.

"It's all over with," Franz whispered. "It was just a nightmare. None of it was real."

"They killed you," Japhet shook. "I saw them. They killed you to get to me."

Franz held him tighter. "It was just a nightmare, Japhet. I wouldn't let them do that, to either of us." He swallowed back his anger and slowly pulled back.

Without a word, he helped Japhet to his feet and led him into the living room. There, he sat him down on the shabby couch, then rushed back into his own room and snatched his blanket off his bed. When he returned to the living room Japhet had his knees pulled up to his chest, his chin resting on them. He looked broken and completely alone in the world.

Biting his bottom lip, Franz flung his blanket over Japhet's shoulders, then tucked it in around him. Once he was done, he went into the little kitchen and pulled out the last of their milk. Pouring into a pot, he heated it on the stove as he had seen Gabi do and dumped it into two mugs once it was warm.

When Franz finished, he took the mugs into the living room and placed one in one of Japhet's limp hands. Without really paying attention, Japhet took the mug. He held it close as Franz sat beside him, close enough that Japhet would be able to feel his presence.

Silently, they drank their milk, neither speaking. The warm

liquid soothed some of Franz's anger and grief and seemed to relax Japhet. The moment he was done, Japhet's mug slipped from his hands and Franz snatched it before it hit the floor. He said nothing as Japhet curled up into a little ball, lay his head on the side of the couch, and drifted off into what appeared to be a peaceful sleep.

Hoping he might get one night of real rest, Franz didn't move, not even when the evening chill crept into his bones. He stayed where he was, watching over Japhet.

***

It was Saturday. Japhet knew because Franz always fried eggs on Saturday instead of boiling them. It was a tradition of Mrs. Kappel's and one Franz had attempted to continue. Of course, his eggs always had black on the bottoms and a hint of charcoal taste but Japhet never complained.

Japhet had trouble waking up that Saturday morning, something he usually had no trouble with. He had to fight his eyes open as the smell of burnt eggs filled the apartment.

Pulling one arm out from the blanket wrapped securely around him, Japhet rubbed his eyes and blinked, slowly realizing he was in the living room. He had to rub his eyes again before he remembered he was no longer at the Kappels' house but at his and Franz's apartment

Japhet couldn't remember coming out into the living room, or falling asleep on the couch. And, when he looked closer, he saw he had Franz's blanket wrapped around him, not his own. He didn't remember stealing Franz's blanket and wondered if he had been sleepwalking. Though, if that had been the case, he couldn't imagine Franz willingly giving up his blanket. Sleepwalking or not, he would have put up a fight.

Pushing himself up, Japhet held the blanket close because the apartment was cold. He turned his head and blearily peered into the kitchen as smoke rolled out of the oven.

Franz jumped back and yanked the little door open. He pulled out two pieces of black toast with his bare hands. Franz yelped when they burned his fingers and he flung the toast across the kitchen, sticking his fingers in his mouth.

Japhet laughed. It came up without warning, escaping his throat and bursting out of his lips. And it wasn't just a light chuckle, but a real laugh. The kind that made him wrap his arms around his stomach and caused his shoulders to shake.

Hearing him, Franz spun around, but he didn't scowl like Japhet thought he would. He had stared for nearly a minute before a smile escaped, followed by a laugh.

It felt nice, laughing as they had done as kids. Japhet could pretend they had just done something to their sisters and were giggling out behind the woodpile while they listened to their screeches.

Tossing the eggs on two plates, Franz carried them out and handed Japhet one plate. He then sat down beside him and poked at his egg. Japhet stared at his slightly black breakfast, surprised to find he was actually hungry.

"How did I end up on the couch?" he asked as he ate. His stomach didn't lurch like normal when he swallowed.

"You were sleepwalking last night. You came in and stole my blanket and camped out here. I tried to steal my blanket back, but you bit me."

Franz's tone and expression were so serious Japhet almost believed him. Almost.

"I don't sleepwalk," he muttered.

"Just keep telling yourself that." Franz glanced sideways

at him and grinned. "Now shut up and eat your breakfast. It's Saturday and we both have the day off."

Japhet did as he was told. Both of them had most Saturdays off and spent them in the apartment or walking the streets of Berlin, trying to gather information on the war and learn things that might help their families. Japhet was certain Franz had something different planned for today.

After they had eaten, Japhet was ordered to go and get dressed. When he emerged from his bedroom a few minutes later – wearing his light blue shirt and black pants, his hair neatly combed – Franz was waiting for him. Franz had gone so far as to put on his gray pants, off-white shirt, and gray jacket.

"What do you have planned?" Japhet asked, suddenly suspicious. Franz didn't wear jackets as a general rule.

"Why? I'm not going to get us into trouble or anything."

"I doubt it. I know you, you always get us in trouble. And you don't wear your jacket...you've never worn your jacket. Do you have a date or something?" Japhet's suspicions deepened. If Franz were setting them up on dates, he would punch him.

"No. I tried, really. I have asked about ten girls, tried to convince them to go out with you, but they kept running away. Sorry, looks like you're doomed to be single." Franz clamped Japhet on the shoulder and steered him toward the door. "Me, on the other hand...I have had plenty of girls begging me to go on dates with them. But don't worry, you can be my best man when I get married. Now come on. We're going to have fun today."

Still feeling happier than he had in a long time, Japhet allowed Franz to pull him out the door and outside the apartment building. Once outside, they mounted up on their bikes and Japhet set off, following Franz wherever he planned to lead him.

Sixteen
A final happy memory

1940

The sun had been out the week before and now the streets were dry and the mornings warmer in spite of the nights being cold.

Most of the buildings near Franz and Japhet's apartment were nothing more than apartments themselves. Soldiers and Nazis lived in some of the apartments, which made Franz uncomfortable, but in the one he shared with Japhet there lived a couple families and some single people. An elderly lady lived on the ground floor and she smiled and waved as the boys set off down the street. Franz didn't know her name, but every morning when he left for work she'd be standing outside and she'd wave at him. Franz had started to consider her his friend, and he always returned her friendly waves.

When they were out of sight of the apartment, Franz picked up speed. Since the sun had just broken over the tops of some of the buildings, frost still covered the street and crunched under their bike tires.

"Where are we going?" Japhet asked as they peddled out into the busier part of the city. They now had to move their bikes to the side of the road and ride single file so they wouldn't risk getting hit by the few cars driving up and down the street. Franz took the lead.

"Stop asking questions. It's annoying."

"I'm younger," Japhet said. "I excel at being annoying."

"Keep it up and I will shove you in front of a car and you can excel at being in pain."

"Maybe I should shove you in front of a car," Japhet countered.

"You have to catch me first!" Franz said and pushed his bike on even faster.

Soon they reached the end of the city and stopped to show their papers to the guards. Franz was happy to see Japhet was more at ease this time. They made it through with no problem and set off down the road, turning off when they came to a side road, and peddled on until they were on a hard packed dirt road and surrounded by trees.

By then the sun had risen up above the trees and Franz had to stop to pull off his jacket. Japhet kept his on, though, a small reminder that he was so thin now he had little defense against the still crisp air.

While they rode, they talked, mostly about their childhood. Franz made sure to avoid painful subjects, though their childhood held a hint of sorrow as it was just a reminder of everything that had changed.

Mostly they talked about some of their best pranks, all pulled on their sisters, Ross, and Hardy. They remembered the time they had gotten into the attic in the Kappels' house and scraped the floor until they had Kirsten convinced there was a giant rat above her room. They'd then sat back and listened to her and her sisters running around the house, screaming.

"Oh!" Japhet exclaimed. "Remember when we put a tack on

our teacher's chair and he thought Gilbert had done it?"

Franz grinned evilly. He'd felt bad for that at the time, but that was before Gilbert had started to avoid Japhet because he was a Jew. Franz had gotten into a few fights with Gilbert, and he still didn't feel any regret over them.

"You put the tack on his chair," Franz reminded Japhet. "It was your first prank, and Gilbert blamed me for it. He got Amell to punch me because he was too much of a coward to do it himself."

Japhet grinned and Franz saw no sorrow in his eyes like he expected. "I know, but I jumped him for you..."

Shaking his head, Franz cut him off. "You jumped on his back and he threw you to the ground like you weighed nothing. I had to punch Amell to save you getting your neck wrung, and we were both sent home early and I had to explain to our parents why my pants were torn and you looked like someone had tried to kill you."

They'd both gotten in trouble for the incident. Franz had tried to take most of the blame, but Japhet wouldn't let him and admitted he had been the one to place the tack in the first place.

By the end of it, Japhet had to confess to the teacher and they both had to apologize to Gilbert, who had readily forgiven them.

"I'm kind of sad you had to tell the truth," Gilbert admitted after they had shaken hands. "Everyone believed it was me and they were telling me how brave I was to do it. I haven't been that popular before."

"Probably won't happen again," Franz had said, feeling better that he had taken away Gilbert's fame and that it now belonged rightfully to Japhet. "But at least you got to enjoy it for a day."

"Thanks," Gilbert had muttered and playfully shoved him.

It had been one of the few conversations Franz had taken part in. He hadn't ever told Japhet, but he used to be painfully shy when he was younger. He still didn't know what it was about Japhet, but he'd been able to draw him out of his shell. After that, talking to Japhet at least hadn't been a problem.

"We're going to Brandenburg, aren't we?" Japhet asked, breaking into the memory.

Franz looked up, just in time to avoid the rock his front tire was aiming for.

"Just because we are heading out of Berlin doesn't mean we are going to Brandenburg," he retorted.

Japhet wasn't about to relent or give up that easily.

"I discovered your secret plans and now you have to confess. We're going, aren't we?"

Sighing, Franz tried to sound exasperated. "Yes," he muttered, "I thought I'd push you into the lake there."

"I can swim, you know. I had to learn, being friends with you."

This wasn't the first time Franz had threatened his lake pushing, and he knew it wouldn't be the last.

"I don't care, I'm still pushing you in." He grinned and peddled faster, outstripping his friend and leaving him behind for a few seconds.

The nightmare came back to him. He knew it would happen sooner or later and was only surprised it took so long. It returned as they were going up the road, heading toward the lake Japhet had only ever heard about. It hit him hard, like the foot in the stomach which had broken his rib the day outside the ice cream shop.

Japhet could recall all of it. He heard the gunshots, just like the night he and Franz had hidden in the forest and had been forced to pick off the Nazis. He heard the shouts and screams and again felt no fear because Franz was beside him. Then the scene changed and there were Nazis holding him and Franz and they were yelling.

"You are not Stephen Achen! We know you aren't! Tell us your real name or he dies!" And one of them shoved a pistol up against Franz's head.

Franz looked at him, his face pale, but his eyes showing an unnerving calm.

"Don't do it," he said, his voice controlled. "Don't do it, I'm not worth it!"

Japhet hadn't believed him. Franz was his best friend, his brother, and that made him worth it.

"My name is Japhet Buchanan!" he had shouted.

"A Jew!" one of them snapped, then there was a shot and Franz hit the ground, his eyes glazed over in death.

The memory was as vivid as the nightmare had been and it took Japhet's breath away, but he didn't stop peddling or let his distress show on his face. Something else stirred in his memory. He remembered someone forcing him awake and hugging him, then he'd been led out to the couch, wrapped up in a blanket, and given warm milk as if he were only five.

Glancing sideways, Japhet saw Franz intently studying their surroundings as if suddenly worried he had gotten them lost, and he smiled. The bike ride made more sense now and Japhet pushed the nightmare away. If Franz were going through all this trouble to make him feel better, then Japhet would enjoy it and not slip back into fear and sorrow over a nightmare he desperately hoped would never come true.

***

They found the lake half an hour later and stopped their bikes, racing each other to the water. Franz had his shoes off before

Japhet reached the small, dancing waves and he turned back to give a look of triumph.

Japhet saw his chance, a chance he knew would likely not come again – or if it did it would be years from this moment. It was not something he could pass up. He dashed up behind Franz, shoving him as hard as he could.

Hitting Franz was like hitting a solid wall, but Franz wasn't expecting it and lost his balance. Arms flailing, he tumbled into the still cold waters and came up sputtering.

"You didn't just..."

Japhet proudly crossed his arms over his chest and grinned as he stood in the grass. He felt he deserved a moment of gloating and didn't wish to waste it.

Pulling himself out onto the grassy bank, Franz grabbed a handful of his shirt and wrung water from it. Japhet watched him, waiting for his reaction. It wasn't like him to take something like this and not put up a fight. Japhet wondered if his calm had something to do with the nightmare. Was this going to be the day where Japhet could do anything he wanted and Franz would just meekly take it? His mind began to turn with the possibilities, but they didn't have a chance to turn into any solid plans.

Without warning, Franz was on his feet and had Japhet swung over his shoulder. In a blink, he threw him forward, tossing him into the lake. Japhet barely had time to hold his breath as the cold water closed over his head. He fought his way to the surface and gasped for warm air as the cold tried to squeeze it all out of his lungs.

Pleased with himself, Franz sat down on the edge of the lake and laughed. Japhet, standing up, yanked his jacket off and tossed it at Franz, then he leaped toward the bank, grabbed Franz's feet, and threw himself backward. Surprisingly, Franz slid into the water with ease and soon both of them were tackling each other, splashing and shouting as the water turned their bodies numb.

They might have stayed in the water all day, at least longer than the fifteen or so minutes they were in if their lips hadn't started to turn blue. Shivering, they climbed out and laid in the sun, looking up at the clouds like they used to do in the field near their village.

Little was said, but Japhet didn't care. He didn't think moments like these were going to be common after this, so he determined to enjoy himself while he could.

When they were mostly dry, Franz pulled his shoes back on and Japhet picked up his still wet jacket. He draped it over his handlebars so it could dry as he and Franz rode into Brandenburg.

All of their effort to dress nicely now wasted, Japhet didn't even bother to try and smooth down his hair and brush grass off his rumpled shirt. He didn't think it mattered much since their sisters weren't there to scold them.

Franz stopped at a little ice cream shop for lunch. Japhet didn't protest the idea of just having ice cream and followed him inside, ignoring the looks they got from a group of five pretty girls who sat together at one of the tables.

Getting their ice cream, which Franz paid for, they took a table one away from the girls and did justice to their lack of actual real food since breakfast. Japhet could feel the girls watching the two of them, but he didn't let it bother him.

He grinned slyly at Franz, who returned the look. He figured they would both have to learn how to behave in public if they really did want to get dates someday.

Seventeen
Franz's idea

1941

Summer passed and still the Kappels and Ruth had not been able to get out of Germany. Warren kept in contact with the boys, bluntly telling them of the complications they were continually running into. Franz was grateful for it. He didn't want things smoothed over and made to look better than they were.

Our forger was caught, he explained in one of the messages he managed to get into Berlin. *We tried to free him but the Nazis sent him to a concentration camp and he was killed in the gas chambers before we could get him out. We have others, but they are being more careful now and it's hard convincing the two we know to help us out. I know of another, but he is going to want a fortune to do it. Right now, at this moment, our biggest setback is money and knowledge. What you are sending, money wise, has been helping and we will have enough by next summer – I'm convinced of it. Not knowing who we can trust, who is going to turn us in, or what the Nazis are planning – or if they are closing in on us – is something I have not found a solution to yet. If you can learn anything while in Berlin, let me know. Just, don't get your stupid heads blown off for it.*

"He really likes insulting us, doesn't he?" Japhet asked as

Franz finished reading the message and then promptly burned it.

A storm howled outside and battered against the windows. The bedrooms were cold so the two of them had opted for sleeping in the living room, in front of the stove.

"Do you think we can get information for him?" Japhet asked.

"It won't be easy. It isn't like either of us has a job where the movements of troops and what the Nazis are doing is easy to come by."

"What do we do then?" Japhet rested his elbows on his knees. They were sharp joints digging into his thin legs. Franz looked away.

"We'll think of something," he said, "don't worry. We always come up with something."

Each day passed in Berlin had slowly grated on Franz's nerves. Each day meant a higher risk of Japhet being found out or of his family being discovered on the farm. There were nights when Franz couldn't sleep because all of his dreams were of his family getting shot, or of soldiers dragging Japhet out into the streets and beating him to death.

Desperate for information, Franz had taken to walking the streets. Each day when he left work he took a new way home, hoping to overhear something.

Two days after Warren's message came, Franz prepared to leave work half an hour after his shift ended. He'd discovered if he stayed half an hour later no one said anything and he could make a few extra dollars.

He'd just clocked out and was in the back room, putting on his jacket and picking up half his sandwich left over from lunch when one of his fellow co-workers joined him.

Franz didn't interact much with the men he worked with. Most of them were husbands or older men, and like Franz, they kept to themselves. A few were friends and would go out for drinks after their shifts, sometimes inviting others to join them.

"Long day," the man sighed as he came into the little room where jackets and packed lunches were kept. The men were allowed a half hour break each day and most of them ate in the room.

"Yes," Franz said. He shoved the paper bag, which contained his sandwich, into his jacket pocket.

"Headed home?"

Since it didn't seem like the man had plans to stop talking, Franz turned to carry on a conversation face-to-face. The man was middle-aged, balding, and portly. Franz recognized him as Mr. Janz. He'd been there since Franz started, greeted everyone as if they were his best friends, and walked with a limp in his right leg.

"Yes," Franz said. He relaxed. Mr. Janz had only ever been friendly, and nothing about him screamed Nazi spy.

"If you hold up a minute I'll walk some ways with you. Not sure if we live in the same place, but we can go together 'till we part ways." And he winked.

"All right," Franz said. He couldn't think of any reason to turn the offer down, and realized he didn't want to even if he could.

Mr. Janz yanked his coat around his shoulders and grabbed his cane, which he never used while he worked. He waved Franz out the door in front of him and together the two left the factory and set off down the street.

Cold air bit at Franz's nose and he kicked himself for not bringing his coat. When he'd left that morning, there had been an illusion of warm weather in the air. Now with the sun gone the night had turned bitter.

As they walked, Mr. Janz talked of rumors he'd heard about the war. Franz nodded to show he was listening though he wished Mr. Janz would pick a subject which would help his family.

"You live with your cousin, don't you?" Mr. Janz asked as they turned a corner and started down another street. Franz had forgotten to watch where they were going.

"Yes." He glanced warily at the man beside him. He never spoke of Japhet at work. He looked around but saw they were still alone.

"Saw you two the other day...bike riding a few Saturdays ago. Probably the last one you'll be able to take now that winter is really here!" Mr. Janz laughed and turned his collar up.

"How did you know we're cousins?" Franz asked, trying to keep suspicion out of his voice.

"My wife was with me. She's friends with your neighbor or something." Mr. Janz shrugged and winked. "Women gossip you know. My wife told me."

Franz nodded. He relaxed his shoulders but still felt tense.

"He looked like a nice kid," Mr. Janz went on.

"He is." Franz cleared his throat and changed subjects. He would rather talk about war rumors that his Jewish friend. "What else have you heard about the war?"

"Not much." Mr. Janz eagerly jumped back to war news. "If you want to know what is going on, though, you need to get a hold of one of those Nazis. Bet they know more than any of us can ever dream of knowing."

Unexpectedly, a knot formed in Franz's stomach and an idea began to haunt him.

Eighteen
Japhet meets the Hitler Youth

1941

The week before Christmas, Franz became quieter and withdrawn. Japhet didn't think much about it. He was the same way. Christmas was hard to celebrate now, it just reminded him of his parents' deaths. He was just as sullen as Franz.

One morning, after they had both choked down hard and lumpy oatmeal, Franz broke the silence they had been spending the last two days in.

"You might want to cook dinner," he said as he washed their bowls and left the pot full of water so the oats all burned to the bottom would have a chance to loosen before he tried to wash it later.

"Huh?" Japhet lifted his head and blinked sleepily. He'd been getting even less sleep, the closer it got to Christmas.

"I know, it's my turn." Franz didn't turn from the sink and his shoulders went up and down. "I don't think I'll be home, though, 'till really late. You don't have to wait for me."

"Oh." Japhet rubbed his eyes and tried to wake himself up. "I don't care. I mean, I don't care that I have to cook. It'll be fine."

Franz finally turned and squinted at him. "Are you okay?" he asked.

"What? Oh, yes, I'm fine. I'm just tired." Japhet knew being fine wasn't required right now, for either of them.

"Maybe...you know, you could not go to work today. Stay here and get some sleep. It wouldn't hurt anything." Franz's eyes filled with concern as he intently studied Japhet.

"No, I'm fine, really." Japhet even forced a smile. "If I get tired, though, or worse, I'll come home early." He didn't think he would actually do it, but he knew Franz would feel better if he heard him say it.

"Okay...if you're sure. Don't try and overdo anything. Some extra sleep wouldn't kill you."

Franz's usual smile didn't follow these words and Japhet was pricked with guilt for worrying him so much. He told himself he was going to sleep that night so Franz wouldn't waste energy and concern over him.

"Go to bed early tonight, don't wait up for me. If you're awake when I get back, I'll wrap you up so tight in your blanket you'll have to sleep all week. I'll see you tomorrow." And just like that he was gone, but Japhet didn't mind, because Franz had sounded like his old self as he slipped out the door.

Japhet didn't mind his job. No one came to the library all that much, which meant he could spend hours quietly reading after putting away returned books. Not that he found many interesting books, not since Hitler had banned and burned many books to "cleanse the German spirit" as Joseph Goebbels had said in his speech at the 1933 book burning.

Hitler's idea of cleansing was banning every book written by Jews, liberals, foreigners, and so forth. The head librarian, a man in his seventies with balding hair and wire-rimmed glasses, had explained it to Japhet.

"Hitler knew what he was doing, he still does. If you want to change a country, what do you do?"

Japhet said nothing at first. Such talks could get a person arrested, or worse, and he hadn't known if Mr. Voelgr was baiting him. He'd shrugged his answer and the old man had leaned in closer to him.

"You start with the children. You present a new idea and make it a truth. You take away their freedom of thought, leaving them only one option. What do you think he's doing with the Hitler Youth? With his nighttime speeches? He is giving the new generation an idea, but only one idea. They are being raised to believe it is the solid truth, and anything else they hear growing up they will assume is wrong.

"Yes, Hitler knows what he's doing. You don't try and change the old men who are set in their ways. No, you start with the young. That's how you conquer a country."

As Japhet walked home from work later that evening – Mr. Voelgr had sent him home early, saying he didn't look well and it was close to Christmas – he again thought of some of their talks. Not that they were really talks as all Japhet ever did was listen.

Snow crunched under his boots as he made his way down the street, barely paying attention to where he walked. The wind picked up and he turned up his collar, lowered his head, and turned down a side street which blocked the wind better than the one he had been on.

Japhet rarely took other paths home. He liked to keep to the one he was familiar with, but the wind bit through his thin coat, making the back streets welcoming.

With his head down, Japhet forgot to look where he walked and before long plowed into another body. Japhet bounced backward, lost his balance, and fell to the sidewalk. When he raised his eyes, his stomach lurched so violently he felt sick.

Sitting on the ground in his own snow bank, his feet out in front of him, was a boy around Japhet's age. A boy dressed in a Hitler Youth uniform.

Japhet's head spun and he fought back waves of panic. In his mind, he screamed at himself, over and over, "Your name is Stephen Achen! Stephen Achen!"

"I'm sorry." The boy stood up and brushed snow and something else off his uniform. His hands shook and Japhet saw his face was pale. Japhet squinted through the gathering dusk and saw something gray spread out in the snow at the boy's feet. A box lay in the snow and something gold glinted beside it.

Pushing himself to his feet, Japhet stretched to his full height though he knew it wouldn't do much good. He was still so thin and worn he didn't look anything close to a man. He wished his voice were deeper.

"I wasn't looking where I was going," the boy murmured. He had trouble taking his eyes off the box.

"What are you doing out here? It's...kind of cold," Japhet stammered.

The boy squared his shoulders and threw his head back as if suddenly remembering he was part of the Hitler Youth.

"I'm on a mission..."

A cold knot formed in the pit of Japhet's stomach.

"A mission?" Japhet whispered as something wiggled into his mind. Now he stared at the box.

"I was supposed to deliver these boxes..."

Boxes. More than one. How many had he delivered? Slowly, cautiously, Japhet lifted his eyes and for the first time saw where he'd wandered while trying to avoid the wind. He was in one of the back streets, one he never had gone to before. All around him a heavy, frightened silence lay. His head started to spin and he staggered forward a step, stopping right above the gold.

It was a ring, just like the wedding ring his father had worn. Japhet was looking down at a box which had contained human ashes and a wedding ring.

"Who are you giving the boxes to?" Japhet whispered, his voice squeaking in a way which would have shamed him at any other time in his life.

"Mostly women...sometimes children. They all live in these apart..."

Japhet snapped. He'd never felt such uncontrollable rage fill him as did at that moment, even when he had watched his mother shot. Something inside him broke and anger filled the space where it had been and nothing he could do stopped it.

Springing forward, Japhet grabbed the taller boy and shoved him up against a building. Filled with a strength he didn't know he had, Japhet rammed his arm against the boy's throat and held him there, listening to his strangled gasps as he fought to breathe. The boy grabbed Japhet's arm but wasn't able to pull it down.

"Do you know what was in those boxes?" Japhet demanded, his voice so cold it sounded like it belonged to someone else. It scared him.

"I was just told to deliver them!" the boy whimpered, struggling to get free. "I didn't question my orders!"

"Of course not," Japhet hissed, "you're a good little soldier, aren't you? Doing what you're told without thinking about yourself. Those boxes – they were filled with human ashes. Dead Jews. You were taking bodies of dead Jews back to their families!"

"At least this way they know what happened to them," the boy garbled, fear in his eyes as he stared into Japhet's.

Japhet saw red. His saw his own fist, but it seemed to come

out of nowhere as he slammed it into the boy's face.

The boy yelled and Japhet pulled his arm back for another blow when someone grabbed him from behind. Strong hands held his shoulders and pulled him back, but Japhet wasn't about to give up without a fight.

"Let me go!" he roared, but whoever held him just gripped him tighter as the boy wrapped a hand around his bleeding nose.

"Shut up before you get yourself killed!" the man holding him snapped, but Japhet didn't care. Horrors he never dreamed possible were staring him in the face and all he felt was anger. Japhet wanted to beat the boy until he felt the same pain as he did.

Japhet struggled against the arms holding onto him, but he couldn't break free. He fought as hard as he could but the lack of food had left him with little muscle and the man was bigger than the boy had been. Japhet could do nothing as he was pulled behind one of the buildings and slammed against a brick wall.

"What's wrong with you?" the man hissed. He was taller than Japhet had thought, towering over him and scowling. "You trying to get yourself killed?"

"He was...the boxes..." It started to sink in what Japhet had seen and his anger slowly drained, leaving him light-headed and weak in the knees. His stomach turned violently and he had to drop his head and concentrate on breathing.

"Calm down!" The man relaxed his hold, gently keeping Japhet on his feet. Japhet sagged forward and relied on the man to hold onto him. He wasn't sure if he could trust him or not, but he didn't trust himself to be on his own.

Shaking, in whatever rage still flowed through his body, Japhet thought of the ring again. How many Jewish women had gotten boxes like the one Japhet had knocked over? How many were left weeping in their homes, knowing they would never see their husbands again?

"Hey, calm down there kid!" The man lowered him to the ground and Japhet buried his face in his hands and breathed deeply. In some ways, he felt like he'd been stabbed in the heart, but he didn't want this stranger to see him falling apart. He forced himself to stand and the man grabbed his arm.

"We have to get out of here. That boy likely left to tell all his friends, and if they find us neither of us are walking away with all our bones in one piece, if we walk away at all. Follow me."

Japhet had no choice but to follow. He had no energy to walk on his own and the man kept a firm hold on his arm. Japhet had no idea where they were going and he didn't pay attention, but neither did he fight it. He no longer cared. He wouldn't even mind if they killed him – he no longer wanted to live in the world his had turned into.

Japhet was vaguely aware of being led down some stairs into a dark room. From there the man nudged him down a hall to a door at the far end. The man opened it and dragged him into a cellar where another man sat at a wide desk. He rose and frowned when he saw them.

"Not again, Seth!"

"This isn't an again, Leb!" Seth retorted. "This one is-"

"What?" Leb cut the taller man off. "Different? Ready to fight for our cause? Stupidly brave? Reckless enough to stand up to Hitler? I've heard it all before, Seth. I thought we agreed you'd stop dragging people down here after you almost got us turned over to the Nazis last time."

"This one is different, Leb!" Seth argued, ignoring the Nazi comment. "He punched a Hitler Youth boy."

Leb's eyes widened. "He what?" he asked.

"He punched a Hitler Youth. I think he broke his nose."

"Really?" Leb came around the desk and studied Japhet, his eyes intent though Japhet had trouble focusing on the face in front of him.

"Yes. You should have..."

"Shut up, Seth," Leb said, cutting him off. He squinted hard at Japhet. "What's your name?"

"Japhet Buchanan."

Japhet knew the old man at the farm would be mad at him, but he didn't care. After what he'd just seen he didn't want to be Stephen. He wanted to stand tall and tell the world he was Japhet Buchanan and he was a Jew.

"Hmm," Leb murmured. "Buchanan, you say? That isn't exactly the kind of name Hitler would like. It's very Jewish."

Leb was hoping for something. Testing him. Japhet didn't care what kind of test it was.

"I am a Jew," he bluntly told him.

"See, I told you..."

"Shut up, Seth." Leb didn't take his eyes off Japhet. "What kind of man openly admits to being a Jew and punches a boy in the Hitler Youth?"

Japhet's shoulders went up and down and his tongue suddenly refused to work. He wished Franz were there, right beside him, ready to help him out of this mess. Who were these men and what were they going to do to him now that they knew the truth?

"Well, you are either very brave or very stupid...likely a little of both," Leb murmured. "And we are always looking for a little of both."

"We?" Japhet finally found his voice though his lips remained dry. "Who is we?"

Leb shook his head.

"Before we tell you that we have some questions for you."

Then, without any kind of warning, a bag was thrown over Japhet's head, his hands were pinned behind his back, and he was dragged off.

Nineteen
Tested

1941

Since Japhet couldn't see he relied on his other senses, hoping they might give him some idea as to where he was being taken. He hoped for certain scents, tried to get a feeling of the ground under his feet, anything that might help him to escape if he was able to get away later. He heard a door open, then someone – probably Seth – shoved him into a chair. His hands were tied to it behind his back and he gave up all hope of escape.

"Another one?" This was a new voice, deep and cold. Japhet's blood turned to ice.

"Yes. I want to know everything about him. He says his name is Japhet Buchanan." That was from Leb, and his words were followed by scuffling feet and the door opened and closed.

"About time. I was getting bored."

Japhet almost whimpered but didn't allow himself. He wanted Franz now more than ever. This man sounded like one of the bullies who had beat him up outside the ice cream shop, only this time Franz wasn't there to try and save his neck. Japhet almost panicked, suddenly frightened that he would never see his friend alive again.

"So," the man pulled the bag off and Japhet blinked in the light of a single bulb hanging from the ceiling, "you're Japhet Buchanan? Great name. Jewish?"

The man probably stood only a few inches taller than Japhet, but he made up for it in muscle. His arms, chest, and shoulders were large and he filled up the small space lit by the light. The sight of him did nothing to make Japhet feel better. Looking up at the man's cold smile, Japhet had an image of a cat toying with a mouse just before killing it.

"Y-yes," he stammered. He saw no point in denying his name. He had already told Seth and Leb.

It came out of nowhere. It wasn't a fist, but it hit him so fast Japhet couldn't get a good look at it. He figured it was a stick of some sort and it slammed into his shoulder. Japhet gritted his teeth together, but it didn't help the pain.

"Jew!" the giant man bellowed, his voice filling up the small confines of the room. "Scum! Worthless, murdering race! Give me one reason I shouldn't kill you!"

Japhet saw his mother shot and recalled every story he had heard about how the Nazis treated and killed the Jews. Now it was his turn, only he wasn't going to the gas chambers. No, an over-sized Nazi would beat him to death in some back storage room.

"Well?" The man stuck his face right in front of Japhet's. "Tell me! Why shouldn't I kill you?"

No answer came to Japhet's mind. He couldn't think of any good reason he should be allowed to live. He couldn't even think of a reason Franz would give, one full of sarcasm, because he was going to die, so why not.

"Maybe I do deserve to die," he whispered.

"Maybe?" the man scoffed. "You do! And I will help you get

what you deserve!"

The stick returned, only slower this time, and Japhet could see it. It cracked into his side, enough to knock the breath from his body but not break any bones. Gasping, Japhet doubled over as far as his bound hands allowed. He struggled to fill his lungs with air.

"Tell me," the man said, walking to his other side, "do you have friends? Family?"

For a moment, Japhet thought of giving a sarcastic answer but he didn't feel like it so he said nothing. The stick slammed into his other side and he tugged at the ropes. He wished they would give just an inch so he could draw in a deep breath of air.

"If you tell me I promise to go easy on you."

Still Japhet didn't speak and again the stick hit him, this time across the back of his shoulders. He sat up straight, pain lacing through his shoulder blades.

"Maybe you have fellow Jews you're hiding? Trying to help them get out of Berlin?"

Whack! This time the stick rammed into his other shoulder, harder than the first time, and Japhet heard a snap. Numbing pain ripped through his body and stars danced in front of his eyes. He was only partly aware of his shoulder dislocating.

"No? Well, I still think you have a family out there somewhere. Friends. Just tell me where they are and this all ends for you."

The stick smashed down on his leg. Japhet felt tears of pain fill his eyes. He tried to show a minimal amount of pain; he didn't want the Nazi to feel like he was doing a good job. Japhet wouldn't give him that kind of satisfaction. He would show him a Jew could die with courage.

"Come on, you don't want to go through this, do you?"

When Japhet said nothing this time, the stick flew so fast he could barely keep up. His other leg was hit then the Nazi rammed the stick against his throat. Japhet choked but looked the Nazi in the eyes, his last act of defiance.

His name was Japhet Buchanan. He was a Jew, and he was going to die like one.

"Give me answers!" the Nazi roared, and Japhet forced a thin smile.

"You're just going to have to kill me."

"I will!" The Nazi drew his pistol and stuck the barrel against Japhet's head. "Are you sure this is what you want?" he snapped.

"It's all you get, I won't tell you anything," Japhet replied, his voice cracking. He swallowed, suddenly glad his hands were tied behind him so the Nazi couldn't see how badly they shook.

"Fine, have it your way." And the Nazi fired.

Twenty
The Resistance

1941

Franz had decided that morning to take a double shift at work. It wasn't that he didn't want to see Japhet. He just needed time alone, to think, and he thought better when he was doing something with his hands.

By the end of the second shift, he hadn't come closer to working out his thoughts than when he'd started his first shift. The idea of joining the Nazis hadn't gone away, and shame filled Franz. When he finally stumbled back into the apartment he was so tired he barely noticed that things were not as they should have been.

It took him a minute or two before he spotted the oatmeal pot still in the sink and the lack of a burned food smell in the kitchen that would indicate Japhet's dinner attempts. Even though it had been Franz's turn to do the dishes, he wasn't used to coming home and finding the ones he hadn't had a chance to wash.

Remembering that Japhet hadn't looked like himself that morning, Franz hurried to his room to check on him. All he found was Japhet's bed, empty and still neatly made.

Franz didn't wait around. He grabbed his coat and charged

out of the apartment, running in the direction of the library.

***

"I think I dislocated his shoulder."

Those were the first words which broke through the ringing in Japhet's ears.

"How many times do I have to tell you to be careful? You're supposed to bruise, not break limbs!" That voice belonged to Leb, who sounded like he stood right behind Japhet.

"I keep forgetting how strong I am," the other man murmured. "And I didn't break his arm, I just dislocated it."

"How can you keep forgetting," that one was Seth, "you're so big you have to walk sideways through some of the doors. And you still forget?"

"I didn't walk through a door today. I spent the night here."

"Shut up," Seth muttered, "and untie him."

"Okay. And I think you're being too hard on me. At least I didn't use real bullets this time."

That was too much for Japhet. His stomach heaved and he coughed violently, lurching forward. Since his hands still held him to the chair, he couldn't move. Pain stabbed through his dislocated shoulder and he yelled.

"Get him off that chair!" Leb shouted.

Hands gripped him, his ropes were cut, and someone lowered him to the floor. Japhet's whole body ached and he cradled his bad arm as he lowered his head to his knees. He fought to breathe normally as Seth knelt in front of him and held a cup of water out to him.

"I wasn't serious about ever using real bullets," the man who had beaten him said. "I only shoot Nazis."

"You're not helping!" Seth snapped. He moved to Japhet's

side, gently pulling his dislocated arm away from his body.

Japhet gasped.

"I know, I'm sorry," Seth murmured. All of the sudden, more than anything in the world, Japhet wished it was Franz holding his sore arm.

"I can pop it back in," Seth said. "Leb, get me some bandages so I can make a sling when I'm done."

Leb dashed away and Seth began to talk as if to take Japhet's mind from the pain.

"So, why are you in Berlin? And how have you escaped the Nazis' notice if you're a Jew?"

"I have papers," Japhet said through gritted teeth. He wished Seth would keep silent, he didn't want to talk, and he was mad. Whatever was going on was Seth's fault, and if there had been a bone in his body that didn't ache, Japhet would have punched him.

"That doesn't answer why you're here. Did you just come in to punch the Hitler Youth? Because that is a daring ambition, but stupid."

Japhet frowned, unsure if he liked this man or not.

"And what about you? Why did you kidnap me and beat me up and try to deafen me?" Japhet asked, his temper flaring again.

Without warning Seth grabbed his shoulder and snapped his arm back into joint. Japhet yelled because it made him feel better. Seth smiled.

"Sorry," he said, though he didn't sound like it, "it's easier if you're mad...it hurts less."

"You know from experience?" Japhet snapped through clenched teeth.

"Yes..." Seth murmured. Japhet didn't believe him but at that moment Leb returned with bandages.

Helping Japhet out of his coat, Seth wrapped his arm close to his chest with a sling and some of the throbbing pain subsided. When Japhet lifted his eyes, all three men were staring intently at him, so he scowled at them.

"Who are you?" he demanded. "I deserve answers after all of this."

Seth didn't seem bothered by his anger. He just grinned.

"You do. We are the resistance."

The resistance. Japhet had never heard of them before, but the name reminded him of the Zealots who had stood up to Roman rule during the days of Jesus and afterward. Also, Seth and his comrades fit the description of Zealots – secretive, bold, hiding out in basements and beating people to see if they could hold up under torture.

Before Japhet could ask anything about the resistance, though he wasn't sure he even planned to, Seth began to explain it. He said it was certain Jews banding together to fight back against Hitler. They gathered information on Nazi movements and gave them to the allies. They also helped other Jews escape Germany. There were groups all over, though Leb's – the leader – worked mainly in Berlin.

The beating and gunshot had been a test to make sure Japhet wouldn't betray others to save his own life. Japhet wished there were better ways to find that out, ways that didn't leave his body bruised, his shoulder dislocated, and his ears ringing.

"Can we count you in?" Seth concluded. He leaned forward eagerly and everything that had been said before became clear to Japhet.

"You want me to join the resistance?" he asked.

"You're a Jew. You didn't turn anyone in when Odis beat you up. And you can't be any happier about what is going on than we are. Why not join us?" Seth's eyes shone with excitement, but all Japhet wanted was his bed.

"Because you kidnapped me, beat me up, and dislocated my shoulder. Do I need more reasons than that? If so, I think I can add your insanity to the list."

Seth didn't punch him like Japhet thought he would. Instead, he clamped a hand down on his good shoulder and smiled.

"Think about it for a day or two. We'll be in contact with you; you can have your answer ready then."

Japhet smiled because he already knew what his answer would be.

Twenty-One
Lies

1941

It was later than Japhet realized. He'd also been led farther from the apartment when Seth had taken him down into the cellar. It took him half an hour to limp home, his whole body protesting each step. Weary and in more pain than he'd ever been in in his life, Japhet dragged himself up the stairs, quietly opening the door.

He hoped Franz would be asleep and not have noticed he'd been out. It was past midnight and, even though Franz said he'd be late, Japhet didn't think he'd be this late.

Japhet was very careful not to make a sound, and only jumped when something rustled on the couch and a flashlight beam connected with his eyes.

"There you are!" Franz exclaimed. He clicked on one of the lamps, relief in his eyes as light flooded the room.

Blinking, Japhet stood by the door as Franz nearly ran to his side and scowled at him.

"Why were you sitting in the dark?" Japhet asked.

"I've been out looking for you for hours!" Franz snapped, his tone edged. "I came back here to see if you had returned and the landlady yelled at me and said I was wasting money because I had all the lights on. I was just going out to look for you again... what happened to your arm?"

Part of his reason for asking about the lights had been to distract Franz from his arm tied up in the sling, but it failed. In one swift, easy motion, Franz had his jacket off and was closely examining the sling, gingerly touching Japhet's arm, trying to find where the damage was. Instead, he touched one of the many bruises which covered Japhet's shoulder. The wince escaped without Japhet's permission.

"What happened to you?" Franz demanded. "Is your arm broken? Who did it?" He stared into Japhet's eyes at the same time he ground his teeth in anger.

It was too many questions all at once and Japhet couldn't get his tired mind around them all. He suddenly had no idea what to say or how to explain it all to Franz. So much had happened to him in just one day and he didn't know how much would be safe to reveal. Franz would charge out and kill everyone in the resistance if he knew they'd beaten him.

"I...I got into a fight," Japhet stammered, feeling even worse as the lie slipped out between his lips.

"Who did it?" Franz asked. His words turned to ice.

He would strangle them; Japhet could see it in Franz's eyes. He could only imagine what the resistance would do if they were confronted by a German who wasn't a Jew. They'd unjustly assume he was a Nazi and use the pistol on him, only with real bullets.

Japhet shuddered and remembered his nightmare. He saw Franz falling to the ground, cold and dead, his eyes glazed over. Very unlike the eyes in front of him, flashing life and anger. He couldn't let his nightmare come true, even if he had to lie to stop it.

"I... ran into one of the Hitler Youth." Japhet decided to tell as much of the truth as he could.

"Did they find out you're a Jew?" Franz snapped.

Realizing he had only made things worse, Japhet rushed his story. He explained how he had run into the Hitler Youth boy and realized what he was doing. He then changed his story. He said the boy had fought back and that was how he'd dislocated his shoulder.

"How bad are you hurt?" Franz said through gritted teeth.

"I'm just a little bruised," Japhet lied. He looked at the floor and tried not to appear guilty.

"You're more than a little bruised," Franz snapped, clearly not buying it. "How bad is your shoulder?"

"I told you, it's just dislocated...it should be fine in a few days."

"Sit down, I'm checking the sling."

Japhet couldn't argue so he obeyed. He sat on the ragged couch. It hurt sitting down, but once he sat, he didn't think he ever wanted to move. His eyes grew heavy and more than anything he wanted his bed.

As Franz undid the sling, all Japhet could do was sit and clench his teeth. He didn't know which hurt worse, his bruised chest or his shoulder.

Franz unbuttoned his shirt and pulled it off his shoulders to get a better look. Japhet didn't think to stop him until it was too late.

"A little bruised?" Franz growled when he got a good look at his chest, back, and arms. Japhet couldn't tell if he was mad at him or the men who'd beaten him.

"What did the boy beat you with, a stick? Japhet, you're

almost completely black and blue!"

"I..." Japhet looked down at his own arms and chest. He'd had been planning on telling Franz it was worse than it looked, but he couldn't do it when he saw how bad it looked. He literally was black and blue.

"He wasn't alone, after a while." Japhet would have shrugged, but he knew it would hurt too much.

"Well, next time, you won't be alone either and then he will think twice..." Franz was using the sling, carefully winding it around Japhet's shoulder. Japhet smiled as he listened to him mutter under his breath. He didn't plan to go through something like this again, but it was nice to have Franz threatening to beat up the entire Hitler Youth. It reminded Japhet of when they were younger and Franz would stand up for him.

With his shoulder bandaged, Japhet let Franz help him into his nightshirt, then allowed him to put his arm back in a sling before crawling into bed. Japhet had no intention of waking up until late the next morning.

Seeing Japhet covered in bruises not only angered Franz but deepened his determination to get his friend out. If the Hitler Youth could do that to Japhet, Franz could only imagine what the Nazis would do if they ever found out Stephen Achen had forged papers and was a Jew.

While Japhet slept, Franz paced the living room, trying with everything in his power not to think about how much joining the Nazis would help. But now it was even harder to keep the idea at bay.

It was three days before Christmas, the same time that Mr. and Mrs. Buchanan had been shot in Hardy and Kristen's home. Franz could still hear Mrs. Buchanan screaming. He used to just hear her in his nightmares, but now it came sometimes in the daytime. He felt his arms around Japhet, holding him back so he couldn't rush to his parents' side and join them in death. He still remembered how it felt restraining him, at that moment only able to think about Japhet and not the Nazi with the pistol in his hand.

Would his parents be next? Would his sisters? Franz didn't want their deaths added to the list of people he had already lost in this war. He'd been trying to get Warren the right information he needed, but even now he didn't know where to start. If his family died, Franz knew he would never be able to forgive himself.

Throwing himself down on the couch, Franz turned his head just enough so he could see Japhet's closed bedroom door. There was something he had left out of his story; Franz knew him well enough to know that. He could guess what it might have been, but guessing only made it worse.

Had someone finally discovered his secret and Japhet was too scared to tell him?

Twenty-Two
Joining the Nazis

1941

Neither Franz or Japhet felt like celebrating Christmas, but they tried their best. They attempted to roast hazelnuts in the oven and prepare a Christmas meal out of a canned ham, two potatoes, and some suspicious looking bread.

The ham was okay, considering it had spent who knew how long in a can. The potatoes were undercooked, but nice since they were so used to eating burned food. The bread they finally opted to throw out, and the hazelnuts nearly caught fire. Japhet was about to throw the nuts away, but Franz suggested they keep them and drop them on the heads of their fellow apartment dwellers when they passed under their window.

The meal wasn't a complete loss, though. Not long after lunch their landlady appeared with a pie which they cut in half and devoured.

After lunch, Japhet lay on the couch and fell asleep. He'd been sleeping more, Franz had noticed, but not from lack of nightmares. He was still bruised and Franz insisted he keep the sling on a little while longer. Japhet slept now because his body had been beaten and needed a chance to recover.

Throwing a blanket over him, Franz left him alone to his nap and pulled on his coat so he could take a walk outside. There were more people out than normal – most of them children. A group of boys ran past him, throwing snowballs at each other. One stopped and waved.

"Hi, Herr Hoffmann!" he shouted before taking off.

Franz waved back before he turned down another street. Down this street, he spotted a group of young men around his age. All wore Nazi uniforms and they talked and laughed as if life were normal. Franz stopped and watched them, keeping back so they wouldn't notice him.

It made him angry to see them happy and carefree. They had nothing to fear, no reason to constantly watch over their shoulders. They weren't the ones curled up on the couch on Christmas, trying to recover from a bruised body. They weren't the ones who had to change their names and pretend to be someone they weren't. They weren't the ones who were kept up most nights because they couldn't sleep from all the nightmares.

Franz ground his teeth together and clenched his hands into fists until they hurt. The Nazis were ruining the lives of so many people and they didn't care.

It was at that moment Franz made up his mind. He knew it would be the most stupid thing he'd ever do in his life, but he wasn't sure he cared. He wasn't going to let the Nazis win, no matter what it took.

Franz didn't do it until the day after his birthday, January 17th. He told himself he would feel braver about it if he waited until he was eighteen. When the day came and passed, he felt no different than when he was seventeen.

That night he was awakened by Japhet's muffled shouts from the next room. He wanted to go and check on him but instead sat up and pulled his knees up to his chest.

Pulling his blanket up over his shoulders, Franz rested his forehead on his knees. Each time Japhet yelled it felt like someone stabbing Franz in the heart.

In two weeks, Japhet would be turning seventeen. When they were boys they had been thrilled to learn their birthdays were in the same month and only two weeks apart from each other. They'd always looked forward to January, now it just brought back painful memories.

Franz could feel a heavy weight pressing down on his shoulders. Responsibilities he never thought he would have, especially not at eighteen, were crushing him. Added to it was the weight of guilt.

Lifting his head, Franz rubbed his scar without thinking and went over his plan once again. He had worked out every possible thing that could go wrong, but he still didn't like it. Mostly because he couldn't tell Japhet about it.

Japhet would never understand, Franz knew that. He didn't blame him. Japhet could be reckless, but he drew the line, and it was a line Franz was about to cross over. Japhet would tell Franz he couldn't do it and would make him see how stupid it was and Franz would listen to him and not go through with it. Then, if anyone died because he hadn't gotten the right information, he would never forgive himself.

He couldn't tell Japhet, ever. No matter what happened, Franz had to somehow keep a secret from his best friend. The biggest secret of his life.

Franz left work early the day after his birthday and did everything he could to walk boldly into the office inside the Gestapo headquarters. He glanced over his shoulder to make sure no one he knew – mainly Japhet – saw him entering. With a deep breath, Franz pushed the doors opened and entered a high roofed building.

It was hard for him, later, to remember details of what happened in that building. He knew his papers were checked, he remembered talking to several men and being asked too many questions. There was only one he remembered in detail.

"Why do you wish to join the Party?" a tall soldier asked, looking down his nose at Franz.

Franz had prepared for this, something he was grateful for because the answer sprang from his lips without him having to think about it.

"I want to make Germany a better country."

He didn't know if his answer worked as he again seemed to black out. He knew he signed his name, and later feared he had put Franz Kappel instead of Rupert Hoffmann, but figured he must have done it right because no one killed him on the spot. Then there was a uniform being pressed into his arms and he was told to report tomorrow morning.

In a daze, Franz left the building and returned to his home. He hid the uniform, continued through the rest of his evening with Japhet, and wasn't aware of what had really happened until that night.

When it finally did hit him, it hit him hard.

Franz Kappel was now a Nazi.

Twenty-Three
Stein

1941

Japhet didn't go back to work. By the time he could move they had given his position to someone else and fired him. Mr. Voelgr apologized for it. He said he hadn't wanted to do it, but authorities higher up had given the word and his job to someone else.

Franz said it didn't matter, that they could still get the money Warren might need without Japhet working, but Japhet felt like he had failed everyone.

Also, the beating had taken a bigger toll on his body than he first realized. He slept more during the next few weeks than had in the last few years.

At first, Franz was always there whenever he didn't have to work, but soon after his birthday he became a less frequent sight around the apartment, though his concern didn't diminish.

When he was there, Franz waited on Japhet hand and foot, scowling whenever he wrapped his shoulder and saw his ribs sticking out from his skinny body.

Not wishing to worry Franz, Japhet tried to eat more but his stomach still rebelled at even the thought of food. He was a failure for losing his job and he told himself he couldn't die and leave Franz on his own. He'd made him a promise, he'd made his whole family one, and he had to find a way to carry it out.

Franz lied to his best friend – again. Maybe it wasn't a flat out lie; Franz hadn't said why he was going to be late, nor had he made up a story for it, but he still felt guilty. It was only worse because Japhet was still so tired and looked like someone who had fallen so far into despair he would never get out. Franz didn't like the idea of him being alone by himself.

Trying to keep his work as a Nazi a secret was harder than Franz thought it would be. There were meetings he was supposed to go to and he had to help with a patrol on some nights. He was out of the apartment more than usual and he was certain Japhet was starting to get suspicious. Franz even had to quit his job, relying on the pay he got for being in The Party.

A few days before Japhet's birthday another meeting was announced. Franz told Japhet he wouldn't be back until late and said he should go to bed early.

During the meeting, Franz had trouble listening. When they were dismissed he had no idea what they'd wanted him to take from the talk. Ten o'clock had rolled around while he'd been sitting and Franz snatched up his coat and attempted to make a break for the door. Unsuccessfully.

"You're the new one, aren't you?"

The voice could have been ignored, but the hand on Franz's arm stopped him before he could escape. Reluctantly, Franz turned to look up at the young man standing in front of him. He was tall, blond, and handsome. His uniform fit him almost like he'd been born in it and he probably broke the hearts of a lot of young ladies. He was Hitler's ideal Nazi.

"Yes." Franz still wanted to run but hoped the nicer he

was the sooner he could cut this conversation off. "I'm Rupert Hoffmann."

The young man – likely only a year or two older than Franz but already holding a rank – held his hand out and his smile deepened.

"Gorge Stein."

Franz wanted to punch the man rather than shake his hand, but he submitted and even went so far as to return the smile. Franz didn't know what to do after that, though. He didn't want to say, "It's nice to meet you," since he really wasn't pleased to meet him.

The silence between them became awkward and was only broken when a man, who was likely the same age as Franz, came up behind Stein and clamped a hand on his shoulder.

"You're coming, aren't you?" he asked as two other young men, about Stein's age, joined them.

Stein moved forward until the younger man's hand was off his shoulder. "Naturally," he murmured though he didn't sound very happy with whatever the plan was.

The young man grinned. "Bring your new friend too."

Franz almost turned and ran. He didn't like where this was headed and just wanted to go back home and try and sleep.

"We're going for drinks," Stein told Franz. "You'll come, won't you?"

His tone left little room for argument. Franz glanced down at his uniform and his stomach flopped. Go out into the streets, dressed as a Nazi? With Nazis beside him? It was the last thing he wanted to do, but he could think of no good excuse to turn them down. His mind drew blanks on possible reasons why he couldn't go.

It wasn't as if he could tell them he had to get back to his apartment because his Jewish friend might need him. That wouldn't get him a bullet in the head – that would get him tortured before they killed him.

"Yes...I'm coming," he murmured.

"Come on then." Stein led the way and the other young men flanked him. Franz had no choice but to follow.

Franz, Stein, and the others approached one of the fancier restaurants Franz never would have gone into on his own. He tried to hold his head high, to act like he did this all the time, as he stepped inside the wide doors and was momentarily blinded by the lights. His only hope was that the evening would lead to some discussion on Nazi movements which might give him valuable information for Warren.

The hall was brightly lit, but the dining area was dimmed. A small orchestra sat on a platform, playing *Lili Marleen*. Franz felt a little better as he listened, though the crowded place set him on edge. There were so many Nazis and Franz wasn't sure he'd be able to keep up his false front long enough to fool them. Someone was sure to catch on.

"Here." Stein led them to an empty table and they all sat down. Soon after, a pretty girl walked over and asked them what they would like.

One of the young men made a crude remark which turned the girl's face red and Franz had to hold back his temper. The girl looked tired, overworked, probably keeping the job because she had a family that needed the money. She didn't need to put up with rude Nazis. Franz wanted to break his companion's nose.

The four young men ordered beers, but Franz stuck with coffee. He'd never had anything alcoholic and wasn't sure now was a good time to start, even with his cover at risk. Also, he managed to get out of the teasing.

"Coffee?" the one closest to his age laughed. "What's wrong with you? Turning into an old man?"

"You have a problem with it?" Franz growled, his tone dangerous. "If you do, then we can go and settle this out back. I've been beating up men like you since I was ten, I've had lots of practice."

Stein laughed as if he approved of Franz's short fused temper.

"No one is beating anyone up tonight. We've all had a long day and we have an even longer one coming up. Just sit back and relax." Stein stretched out his legs and leaned back in the soft chair, smiling in contentment.

Franz couldn't relax. His nerves were strung so tight, all he needed was someone to poke him and he'd have a breakdown. What would his parents think if they saw him in this place, wearing the uniform? What would Japhet think? Not that it mattered now, he was already too far in to back out.

Right now, all Franz had to do was drink some coffee, try to gather information, and leave.

Franz somehow survived the night, but when he got back, he was so tired he was barely aware of his surroundings as he fell into bed. The next morning, he overslept but since it was Saturday, he didn't worry about it.

When he finally woke up, Japhet was laying on the couch, his feet propped up on the backside of it, a letter resting on his chest. He held it up when Franz stumbled into the living room.

"This came yesterday, I think Warren dropped it off," he said. He lifted his head so he could peek over the couch. "It is from Munich."

Taking it, Franz dropped to the floor and threw his feet up on the arm of the couch. He looked at the letter, written by Leah. Unfolding it, Franz read out loud.

Franz and Japhet,

We heard about what happened to Karl. We've sent our condolences to poor Gabi, but we know it has to have been hard on the two of you. Even though you didn't know him as long as you did Hardy and Ross, we know you loved him like he was already a brother. This war has been so hard on everyone, but in many ways it seems to be affecting the young even more. Please remember to keep your trust in God. He and He alone can help us survive this time – and not just survive but move on when this war ends.

None of us were happy to hear you had gone into Berlin alone. All of the antics you two have pulled, the dangers you have placed yourselves in, and you have found a way to top it. We have taken to calling you two Daniel, since you have entered the lion's den much the same way he did. We all three caution you to be careful. In spite of the torment you put us through growing up, we would hate to lose our baby brothers.

We are constantly being told by the Kappels that we are no better than the two of you, remaining in Munich instead of allowing Warren to take us to the farm. He is a persistent young man. He shows up every other week, almost like clockwork, and spends hours trying to get us to leave. Also, I'm not so convinced his constant visits just have to do with making us leave. You know how good Elsa's coffee is. I've never seen a man drink that much coffee. I'm surprised he is able to sleep.

I know the two of you are concerned for us, just like everyone at the farm. I wish I had some reassurance for you, to make you able to sleep at night. We haven't been idle here, just as the two of you haven't been. I'm sure you have heard how Hitler had a lot of books burned. He has also been stealing artwork. The three of us have been working to save and hide as many books and saving as many paintings as we can find. I know that is unlikely to bring you any form of comfort, as you both know the danger that puts us in, but I think you will understand why we are doing this better than anyone else in our family.

So much is being lost in this war. Hitler is taking much away from us. If he takes everything, he threatens the existence of the Jews. Until we leave Germany, Bea, Elsa, and I believe this is one small way we can help stand up to and fight against him. Hitler is about to find that he is attempting to kill a people who has been fighting for more than a hundred years to survive. We do not die without a fight, and we do not just vanish.

You both understand that, don't you? We have to fight for ourselves, in whatever way we can.

Pray for us, as we pray for you. May God grant that someday soon we will all see each other again and be reunited as a family.

Your loving sisters

Bea, Elsa, and Leah

When he was finished with the letter, Franz folded it and set it on the floor beside him. He rested his head on his arms and stared up at the off-white ceiling.

"It isn't strange I'm worrying about them, is it?" he asked. "Even though they're older."

Japhet dropped his healed arm to his chest. He shook his head and swallowed once or twice as if he were trying to hide tears.

"They're our sisters, I think we're supposed to worry about them."

Franz wearily looked at Japhet. He was relaxed, as relaxed as he could possibly be. His shoulder had healed and most of his bruises were fading, but Franz still worried.

All of his threatening to make Japhet eat once they were sharing a place together hadn't worked. He had tried, but Japhet refused to swallow more then he needed to keep him barely alive. He was changing, becoming distant, and Franz didn't know how to help him. He hated not knowing.

Now, if Japhet started worrying about Leah and the others, he'd only get worse and Franz would be forced to watch him waste away right in front of his eyes.

Franz wished he believed in the God Leah, Bea, and Elsa did.

Twenty-Four
Joining the resistance

1941

Seth didn't contact Japhet in the two or three days he said he would. He didn't show up until two days after Japhet's birthday and by that time Japhet had forgotten about him.

When he did arrive, Japhet was nearly healed from his beating. His body still protested to certain movements, but he didn't get as tired as easily. Mostly he suffered headaches from worrying about his family so much; Leah's letter only added to his mounting concerns.

After he had healed, Japhet planned to find a new job despite what Franz said about him not needing one. He tried to think of ways to get easier access to forged papers and contact anyone who aided in Jew's escapes.

When the worry got too much, Japhet would sit and draw. He ate even less, his stomach in so many knots just the thought of food made him sick.

The day the knock came Japhet was drawing. In the last few weeks, he'd completed ten different pictures.

The knock sounded like the landlady, so Japhet didn't hesitate to open the door after he closed his sketchbook. Instead of a blond haired woman, though, Japhet came face-to-face with Seth. Japhet didn't even bother asking how Seth had found out where he lived, Seth was just the kind of person who would know. He'd probably followed him home the night after they'd beaten him.

"Look at you!" Seth said, inviting himself in and sitting down at one of the chairs at the small dining table. "All recovered. I knew it wouldn't take you long."

Japhet's temper flared just looking at Seth. Glaring, he walked over and sat in the other chair.

"Still mad at me?" Seth asked. "Just be glad it wasn't the Nazis who got a hold of you. You'd be in worse shape now, likely have some broken limbs if you were allowed to live. What kind of idiot openly gives his name like that? You had to have known Buchanan is a Jewish name. And Japhet...Japhet is a dead giveaway. And I do mean dead."

"Are you here to criticize me or do you have another reason for coming over?" Japhet asked, glad that Franz wouldn't be back until late that night. Japhet didn't want him coming home and having to put up with a radical Jew. Especially if that radical Jew found out Franz wasn't a Jew.

"You know why I'm here. What have you decided?"

Japhet wasn't ready for that question. He hadn't thought it over at all. He'd all but forgotten Seth, though he hadn't forgotten the dark cellar and Odis' stick. Now that he sat in front of Seth, Japhet remembered how much he didn't like him. He seemed like one of those fighters who wanted to throw away his life in some desperate act of courage.

Yet, looking into his eyes, Japhet remembered how upset he'd once been that he couldn't fight in the war. He would never join Hitler's army, and it wasn't as if he could leave the country with the intent of joining the allies. He also knew the resistance might be able to aid him in helping his family escape.

Japhet didn't like this new turn in his thoughts. And he didn't know how he'd explain it to Franz if he did join.

I'm part of the resistance now. They are like the Zealots in the days of the Romans. Kill now, ask questions later. They probably kill men like you, since you're not a Jew. But don't worry, I'll be fine.

Franz would wring his neck. Franz took his protection of Japhet seriously and wouldn't hesitate to kill him if it meant keeping him alive. He'd send him off to the farm and stay in Berlin on his own. Japhet couldn't let that happen. Deep down he knew Franz needed him as much as he needed Franz.

"I'm joining." The two words came out before Japhet was aware they were even on his lips. He wanted to take them back the moment he uttered them but pressed his lips together to stop himself.

Seth smiled like a little boy at Christmas.

"I knew you would!" he said jubilantly. "You're a brave man and I knew you wouldn't let us down."

Japhet didn't think of himself as a man. He was only seventeen, but he wasn't going to argue. Let Seth think of him as a brave man for now; his opinion would change soon enough.

"Do you live here alone?"

The question was unexpected and Japhet wondered if he had missed part of the conversation before it.

"No, I live with a friend of mine," he said.

"A Jew?"

Japhet could have slapped himself. This was what the old man at the farm had warned him about. He had to think before he spoke, only now he hadn't – again.

Racking his brain for ideas, Japhet tried to keep his face blank so Seth wouldn't catch on that he was trying to think of an answer. It didn't work. The man raised both his eyebrows and leaned forward.

"He's not a Jew? He's...a German?"

Gritting his teeth, Japhet tried to keep his anger in check. "I'm a German," he said. "I was born and raised here."

"So? I was too, but that means nothing!" Seth snapped. He slammed his hand down on the table, stood up, and paced. Japhet kept glaring at him.

"The Germans don't want us, or did you not get that when they started dragging people into the streets and killing them? We can't be Jews and Germans, not anymore. You have to get that through your thick head, Japhet Buchanan. You're a Jew and only a Jew."

Japhet opened his mouth to protest, but Seth didn't shut up long enough.

"Who is this man you're living with? Some friend who has told you he's completely opposed to the Nazis and what is going on in his own country? You know it's just a lie, don't you? Germans care only about their country and thinking they are better than everyone else. He cares nothing for you, just like all the other Germans out there."

Japhet lost his temper completely. It wasn't enough that this man had arranged for him to be beaten black and blue, but now he was insulting Franz.

"I'm just as German as Franz!" he snapped, standing as well. He tried to look as intimidating as Seth. "And it isn't his fault all of this is happening. He has been there for me since we were kids! You don't know what you're talking about. He's my best friend and I trust my life to him."

Seth scoffed. "He is just like all the other Germans out there and he will betray you one day, just you watch. Give up this foolishness and get out while you still have your sorry head attached to your sorry neck!"

"Franz would never turn me in!" Japhet yelled. "He isn't a Nazi!"

Without warning, Seth jumped forward and clamped a hand over Japhet's mouth.

"Keep your stupid voice down!" he hissed. "Walls are thin these days. Do you want to get us both killed? I'm a wanted man you know."

Pulling free, Japhet scowled.

"That's your problem, not mine," Japhet hissed, though he did lower his voice.

"It's going to be your problem if you join us," Seth snapped back. "You should know what you are getting into if you do join. We are in constant danger of losing our lives, and we can't have idiots like you making it worse by buddying up to a Nazi."

"Franz is not a Nazi!" Japhet hissed savagely. "And if you keep it up I won't-"

"Join?" Seth huffed. "We don't need you and your idiocy then! Make a choice, right now, Japhet Buchanan. How much do your people mean to you? Are you willing to let millions die because you won't give up friendship to a man who has every intention of one day betraying you?"

Japhet thought of his sisters, of Franz's, of the Kappels. Of Franz himself. Seth was an idiot, Japhet was convinced about it, but this might be his only chance to help everyone he loved. Working with Seth would be worth it for them.

"I won't tell him what I'm doing," he said, the only promise he could think to offer. "Not a word."

The look in Seth's eyes showed he still wasn't pleased, but he nodded curtly.

"One word and I'll personally kill you," he warned.

Japhet's blood turned cold, but he nodded. "Not one word."

"And you keep an eye on him. One hint of suspicion and I expect you to deal with it, understood?"

Thinking of the pistol in his bedroom and the knife strapped to his side, Japhet feared he understood all too well.

***

"You seem distracted," Stein said, waving his hand in front of Franz's nose.

Blinking, Franz focused on the face in front of him and shrugged. He didn't bother smiling, not sure why he should have to smile at a Nazi.

"Haven't been sleeping much," he said.

"You're staring off into space because you haven't slept?" Carsten laughed.

Franz was slowly getting used to Carsten. He had been the one who had dragged them out for drinks the first night Franz had met Stein and – while Stein didn't seem to like it – wherever he was Carsten was not far behind.

"Seemed like a good idea," Franz muttered.

"You're grumpy when you don't sleep."

"I'm always grumpy." Franz forced another smile, this time at Carsten. "Get used to it."

Stein laughed, though it sounded stiff, just like him. Franz had never seen someone sit, stand, and walk so ramrod straight.

They were back at the restaurant they'd visited the first night. Franz sat across from Stein at the same table they'd used during that visit. Carsten and Stein seemed to like it, Franz could have cared less. He kept thinking about Japhet. Something had been bothering him the last two days and Franz hadn't been able to figure out what – he'd even started drawing again. It wasn't like his friend to keep secrets.

It isn't like you to keep secrets either, he reminded himself. He would have looked down at his uniform, but he hated the sight of it on him. It was bad enough seeing it on Stein and Carsten.

"You heard the rumor, though, didn't you?" Carsten asked.

"What rumor?" Stein asked, bored.

"There's a Jew living in Berlin!"

Franz dropped his coffee cup. He didn't mean to, but it slipped out of his fingers, crashed to the table, and spilled hot liquid onto his lap.

"Watch it, stupid!" Carsten leaped up as the coffee came for him. Stein tried to mop it up with a pure white napkin and a waitress appeared to fix the matter.

In moments, they were at a different table with new drinks and Franz was trying to sop the coffee off his uniform. He could feel Stein's eyes on him but ignored them, until the Nazi spoke.

"What were you saying, Carsten? Something about a Jew?"

He knows! Panic seized Franz and he glanced at the door, ready to run as Stein quietly studied him.

"Yes, there's a Jew in Berlin."

"More than one I should think," Stein said, taking a sip of his drink. "Why bring one Jew up?" He broke his stare and Franz breathed easier.

"Because, from what I heard, he's been hiding and he was finally found out. If his papers come through and he is who the soldiers think he is they are going to get him tomorrow night. Drag him out of his home and deal with him." Carsten smiled.

Franz gripped his coffee and tried not to shatter the cup. He kept his face blank and tried to feign interest, but his thoughts rushed to Japhet. Had he been found out? Was he the Jew they were going to drag into the streets and beat until he was dead or wished he was?

"Hmm, that will liven things up around here. I had heard we, the new recruits, are to be given a special mission soon...but until then, we can at least go and have some fun tomorrow."

The cold in Franz's blood turned to ice. Stein thought it was entertainment, watching a man getting beaten to death? He swallowed. He had to make Stein believe he was as interested in this as he and Carsten. And he also wanted to make sure the Jew was not Japhet.

"You two are going to watch tomorrow, then? I'd like to come with you." He hoped his request sounded like one a good Nazi would give and not a little kid asking to tag along with his older boys.

"You have to come," Carsten said, scoffing.

"What is the address then? That might be helpful." Again, Franz kept his voice even.

"You can just come with us," Carsten said, "since we will be going."

"Walk there, with you?" Franz got his brain to work finally and the words slipped out almost on their own. He rolled his eyes for added effect. "I don't want every Nazi in the city knowing I'm associated with you. Just give me the address and I'll meet you there. Besides, I don't have time to hang around with you all day tomorrow."

Stein actually laughed. "Give me the address too. I'd rather not let everyone think I spend all day with you."

Grudgingly, Carsten gave them the address and Franz breathed easier since it wasn't his. He finished his coffee and said he had to go home and try and clean his uniform. He left without a goodbye, which wasn't unusual for him.

Once out of sight of the restaurant, Franz ran and didn't stop until he had crashed through the main door of the apartment. It was late, so no one was around, and he had no trouble slipping into one of the closets and changing back into the clothes he had left there that morning. He wondered how many other Nazis had to change in secret.

When he left the closet, he looked around for the sweet lady who liked to wave at him and Japhet. It had been hard avoiding her as well as Japhet. He didn't want her to see his uniform and mention it to Japhet in passing.

When he again saw no one around, Franz ran up the stairs and shoved the door to his and Japhet's apartment open. Japhet lay on the couch, his sketchbook open on his knees. His hand flew over the page.

He looked up when Franz entered and smiled. His real smile, the one that had been gone for the past two days.

"You're earlier than I thought you'd be," he said.

Franz returned the smile. He sat down beside him, shoving Japhet's feet off the couch so there would be room. Japhet closed the sketchbook but not before Franz caught a picture of the street they used to play on as boys.

You're still boys, Franz told himself. He quickly shoved the thought aside.

"What are you doing tonight?" he asked.

"I have a feeling I'm going to be helping you with something," Japhet said, squinting sideways at him. "You have that look in your eyes."

"I don't have any look in my eyes," Franz retorted.

"Yes. The one you always get when you have a plan you know I won't like."

"I don't think you will mind this one, it is...I'm just not sure how we're going to do it."

Japhet sat up straighter. "What's going on? What are we going to try and do?"

"Save a Jew."

Twenty-Five
Refusing to be moved

1941

They ran down the dark streets, Franz in the lead while Japhet tried to process the idea of a Jew, hiding in Berlin, and being discovered. How had the Nazis found him? Would Japhet be next? Even if he was part of the resistance now, would they be able to keep him safe? Would Franz? Would Franz get shot protecting him?

"This way," Franz whispered. He ducked into a dark alleyway. Japhet followed, stumbling.

For the first time since doing it, Japhet didn't feel as guilty about joining the resistance. He would have done anything, or almost anything, to save Franz. Who cared what Seth thought about Germans and there being a difference between a German and a Jew? Seth had never met Franz, and if there was one thing Japhet could rely on, it was Franz.

"How are we going to get him out?" Japhet whispered as Franz stopped and pointed to a row of small houses. The address he had given Japhet was on one of them.

"We have to warn him. I don't think we can get him out, but there have to be people who can help him. We can at least warn him," Franz whispered, looking left and right down the street before he left the alleyway and darted into the yard.

Japhet followed. Once they were across, they were able to use the two trees in the yard for cover before darting up the steps and knocking on the door.

Franz had to knock three times before the door finally opened a crack. An eye peered out at them, squinting, angry, and scared.

"Who are you and what do you want?" the man behind the door demanded.

"My name is Rupert," Franz whispered, "and this is my cousin Stephen. We have come to tell you that you have to leave your house, tonight."

"Why?" the man asked. "Is this some kind of prank? Shouldn't you two be in bed?"

"You're a Jew, aren't you?" Franz's whisper became desperate. "Living here under a false name and with false papers?"

"Who do you think you are?" The words were sharper this time and they were followed by the glint of a pistol barrel. Japhet grabbed Franz's arm and tried to pull him back, but he would not move.

"I'm trying to help you," Franz insisted. "I found out about you being a Jew, and I also learned that Nazis are coming tomorrow night to take you to the camps. You have to get out of here!"

"How did you hear this?" the man asked sharply.

Japhet had wondered the same thing but hadn't wanted to ask. He wasn't sure why, but he didn't want to know the answer.

"Does it matter?" Franz asked. "I'm trying to save your life! You have to flee!"

The man lowered his pistol. "How do I know this is not a trick?" he asked.

"You really think I'd lie about something like this? If it is a lie then how I would I even know you're a Jew?"

Sighing, the man leaned his head against the door jamb.

"I'm a German. I was born and raised in Germany. Why doesn't that matter anymore? Why am I suddenly a threat?"

"It doesn't matter," Japhet whispered. He hadn't meant to speak, but he wasn't able to stay quiet. "What does matter is living. Not giving up. You have a chance to continue on with life; take it while you can."

"Yes, of course," the man murmured, then he lifted his head and looked at them again. "But you have to get out of here before someone sees. Thank you for your warning, but leave now!" And he closed the door before they could say anything else.

***

When Carsten convinced Franz and Stein into walking with him to the Jew's house the next night, Franz didn't object. He wanted to see the look on Carsten's face when they opened the door and found the house empty. That would ruin Carsten's night. The only problem with going along was that Franz kept catching strange looks from Stein. How much did the man suspect?

There were soldiers outside the house by the time Franz, Carsten, and Stein arrived. They stood in the yard as the sun cast its last light down oo the streets. The shadows were long, stretching out as if they wished to escape the dying light.

"What are they waiting for?" Carsten asked, but Stein rammed his elbow into his side and shut him up.

Franz bit the insides of his cheeks, keeping back his smile, as one of the soldiers walked up the same steps he and Japhet had run up the night before. He watched as the soldier knocked – once, twice, three times. Nothing.

Hitler hadn't counted on Franz Kappel, foiling his plans. It would teach the Nazis to—

The door opened.

The Jew stepped out of his house and stood before the Nazi soldiers with his head held high.

"Jacob Cohen, you have been found guilty of crimes against the Fuhrer." The Nazi standing on the top step thrust his shoulders back as he looked Mr. Cohen in the eyes. "What is your answer to these accusations?"

Franz wanted to yell. He fought to control his emotions.

"The Fuhrer believes it is a crime to be a Jew. I cannot help who I am, and I'm proud of my heritage. I have hidden it, to save my own life. I have hidden and become what Hitler wanted of me, and now he still wishes to kill me." Jacob Cohen straightened his shoulders. "I know what waits for me, and I want all of you to hear me. You have been told nothing but lies, and one day soon you are going to have to pay the price for those lies. Ask yourselves now if they are worth it."

"Kill him!"

It was never found out who yelled the order, but no one needed any more motivation than that. The soldier in front of Jacob Cohen grabbed him and threw him down into the snow. Before Cohen had a chance to rise, the Nazis were on top of him, kicking him and beating him with the butts of their rifles. Carsten rushed to join in and Franz had to refrain himself from trying to stop them. There was nothing he could do, and he couldn't get himself killed, not when Japhet still needed him.

As he stood by, silently seething, Stein slipped an arm around his shoulders and smiled. "Glad he was still here, Hoffmann. If he hadn't been, I would have been under the impression you had warned him and helped him escape." His smile deepened. "Silly of me, wasn't it?"

Somehow Franz kept his face expressionless though his thoughts were in turmoil. Jacob Cohen could easily be Japhet.

"Silly. Silly of you not to trust me," he murmured as Jacob Cohen's groans fell silent until the only sounds were the rifle butts hitting his dead flesh.

Twenty-Six
Protective walls

1942

The resistance hid in various basements and cellars. They never held their meetings in the same place two nights in a row. The rule was to make sure they weren't followed when they entered a meeting or got together after a mission.

Japhet told himself this, over and over, as he ran past the house where he was supposed to meet up with Seth and Leb. Behind him, a Nazi soldier gave chase, closing in on him.

It had been more than a year since Japhet had joined the resistance. Spring had begun to melt the snow and cover the roads with muddy slush. Cold, melted snow got into Japhet's boots and numbed his feet. Still he pressed on, knowing Seth would yell at him for an hour if he risked leading this Nazi anywhere close to the others.

Just the night before Japhet and Seth had gotten into another fight, and again it had been over Franz. It started when two men smuggling supplies had been caught by a group of patrolling Nazis.

"Wouldn't be surprised if your Nazi friend was one of them!" Seth had shouted.

"Franz is not a Nazi!" Japhet had yelled back.

"Well, he's not a Jew either!"

"Shut up!" Odis, the big man who had beaten Japhet, had finally gotten in the middle of them. No one fought when Odis said to stop and they both went their separate ways in foul moods.

The steps behind him got louder. Japhet turned a street corner and paused for a second, looking around. His eyes landed on a rubbish bin, but he ran past it, pushing his shaking legs on. He went up another street, turned, and then stopped. The steps were farther behind now and he took his chance. Japhet climbed into another bin, pulled the lid over his head, and steadied his breathing. And waited.

With his eyes closed and his head inches from his knees, Japhet again thought of what Seth had said. What he hated most about his fights with Seth is that he knew something was wrong with Franz. It didn't help that a rift had grown between the two of them.

Japhet hated it, every second of it. When they saw each other, which was rare with Japhet out most nights, they barely spoke. Japhet didn't want to risk slipping up and telling Franz what he did each night, and he knew Franz was keeping something from him as well. He hated the silence, but he didn't know how to break it.

The Nazi ran past his hiding place, but Japhet didn't bother coming out. He wanted to be left alone and wasn't ready to face Seth yet.

***

Stein was put in command of a special mission group which consisted mostly of younger recruits. They were told to remain in Berlin and hunt down and kill the resistance fighters. Stein readily asked Franz to join.

Franz didn't want to hunt anyone down and kill them, but searching Berlin for the resistance would keep him from being shipped to the front lines where he wouldn't be able to keep an eye on Japhet, so he joined. It also gave him a chance to try and get the information Warren still needed. He worked hard at securing it, and one day finally discovered something useful.

Messages between him, Japhet, and Warren came and went, followed at last by one Franz had been hoping for.

"Gabi is out," it had read, "it was easier getting her out than Ruth, and we couldn't get all four at once. The information you sent was just what we needed. If you can keep it up, I can get Ruth and your parents out soon. We're having more trouble with Ruth, though. Gabi, with her blond hair, looks German. Ruth doesn't. And your parents refuse to leave without her, so when she goes all three go, which puts more risk on the escape. Don't give up, though. Keep doing what you're doing. I'm not resting until all of you are out of here."

All of them meant Leah, Bea, and Elsa as well. Franz still heard from his sisters and the work they continued to do. He worried, but he felt hopeful. Gabi had escaped. He was able to use the knowledge he'd gained as a Nazi to save his sister. He didn't want to stop, not until he'd saved the others as well.

Franz listened, day after day, but usually all he overheard were the men talking about how they were winning the war. They all believed it would be over before the year was out and Germany would emerge a country more powerful than Europe. No one would ever look down on the German people again.

"And just think," Stein liked to tell Franz, "you're going to be part of it. These resistance fighters are doing everything they can to pull Germany back into darkness and depression. They do not think we deserve freedom and respect. We have to show them differently."

Franz usually just nodded when Stein gave him these speeches, pretending to be interested so Stein wouldn't suspect him of anything. Things had been better since Jacob Cohen had been killed, but Franz knew Stein still had his doubts. He'd catch the man staring at him sometimes, almost as if he were trying to see into his soul and find the secrets hidden there.

Your best friend is a Jew. Your papers are forged. What is there to hide? Franz would sometimes scoff himself.

Then, on top of his problems there was Carsten. Carsten tested his incredible lack of patience.

"What do you plan to do with the first resistance fighter you find?" he would ask at least once a week. He would grin like an eager little boy and Franz imagined himself tripping Carsten and breaking his neck.

"I plan to give him your address and tell him you threatened to cut his fingers off," Franz would mutter irritably. He had a list of threats he went through whenever he had to answer.

Stein usually smiled at them, slightly amused though he never commented on their conversations. After a year, he had become used to Franz and Carsten not getting along. Now the three of them were walking down the street, the muddy slush of melting snow squelching under their boots.

"No resistance soldier in his right mind would be out in this kind of weather," Carsten grumbled as he walked a little behind Stein and Franz. "It's going to take me forever to clean my boots after this."

"Are you questioning our orders or complaining? Nazis don't complain, do I need to remind you of that?" Stein looked over his shoulder, his gaze cold. Carsten clamped his jaw together.

Franz almost sighed in relief. He was tired of Carsten's constant whining and complaints. So much for the Nazi army and showing no emotion.

They had been patrolling the streets since early that morning and it was now well past noon. Franz's boots had so much water in them he didn't think they would ever dry. Also he, Stein, and Carsten had found no signs of the resistance.

Franz ran over his knowledge of the resistance. They were some type of radicals, according to Stein. It was their sole purpose to divide Germany and bring about its downfall. They were working from the inside, hoping to weaken the country so the allies could get in.

Over the past year, Franz had helped capture at least three men from the resistance. Stein and Carsten had apprehended even more.

After catching the three he did, Franz never saw them again. He didn't talk to them nor was he present for their interrogations. He had no idea what happened to them after they were dragged away, but he also didn't care.

"We are doing this for Germany," Stein told him over and over. "It's our duty, as Germans, to fight for the Fatherland in whatever way we can. You understand this, don't you, Hoffman?"

Franz felt he did. He loved Germany, even now. He had been born and raised there. Hitler might be insane, but it was still Franz's country and he did want to help. He suffered doubts, ones Stein seemed to pick up on and talk about. Franz talked to him more than he would have liked.

"What about the Jews?" Franz asked once. He hadn't meant to put his question into words, but it just happened; it was soon after he'd heard something about the resistance being Jews.

"This has never been about Jews," Stein told him. "All of that has been a lie, saying we are only locking up Jews because they are Jews. The world has decided that is what we do and now everyone believes it. They needed an excuse to attack us, so they turned us into monsters.

"We were never monsters, though. Hoffmann, what we are doing is saving Germany. The world is out there, ready to crush us and we have to fight back. Jews, gypsies, they are trying to tear our country apart, but they are not the only ones. There are plenty of others we are forced to lock up in order keep our country alive. I will admit most of them are Jews, but we have people of other religions and beliefs who we have been forced to arrest. Should a man go free just because of what he believes?

"Most of them, but Jews especially, have never felt a part of Germany. The Jews have always been their own separate race and now they have a chance to rise up. But they don't want to go back to their own country. They want to take Germany and make it their new Israel. We would fall if we didn't stop them. That is why we are arresting Jews. No other reason. Everything else you've ever heard is a lie."

Franz swallowed because he felt like he was choking. He had nothing to say and for the first time in his life he was completely shaken. If everything Stein had said was true, then how was he to know which was truth and which was lies?

It confused him, trying to make sense of all Stein told him and he tried not to think about it too much. Franz instead spent most of his time working on helping his family.

The melted snow splattered up and into his boots, bring Franz back to the present for a few seconds. It didn't last, his mind wandered again. This time to Japhet.

***

He rarely saw Japhet now. When he wasn't out late Japhet was. The times he had seen him, Japhet had been sitting at the table, hallow and thinner than ever, drawing feverishly. His eyes were haunted, but he wouldn't talk about it, and Franz felt bad demanding answers. Why should he ask for Japhet's secrets when he refused to share his own?

Then there were the nightmares. Somehow, they had gotten worse. Every night now Franz woke to Japhet yelling. It had been a long time since Franz had gone in and tried to comfort him. He hadn't realized he'd pulled back until it was almost too late to fix it.

It started after Franz had seen Jacob Cohen killed in his own yard. He had his own nightmares about it; the man bloody and bruised, struggling to breathe. In Franz's nightmares, the Jew was always Japhet and the Nazis had found him because Franz had let something slip.

Franz pulled back so that wouldn't happen. He did what he could for Japhet without getting too close. He was not going to lead the Nazis to him, no matter what.

With each passing night, with each nightmare Franz lay awake listening to, his last hope in God vanished. If there really was a God out there, the God his family talked about, why had He turned his back on Japhet? Japhet was a Jew, one of His own people, and he was suffering. Where was his God when he needed Him?

Fight the resistance, save Japhet, Franz told himself. If God wouldn't save him, then he would. That soon became the one thing that got him through each new day and night. He would do this to save Japhet.

Twenty-Seven
Meeting the Americans

1942

"How is your German friend?" Seth asked as Japhet slipped into the basement where they were holding one of their many meetings.

Japhet gritted his teeth and said nothing as he sat down in one of the corners. The basement was slowly filling, men sneaking in under cover of darkness. Most everyone ignored Japhet, which he was grateful for. He wished Seth would follow their example.

"Are you ever going to get tired of asking me that?" Japhet demanded.

"No. I'm going to keep asking 'till you are no longer living with him. You're going to get us all killed, I just know it."

"Then why do you keep insisting I fight with you?" Japhet asked.

"Fight, Japhet Buchanan? Fight? When have you actually fought? We get into scuffles with the Nazis and you hide in the alleyways. All you ever help with is smuggling supplies from them. You're no help when it comes to real fighting." Seth glared, his eyes glinting in the candle light.

"Why do you keep asking me to come back then?" Japhet

asked, rephrasing his question. He wasn't sure if he wanted to be kicked out, but he also didn't think he would really mind. He wasn't making much with the resistance, but he was finding out valuable information which could help his family escape. Yet, he wasn't sure if it was worth the added nightmares.

He had seen so much in the time he'd been with the resistance. Nazis being killed while on patrol. And not just killed, but beaten until they were barely alive, then sneered and laughed at as they fought to breathe, finally giving up.

Seth was the worst. Not all of the resistance fighters were as cruel as he was. He seemed to think he could do whatever he wanted to the Nazis because they did whatever they wanted to the Jews. On top of that he robbed Germans – even poor ones who barely had anything. More than once Japhet had skipped meals, sneaking his portion of his and Franz's dinner to the families Seth thought it was okay to steal from.

Leb wasn't as bad. He understood they had to be better than the Nazis. He was of the few able to keep Seth in line. He put a stop to most of Seth's ideas and kept reminding everyone why they were doing what they were doing.

"We are trying to help the Jews. We want to show the Nazis that the Jews are just as human as they are."

Japhet rubbed his face, not sure he believed that anymore. His whole country thought he was less than human and he had trouble not believing it. His tired mind no longer had the will to fight off the lies.

"If you really want to prove yourself then you should join in the next time we have an actual fight."

Seth wasn't letting Japhet off easy tonight. He sat down in front of him and scowled, so Japhet scowled back.

"Who said I want to prove myself?" Japhet snapped.

"You should. I'm starting to think you are helping out that Nazi friend of yours."

Seeing red, Japhet stood up and curled his hands into fists. He didn't care that Franz wasn't there to help him when he got into another fight, he'd teach Seth to call Franz Kappel a Nazi. However, before he had a chance of rearranging Seth's nose, the basement door opened and their last member arrived, with two men at his side.

Japhet easily recognized Leb; the other two were men he'd not seen before, though he had a hard time getting a good look at their faces. They wore hats which added more shadows to the ones the candles cast.

Leb walked to the front of the room where he could be seen by almost everyone in the room. He remained standing when he got there, the two men at either side of him.

"We all came here tonight to talk about our next move against the Nazis, but that is no longer our top priority," Leb announced with no other sort of introduction.

Seth snorted in anger. "What can be more important than making Nazis pay for what they have done for us?" he snapped, trying to get everyone riled up and on his side. Japhet again thought about punching him.

"You've all heard of reconnaissance pilots, I hope?" Leb looked right at Seth so even those who didn't know nodded because they didn't want to be lumped in the same category as him.

"Good. Well, a few nights ago a reconnaissance plane was shot down while flying over Berlin."

"How were they shot down?" Seth scoffed. "And why were they flying over Berlin?"

"They were probably shot down with guns," one of the other

men answered. Japhet smiled as Seth clamped his jaw together.

"The two pilots somehow managed to survive the crash. They were captured by the Nazis and brought into Berlin." Leb went on. He ignored Seth. "Myself and three others saw them and managed to free them. Now we have to keep them safe until we can get them out of Berlin."

"Pilots?" Seth roared. "You want us to hide pilots? What is wrong with you? We are the resistance, not babysitters!"

Leb walked over to him, his steps measured and clipped. Japhet shrank back, not wanting to be close to Seth.

"We are here to help those we can," Leb snapped. He stopped right in front of Seth and stared down at him with anger flashing in his eyes. Even though Leb was shorter, Seth moved back and seemed to wilt.

"Understand that, Seth?" Leb went on. "I'm tired of your complaining. We are going to help them and if you have a problem with it, you can leave now."

Swallowing, Seth nodded and Leb walked back over to the two men. He motioned to them and they pulled off their hats and moved into the light. One was tall with shaggy brown hair; Japhet guessed him to be close to Franz's height and age. The other was shorter and older with blazing red hair.

"I don't know much English," Leb admitted, "but I know enough that I was able to get their names and some of their story. This is James Rodgers and Samuel Winters. If there is anyone here who speaks English I would be grateful if he would translate."

Japhet knew it would anger Seth even more if he knew about the time Japhet spent studying English, which was why he stepped forward. With his head held high, he walked over to Leb and smiled.

"I speak English," Japhet said.

***

Japhet wasn't in the apartment when Franz got there. He peeled off his wet and muddy boots and stuffed them in the little closet in the hall, then ran down and pulled his uniform out of the closet. He had no idea where Japhet was on nights like this, but every time he was gone, Franz took the opportunity to press his uniform. And tonight it really needed it.

***

When the meeting was over Japhet stayed in the basement with Leb and the two American pilots. All three stared at him, which made him nervous.

Hoping to distract the Americans from staring, Japhet cleared his throat twice, then stammered, "Hi." His voice cracked and he cleared his throat again.

"You speak English?" Samuel Winters gasped in surprise. He had a funny accent, one Japhet had never heard before. Now that Japhet had a chance to get a better look at him, he guessed Samuel to be in his late twenties or early thirties.

"Or do you just speak it like your buddy there? Because, let me tell you, that ain't English." James Rodgers had an accent too, one Japhet thought he should be able to place.

"I...I taught myself how to speak it," Japhet stammered, not liking the way the American watched at him. He seemed to be looking for some hidden secret.

"Listen, kid." James Rodgers stopped staring and sighed as he leaned back in his chair. "Can you tell us what's going on around here? Your buddy there, Heir Kraut, he pretty much kidnapped Sam and me and dragged us here. You ain't with Hitler, are you? Because we aren't going down without a fight, and Sam is pretty deadly in a fist fight. I saw him take down a six-foot-something giant once..."

"I..." Sam interrupted, but James Rodgers wasn't done.

"We just want out of here, got it? And I don't know what you and your buddies want from us, but you aren't going to get it. We're Americans. We don't crack under torture, so do your worst."

"Um, Jim..."

Japhet shook his head and blinked.

"Well, Jerry, what do you have to say for yourself?" And this time the pilot leaned forward and stared.

"Jimmy! Stop talking," Sam ordered.

Since Jimmy kept staring at him, Japhet decided he was waiting for something.

"My name isn't Jerry," he said, finally finding his voice. "My name is Japhet Buchanan."

"He's a Jew!" Sam gasped, then to Japhet, "You're a Jew, aren't you?"

"How do you know he's a Jew, Sam? He looks like the rest of the Krauts!"

"What's a Kraut?" Japhet asked.

"You are," Jimmy snapped, "you and him and everyone else in this stinking country! I know my rights as a prisoner of war, and I demand you fulfill them!"

"What's he saying?" Leb whispered to Japhet.

Japhet shrugged. "I don't know," he admitted.

"What are you two talking about?" Jimmy shouted. "If this is some conspiracy against us I will break your nose! I demand you take me back to my plane!"

Without warning, Sam jumped up and grabbed Jimmy's shoulders, shoving him back into his seat. Japhet stared in surprise, not sure what to do or say.

"Jim, will you just shut up?" Sam said, his accent growing thicker. "I think they're trying to help us and you're making it worse! Your plane is gone, they shot it, but we're alive. You can be thankful for that."

Just like that Jimmy shut his mouth and Sam sat back down. Both turned their attention to Japhet. Japhet just smiled because he could think of no other response.

***

It was late when Japhet got back to the apartment, so late it could almost be considered morning. His feet dragging, he climbed the steps and crashed through the front door, no longer sure what he thought of Americans.

Shoving the door opened, Japhet tripped into the living room, surprised to see Franz up and sitting at the kitchen table with two glasses of milk. He looked up and smiled when Japhet came in, the first real smile he'd offered in a year.

"I thought you might need a chance to sit down and rest when you got back," Franz said, motioning to the other chair.

Japhet smiled. He didn't know what had been wrong with Franz before, but it didn't seem to matter now. Franz still cared about him, despite what Seth thought.

Twenty-Eight
The Nazis attack

1942

Summer arrived, hot and miserable. Japhet, who had a chance to get out in the fresh air every day, didn't know how Jimmy and Sam endured it. Both pilots had been hidden away in the basement of a widow named Mrs. Schmidt. Even though her husband had fought with Hitler – before he'd been killed in battle – she helped the resistance.

Japhet spent a lot of time with Jimmy and Sam, since he spoke English. One day in July he smuggled them a newspaper, which he had to read to them since it was written in German.

When he finished, Jimmy smacked his fist into the palm of his other hand.

"Stupid, Krauts!" he snapped. "Just get me out of this basement and I'll teach them not to mess with us!"

Even though he never talked much, outside of war news, Japhet had learned Jimmy was from New York. He had first claimed his accent was from Brooklyn, but Sam had set him straight and told Japhet that Jimmy was from Queens. Japhet had looked it up later, learning Queens was in New York City.

"Right." Sam had a bedroll under the stairs. He liked to sit there most days, whittling. When he wasn't doing that, he and Jimmy would play a game of chess. "The farm boy from New York is going to win the war single-handed."

The day Japhet learned Jimmy was from New York he'd been told Sam had lived in Ireland until he turned seven. His parents were immigrants who had traveled to America, where Sam's dad had changed their last name in an attempt to fit into their new home.

"Farm?" Japhet asked. He folded the newspaper and tucked it into his shirt before Jimmy could rip it up in irritation. "Like Dorothy from The Wizard of Oz?"

"How do you know about The Wizard of Oz?" Jimmy asked. He squinted suspiciously. "Didn't think you Krauts knew about American movies."

"I'm not a Kraut," Japhet grumbled. He had discovered Kraut was an American insult for Germans. "I saw it once with my best friend." He almost smiled when he thought of how he and Franz had hidden behind the chairs, scared of the flying monkeys. He had had no idea at the time that he'd be facing things worse than flying monkeys.

"How did you see it in Germany?" Jimmy scoffed, sounding so much like Seth at that moment that Japhet decided not to give a straight answer.

"We didn't," he said, "we traveled to America the day it went into the theaters and saw it."

"Oh, you're a sarcastic one, ain't you?" Jimmy sat back against a bag of flour and crossed his arms over his chest, frowning, but Sam laughed.

"What's your friend's name?" Sam asked.

Japhet crossed his legs even though he knew it would only solidify Jimmy calling him a kid. He'd been annoyed with the term at first, even more so when he found out Jimmy was only twenty and believed Japhet was no older than fifteen.

"Franz Kappel," Japhet replied.

"Is he a Jew too?" Jimmy asked.

"Kappel isn't a Jewish name," Sam replied before Japhet could.

"How do you know this?" Jimmy asked.

"I studied, I wanted to know about the Jews when I heard rumors about what Hitler was doing to them," Sam answered, staring at the hard dirt packed floor. Japhet did the same, unsure what to say. During the long struggle to get his family out of Germany he had never taken the time to consider that there might be people out there who actually cared about him and his people.

"Yeah, well, I didn't think I'd end up in Germany," Jimmy muttered. "I joined up to fight the Nips."

"Nips?" Japhet asked, glad to change the subject.

"Nips, Japanese." Jimmy shook his head. "You know, the little Orientals who bombed Pearl Harbor."

"Oh, right. Seth was talking about that, so I didn't listen." Japhet smirked and Jimmy actually laughed.

"You have issues with Seth, don't you?" he asked.

Japhet shrugged. "I have my reasons for disliking him." And he looked at the floor again.

"So, your family in Berlin?" Jimmy asked after they'd sat in silence for a while.

"No, just me and Franz. We have sisters in Munich, and Franz's parents and my other sister are staying at this farm. They're trying to get out of Germany, but it hasn't been working well..." Japhet let his voice trail off, thinking that might be something Sam and Jimmy could understand. So far no one had come up with any plans on how to get two English speaking Americans out of Berlin, let alone Germany. They kept running into different complications and the only thing they could do at the moment was to have Sam and Jimmy try and learn German so they would be ready if the chance came to escape.

Leb had been teaching the two pilots, but the lessons were slow and Japhet knew Leb was being pushed to the limits of his patience. Sam was a willing student, though his accent proved to be their biggest concern. Jimmy, on the other hand, acted like each lesson was pure torture.

"I'm sorry, Japhet. I'm sure that must be hard for you," Sam said, cutting off Japhet's thoughts. "I will pray that God provides a means of escape."

Japhet nodded but said nothing. The mention of God no longer made him mad, just numb. God didn't care about him or his family, and He never would.

He decided to change subjects again.

"So, you two joined the war because your Pearl Harbor was attacked by the Japanese?"

Jimmy sat upright and scowled and Japhet wondered what he'd said to make him bristle.

"When you put it like that..." he huffed, then stopped and scowled. "That isn't the only reason I joined...I had other reasons!"

Sam leaned back, positioning his back to rest in the middle of a pole. He said nothing, but he kept throwing Jimmy quiet, strange glances.

"What other reasons?" Japhet asked, curious. America had always been so far away, the place he and Franz joked about going to, disconnected with the war. A little island where, if he and Franz ran to it, they would be safe. Japhet couldn't think of any reason someone would want to leave that.

"I..." Jimmy paused and glared hard. "I just had other

reasons!" he snapped.

Japhet looked at him for a second or two then shrugged. He hadn't known Americans could be so short tempered, so he let the subject drop.

Seth was furious over Jimmy and Sam. He gathered together some of the resistance that night and talked to them about it, laying down his argument as to why they should no longer help them.

"It has been three months since they arrived!" he shouted as Leb glared at him. "We are risking our lives keeping them here and they are eating food we're already short on. Also, they've offered us nothing in return!"

"Our lives were at risk before they came," Leb calmly reminded him. "And what would you have them offer us? They cannot fight beside us, don't you think the Nazis would notice two Americans in Berlin?"

"Leb, we owe them nothing, why do you insist on keeping them hidden? Who knows when we will be able to get them out? It could be years! It could be the end of this blasted war! We can't keep them that long!"

"Maybe he has a point," one of the other men said, keeping his voice level and more rational than Seth. "Leb, you have been spending all your extra time with them, trying to teach them German...but we have to be honest with ourselves. Even if they are able to learn German, which could take years, we will still have problems. Problems which we can't fix as easily as teaching them to say a few words in German. What about Sam's accent? Don't you think the Nazis will catch on when he does say something?"

"And in the meantime," another added, frowning deeply, "our leader has his attention divided." He looked right at Leb. "You're one of the best we have, Leb. We need you if we plan to stay alive."

"What would you propose?" Leb asked. He looked from one to the other – even at the men who were nodding in agreement – but lastly resting his gaze on Seth. "You want to take them to the Nazis yourself?"

The other men who had spoken stared down at the floor or their hands while Seth opened and closed his mouth and Odis glared until he shut it completely. Silence swallowed the room and Japhet quietly looked from one of the fighters to the other. He thought of the two men in Mrs. Schmidt's basement, one only two years older than himself, and something stirred in his chest. Without knowing what he was doing, he stood up and walked to the center of the room, his legs shaking.

"There are Nazis out there, killing people because of their beliefs and nationality," he said, his voice cracking until he swallowed twice and steadied it. "We've seen death everywhere we turn. Soldiers are killing soldiers; civilians are caught in the crossfire. We're surrounded by hate and anger, but if we allow ourselves to feel the same and kill those who come to use for help, are we better than the Nazis? Jimmy and Sam need us. Do we really want to betray them?"

Leb stood as well and laid a hand on Japhet's shoulder as his eyes again roved over the room.

"Well?" he asked, as calm as always. "Since we started the resistance we've been claiming that we are better than the Nazis, but how true is that if we don't help those who need us? It doesn't matter if it's Jews or American soldiers. All of us are at risk of the Nazis finding us; that should make us sympathize with those two young men. Can any of you look me in the eye and say you would really be able to turn them out into the streets and let them try to fend for themselves? Japhet has a point. Are we going to let ourselves be filled with the same hate and anger as the Nazis? Because if so, it's time we give up fighting and let the Nazis do what they want with us, because they have already won."

Seth was seething, Japhet could feel his eyes on him, trying to burn him where he stood. For a second or two all Seth did was glare, then he finally lowered his eyes and sighed.

The sound of pent up breath escaping his lips reminded Leb of his presence and he walked over to stand in front of him.

"You're better than them, Seth," he whispered. He rested a hand on his shoulder. "I know you've been through a lot, but you can't let the Nazis win."

Seth raised his head and gave Leb a faint smile and Japhet breathed easier until the basement door was shoved open and the man they'd posted on watch stumbled down the stairs.

"The Nazis!" he hissed. "They've found us!"

With no other warning needed, the men quickly rose and moved toward the exit, hardly making a sound even though they were rushing. Japhet was hardly aware of himself moving until he stood outside and looked up into the starry sky overhead. He didn't realize Seth was shoving him behind a building until they were there, his back pressed against the rough brick wall, the shadows hiding the two of them as the other men disappeared.

"Shh!" Seth hissed as a window in the house shattered, men shouted, and grunts filled the night air. Japhet saw flashes of light even though none of them reached his and Seth's hiding place.

"Shouldn't we be helping or something?" Japhet hissed. He tried to pull free of the hold Seth had on his shoulders. "What about the family?"

"Almost everyone got away," Seth whispered, scowling. "And you know the family living there had a plan to escape if this happened. They're safe. Those that didn't get away...there isn't much we can do. Not unless we want to join them."

Japhet would have argued, but he stopped when he saw tears in Seth's eyes. He lowered his head and swallowed, trying to block out the sounds of windows breaking.

"I think I caught their leader!"

At the shout, Japhet's head jerked up and Seth released him in surprise. Together they peered around the side of the building. Holding their breath, both watched in horror as Leb was pulled out under one of the streetlights and thrown to the ground. He appeared to be the only one the Nazis had caught and ten of them surrounded him. Japhet lunged forward, but Seth grabbed him and held him back as Leb rolled to his knees and looked up at his captors.

"Now, Jew," one of the Nazis spat, "where are all your friends? Left you, didn't they? And I was under the belief that Jews stuck together."

The others laughed and the one who had been talking yanked Leb to his feet, lifting him until his toes just brushed the ground.

"Where are the others? Come on, tell us and we'll let you go."

Japhet kept struggling. It reminded him of the night his parents had been killed, only this time it wasn't Franz that held on to him. Japhet keenly felt his absence.

Leb smiled and Japhet felt his heart drop to his boots. "You won't get anything from me," Leb said.

The Nazi dropped him and Leb hit the ground hard. "Stinking Jew!" the soldier snapped. "We'll see about that!"

Without warning, he pulled his foot back and kicked Leb hard in the ribs. Even from the distance he was at, Japhet heard a crack and he sagged against the wall.

"Um," one of the other soldiers murmured but it was too late. The first blow had been delivered and others were fast to follow.

Japhet fought to break free of Seth's hold again, but Seth just shoved him back and held him there.

"We can't help him," he whispered, tears escaping his eyes, "we would only get killed ourselves; there is nothing we can do."

Japhet knew Seth was right, but he didn't feel any better about it. He could hear each blow as it fell. He closed his eyes and fought nausea twisting his stomach, wishing for it to be over, not so much for himself but for Leb.

He didn't deserve to die this way.

***

Franz wasn't on patrol that night. It was one of his nights off and he had decided to stay in. The only problem with this was that Japhet had gone out, and Franz realized he missed his company.

With his eyes closed, Franz lay on the couch and tried to enjoy the peace and quiet. But his mind refused to slow down, spinning with worry. He couldn't shake the feeling that something was wrong.

***

Japhet wasn't sure how long the soldiers beat Leb, but Seth didn't release him until they were gone. The moment he did, Japhet staggered forward, then shoved past Seth and rushed to Leb's broken body. He could barely see through his tears and wasn't aware of himself tripping and landing hard next to the man he had been slowly come to admire.

Leb was on his side, curled up into a tight ball and Japhet hoped he might still be alive. Japhet rolled him to his back, part of him expecting Leb to smile at him and say he only had a few broken ribs.

The eyes which stared up at Japhet were lifeless. A sharp stab cut through Japhet's heart as he looked into those eyes and once again his world shattered.

How could this keep happening? His parents, Karl, and now Leb. How many more did he have to lose? Lowering his head to Leb's chest, Japhet lost control over his tears and sobbed until Seth interrupted.

"Crying isn't going to do us any good," he snapped, his voice thick with his own tears. "He's dead and we can't fix that. Unless we kill some of those Nazis to avenge him!"

"What good would that to?" Japhet asked. He lifted his head and brushed away some of his tears. "It won't bring Leb back."

"No, but at least we can make them understand what it feels like!" Seth shouted. "We can show them! All of them! Do you understand now, Japhet? Your friend, your Nazi friend, think of Leb when you see him next!"

Japhet didn't think he could feel anger after such stabbing grief, but he was on his feet before he knew it and he shoved Seth hard, satisfied when the taller man hit the ground.

"Franz is not a Nazi!" he shouted.

"Prove it then!" Seth shouted back. "If you're so sure of your German friend then prove it! Because as far as I'm concerned, he's no better than the men who killed Leb!"

"I will," Japhet hissed, backing away. "I will prove it." And he turned and ran off, unable to look again at Leb's bruised and twisted body.

Twenty-Nine
The fight

1942

Japhet didn't return to the apartment that night. Franz stayed up waiting for him and almost didn't go to meet with the Nazis the next morning. In the end he decided he had to, or risk Stein looking for him. If that happened, there was a chance he'd run into Japhet.

When Franz went downstairs, the little old lady from the first-floor apartment was coming in from outside. She smiled at Franz.

"Rupert!" she greeted with a smile which make crinkles appear around her eyes. "It has been a long time since I've seen you!"

Some of the tension drained from Franz's body and he smiled in return, glad he hadn't been coming out of the closet when he ran into her.

"I've been busy," he explained.

The woman patted his arm as she passed him. "I'm sure. Don't overwork yourself. You're still young. Take that cousin of yours out and have some fun. You both need it. He's getting so thin and pale." She clicked her tongue.

The knots came back and Franz nodded. "I will," he promised

as she entered her apartment.

All the way to the headquarters Franz worried about Japhet. He didn't stop even when he spotted Stein and Carsten standing outside with some of the other young men. All were laughing and talking. Franz didn't think he would like to know what they were so happy about, but he joined them in spite of that.

"You missed it!" Carsten said the moment he saw Franz. He waved him over and beamed him his friendliest grin.

"Missed what?" Franz asked as Stein smacked him on the back.

"You picked the wrong night to have off of patrol!" he said, beaming as well. "We found some of the resistance fighters!"

The others nodded eagerly and Franz disguised his racing heart behind a smile. He reminded himself, over and over, everything Stein had told him about the resistance, but it didn't help.

"You brought them in?" he asked casually.

"Only two, the rest got away," Carsten muttered.

"But we killed one," another of the men said before Franz could process.

"Oh?" he asked. It was easy to fake feeling nothing right then since that was all he did feel.

"He was one of the leaders," Carsten continued. "He flat out refused to tell us anything, so Stein kicked him. I think the man would have died from internal bleeding on that kick alone, but you know...we had to help out."

Franz's stomach tied into a violent knot, but he ignored it. This was what happened in wars, wasn't it? Men died, men were killed. The resistance leader was a soldier, same as anyone else who put on a uniform and went out to the battlefield to fight. And soldiers were killed every day.

Hoping to hide his nausea, Franz smiled at Stein. "Way to go," he said, though he didn't feel it. Soldier or not, had the man really deserved to be beaten to death?

For Japhet, Franz told himself.

"Yes, but we could have gotten information from him. Since he was their leader," Stein muttered.

"Oh well," Franz said, hoping his smile didn't look forced now, "we'll catch more of them, then you can get all the information you need."

***

Japhet had gone back to the apartment that night, he just hadn't gone in. Instead, he had sat in the alley and waited for Franz to come out. He was determined to clear Franz's name to Seth, but the moment Japhet saw him it was like walking into a living nightmare.

Franz Kappel left the apartment in a sharp Nazi uniform and Japhet's world twisted so suddenly he was thrown to his knees. He didn't stay down long, though.

There had to be a reason behind it, he yelled at himself. Franz had stood by him too long to be a Nazi now. So Japhet followed, hoping something might wake him up and end the horrible sight right in front of his eyes.

He followed Franz all the way to Prinz-Albrecht-Straße 8 , which everyone knew to be the Gestapo Headquarters. Japhet slowly edged his way close to the building as Franz joined a group of Nazis standing outside.

By the time Japhet made it close enough to hear the conversation, the Nazis were talking about Leb and his death. He listened as Franz told one of the Nazis he had done well, and just like that everything Japhet thought he knew about the world crashed down on his exhausted head.

Escaping, Japhet wandered the streets, unaware of where he went. He couldn't make sense of his own thoughts or the fact that Seth had been right all along. He didn't understand what kind of horrible joke was being played on him or how it could be possible what he had seen and heard was true.

Franz had promised to look after him when they moved to Berlin. How could he do something like this, after all the times he had taken a beating for him? More than anything Japhet wanted to deny it, but he kept seeing Leb's body, heard his bones breaking, and saw Franz talking to Nazis like they were old friends. His tired mind had trouble processing, but he couldn't deny the things he'd seen.

It was only when darkness settled over Berlin that Japhet found himself back at the apartments. He stopped outside the building and looked up, thinking of the first time he and Franz had seen it. They'd been nothing but scared boys then; what were they now? Japhet thought again of Leb's death and remembered how he had just stood back and done nothing.

Was that the kind of man he was? The one who didn't have the courage to stand up to the Nazis? He had never had the same kind of courage as Franz, but at least he hadn't turned his back on his friends.

Taking a deep breath, Japhet stepped into the building and climbed the familiar steps. With each one his exhausted mind replaced his sorrow with anger.

Franz had promised to be there, and now he was part of the organization that had killed Japhet's parents, which had killed Karl and Leb and would kill his sisters if they got the chance. Franz hadn't just betrayed him, he'd betrayed everyone – their families, their friends, even Warren. Japhet couldn't stand back and do nothing, not like he had done with Leb.

Reaching the door, Japhet shoved it open, not sure if he was pleased or dismayed to find Franz still up, laying on the couch.

"There you are!" Franz leaped up the moment the door opened. "I was starting to get worried when you didn't come home at all last night."

Franz had noticed he hadn't come in. For some reason, that made Japhet feel slightly better. That at least meant he hadn't been one of the ones to kill Leb.

"I didn't think you would be here," Japhet whispered, his voice cold in his own ears.

"Why wouldn't I?" Franz asked. He studied him for a moment before he added, "Are you okay? You don't look so good."

"I'm doing okay, for a Jew." Those words were so bitter even Japhet winced. He tried to get a hold of his emotions. This was Franz, his best friend, his brother. Deep down Japhet knew he deserved a chance to explain himself, but Japhet's unreasonable, jumbled words wouldn't stop.

"What are you talking about?" Franz asked. He came around the couch but stopped when Japhet moved back. His forehead wrinkled in concern. "Come on, Japhet, tell me what's wrong!"

"I saw you," Japhet whispered, lowering his eyes and staring at the floor.

"Saw me?" There was a hint of fear in Franz's voice and Japhet sagged against the wall. It had to be true. Franz wouldn't sound like that unless it were.

"You're a Nazi." The words tasted bitter and a shiver went up Japhet's spine.

"What?" Franz whispered, almost as if someone punched him in the stomach and he was trying to breathe.

"You're a Nazi!" The anger came back so suddenly Japhet felt a new wave of energy tear through his body. He straightened up and glared. "You're a Nazi, Franz Kappel! A Nazi!"

"Japhet, I..." Franz held up his hands, but Japhet wasn't about to listen.

"How could you?" he shouted. His voice cracked. "How could you do that to all of us? What about our sisters, your parents? Do they know? How could you join them, Franz? You know what they do to Jews!"

"Japhet, you have to listen..."

"I don't have to listen to you!" Japhet yelled. "All of your promises, you didn't mean them! You didn't just betray me, you betrayed them! Your own family!"

"Japhet, I haven't...it isn't like that! And you're my family, you and your sisters. Do you honestly think..."

"You congratulated the man who killed Leb! Killed him, in cold blood! You're with them, you help them. I trusted you!" Japhet felt tears sting his eyes, but he fought them back. Now was not the time to start crying.

"You have to shut up and let me..." Franz moved toward him, but Japhet leaped toward the door.

"You're not my father!" he shouted. "I don't have to listen to anything you say!"

"Japhet!" Now it was Franz's turn to shout. "How can you think I'd hurt you? What about all those times I stood up for you? Do you really believe..."

Japhet shook his head violently. "I don't know what to think," he hissed, "but I know what I saw. You're a traitor, Franz Kappel! A traitor!"

"A traitor? You really think that?" Franz shouted. He stood up straighter and Japhet glared at him as he glared back. "You think I'm a traitor? After everything I've done for you?"

"You're a Nazi!" Japhet yelled. "If that isn't a traitor then what is?"

"If you would shut up and just listen!"

"Listen? To what?" Rage flowed through Japhet's body and he began to shake. "To your lies? Because we both know Nazis are good liars!"

"I'm not a Nazi!" Franz shouted. He stepped closer to Japhet and this time Japhet didn't back up but tried to make himself as threatening as Franz.

"You were with them, wearing a uniform!" Japhet reminded him. "If you're not a Nazi then what are you?"

"I..." Franz froze for a second or two and Japhet felt something prick him, right in the heart.

"You don't have a good answer, do you?" he whispered, feeling defeated. "That's because you are one and you can't deny it."

Franz snapped. His head shot up and he threw himself at Japhet, grabbing hold of him and shoving him back into the wall. Japhet twisted and fought to pull free, suddenly scared. He had never seen Franz look at him the way he did at that moment. It was the same look he had given Amell once before punching him in the stomach.

"How can you think that?" Franz yelled as he pinned Japhet. "Do you have any idea how many times I got beat up for you? I never told you all of it! Never! There were days when I couldn't even come over because I was afraid to let you see me! I was hated by everyone in school; I couldn't even walk down the halls without them taunting me. Do you have any idea what that was like? I was hated, for you!"

Japhet continued to fight, trying to break away. "I'm sorry I was such a burden!" he snapped. He felt an overwhelming amount of guilt, imagining Franz at home, black and blue with bruises, but he still couldn't shake the rage which had gripped him. "Is that why you joined them, so you would finally be accepted?"

Franz slammed his hand into the wall right beside Japhet's head.

"Shut up!" he yelled. "I'm not..."

Not wanting to hear more, Japhet swung, punching Franz in the chest. It was like hitting a wall, but Franz moved enough that Japhet was able to get out of his hold. He turned and rushed for the door, but Franz grabbed his arm, yanking him back. Just in time, Japhet saw Franz's fist coming for his head and he ducked and kicked Franz in the leg. Franz finally loosened his hold and Japhet pulled his arm free.

Stumbling, Franz kept upright and swung another punch but Japhet backed away from it, then delivered his own, swinging as hard as he could. His fist connected with the side of Franz's head. Japhet was certain he hurt himself more than Franz and was even a little concerned that he might have broken his hand, but he didn't wait around to examine the damage.

As Franz staggered back from the punch, Japhet ran out the door and down the steps, ignoring Franz yelling his name behind him.

Thirty
Seth's confrontation

1942

Stunned by the blow to his head, Franz stumbled and crashed on the couch, where he tripped and fell to the floor. For a minute or two he just sat on the floor, waiting for the room to stop spinning while his brain screamed at him to get up and go after Japhet.

When he finally was able to stand, Franz stumbled out the door and almost broke his neck tripping down the stairs. Once out the door and into the fresh air, his head cleared and he ran down the street, desperate to catch sight of Japhet.

Franz searched all night but didn't find even the smallest trace of Japhet. An hour after the sun rose he was exhausted and frantic.

He and Japhet had never fought before. They'd disagreed on things, but that never had lasted long. They'd never gotten really angry and Franz had no idea hat Japhet would do after something like that or where he would go.

Two more hours passed before Franz, bone weary, sat down on the edge of the sidewalk and lowered his head into his hands.

His head hurt, he could feel his eye bruising, and his thoughts wouldn't slow down long enough for him to try and think of somewhere Japhet might have been hiding. Franz feared Japhet had done or would do something stupid; he'd been upset enough.

Be reasonable! Franz snapped. *This is Japhet you're talking about. He isn't an idiot. He wouldn't turn himself into the Nazis or anything like that. He's just hiding out somewhere until he cools down. And he has a good reason to be mad; you should have told him right off about the Nazis and all of this could have been avoided. But Japhet knows the truth. He knows you well enough to know you would never —*

He stopped and rubbed his forefinger over his scar.

Never what? Never join the Nazis? Because he had already done that and Japhet had seen him. Franz had no idea how he was going to try and explain it to Japhet when he found him. The uniform hanging in the supply closet downstairs was incriminating. How could he make Japhet understand what was going on when he barely understood it himself?

Could he explain it to Japhet the same way Stein had explained it to him? Franz wasn't hunting down and killing Jews; he was fighting soldiers to help save his country. And he could help his family at the same time. He highly doubted Japhet would see it that way. He wouldn't see the truth behind the things Franz was struggling with. If only Franz could find him, so they could work this problem out.

He might be back already. He just needed some time alone to process what he saw, but he is sure to come back and talk it out. He is probably at the apartment now, waiting for you, to yell at you again.

Smiling, Franz staggered to his feet and ran back to the apartment, but when he entered it was empty and lifeless. There was no sign of Japhet anywhere.

***

Part of Japhet, deep in his exhausted mind, knew he had to go back and give Franz a chance to explain himself. Way deep down Japhet knew Franz would never do something like this to him but at the moment he couldn't comprehend what he had seen. He walked the streets and fumed and somehow ended up at the house where Jimmy and Sam were hiding. He was about to go down, planning on spending the night with them, when someone grabbed him.

Japhet's first instinct was to fight back and he tried to twist around and punch his attacker even though his hand still hurt. Before he could connect with anything his attacker clamped a hand over his mouth and Seth hissed in his ear.

"Quiet! Unless you want to get us both killed. Follow me, we need to talk." Seth released him and hurried behind the house.

Knowing he wasn't going to like what was coming, Japhet followed, his steps less eager than Seth's. Once in the small backyard, Japhet faced Seth as they stood under the tree.

"Well?" Seth asked and his smug smile brought Japhet's temper back to the surface.

"Well what?" he snapped.

The smile deepened. "As I thought. You followed him, didn't you? Like I said you should. And what did you find? Your friend is a Nazi, isn't he?"

Japhet's vision blurred and his fist seemed to come out of nowhere. It connected, satisfactorily, with Seth's jaw and Japhet didn't mind that he'd made the pain in his hand worse. The next thing Japhet knew he was standing over the man, glaring down at him.

"You think you can deny it?" Seth snapped, rubbing his jaw. "I followed you...did you think I wouldn't? I saw what you saw.

One of those Nazis you were watching, one was your so-called friend, wasn't he? Admit it, Japhet! He betrayed you!"

"Shut up!" Japhet yelled, unconcerned that they might be overheard by a patrol.

"You can't ignore the truth!" Seth said, suddenly too calm. "You saw it. Right in front of you. What excuse did he make for it? What did he say, to explain why he had stabbed you in the back? The same one my supposedly best friend made?" Seth pushed himself to his feet and Japhet staggered back.

"Your best friend became a Nazi?"

"I thought he was my friend. We grew up together," Japhet was surprised to see real hurt in Seth's eyes, "but the first chance he got, he joined the Nazis. He turned his own father in, made up some lie about him. Not that his dad didn't deserve it; he beat him all the time. But the Night of Broken Glass, you heard of it, right? My friend helped. He killed Jews." Now Seth looked away. "He shot my family. He let me escape, but I wished he hadn't. I think he wished he hadn't too when I found him two nights later and I killed him."

Japhet shivered in the warm summer air. "You killed him?" he whispered.

Just like that, Seth snapped out of his sorrow. "Yes, I killed him! I choked the life out of him and I enjoyed it! He killed my family! Shot them in the streets! My kid siblings, all three of them, even though they were screaming and crying. Looked them right in the eyes and pulled the trigger! Don't you dare give me that look, Japhet Buchanan! He deserved to die!"

Walking closer, Seth grabbed both Japhet's shoulders and dig his fingers in, holding him in place as he looked him in the eyes.

"We can't trust them, Japhet. None of them. Us Jews have to stick together because right now the whole world is out to kill us.

You have to accept that. It doesn't work, a Jew and a Nazi being friends. The boy you grew up with, he's gone. And now you have to decide, are you going to go back and get yourself killed...or are you going to fight for your people?"

Part Three
The dreams that you dare to dream

Thirty-One
Believing the lies

1943

A grenade exploded near him. Japhet heard it hit the ground and he threw himself to the side even as it blew. Dirt and rocks flew into the air with the explosion and showered down on Japhet as he covered his head with his arms.

"The left! The left! They're in the trees!"

The shout came from the newest recruit, an energetic young man named Levi. Japhet was certain Levi would get a bullet in the head before too long. He had a bad habit of jumping up at the wrong moments during fights.

"Get down!" Odis growled. He yanked Levi into the ditch running along the side of the road. The moment Levi's head was out of sight, bullets filled the evening air.

"Japhet!" Odis bellowed.

Japhet had no time to assure Odis he was all right. He had dodged closer to the other side of the road and had just enough time to roll into the ditch as bullets struck the ground where he'd been lying. As he rolled, the grenade he had been carrying dug into his side, reminding him it was still there.

"This isn't supposed to happen!" Japhet snapped as bullets

tore into the dirt road.

The mission was supposed to be relatively simple. Seth had learned that there were three supply trucks moving out of Berlin. Japhet had appointed himself, Odis, and Levi to sneak out and bury some mines in the road to stop them. Japhet hadn't thought they would need any more than three men, and the less they took, the less chance they had of getting caught.

Setting the mines had been easy but the three of them were spotted before they could flee, as the grenade and bullets testified.

"Japhet!" Odis' worried shout could still be heard above the gunshots.

Japhet groaned. Even after a year of fighting together, after the times Japhet had gotten out of messes worse than this and even saved Odis' life twice, the man who had dislocated his shoulder when they first met still worried about him. It made Japhet smile, but only when the large man couldn't see. He didn't want Odis to know he liked being looked after – he didn't want anyone to know.

"I'm fine!" Japhet shouted back, not sure if his comrade heard or not. He just hoped Odis wasn't foolish enough to try and come after him.

"Move in!" This shout was from the Nazis firing at them and Japhet ground his teeth. He, Levi, and Odis didn't stand a chance if the Nazis advanced.

Drawing his pistol, Japhet carefully lifted his head. The trucks were heading off down the road, right for the mines. If they reached them before the Nazis reached Japhet and his companions, then there was a chance the three of them could still get away.

The Nazis were on the open dirt road now, advancing in tight formation. There were at least twenty of them and they were all heavily armed. Japhet knew he could take out some with his grenade, but the Nazis had spaced themselves, ten in front and ten a little further back. The grenade would only daze the ones behind and then Japhet and the other two would still have to deal with them.

Sighing, Japhet grabbed his grenade and gripped the end of it. Grenades were hard to come by. He'd been saving this one for a special occasion, but he figured if he died now that occasion would never come.

Japhet twisted the end off and stood up long enough to throw. As he did so, someone fired and pain tore through his shoulder. He hit the ground as one of the Nazis yelled grenade and it blew.

Clamping his eyes shut, more to keep dirt out than to try and block out the pain in his shoulder, Japhet waited until the dirt settled before shoving himself up again. Keeping low behind the ditch, he began to fire at the Nazis who had survived the grenade blast. Odis and Levi joined in, though Japhet wasn't sure how many soldiers Levi actually hit. Japhet decided that next time he'd leave Levi behind. Let him put up with Seth; it wasn't as if Japhet had to babysit him.

The Nazis fired back, but there were only a few bullets exchanged before the first truck hit a mine and blew. It flew a foot or two into the air and tipped to its side, smoke billowing out of the bottom as the windows shattered. The Nazis on the road spun around, then rushed to check for damage as the other trucks slid to a stop. Japhet didn't wait around to admire their handiwork. Instead, gripping his shoulder, he ran off into the woods, knowing Levi and Odis wouldn't be far behind.

***

"They attacked, again!" Stein slammed his fist down on the

table. His coffee cup jumped and some of the cold liquid sloshed over the side. Carsten had brought it to Stein that morning; now it was probably as cold as ice.

"What did they do this time?" Carsten asked. He pulled a cigarette from between his lips and blew smoke into the air.

"They blew up two of our supply trucks!"

"How did they get two?" Franz stood near the door, arms crossed, foot propped up against the wall because it annoyed Stein to have muddy boots on his walls. Franz wore his hat pulled lower over his eyes and squinted out from under it. "If one of the trucks blew, the driver of the other one should have stopped to let someone make sure the road was clear." He didn't bother pointing out they had to learn that from experience when they'd lost two trucks the first time the resistance took to burying land mines.

"They placed them further apart," Stein muttered. He clenched his teeth together and Franz heard his jaw popping. He was mildly surprised Stein still had teeth. One of the great mysteries of life. "There were no mines for three miles in front of the first one. Three miles. They went three miles to place another!" Once more Stein's fist connected with the table and this time the map jumped.

Teeth and still intact bones. Two of life's greatest mysteries.

"How are they even getting their hands on mines?" Franz asked, watching one of the tacks, which had been in the map, roll to the floor.

"That's what I want to know!" Stein shouted.

"What are we going to do?" Carsten asked, casually catching a pen as it rolled off the table. He flicked ashes to the floor.

"We're going to stand back and let them overrun Berlin," Stein said, his voice suddenly calm.

"Wha..." Before Carsten could finish, one of the other pens left Stein's hand and struck Carsten's shoulder.

"We're going to find them and kill every one of them! And not just the fighters, I want leaders! You saw how inactive they went when we killed that one leader a year ago! I want all of them. Alive. Because we are going to send a message to those Jews. We are going to put them in their rightful place!"

***

Japhet always entered the basement through the small window, the only source of fresh air for Sam and Jimmy. He was one of the few small enough to fit through the window.

As Japhet wiggled through, Jimmy's soft singing of the song *Don't Sit Under the Apple Tree (with Anyone Else but Me)* reached his ears. Jimmy stopped when Japhet dropped to the floor and caught his attention. He and Sam looked up and Japhet again admired them for lasting a whole year in the basement.

It wasn't that the resistance wasn't trying to get them out. Ever since Leb's death and Japhet's promotion to leader he had made it one of his goals to find a way to help the Americans escape. He had even taken over teaching them German, but it wasn't as easy as that. Trying to help them speak just a few words fluently took time and there was still the complication with Sam's accent.

The black curtain which Mrs. Schmidt kept over the window fell back into place and Sam looked up from a book. He sat beside a candle, bent over as he held the pages dangerously close to the flame.

"Why if it isn't our fearless leader, come back covered in dirt, again," Jimmy said. He sat against one wall, his feet thrust out in front of him.

"About time," Sam said. "He's been singing that song over

and over for the last hour. I was about to kill him."

Japhet leaned against the wall nearest him, feeling the blood loss now that the adrenaline had worn off.

"What happened to your shoulder?" Sam demanded. He jumped to his feet and squinted at Japhet in the dim light.

"I'm not your fearless leader," Japhet told Jimmy, then forced a smile at Sam. "Nothing, it's fine. Just a graze I think."

He knew it was more than that; the bullet had gone clean through. He had done his best to stop the bleeding, but he could still feel blood running down his arm. He swayed back and forth.

"Right, just like the bullet you took five months back. Be glad that one didn't cripple you," Jimmy snapped. He walked over, lead Japhet to the one chair Mrs. Schmidt had brought down for them, and shoved him into it. "Now let Sam look at your shoulder before you die on us."

Japhet couldn't protest, but he wanted to. He already had Odis constantly worrying about him, he didn't need Sam to worry as well.

Moving the candle closer to the chair, Sam helped Japhet out of his shirt and examined the wound. Japhet kept his eyes straight ahead. He'd gotten into so many scraps over the past year his body was now covered in scars. He had one on his left arm where he took a piece of shrapnel, one on his side from the bullet which had nearly crippled him, and a jagged scar across his stomach.

"A graze?" Sam demanded, all hints of his American accent gone.

"Well, it wasn't like I took time to look. I was trying not to get killed at the time," Japhet muttered, his teeth clenched. The bullet hole had gone numb until Sam started poking it.

"Now it's bleeding again!" Jimmy yelped.

"That's what happens when you're shot!" Sam said.

"What's going on here?" Odis' voice filled the basement the same way his large figure did. One moment he stood on the stairs that led to the house above; the next he was beside Japhet. Grabbing the candle, he bent to get a good look at his bleeding shoulder as Levi stood on the steps and swayed back and forth.

"Is that blood?" he whispered faintly.

"Yes. Go and ask Mrs. Schmidt for bandages and hot water," Odis ordered. "Hurry!"

Levi tore up the stairs and Sam pushed Odis back.

"Tell him to leave you alone," Sam told Japhet, his accent betraying his outward calm. "I need to clean the wound before he starts poking and prodding."

Odis glared at Sam and Sam glared back and once again Japhet felt caught in the middle. Another reason he didn't want them both worrying over him.

"He sent Levi for bandages and water," Japhet told Sam, wishing his eyes would stop turning everything fuzzy. If he blacked out now, Odis would never let him go on another mission – even if Japhet did outrank him.

"How could you have gone and got yourself shot again?" Odis demanded, diverting his glare from Sam to Japhet. Sam pressed a cloth to the wound and Japhet closed his eyes against the burning pain.

"Look at you!" Odis exclaimed. "You're dying! I knew you'd die on me, you're too idiotically brave for me to keep alive!"

"I'm not dying," Japhet whispered, the crack in his voice not helping matters.

"What's he bellowing about now?" Jimmy asked.

It was hard concentrating, harder than it was keeping conscious, and Jimmy, Sam, and Odis weren't helping by shouting at him in two different languages.

"Did he say you're dying or that he's hungry?" Jimmy asked.

Fiery fingers seemed to be burning Japhet's shoulder, and in the jumble of voices flying around him, a new one joined in.

"He's going to be all right, isn't he, Mrs. Buchanan?" Franz was worried, but Japhet's feverish mind couldn't understand why.

"Of course he is," Mrs. Buchanan answered, her voice like a cool rain falling on his burning body. "It's just a fever."

"He doesn't look very well," Franz murmured.

"Now don't start worrying, Franz Kappel," Mrs. Buchanan scolded. "Worrying won't help anything. Why don't we let him rest; you can come down and have some of the cake Ruth made."

"If it's all right, I'd like to stay here for a little while longer," Franz murmured.

"Stay as long as you want," Mrs. Buchanan whispered.

***

It had been a year since the day Japhet had disappeared. A whole year.

Franz kept it secret from everyone. He hadn't told his family or Japhet's sisters; he couldn't bring himself to. Part of the reason he didn't tell them was because he believed more than anything he would find Japhet. He hadn't given up looking. Every moment he wasn't with the Nazis, trying to sleep or forcing himself to eat, he searched. He determined not to rest until he found his friend.

There were days, in the passing year, when Franz had moments of doubt that Japhet was even alive. He couldn't believe Japhet would just leave and not come back to at least try and work things out, and the only explanation he could think of was Japhet being dead. During those days, Franz wanted to give up on everything. If Japhet were dead what reason did Franz have to live?

Stein helped to keep him distracted. Stein had given him a purpose, something to keep his sanity intact while he searched. It wasn't much. Most of the time he just patrolled streets with Carsten or one of the other men under Stein's command. They raided basements and cellars, walked through dark alleys, and set traps hoping to catch even one from the resistance.

The traps weren't elaborate. Stein would let false information leak sometimes, hoping the resistance would get word about shipments being moved which were just decoy trucks filled with Nazis. Sometimes the traps worked and fighters would be captured; other times the Nazis had to return to Berlin, mostly with their tempers rubbed short.

During the past year, the resistance was not only getting bolder in their schemes but smarter as well. Though Stein didn't use the same decoys and traps every time, the fighters most often seemed to know what was real information and which was false. Franz wished he could see through the lies and truths in his life as easily as they did.

The day Stein tried to impale Carsten with a pen was the same day Stein appointed Franz to patrol the streets with him. After giving his orders to Carsten to be delivered to everyone, he and Franz left the headquarters and turned toward one of the less populated streets.

The warmth of the sun hadn't yet left even though it had sunk behind the buildings and long shadows fell over the streets. Franz might have considered the evening pleasant if he wasn't stuck in Berlin with Stein for company.

"You seem to be adjusting better," Stein said after they had turned down two different streets. "When you first joined I honestly wasn't sure how long you were going to last."

Franz shrugged, his favorite response to most of Stein's

remarks. He preferred patrols when he was paired with a less talkative companion.

"I guess I can kind of understand, though." Stein easily rested his hand on his pistol and glanced down side streets. "You grew up outside of Berlin, didn't you?"

The only thing Franz hated more than Stein talking was him trying to get Franz's back story.

"Yes." Franz had learned it helped to keep his answers short. It usually discouraged further attempts at conversation.

"That explains why you had so much trouble when you first joined. I've seen it before. Those who weren't right in the middle of everything going on, and didn't witness it first hand, have a harder time believing how bad things really were before the war. You weren't here, the Night of Broken Glass. If you had seen what some of those Jews did to our soldiers..."

Franz ignored him. He'd heard all of this before. All Stein ever talked about was how the resistance was tearing Germany apart from the inside out and how if the Allied forces ever got in, Germany would fall because of them. Franz had every intention of doing his part to keep Germany standing, but he didn't think he had to listen to Stein repeat himself to make that happen.

Just do it for your family, he reminded himself. *You have to stay until they are safe.*

Thirty-Two
Trying to break through the wall

1943

"You really have to stop getting shot. You're going to give Odis a heart attack."

Odis had insisted Japhet rest for a full day. Jimmy didn't think he'd do it; he even had plans to tie him to the chair, before Japhet said he'd stay in the basement and rest. He now sat on his bedroll, bent over his sketchbook.

For the past year, Japhet had been living with Sam and Jimmy. One day he just climbed through the window, laid a pile of blankets on the floor, and went to sleep. Since then he returned every night, even coming back after Jimmy lost his temper from cabin fever and threw his shoes and chess pieces.

"I don't make it a point to get shot," Japhet said. He didn't look up from his drawing.

"Really? Because you sure do get shot a lot for someone who's supposed to be avoiding it. If I didn't know any better, I'd almost say you were trying to get yourself killed." Jimmy honestly couldn't be sure if that wasn't what Japhet was trying to do.

Japhet said nothing more and Jimmy didn't press him. Instead he glanced over at Sam, once again bent over his book. He'd already read it three times, but it was the only book Japhet had been able to find written in English.

Jimmy remembered when he'd first met Sam. He'd been sent to fly reconnaissance missions near Germany. He'd landed and almost immediately been introduced to Master Sargent Samuel Winters and been told Sam would be his copilot.

It had been the captain who'd done all the introductions. "This is Second Lieutenant James Rodgers." "He was a bomber pilot in the Pacific."

Sam had smiled. But Sam always smiled, Jimmy soon learned.

"Bomber pilot!" Sam's eyes widened. "Always admired bomber pilots. What did you fly? A B-17 or B-24?"

Jimmy hadn't wanted to talk about it, but he also didn't want to start off on the wrong foot with his new copilot. That could end in disaster for both of them later on.

"Seventeen," he'd said.

After that, Sam tried to get a conversation going but Jimmy continually cut him short. Instead, Jimmy had gathered information on Sam from the other men in the squadron. All of them had only praise for the Irishman.

"You won't find a better man than him," they liked to say. "He's a great copilot, but also a really great man in general."

None of that brought Jimmy any comfort. He wasn't sure how much his new captain had been told of why Jimmy had been transferred, but he didn't think he got all the details—not if he wanted him to fly with someone like Samuel Winters. Jimmy had gotten enough people killed; he didn't need a good man like Sam added to the list.

Doing all in his power not to get close to Sam, Jimmy had spent all his ground time with the wilder bunch of men. He joked and laughed and drank with them – though never getting drunk because he knew his best friend Danny would have his head if he ever found out. It helped, though. Drinking helped dull the pain and guilt.

He'd also started pulling stupid stunts. He would fly off course on missions, though no one ever reported him. Jimmy didn't do it for the thrill, though, but to learn something important, to prove to everyone in his old squadron he wasn't a failure worthy of being shipped off. Though he wasn't sure he believed that himself.

Now his flying off-course had gotten himself and Sam shot down. And stuck in a basement. All Jimmy could do now was make sure Sam got out of this alive. He wasn't about to get someone else killed.

***

It was always around midnight or a little after that the heat of the day finally cooled enough where Franz didn't feel like he was sweltering in his jacket. He was ready to be at the end of his patrol, even though the air wasn't heavy with heat, and get out of his uniform.

"One more round, up this street," Stein said, taking the lead once more.

Turning, Franz took two long strides which brought him up beside Stein again. He slyly kicked a pebble which was directly in front of his foot and flashed back – for one or two seconds – to a blond haired, barefooted boy who ran down a grass covered hill.

Beside him, with no warning, Stein stopped and Franz snapped his head up in time to see shadowy movement in front of him. Stein drew his pistol and Franz followed his example without thought.

"Who's there?" Stein called into the shadows where the figure had vanished.

There was no answer, which in a way was answer itself. Franz and Stein took off, running down the street and the figure emerged in front of them. It was the figure of a man, tall and well built, flying down the street like his life depended on it.

"Halt!" Stein ordered.

The man didn't listen but instead pushed himself on even faster, trying to put distance both the Nazis chasing him down. Realizing they were going to lose him, Franz slid to a stop and raised his pistol, squinting down the sights in the uncertain light. He took a deep breath and pulled the trigger, watching as the man crumpled and fell to the ground.

***

Japhet often didn't attempt to draw people. They weren't in his skill range and he stuck to drawing scenery as often as he could. However, sometimes he would try and draw his sisters, his parents, or even the Kappels. It helped when he ached from missing them all.

"Hey, Sam." Jimmy's voice broke through the fog Japhet had wrapped around himself. He liked to ignore his two companions as often as possible, but something in Jimmy's tone caught his attention.

"What?" Sam closed his book. He used his finger to mark his page.

"You ever eat a steak?"

"What kind of stupid question is that? Of course I've eaten steaks."

"Well, just asking. I wasn't sure, you being Irish and all."

When Japhet looked over at Jimmy, he was grinning. Kept out of the sun, living on little food and activity, Jimmy's face was no longer tanned. He was pale and gaunt, but he hadn't lost any of his spirit.

"Just because I'm Irish doesn't mean I don't like a good steak," Sam grumbled.

"What about you, Japhet?" Jimmy asked, ignoring Sam.

"He's a Jew," Sam said. He looked at Japhet. "You don't eat steak, do you? Or do I have my meats wrong?"

Japhet shrugged. "My parents were Christians. We celebrated some of the Jewish holidays, but we ate like everyone else...most of the time."

"You could've just said yes," Jimmy said.

"What's this sudden interest in steak?" Sam asked when Japhet said nothing. He had already gone back to his picture, though instead of working on it, he frowned at it. Something about Leah's nose wasn't turning out right.

"I just really want a good steak. I'm sick of hard bread and sauerkraut soup."

"I want a slice of apple pie," Sam said. "A thick slice. My mom used to make it. With heavy whipping cream and we'd pile it on top."

Again Japhet drifted. He bent over his picture, only coming back to the present when he heard Jimmy calling him Jerry.

"My name's not Jerry," he grumbled, raising his head.

"I know, but it's the only way I can get your attention, kid."

"What did you want?" Japhet muttered.

"I said, do you have a girl?"

Japhet squinted at him and rubbed his nose. "A girl?" he asked.

"Yeah. You do know what a girl is, don't you? Female version of the male? Whole lot prettier. Sweet, pleasant features. Heard they're great for marrying. Thought a handsome, half-starved and nearly dead Jew like you would have one of those by now."

For a moment, Japhet said nothing. He wasn't sure how the conversation had jumped from food to girls and wondered how much he'd missed in between.

"Do you think I have a girl?" he finally asked.

"He has a point." Sam laughed. "I don't think he'd be here every night if he had some cute girlfriend to visit."

"Guess you got a point."

Japhet had no idea what had put Jimmy into such a talkative mood, but he didn't think he'd get him to shut up unless he talked a little. He closed his sketchbook.

"Do you have a girl?" he asked.

"Naw." Jimmy stared at his hands. "I was always too busy keeping an eye on Danny."

"Who's Danny?" Sam asked.

"My best friend from back home. Something like a little brother. He used to follow me everywhere."

The pang in Japhet's chest made it hard to breathe, but he ignored it.

"If he used to follow you everywhere, why didn't he follow you into war?" he asked.

Jimmy raised his head and Japhet was surprised to see worry and fear in his eyes. It passed quickly, but it had been there.

"We couldn't join up together," he said quietly. "Air Force wouldn't let us."

"Too scared he was too much like you?" Sam teased.

"Funny." Jimmy tossed a rook from the chess game at Sam, then shook his head. "No. Danny's black."

"Oh," Sam murmured.

Japhet said nothing. He remembered something Franz had told him once, something which happened during the Olympics.

He'd said that Hitler had publicly humiliated – or something like that – the black American runner Jesse Owens. Japhet hadn't thought Americans thought of blacks the same way as Hitler.

"Not easy, living in a world where someone gets to decide who can be friends and who can't based on something like skin color," Jimmy muttered.

Lifting his head, Japhet met his eyes. They stared at each other, and Japhet had a feeling there was more behind Jimmy's words than what appeared on the surface.

"Same with religion," he said.

"I guess." Japhet looked away and Sam stayed silent.

"Crazy world we live in," Jimmy muttered, then said nothing more.

Thirty-Three
Seth intervenes

1943

Jimmy didn't sleep much at nights. Sleep brought back memories and dreams he didn't want to relive. He usually stayed awake, listening to Sam's snores, staring at the black ceiling, until exhaustion overcame him and allowed him a few hours of sleep.

Not that his dreams were the only thing which kept him up. Often, just as he drifted off, Jimmy would be awakened by Japhet's tossing and turning, and sometimes his muffled cries. The night after he'd gotten shot in the shoulder, Japhet woke him from a deep sleep when he started to shout.

"Franz, please don't."

Jimmy sat up and squinted in the heavy darkness of the basement. Sam still snored on his bed under the stairs, but Japhet tossed and turned only a few feet from Jimmy.

At first Jimmy feared Japhet's shoulder was bothering him and might have become infected. He prepared to wake Sam, who would know what to do more than Jimmy, when Japhet again called out. Again with the same name.

The words shook and cracked and Jimmy remembered the time he'd dragged his brother Allen to see The Wizard of Oz.

The poor kid had awakened Jimmy up in the middle of the night, sobbing over a nightmare about the flying monkeys.

Japhet wasn't thrashing around from an infected shoulder, but one of the many nightmares he had. Only this one was worse. Jimmy could see it, now that his eyes had adjusted to the darkness. Japhet's pale face, his mouth twisted into a frown, his hallow cheeks drawn.

Jimmy didn't know much about the kid. He did know he was only nineteen, too young to be leading a bunch of men into scuffles with the Nazis. Jimmy couldn't be sure, but he believed Japhet had seen his own parents killed, from the garbled English he'd gotten from Odis – a surprise he hadn't been prepared for. He did know the Japhet who had moved into the basement a year ago—the soldier who rushed out and got himself shot—was not the kid who had sat in front of him when before Leb died. There was a hardness about this Japhet, a wall that Jimmy wasn't sure anyone would ever be able to break down.

Except for maybe right at this moment. This kid, crying in his sleep and yelling for his friend, was the real Japhet – all of his walls broken down. A scared kid who had seen too much in his short lifetime.

You're just a kid yourself you know, Jimmy told himself. *You're only twenty-one. This is what the war has done to you, to Danny...to Japhet. It's turned kids into soldiers and killers.*

"Franz," Japhet said again. His thin body shook and he curled up into a tight ball.

At first Jimmy didn't move. He stared at him, the skinny Jew who was slowly killing himself even if he wasn't aware of it. The Jew who had lost so much he didn't seem to think there was any point in living. The kid who had had his childhood ripped away from him.

Then, at that moment, Jimmy realized something. He figured he should have noticed it before then. He'd never cared about races and what the world said, one couldn't if he were a white kid whose best friend was black. But somehow, Jimmy had always seen Japhet as different. They'd lived worlds apart; they never would have met if Jimmy hadn't been an idiot. But somehow, that suddenly didn't matter, because Jimmy wasn't seeing a Jew who he'd always secretly believed to be of the race who had somehow caused the war. No, for the first time since meeting him, Jimmy saw a scared kid. Much like his brother, or even Danny, fighting off somewhere on his own because the world said he and Jimmy couldn't fight side-by-side even though they'd done everything else together.

Without thinking, Jimmy pulled Japhet up, waking him. He said nothing, but when Japhet looked at him, that didn't matter. They just stared at each other and enough words passed between them to fill a book; and Jimmy Rodgers, the kid from Queens, New York, and Japhet Buchanan, the Jew trying to live in Berlin, Germany understood each other.

The nightmares had only gotten worse since moving into the basement, but Japhet had trained himself not to wake up yelling. He thought he no longer had anything to worry about until he woke up and Jimmy Rodgers was holding his shoulders. One look and Japhet knew he'd been saying something in his sleep.

Jimmy didn't say anything. He grabbed Japhet's blanket and flung it over his shoulders. The gesture made Japhet wonder if Jimmy had younger siblings.

For a long while, they sat in silence. Japhet pulled loose strains out of his blanket, awkwardness making him tongue-tied. He stared at his bare feet and held to the blanket with his one good arm.

Seconds wore by, then Jimmy spoke.

"I found out Odis speaks some English. It's broken, but he does his best."

"He does?" Japhet looked up in surprise. What else about the man didn't he know?

"Yeah. And he told me something, about you." Jimmy raised his head and looked at him briefly through the darkness before turning away. "He said you had a friend, who joined the Nazis."

Thoughts of Franz filled Japhet's head, along with memories of the nightmare. Of Franz on the other end of the pistol pointed at Japhet's head. He didn't know what to say. He wanted to deny Franz being a Nazi, but he couldn't.

"Danny and I had a strange friendship," Jimmy's voice was quiet and level. Japhet sat quietly and listened. "I'm older than him by two years, but he was always the one who acted older and planned things out. Me? I just jumped into the middle of everything and paid the price later on. I spent a lot of time grounded, especially because I kept stealing my dad's crop duster and flying around the local farms. Of course, Danny was with me every time, he loved the air as much as I did."

Japhet shifted but still didn't speak.

"When Pearl Harbor was attacked we were going to join the war together. Danny kept giving me those looks he gets, like he knew the whole thing would blow up in my face, but I didn't bother slowing down long enough to think. Never do. The short version of it? The Air Force took me but not him because of the color of his skin. Stupid reason because Danny can fly better than most of those wise guys I've flown beside."

"Wise guys?" Japhet asked. His voice cracked.

"Yeah, you know, not intelligent or anything. What do you call them? Dummkopfs?"

Something bubbled up in Japhet's throat. He thought it might have been a laugh but since it didn't come out he couldn't be sure. "Okay, if you want."

"Yeah, I want. But that doesn't matter. What does is Danny ended up with the Tuskegee Airmen."

"The what?"

"Tuskegee Airmen. They are a band of special pilots, all black. Gave Dan a chance because they're black like him. Danny, he's doing good with them. Flies with the 99th Pursuit. We write. I mean we used to write, and he was always better at writing than me."

Japhet had talked to Odis about letters after Sam asked if he and Jimmy could write home. Odis had said the risk was too high.

"The Nazis don't know they're here. But if letters fall into the wrong hands it could mean the death of those two. Better to let their families think they're dead and get them home alive then risk them really dying," Odis had explained.

"Now he and I are fighting the same war, just not together," Jimmy continued. "It ain't the best arrangement. We were always there for each other. Now, he could walk into a land mine and I wouldn't be there to save his neck."

Long seconds passed. Japhet wiggled his toes and bit his lip. He wasn't sure what to say at first, but when he opened his mouth words just came out.

"I was more like Danny," he whispered. He pulled his knees up to his chest and wrapped his arms around them. He wished his voice would stop cracking so badly.

"Franz...was the one who kept getting into trouble," he continued. "He got beat up a lot. Most of it was for me, though. He'd punch anyone who insulted me and get a black eye for it. I don't know if I was much better, though. I had some of my own stupid ideas, and there was one time when we both got beat up pretty bad. I even got a broken rib, and he still has the scar from it." He paused, but couldn't seem to stop now that he'd started. Cautiously he kept going.

"We...we didn't meet like you and Danny. I didn't know him until I was seven, and I think the only reason we became friends was because we both had older sisters. We became the brother we both wanted.

"It wasn't easy when things began to change – especially after my parents were killed. But I always knew I could count on him. That's why I've been having so much trouble with him..."

"Your parents were killed?" Jimmy whispered after Japhet let his voice trail off.

"Shot. By a Nazi." Japhet jumped at the conversation change even though it made his chest hurt to think about it.

"I know it's not the same, but I have a kid sister. A cute sister. Blond curls...looks kind of like..."

"Judy Garland?" Japhet suggested.

"How do you know what Judy Garland looks like?" Jimmy asked, amusement in his voice.

"I told you, Franz and I saw The Wizard of Oz."

"You've got to tell me that story sometime. Okay...yeah, she looks like Judy Garland. Why not. But a year before we left for war Danny went and fell in love with her. And... I'm her big brother, so I've always been looking out for her. I don't know if you realize how weird it is having your best friend dating your kid sister. It just isn't right.

"I was upset by it too. Got into this big fight with Danny and we didn't speak for a week. But I realized something. Japhet, sometimes you met this one person, and you might not be anything alike. You might not always see eye to eye, and you might have days when you want to kill him. But there will be something special about him, something you know you need. I think you feel like he belongs in your family, only closer. And when you met that person you've got to fight for them. Because you'll never have a friend like that again, never in a million years. And that's a pretty good excuse to keep them around."

Japhet knew what Jimmy meant, but it didn't offer him a lot of help.

"But he's a Nazi..."

"I think there's more to that than you know. I think you need to go back and at least let him explain what was going on. If he was there for you for so long, I think he'd want to be with you for whatever is going to happen next."

Japhet had left before Jimmy woke the next morning. He didn't want to face him after their talk in the middle of the night. Even before he and Franz had fought, Japhet wasn't the sort to sit and tell his thoughts or feelings.

He still wasn't sure what he thought about the whole thing. He hadn't meant to wake up from a nightmare about Franz shooting him and spend the rest of the night talking to Jimmy and telling him about his boyhood with Franz. Now because Jimmy knew Japhet was walking back to the apartment.

The closer he got the more his feet dragged and he would have run off in the other direction if it wasn't for Jimmy. He'd promised to listen to Franz and now he had to do it.

He wasn't sure Franz would even want to talk to him. It had been a year and Japhet had not let him know once where he had gone. Franz would be mad, so mad he might not forgive him. Not that Japhet could really blame him. He'd be just as mad if he were in Franz's shoes.

"What do I even tell him?" he whispered since there was no

one around to hear him. "Hi, how've you been? Still a Nazi I see..."

He stopped and took a moment to remind himself he had to give Franz a chance. He couldn't try to talk to him if he was still angry.

What would Franz be like, after a year? Japhet knew he had changed and he didn't really want to think about the changes Franz might have gone through. If Japhet was harder and colder now, would Franz be worse since he had spent the year with the Nazis? What if Franz really did hate Jews now? What would he do when he saw Japhet standing in front of his door?

"You can do it," Japhet whispered, "it's just been a year. And this is Franz..."

"What?"

Japhet spun around in surprise and saw Seth standing behind him. How he got to be there Japhet wasn't sure and he wasn't given time to react. With no warning, Seth grabbed him and yanked him off the street. He pulled Japhet behind one of the apartment buildings and only let him go once they were out of sight.

Without Seth yanking him around Japhet stumbled and caught himself by placing a hand on the wall next to him. The jarring made his bullet wound ache. After he stood, he turned and glared at Seth.

"What do you think you're doing?" Seth snapped before Japhet could speak.

"I was walking; what do you think you're doing?" Japhet didn't break off his scowl. He didn't look intimidating, but he did his best.

"You were going to see that Nazi?" Seth lowered his voice, anger seeping out of every word he spoke.

"You were following me?" Japhet demanded instead of answering him.

"Of course I was following you!" Seth nearly shouted.

"And who gave you the right to follow me?" Japhet squared his shoulders, wincing in pain at his bandaged shoulder, and tried to look older than nineteen.

"I was assigned to watch you," Seth muttered bitterly. "Everyone is worried you're going to do something stupid since you've been so upset lately that I've been keeping an eye on you while you're in Berlin. Odis keeps an eye on you when you go out on missions."

Japhet was glad the wall was behind him. He didn't let the strange emotions flowing through him show on his face, but he felt something shift inside him. He wasn't sure what it was, though – shock, anger, sorrow, or all of them at once.

"They think I need someone to look out for me?" he asked, speaking as calmly as he could, forcing his voice not to crack.

"Someone has to keep you alive. Whether you realize it or not, you've become important to the resistance since Leb's death. A lot of the men look up to you and depend on you." Seth's scowl turned bitter.

Japhet knew this was a sore subject for him. Seth had been the one who wanted to become a leader. He'd worked hard for the position, and then Japhet had lost his best friend and thrown himself into fighting. The next thing Japhet knew he'd been made into a leader and had everyone asking him for orders and coming to him with problems. He hadn't wanted it—no more than he had wanted to be assigned to helping Jimmy and Sam learn German—but it helped keep his mind off Franz, so he didn't turn away from the responsibilities.

"It's a good thing they thought to send someone to watch

you. I've always known you'd go back to him. Everyone else trusts you, but I've always wondered how much we can. You were friends with a Nazi once, who's to say..."

Hearing enough, Japhet straightened up.

"He wasn't always a Nazi and I wouldn't betray everyone!" he snapped loudly.

"Shut up!" Seth looked around, then leaned closer. "You knew you couldn't trust him. He wasn't a Jew, you had to have known he would betray you one day!"

Japhet glared, hating how persuasive Seth could be. He'd always been sure of himself. Japhet, on the other hand, continually doubted himself and felt like his thoughts were constantly being swayed to whatever Seth wanted them to be.

"He was always...he..." Japhet wished his voice didn't waver, "I trusted him."

"And it was foolish of you. You have to admit that and move on. You can't keep doubting yourself and letting yourself think he can change," Seth murmured, his tone soothing and understanding. "You made a mistake, but it's okay. No one has died over it. You can still fix this, as long as you don't go back there. He's a Nazi, Buchanan. You have to accept that. Nothing will ever change it. He's a murderer, and he'd kill you and all of us as soon as look at us. You have to keep everyone safe. You can't endanger them."

Sometime during Seth's speech, Japhet had begun to nod his head. He didn't know if he believed everything he heard, but he couldn't stop nodding. And part of it was true. He was a leader now; there were people looking up to him to keep them alive. Could he really risk their lives just because he had hopes Franz might still be the same boy he had grown up with?

"I won't go back," he whispered. It wasn't easy to say the

words out loud and as they left his lips, Japhet felt like his heart was being broken again. He wondered how many times could it break before it stopped beating altogether.

Thirty-Four
The battle

1943

Odis had taken to doing a bit of spying during the first days of fall. There had been little activity and he became restless so he began to look for some. Japhet didn't like the idea, but Odis shut him up by saying he should keep it in mind the next time he ran out and did something stupid.

It was nearing the middle of fall when Odis discovered an important Nazi message. They were bringing three important Jews into Berlin. Who they were Odis hadn't been able to learn, but it was obvious why they were being brought into the city. It was decided Japhet would lead a mission to save them before they even got into the city.

Japhet requested Odis and Levi to come with him and some of the other leaders appointed Caleb – a recruit who had a thing for bombs – to go with them.

***

It was Stein's idea to spread the false message of bringing three Jews into the city to be tortured and killed. Carsten acted like it was the best trap they had ever come up with and kept raving about it until Stein told him to shut up.

The idea was to fill the truck the Jews were supposed to be in with soldiers, armed and ready to fight whenever the resistance attacked. Franz, Carsten, and Stein – along with a few other Nazis from Berlin – were to remain posted in the woods alongside the road to help since only ten soldiers could cram into the truck.

Franz didn't admit it, not even to himself, but he was looking forward to the fight. He needed the distraction and shooting a gun proved to be one of the best means of getting it.

Leaving Berlin wasn't ever easy. Passages out of the city had to be paced to keep suspicions down. Japhet was given his orders the day before the mission.

"Fighters outside of Berlin are hiding the supplies you will need."

"Good. We won't have to explain why we're biking out land mines," Levi said.

"You should be joined by the other fighters before the trucks reach you." Japhet was handed a map with the spot for the planned rescue marked on it. He quickly memorized it and passed it on to the others.

"Fine. As long as they share the bombs," Caleb said.

***

Stein had moved his men out of the city the night before and set up points farther down the road than where Japhet and his men were. When the sun rose above the trees, he and the other Nazis took up their positions and waited, watching for the band of fighters.

***

"We don't want to blow anything up until we have the Jews

safe," Odis said as he stood in the middle of the road. The sun shown down on his face, showing the wrinkles at the corner of his eyes.

Caleb frowned. Japhet had been trying to guess Caleb's age, finally deciding he had to be in his late twentieths. About the same age as Warren.

"We are going to use the bombs, though, aren't we?" he asked. He cradled a burlap bag filled with land mines and grenades.

"Yes. But if we blow up the trucks without carrying out our rescue mission then there's no point in even attempting a rescue mission," Odis said patiently. As he spoke, he pulled a coil of piano wire from one of the other sacks.

"Oh." Caleb blinked. Japhet had noticed something strange about his eyes before, they were vacant and darted from side-to-side sometimes. Japhet started to wonder about his sanity even though he didn't know Caleb as well as some of the other men. He'd only seen him a couple of times.

Using pliers and a kind of ratchet, Odis strung the piano wire across the road and pulled it tight. When he was done, he stood back and admired his handiwork, even though the wire was almost invisible.

"It works best with motorcycles," he said, smiling at Levi who stood beside him. "I've done it to them before, but this is my first time trying it on a truck."

"You haven't done this before?" Levi asked. He frowned at the wire with sudden criticism.

"No. But it's the same idea. The truck will hit it and be stopped." Odis shrugged.

"And the mines?" Caleb asked. His eyes were twinkling.

"We're setting them further down the road," Odis told him.

"Can we take some back with us?" Caleb asked.

"No. How do you plan to get them back in? Stuff them under your jacket?" Odis asked.

"I've done it before," Caleb answered. He pulled a land mine out and smiled at it.

"You're insane," Levi murmured.

If Caleb took any offense to the insult, he didn't show it. He kept his eyes on Odis.

"Can I bury them?" he asked.

"Sure," Odis answered. Japhet saw pain in his eyes.

"Good!" Caleb hurried off with his beloved sack and they watched him go.

"He's insane!" Levi whispered when he was out of earshot.

Odis' eyes clouded and he frowned. "Caleb has been through a lot."

"You know him?" Levi asked. He squinted in suspicion. "You seem to know almost everyone. Are you some kind of spy or something? Do you hang out of tree branches and stare into our windows at night?"

A smile flickered over Odis' lips, but he shook his head. "No. I was their teacher."

"Their?" Levi asked. Japhet's ears pricked.

"Well, I was a lot of boys' and girls' teacher. I taught math at a university, but there were three boys I was particularly fond of. Caleb was one of them; Warren and Karl the other two." He smiled at Japhet as he spoke.

"Caleb, Warren, and... Karl? The Karl who was going to marry Franz's sister? He knew Caleb?" Japhet didn't really believe it.

"Yes, that Karl. They were best friends, those three. Always getting into trouble, though Warren came up with most of the ideas. They would sometimes come into class covered in dirt and leaves, with black eyes and bloodied lips and would limp to their seats. I'd later find out Warren convinced them to jump off small cliff faces to see if they could survive the fall. I was convinced that one day I'd open the paper and find all three had been killed."

"You were a math teacher?" Levi's tone held a strong note of disbelief.

"Yes." Odis threw his shoulders back, which didn't help Japhet's mental image of him as a teacher.

Levi said nothing more about the teacher position. He moved back to the subject of Caleb.

"From what I've heard of Warren he hasn't really changed, but was Caleb always..." He flapped his hand around.

"No." Odis shook his head and all amusement and joy faded from his eyes. "Caleb used to be one of the brightest boys I'd ever met. He graduated high school at age fifteen and he had so much going for him. While at college he was offered a lot of high paying jobs but he didn't take any of them at first. He had plans."

"What plans?" Japhet whispered. He didn't want to know the answer, but the question slipped out.

"Marrying his best friend. She'd been at his side nearly as long as Warren and Karl and the other two boys adored her. But not like Caleb. I've never seen two people love each other like those two. They courted all through high school and got married after he graduated college. They moved to Berlin where he was hoping to get a doctor position."

"Where is his wife now?" Levi asked. His voice shook.

Tears filled Odis' eyes and he looked at his hands rather than the boys in front of him.

"I only heard about it. It was the Night of Broken Glass. Soldiers barged into their house, dragged them out into the streets, and shot Annie in the head...right in front of Caleb. That shattered him. He's never been the same since."

Japhet's rifle dug into his shoulder and he felt sick. Levi met his eyes and stared at him, his face completely white. Japhet wondered if the same look of horror was plastered all over his face.

"Something like that would drive any man insane," Odis quietly finished.

At that moment Caleb reappeared, running up the road, holding a grenade, a grin on his face. He joined them, proudly reporting he'd buried the mines. Japhet nodded to show he'd heard then ordered them all into the woods. He wanted to say more to Caleb but couldn't find the words.

"Wait until the truck hits the wire," he said before they moved off the road, "Odis said there is only reported to be one truck and some guards on motorcycles. When the truck hits pick off the guards and the driver. I'll go down and get the Jews out...be ready to run when we have them."

"I still think I should be the one who goes to get them out," Odis grumbled.

Japhet glared at him and again pointed to the trees. "Get into position. Levi and Caleb, you two on the left side of the road, Odis and I will take the right."

Nodding, they split up.

***

The truck and motorcycles rolled into sight around an hour after noon and Franz and the others followed as it clattered down the road. They stayed in the trees, moving silently, keeping their eyes sharp for any signs of the resistance.

Franz had all his attention diverted to looking for wild-eyed rebels that he missed seeing the truck slam into something like an invisible wall. Metal crunched and he stared in confusion as steam rolled out of the truck's radiator and rose hissing into the air.

Before any of Stein's men had time to understand what was happening, rifle shots cracked above the hissing and the thrumming of the now idle motorcycles. There were six motorcyclists altogether. Four dropped dead at the same time, the other two before they had a chance to do anything other than jump off their bikes.

"In the trees!" Stein shouted though Franz didn't see the point. They already knew the fighters were in the trees; they just couldn't see them.

The driver of the truck kicked his door open. Franz watched as he leaped to the ground, a bullet taking his life before he landed. He crumpled and Franz swung his rifle around, pointing it in the direction he thought the shot had come from, somewhere in front of him. He thought he saw movement and made his way towards it as the Nazis in the back of the truck leaned out and opened fire at the same time as Stein and the other men.

There was some organization to the bullets flying around him, but Franz didn't care. All he wanted was the fighter now right in front of him, his back pressed to a tree every time he wasn't swinging out to spray the area in front of him with bullets.

Franz tried not to take in too many details the closer he got. He tried to never look into the faces of the fighters he shot, scared of what he might see if he did. This time, he stared too long until he couldn't take his eyes off the man.

This one was younger than any of the others had been. He looked to be close to Franz's age, maybe a year or two younger at the most. His hair was shaggy and his cheeks drawn. Franz stopped to stare at the same time someone near him yelled.

"Grenade!"

It landed about two feet away from Franz and he jumped, throwing himself backward. The fighter in front of him did the same as it blew, shoving Franz back before he had a chance to duck. He hit the ground hard, his ears ringing from the blast, his mind discombobulated as he tried to make sense of his surroundings.

***

After the motorcyclists had fallen, Japhet started to hurry down to the truck. He didn't make it far before the rifle exchange started, but he had no way of getting back to Odis without getting himself killed. Rolling down into the ditch, he lay still, lifting his head to fire only when he thought he could safely do so.

He lifted his head once to see Nazis spilling out of the truck and his heart fell. It had been a trap. Grinding his teeth, Japhet pulled out his pistol and took aim.

The men in the truck didn't stand the chance they were hoping for. With Odis, Levi, and Caleb still hidden in the trees, they were able to pick the Nazis off, Japhet helping when he could.

When it became apparent they couldn't see who to shoot, one of the Nazis grabbed a grenade and hurled it into the trees, in the direction of Levi and Caleb. Japhet used his chance to roll out into the road and under the truck, giving him a better view point where he hoped to find the Nazis who were in the trees and shooting at them. At the same time, he hoped more than anything that Levi and Caleb had escaped the grenade.

***

The ringing wouldn't stop and Franz had trouble focusing on anything, let alone the fighter in front of him. Nevertheless, he tried to crawl toward him.

The young man lay on his back and held to his rifle like it was the only thing that could save him. Franz stopped when he was five or so feet away and pushed himself to his knees. He held to a tree branch to keep himself upright. He kept blinking, waiting until his head was clear enough that he could raise his pistol and get a better aim on the fighter.

Franz's hand shook and he couldn't steady it. The ringing started to fade and he could now hear the fighter groaning softly as he shifted himself and tried to sit up. Franz watched as he put his hands behind him and shoved, the rifle rolling off his chest and onto his legs.

That was what did it. As the rifle clattered to his legs, Franz saw him without a weapon. He saw what the young man should have been, a boy with the freedom to go for a walk down the streets of Berlin without Nazis hunting him down. Instead, he sat out in a forest, armed with a rifle, unaware a Nazi had him in his sights.

Nazi.

Franz's hand shook even more. Since when had he become a Nazi? What had brought him to this point, that he would sight down a pistol barrel at a half-conscious young man? When had he become the kind of man who picked off people when they weren't looking?

At that moment, the fighter looked up, his eyes landing on Franz and his pistol. His eyes widened and he froze. He and Franz stared at each other over the pistol, maybe for the first time in years seeing themselves as they should have been, not what they had been forced to become.

Franz suddenly realized his heart was hammering wildly in his chest. Something burned his eyes and he didn't realize they were tears until he began to lower the pistol.

No sooner had he dropped it to his side then a middle-aged man rushed up to the younger one and hauled him to his feet.

"We have to get out of here!" he shouted. He dragged the young man off without once noticing Franz as he held onto the tree and stared down at the pistol lying at his knees.

***

The rifle shots were dying down. Japhet spotted some of the Nazis in the trees, but he had a feeling it was Odis, Levi, and Caleb who were doing most of the shooting. He could only hope all three were still alive and now taking their chance to escape while they had it.

Things became even quieter, with just a few shots breaking the silence of the forest, but they were fading away. Japhet knew there was still a chance there were Nazis waiting for him, but he didn't want to waste any more time. If Odis and the other two were safely away, he had to follow or Odis would come back for him.

Pushing the rifle in front of him, Japhet crawled out from under the truck and waited beside it, crouched down. He scanned the trees but saw nothing, though it didn't make him feel any better. He wasn't sure he wanted to enter the trees again, not if there was still a chance of Nazis being there. He glanced at the motorcycle lying nearby and stood up, slinging the rifle on his back and holstering his pistol.

Listening for any sounds of danger, Japhet picked up one of the motorcycles and pushed it under the wire. Then, again scanning the trees for any movement, he jumped on and kick started it, roaring the engine to life. He didn't wait to see if anyone heard but sped off down the road, kicking up a trail of dirt behind him.

Thirty-Five
Losing himself

1943

The pistol was cold. Franz didn't remember it being so cold before. It felt like ice gripped in his fingers. He looked down the sight, like he'd done so many times before. He lost count of how many fighters he had killed, mostly because he didn't want to keep count. He didn't want to remember all of the dead eyes staring up at him or the bodies he had to help drag off the streets. Franz didn't like to think of the Fatherland and how he was helping to make it better.

This time was different, though. Whenever Franz had looked down the sights before it was at a soldier. This time, a woman stood at the other end of his barrel.

"Pull the trigger," Stein whispered in Franz's ear. "You can do it. Just remember, she is the reason Germany is falling apart."

Of course she was, Franz already knew that, but there was something so familiar about her. He wasn't sure if it was her black hair or her eyes. Those eyes, he knew those eyes staring back into his.

"You have to do it, Kappel," Stein whispered, his voice filling

Franz's head and muddling his thoughts. "You have to. For Germany. For our country. For your people."

Sweat dripped into Franz's eyes but didn't break his focus. He was a patriot, he had to do this, just as Stein said.

Holding his breath, Franz closed his finger over the icy trigger and fired. The moment he did the woman screamed – not just anything but his name – before she fell dead at his feet. Horror twisted Franz's insides and he dropped the pistol, for the first time noticing the man's body already lying in front of him. His whole body turned to ice as he stared into the dead faces of Mr. and Mrs. Buchanan.

Franz screamed and kicked his blankets off, fighting his way out from beneath them. He jumped to his feet but tripped over the sheets now lying the floor and fell. He landed hard and had to stay down while he tried to catch his breath, only lifting his head when all threat of tears was gone.

It wasn't Franz's first nightmare like that, though usually all he ever dreamed about was killing the men he had already killed. This nightmare was a hundred times worse and sent ice into his normally numb heart. He clenched the sheet to his chest, then buried his face in it and took a deep, shuddering breath.

Slowly, stumbling a little, Franz finally got to his feet and walked over to his bedside lamp, flicking it on. A little mirror hung on one of the walls and when Franz turned he got a good look at himself. He froze, staring at the man scowling back at him.

The man's blond hair stood up on edge, his blue eyes were wild and bloodshot. His face was hard and cold, a frown twisting the lips down. The only thing Franz recognized was the small, white scar right above his eyebrow. His hands shaking, he reached up and touched it and had a brief image of a carefree, bright-eyed boy who had been so determined to keep his little brother safe.

"I'm not going to let anything happen to him."

The promise rushed through his brain and Franz ground his teeth, slamming his fist into the wall beside the mirror. It came loose and crashed to the floor, shattering at his bare feet. Small shards cut him, but he didn't care; it was nice to feel pain again.

Picking his way out of the glass, Franz stumbled into the living room, where he was greeted by a fresh fall breeze coming in through the open window. Sighing, he sat down on the couch and dropped his head into his hands. He knew he wouldn't be getting any more sleep for the rest of the night.

When morning dawned, Franz hadn't moved. He would have sat there most of the day, ignoring his now throbbing feet, if he hadn't heard movement outside his door. When he lifted his head to think about investigating, he spotted a note under the door and hurried to open it. Warren's handwriting stared up at him.

> *They took Leah. I was able to get to Bea and Elsa before they were taken too, but the Nazis found out what Leah was doing and took her. I don't know where. I don't think she is in Munich, but I don't know for sure and I need to find out, soon, if I'm going to save her. I need help. I need information. Franz, Japhet, I'm counting on you. There should be something in Berlin by now. Get it for me so I can save your sister.*

Japhet wasn't there. That was the first clear thought Franz had after reading the message. Japhet should have been there. Even though Franz considered Leah his sister she wasn't his blood sister and Japhet needed to be there, to know. If she didn't make it out, he had to know.

Franz cut that thought off as quickly as he could. He wouldn't allow that to happen. Blood sister or not, he wasn't going to let the Nazis hurt Leah. He didn't know where Japhet was, so he would do it alone.

He could get into the Gestapo Headquarters. That was easy; they knew him there and he walked in the front door almost every day. Franz didn't have the authorization to get the papers he needed, though, but he decided he could deal with that problem when he got there.

Running back into his room, careful not to step on the glass, Franz dressed, washed his feet, and yanked on his boots. He forced himself not to run all the way to the headquarters and tried to look like he was not suffering a swarm of mixed emotions when he walked in.

Stein wasn't there. He had patrol that night with Carsten and a few of the other men. That was at least one problem Franz wouldn't have to deal with.

With his shoulders drawn back, Franz marched down the halls. Important papers and documents were kept under lock and key and only a few people were allowed to enter the room they were held in, but Franz didn't think the things he was looking for would be there. Leah had just been taken; his best chance to find where she'd been taken to would be in the room where the papers first arrived. He knew three or four rooms where they would be kept. He just wasn't really sure how he was going to find them without attracting undue notice. Poking his nose indoors wasn't exactly inconspicuous.

He tried to think up a good reason to be looking for papers when an idea hit him. It wasn't his best idea, but Franz had not been known for great ideas. Japhet had done that.

He's not here! Franz snapped at himself, for the first time in a year realizing he was actually angry with him. He hadn't been before, taking all the blame by himself. He should have been the one who talked first; he should have explained what was going on, but he hadn't and Japhet had run off.

Franz wasn't sure if he was willing to put some of the blame on Japhet, but he did allow himself a moment of anger. If Japhet hadn't run off, he would have been there, right beside Franz, thinking up a fail-proof plan to save Leah. Franz needed him and he feared if he was unable to keep Leah alive, there would always be part of him which blamed Japhet for it.

Trying not to think about the possibility of her dying, Franz stopped at the first office-like room he came to and stood for a moment, wondering if he should knock or just go in. Finally deciding it seemed more Nazi to just walk in, he opened the door and strolled inside as if he owned the place.

A man sat behind a desk, his glasses shoved up so close to his eyes that his eyelashes brushed the lenses whenever he blinked. He looked up when Franz entered and glared.

"Who gave you permission to walk in here like that?" the man demanded. He stood up and came around his desk and suddenly looked much bigger.

"Stein." It was easy to snap; it was even easier to throw the man a look as cold as ice.

"Stein?" the Nazi asked, his shoulders drooping just a little. Just as Franz hoped for.

"Yes. Stein. He has me hunting down some paperwork for him."

"Of course he does," the man muttered, nodding but looking toward the door as if he feared Stein would come running in on them. "What papers do you need?"

"Some Jew was just taken. She was stealing artwork and books.

Stein wants to know where she's being kept. Her name is Leah Buchanan." It cut him to say Leah's name. Franz remembered her warm smile and hug before she'd left for Munich.

"Leah Buchanan, sounds familiar." The man walked back around his desk and went through a pile of papers. "I get so many, though, it's hard to keep them all straight. You can't imagine how much of this I have to go through every day," he said as he continued to look. People's lives, and he didn't even pause to think about how many were being tortured and killed. Franz wanted to punch another wall.

"Leah Buchanan, hmm, I was sure I saw her name in here. Maybe I sent the files already. I know who can help you. Go down to Karla, she probably still has everything." The man smiled and pointed to the wall. "Down the hall out there, two doors, and you'll get to her office. She will get you what you need."

"Thanks." Franz turned to go, but the man clicked his heels and thrust his hand out in front of him.

"Heil Hitler!" he shouted.

The salute used to anger him, but Franz now reacted without thinking.

"Heil Hitler," he said.

Karla was around Franz's age. Her hair was blond and curly and she might have even been considered cute if she wasn't wearing a uniform. But she smiled when Franz entered her little office and under her hard expression he saw a girl who, had things been different, would have been carefree and happy. A girl who would have been concerned about makeup, boys, and dates. Franz almost touched his scar, wondering if the boy he no longer was would have been interested in the girl she used to be.

"Can I help you?" Karla asked, her tone friendly and warm, everything her uniform said she shouldn't be.

Something warm tried to break through the icy wall Franz had been holding up for so long, but he held it back, though he did return her smile.

"I hope so," he said, crossing his arms over his chest. "I'm looking for a file, on a Jew named Leah Buchanan. I was told you might be able to help."

"Who are the papers for?" Karla asked, her tone conversational as she went through the files on the side of her desk. She sat on the edge of it rather than in her chair and swung one leg back and forth.

"Stein."

She nodded, her curls bouncing. "Good thing I still have them then," she said, smiling and looking up, her blue eyes twinkling. She held a file out to him.

For a moment Franz stared into her eyes, again catching a glimpse of the girl the Nazis had stolen, then he reached for the file and tucked it securely under his arm. Leah's life; he now held it securely in his hands.

"I'll be sure Stein gets it," he said, turning to go. Something stopped him, though, half-way through his turn and he looked back at her one more time, but by then it was too late. Her smile was gone and all traces of humanity had left her eyes. The girl was gone, killed by the Nazis.

Thirty-Six
Franz interrogates

1943

"There were files missing this morning!"

Stein was shouting just as Franz walked into the building and he knew it would be a long morning. Not something he needed after his long night. Even though he'd been successful getting the papers he needed, Franz wouldn't be able to rest until Warren told him Leah was safe.

"How do you know papers are missing?" Carsten asked as Franz entered Stein's office. They were facing each other and glaring. A cup of coffee sat on the desk yet again and Carsten was smoking. Franz didn't understand why he had taken it up all of a sudden,

"Don't you think it's a bit too early to be yelling?" Franz asked, yawning.

Stein raised his head and took sudden interest him, a habit he'd had since Franz first joined. Franz knew most of it came from Stein's lack of trust in him, but today it was different. Something like triumph gleamed in his eyes as if Stein had finally caught him at something he'd been wanting to for years.

"You're late this morning," Stein said.

"Yes. I was hungry and ate a bigger breakfast than usual."

Franz was irritable and he didn't mind if Stein knew it.

"Really?" Stein leaned in, squinting. "You look worn out. Didn't you sleep last night?"

Franz shrugged and forced himself not to lean back. "I slept as much as I needed. Everyone sleeps too much around here, haven't you noticed? Take Carsten, all he does is sleep."

"I..." Carsten shouted indignantly, but Stein cut him off.

"Never mind. Sleep isn't important," he said. Stein leaned back and smiled and Franz's frown deepened.

"Hmm...well, I'm sure it's important to some people," Franz grumbled. Personally, he could have done with a few more hours of sleep.

"Maybe." Stein rested against the desk. "Have you heard? A resistance fighter was caught last night." He picked up the cup and took a sip of the strong smelling coffee. Franz always caught a slight whiff of alcohol in Stein's coffee, but he never remarked on it.

Since the battle in the woods, Franz was no longer sure what he thought or felt about the resistance. Every time he thought about them now all he saw was a young man, staring at him over the top of his pistol.

"Aren't you excited?" Stein asked when Franz didn't remark on the news.

"Sure." Franz could be excited if they wanted, he could be anything they wanted. He was already the murdering monster they wanted.

"You know what I just realized?" Stein's casual pose against the desk didn't change. He took another long sip. "You've never helped with an interrogation. I was going to have Carsten help with the one this morning, but I think he deserves some time off.

He hasn't even had breakfast yet and you have. What do you say?"

Franz was suddenly grateful for the wall behind him. He sagged the same way he might have if someone punched him. Up to this point, he'd found ways to keep out of interrogations. Now he'd been backed into one.

You've shot resistance fighters before, what's the difference of interrogating one? He asked himself, but all he could see were those eyes staring into his. Was he really going to get information from a soldier, or was this just another lie disguised as truth?

Franz's hands were sweating and shaking as Stein led him down the interrogation room. It had been so long since he'd felt any kind of emotion and he was ashamed of it. It didn't help that Stein was beside him, watching his every move. If Franz didn't carry out the interrogation to Stein's standards, Franz would be joining the fighter.

Franz did everything he could to turn off his emotions. He wanted to block out those haunting eyes and the nightmare of himself pulling the trigger on Mr. and Mrs. Buchanan. He reminded himself that he did this for Leah and Japhet, but none of it stopped his hands from shaking.

Most interrogations were held in a small back room with only one light on the wall opposite the door. The resistance fighter was tied to a metal chair in the center of the cold room, his face hidden in shadows as he kept it lowered almost to his chest.

"His name is Levi," Stein said, entering the room behind Franz and closing the door. "We haven't been able to get a last name from him."

Hearing voices, Levi raised his head and for the second time that morning Franz almost fell over. In the light shining behind Levi's head, Franz recognized his face. It had been haunting him since the fight in the forest. He was staring at the resistance fighter he should have shot but hadn't.

Levi stared back at Franz, fear clouding his eyes, though Franz saw that Levi remembered him. Neither spoke nor moved and more than anything Franz wished he were a hundred miles away. It was a useless wish. He'd never gotten the things he wished out of life and never would. The world had decided his future for him. They'd decided everything else about his life. Killing people he loved, taking Leah, telling him he couldn't be friends with Japhet. Now they wanted him to be the perfect Nazi and he didn't know how to fight it.

"Well?" Stein moved so he stood in one of the dark corners and nodded his head to Franz.

Franz wasn't sure what to do. His mouth was so dry someone might have stuffed it full of cotton and he feared he'd choke if he tried to speak. But the world didn't want a Nazi who choked, they wanted a Nazi who beat people without emotion.

"You know, not telling us your last name isn't going to help you. Do you think you can save your family by keeping it secret? Do you really think the Nazis are that stupid? We know everything about you already." The cold words came out on their own, startling Franz.

"No...no you don't." Levi stared down at his shoes and shook his head.

"Really? Are you willing to bet the life of your mother and father on that? Do they really mean so little to you that you're ready to just sit here and do nothing, nothing at all to help them?"

"What will you do to them?" Levi's voice started to shake; it reminded Franz of the way Japhet's would crack.

"What we do to all of Germany's traitors." Franz had been circling Levi, but now he stopped right in front of him. "We will shoot them."

Levi's face satisfactorily drained color.

"Imagine it, Levi, if we don't go easy on them," Franz whispered. "Your mother, slowly dying of starvation. Your father dying of dehydration. Is that what you want? Do you want to be the one who killed your parents?"

"I..." Levi stopped looking at him so Franz slammed his palm into the side of the chair.

"Is it?" he yelled.

"No!" Levi whimpered.

"Then tell us where the resistance is hiding." Franz lowered his voice persuasively.

"I... I can't." Levi looked at him again, this time as if he were searching for the same man who hadn't shot him in the forest. Franz stared back, wishing he knew if he were the Nazi or the man who hadn't shot a Jew when he had the chance.

The interrogation took more out of Franz than Levi, at least that was how Franz felt. When he finally left the room, every emotion had been pulled out of his body and wrung to death.

"You did good, I'm kind of sorry I had my doubts," Stein said as they walked together down the hall. He wasn't smiling and he didn't sound happy, but Franz didn't care either way.

"He didn't give us anything, of course," Stein went on.

"Well, he's a soldier. They don't reveal information," Franz muttered. His head pounded and he didn't want to listen to Stein's rambling voice.

"Don't worry, we have methods. You will get him to talk...I have faith in you, Hoffmann."

Franz stopped listening. It wasn't easy, but he blocked out Stein's voice, and allowed the emotions to surface he had tried so hard to bury. He saw himself standing on a cliff, his future as a Nazi stretching out in front of him, and his foot dangling over the blackness waiting to swallow him up. It was time he made a choice, he realized, now, before he went too far and could never go back.

Thirty-Seven
Gone too far?

1943

Odis brought them the news of Levi. He was devastated and blamed himself, pacing the basement for two hours before finally listening to Japhet and going back to his own place to try and sleep. The moment he left, Japhet punched his pillow.

"Idiot!" he hissed, not sure if he was mad at himself, Odis, or Levi.

He'd been the one who had sent Odis and Levi out on a mission together. All they had been asked to do was gather information on troop movements. He'd been planning on going with Odis himself, but the big man had talked him out of it and now Levi was in Nazi hands.

Jimmy and Sam watched him as he stood up and took over the floor where Odis had been pacing. He strode back and forth and ground his teeth together.

"I knew they shouldn't have been out there alone! I should have gone with Odis!" He looked for something to kick but couldn't find anything that wouldn't make a lot of noise.

"This isn't your fault or their fault," Sam said. He stood up and stepped in front of Japhet, putting a stop to his pacing. "You have to calm down."

Japhet didn't think he could calm down. He was exhausted from lack of sleep and worry over the heavy responsibilities now pressing on his shoulders. He hadn't come any closer to helping Jimmy and Sam escape. Seth was starting to question his orders and continually asked if Japhet had met up with anymore Nazis. The pressure kept building. Now Levi was captured and likely being interrogated and Japhet wasn't sure how they were going to save him before the Nazis broke him. "If it isn't my fault, then who's fault is it?" Japhet snapped.

"This is war." Jimmy joined in, moving so he stood in front of Japhet as well. "Japhet, things like this happen, they will always happen. You can't take all the blame on yourself."

Japhet glared at them, his teeth clenched together so tightly his jaw hurt. They were starting to sound like Odis, patronizing him because he was younger, and they felt responsible for him.

"Shut up!" Japhet yelled, not caring if Mrs. Schmidt scolded him for being loud. "I'm not a kid anymore and I don't need all of you babysitting me! They've made me a leader for a reason, and if I don't keep everyone safe then no one else will! This is my fault!"

"Who said it has to be anyone's fault?" Sam asked quietly, unfazed by Japhet blowing up.

"Because the world is falling apart, so someone has to take the blame," Japhet said, lowering his voice. "Is it the Nazis' then? Hitler's? How about God since He is allowing it to happen?!"

"God? You're blaming God?" Jimmy stared in surprise. "But you're a Jew...I thought you believed in God."

"What?" Now Japhet turned all of his anger on Jimmy. "Just because I'm a Jew, I have to believe in a God who allows the world to be ripped apart and who let's so many die? Where is He, if He's real? Why does He allow this to happen, and why should I trust Him if He does? Who wants to serve a God like that?"

"That's what you think?" Sam asked, his accent thickening. When Japhet looked at him, he was as calm as always, but something was different in his eyes.

"Well, yes," Japhet murmured, no longer so confident. "Everything I've been told about Him; if He is who everyone says, why hasn't He stopped this?"

Japhet was surprised at how earnest the question came out. He hadn't meant to sound so genuine, but he realized that, for the first time since asking, he wanted an answer. Where was the God his parents had loved and worshiped?

"The trouble with that is we have the wrong mindset. We are keeping all our focus on us and not God and we have to change that," Sam said, all traces of his American accent long gone.

"It's kind of like in school, when you first hear the earth is round, or that it's spinning, and you can't get your mind around it because the earth – as far as you can see – is flat and still. You have to train your mind to accept a truth you can't see."

Japhet stared, not sure if he wanted to interrupt and shout or stay silent and listen.

"And, of course, no one ever said life was supposed to be easy, but we get it into our heads that if things are going bad for us then God must not love us or must not exist. We want Him to make everything good for us, then stand back and not get involved. But that isn't how God is.

"It's kind of like a father. A father will be there for his kid when he is going through hardships, but he isn't going to take those hardships away or take the kid out of them. He can't, he would be a poor father if he kept stepping in and stopping bad things from happening. It might hurt the father to see his child suffering, but he's going to let him go through it because he knows by the end his child will be a better person...if he keeps his focus on what's important and doesn't allow anger to rule his heart."

Jimmy shifted back but said nothing either.

"God is with us through everything, and like He says in 1st Peter 1:7-9, 'These have come so that the proven genuineness of your faith—of greater worth than gold, which perishes even though refined by fire—may result in praise, glory and honor when Jesus Christ is revealed. Though you have not seen Him, you love Him; and even though you do not see Him now, you believe in him and are filled with an inexpressible and glorious joy, for you are receiving the end result of your faith, the salvation of your souls.'"

Japhet remembered the verse. He'd heard it in church once, though he didn't know why this one should be familiar when he'd forgotten so many others.

"We are put through trials to be refined, to become better," Sam went on. "To turn our thoughts to God. If we keep them on ourselves, we will become bitter and empty. And you have to remember, Japhet, you're not the only one going through pain and suffering. Everyone has their own trials in front of them. Even...look at Jimmy and me. We've been stuck in a basement for a year. My dad is fighting in the Pacific, last I heard. He could be dead and I might never know it. Jimmy has a sister spying in France. His best friend is off flying who knows where. His family is struggling to keep going while he and his dad are fighting. People are dying all over, families are being torn apart. You're not the only one going through this kind of pain and worry."

Japhet continued to glare, but he couldn't get Sam's message to stop bouncing around in his head.

***

Franz didn't sleep the night after the interrogation. Stein had said they would return the next day, after leaving Levi tied to the chair and with nothing to eat so he could think things over. Instead, it gave Franz time to think things over.

For three hours, Franz walked the streets before going home, cringing whenever he caught his reflection in the store windows. The hardened killer who stared back at him scared Franz and he finally went to his apartment and changed out of his uniform, no longer able to bear the sight of it. Throwing it in a corner in his room, Franz went and lay on the couch, where he spent the rest of the night battling a headache.

Even if he wanted he couldn't get Levi out; that was clear even in his pounding head. Stein was already suspicious over the missing files. If a Jew turned up missing, Franz would be his first suspect. At the same time, Franz didn't think he could spend another day standing in front of a man tied to a chair, yelling at him. He'd never been close to one of the fighters before, never seen them so helpless and scared, and all he could see in Levi's eyes was Japhet.

He's not Japhet, Franz told himself. *He's a soldier tearing Germany apart. And you're a soldier fighting for Germany.*

It had always worked before, but this time Franz didn't believe it. He wasn't a soldier, he was a Nazi, and he had to decide if he wanted to continue being one and let Stein destroy that last part of Franz Kappel still holding on, or if he would stand up and fight.

When morning dawned Franz's eyes were so heavy, he had trouble keeping them open. He tripped into his room and pulled his uniform up off the floor. When he did so, some of the shattered glass he hadn't cleaned up from the mirror caught onto the fabric, falling away from his pants. He watched the bits of glass clatter back down and remembered the man he had seen before the mirror shattered.

Clenching the uniform tightly, Franz found the answer which he'd been searching for all night.

The building was mostly empty and there were no signs of Stein around. The few people who were there didn't bother acknowledging Franz as he marched down the halls and to the room where Levi had been left. A guard had been posted outside, but he let Franz enter when Franz mentioned he was one of the Stein's men.

Levi had his chin resting on his chest and when Franz entered he didn't move until Franz poked his arm. Even then, it took a while before Levi was able to get his head up and his eyes focused. His face was white and his eyes red. He stared at Franz without a word.

With the door still open and the guard looking in, Franz circled the chair like he'd done the day before. He began to yell until he came back around and glared at the guard. Getting the message, the Nazi closed the door and Franz and Levi were alone.

Making sure the door was securely closed, Franz bent, bringing his face level with Levi's. Levi didn't blink but continued to stare.

"Listen to me," Franz whispered, not wanting to waste time exchanging glares. "I have a plan, but you're going to have to trust me."

"Trust you?" Levi's words were garbled and his voice cracked.

"Yes. I could have killed you once before and I didn't...and I want to save your life now, but you have to trust me." Franz looked over his shoulder just to make sure the door was still closed before rushing on, wishing his heart wasn't trying to escape his chest. "That man who was with me yesterday, he's going to kill you and, I'm sorry, but if you want to live I'm going to have to do the interrogation and I'm going to have to beat you."

Levi said nothing.

"I've tried to think of a way out of this, but there isn't one." Franz could only hope Levi would understand. "I need you to, no matter what, not tell me anything about your resistance; no matter how hard it gets."

"What makes you think I'd have told you anything in the first place?" Levi croaked.

Franz had no answer. He shrugged and went on. "Fine, but we have to make this work and make it look real. You have to pretend to die in here, do you understand me? You have to put up with whatever I do with you and then...make it look like I overdid it and killed you. I will be able to get you out if you can convince the other man who will be in here that you are really dead.

"I'm sorry, really. I wish there were another way out of this, but I promise I'm not going to hurt you more than I have to. I can make the beating look convincing without leaving any lasting damage."

"Of course you can, you're a Nazi." Levi's bloodshot eyes flicked with defiant fire. "Is this some kind of trick? You pretend to help me so I'll tell you what you want to know?"

"No!" Franz didn't have time for this. Stein would be there soon and he had to make Levi believe him before Stein arrived. "I could have shot you back in the forest if I wanted you dead. You know that; you know I was the one at the other end of that pistol. I didn't kill you then and I won't now, but this is only going to work if you cooperate!"

Frowning, Levi looked away but not before Franz saw tears

in his eyes.

"Please," Franz whispered, "I want to get you out of here as much as you want to get yourself. And I'm the only one who can help. You have to trust me and go along with this."

Shaking his head, Levi squinted but Franz still saw the tears. "Why didn't you shoot me that day? Why'd you let me get away?"

Franz didn't want to tell him, but he wasn't able to stop himself.

"I saw you for who you were, not who the Nazis told me you were. And...I saw my little brother in you."

Levi looked him in the eyes again, then nodded once. "I want to go back home. I want to live, to see my parents again. I'll trust you," he murmured at the same time the door opened.

Snapping upright, Franz slapped Levi with the back of his hand. "Answer me!" he shouted.

"Here already?" Stein asked, behind him.

Franz turned and nodded curtly, not wishing to speak to him — then or ever again. "Well, we need the information," he said as civilly as he

could. "I thought I would get an early start."

Nodding, Stein smiled. "Don't let me stop you, then," he said.

When Franz turned back to Levi his shoulders ached; he hadn't realized he'd been that tense. Levi glanced at him for a second, but it was enough for Franz to catch the trust in his eyes. Raising his hand, Franz hoped he hadn't made a promise he couldn't keep.

Franz had been taught how to cause the most pain without pushing it too far and killing the victim. Even though he had never done it before, Stein had made certain he and the others had the training for it.

Levi bore each punch silently, with only a few grunts. Most of the time he had his teeth ground together and never once did he say anything about the resistance.

Most of the interrogation Franz spent in yelling and threatening. He made up lies about Levi's family, about how the Nazis knew where they were and what they were going to do to them if Levi didn't cooperate.

Through it all, Stein stood by the door and watched. Sometimes Franz would turn and see him smiling. Whenever that happened his blood turned to ice. Franz didn't see Stein in those moments but himself.

"He's very persistent," Stein said after three hours of Franz punching Levi and yelling at him.

"He is," Franz snapped. He didn't like that Stein was suddenly speaking and taking an interest in the interrogation.

"Let me give you some help," Stein said. He picked up a rod which had been lying at his feet. It was a metal rod; thin, long, and hollow on the inside.

"So, you're trying to be a hero, is that it, Jew?" Stein asked, walking slowly around Levi's chair. Franz and Levi glanced at each other, Franz wishing to assure him it would be all right.

"Being a hero won't get you anywhere," Stein said. He stopped circling when he reached Franz's side. "Helping us out, though, that will save your life. Don't you want to live?"

"I think we all want to live," Levi murmured, his voice rough from lack of water.

"You will tell us then?" Stein asked, smiling icily.

Levi didn't answer, only shook his head.

Stein moved the bar so fast Franz almost didn't see it as it smashed down onto Levi's knee. Levi screamed and yanked against the ropes holding him down. The chair rocked, but the ropes held tight.

"That is how you get what you want," Stein said, turning and throwing the bar to Franz. Franz barely caught it before it hit him in the face. "Break his fingers. He doesn't need those to talk."

The pipe was in his hand, Franz could see it, but he couldn't feel it. It was just there, with his fingers curled around it. He stared at it, his mind spinning as he tried to comprehend what had been asked of him. All the while Stein stood and glared at him, watching until Franz could feel his eyes boring into his soul – just like in his nightmares.

"A few broken fingers are better than dying," Levi whispered. He sounded broken and tired.

Franz's fingers curled tighter around the pipe but even then he couldn't feel it. He didn't even feel his legs moving, just watched as he was carried around behind the chair. He stared down at Levi's bound hands and perfectly formed fingers.

"Well?" Stein asked.

The pipe came up and somewhere in the back of Franz's mind he heard his own voice screaming at him, but no sense of panic or emotion broke through the cold which had wrapped around his heart. All he could do was watch as the bar slammed into Levi's left hand, shattering the bones in his fingers.

Once again Levi screamed and it cut through the wall. Franz could feel his heart slamming against his ribs and the bar slipped from his fingers, hitting the floor with a clatter loud enough to burst his eardrums.

Before he could react, Stein was in front of him, holding the bar in one hand and his shoulder with the other.

"Hoffmann!" he shouted, his voice reaching into the fog Franz was drowning in. He blinked at the same time Stein lifted his hand from his shoulder and slapped him. The sting brought him back to the interrogation room and Levi's groans.

"This is for Germany!" Stein told him, gripping his shoulder once more. "You can do this! Just don't forget, this is for Germany!"

Germany. Franz accepted the pipe but when his fingers closed around it, everything went numb again. It felt like someone else was using his body as he went back to yelling and beating Levi with the bar.

Another hour passed. By the end of it Levi was whimpering and his head hung to his chest, but still he said nothing. Franz began to hope they could soon convince Stein he was dead.

Sighing, Stein finally rejoined Franz, shoving his hands down into his pockets as he shook his head at Levi.

"I really thought you were smarter than this, Levi," Stein muttered. "I had such high hopes for you, I'm almost sorry you have failed me like this. Really, I thought I'd finally met one smart Jew."

Levi slowly lifted his head and looked quietly at Stein. His eyes were glazed over in agonizing pain, but Franz didn't feel the guilty prick he thought he would.

"I'm smart enough not to betray my friends," Levi finally whispered.

"I know. That's why I know there is no hope getting information out of you. That is why I'm not sorry to do this."

In one fluid movement, Stein had his pistol out and pointed at Levi's head. There was no time for Franz to do anything other than meet Levi's forgiving glance as Stein pulled the trigger.

Thirty-Eight
James Rodgers

1944

The dream came back. Jimmy knew it would. It wasn't easy, working himself exhausted in a basement with nothing to do. And there was no drink strong enough Japhet could smuggle down to help numb the pain.

So the dream came back.

Jimmy knew it was the dream. It felt vivid, exactly the same as the days he'd lived it. It always started this way and Jimmy never wanted to wake up – not until it turned into a nightmare and was too late.

The sun shone down from a clear blue sky. Palm trees waved on the island as Jimmy brought his B-17 in for a landing. Beside him sat his co-pilot and good friend, Joe Russell. Joe was from Washington state. He was dark haired and handsome and broke the hearts of all the nurses because he had a girl back home.

As the B-17 coasted to a stop, Jimmy's crew whooped and Joe grinned.

"Nice one, Rodgers," Joe said as he pulled off his microphone and hat. He ran both hands through his hair, then patted it somewhat back into place and replaced his hat.

The bombing had been successful. The bombardier, Ohio native Billy Knight, made his way up to the cockpit and grinned at Joe and Jimmy.

"We showed those Nips! Did you see how I blew their whole airfield?"

"Yeah, Knight, we saw," Joe muttered. He pushed his hand against Billy's head and shoved him back and Jimmy laughed.

He liked Billy in spite of his constant bragging. Though Billy did have a reason to brag. There were few bombardiers on base as skilled as he was.

"Come on, Russell." Jimmy stood up and pushed past Billy. "We've got to make our report."

Joe followed behind with Billy trailing them like a lost puppy.

After they made their report, they joined up with the rest of the crew in the mess hall. A couple of nurses were there and Billy made his way over to them, his shoulders thrown back and his best charming smile plastered all over his face.

"Someone needs to get that kid a girl," Joe muttered.

"Hey, not all of us are lucky like you, Russell. We come from towns with more than one guy. Not our fault you were the only eligible choice for poor Cecilia. Take Billy home with you. She might swap up."

Joe rolled his eyes, but there was some wild glint in them that Jimmy had noticed showing up over the past week. As if Joe had some secret he didn't want the others to know about yet.

"Right, Rodgers. As if any girl would trade me up for Billy Knight."

"Lieutenant!"

The shout came from the mess hall doorway and Jimmy recognized the voice. He spun around as the pilot of a shabby B-24 walked in. He grinned and held a pile of letters over his head.

"Serge said I can pass out letters today," he said. He grinned right at Jimmy as the other men turned from whatever they'd been doing before. Joe glared at Jimmy, but Jimmy ignored him.

The pilot began flipping through the letters. He made low murmuring noises in the back of his throat and sometimes said a name. When he got to one letter, he stopped and snorted.

"Someone wrote Billy Knight?" He looked at Billy. "Who wrote you, kid? Thought even your own mom wouldn't do that!"

Laughter filled the room and Billy crossed his arms over his chest. When he'd first arrived he'd been stuck with the nickname kid because he was only eighteen. He'd fought it at first, but had finally given up.

"Just give it here," he said.

The letter was tossed and then another pulled up. The pilot grinned.

"Shocker! Look here! A letter for Joe Russell."

Jimmy didn't lose a second. He darted forward and snatched it from the pilot who held it out to him. It was a tradition now. Jimmy always stole Joe's letters.

He paused with the letter in his hand and grinned at his copilot.

"She used her rose perfume this time, Russell," he said, sniffing the envelope. "Must be something important in this one!"

"Rodgers!" Joe shouted and lunged for him.

Jimmy took off. He turned and ran out the door, through the sand, trying to reach the road where he could get better footing. Behind him howls of laughter filled the air, then they were replaced by Joe's pounding feet and shouts of "Rodgers."

The sand offered no traction. Jimmy kept slipping but pushed on. He could see the road in front of him and knew he'd gain a few inches on Joe if he could only reach it.

Joe tackled him from behind. He used to play football in his college days, at least from what he'd told Jimmy. Now he launched himself and wrapped his arms around Jimmy's ankles. Both went down hard, but Joe was up in seconds and had the letter even faster.

"Nice try, Rodgers," he said. He brushed sand off his pants as Jimmy rested his chin on his hands.

"Well, what's Cecilia say today?" he asked, not bothering to rise. "Can't believe you two write each other every day. Doesn't it get boring? 'Dear Joseph, I went to town today and bought an egg. Then I boiled it and had breakfast.'"

Joe said nothing. He had the letter opened and a wide grin spread from one end of his face to the other.

Joe had proposed, in a letter. And Cecilia had said yes, which explained the grin. When the other crewmen found out, they ribbed Joe for three days over it.

"Thought you were more romantic than that, Russell! Did she think it was a letdown, getting proposed to over a piece of paper?"

Folding the letter, Joe stuck it in his breast pocket. He kept it there day and night and had it on him during the fateful flight.

"She said yes in bold letters and is already looking for a dress. We're getting married in three weeks when I go home on leave." His grin turned dopey. "We're going to dance to *Don't Sit Under the Apple Tree*, since that was the song we danced to on our first date."

Jimmy remembered that. He remembered the look in Joe's eyes and the way he would pat his pocket which held the letter. He remembered it when he fought to get his crippled B-17 back home.

It was a week after Joe got Cecilia's reply that they were sent on another bombing mission.

"Be careful," the captain instructed before they flew out.

Joe had laughed and slapped Jimmy on the back.

"With Jimmy flying you have nothing to fear. He will always bring us back."

Laughing, feeling sure of themselves, they'd all climbed into the B-17 and flown out, over the Japanese base where Billy dropped his bombs with a cry of "Bombs away!" followed by, "Look at that amazing display of fireworks! You boys be sure and tell this to that nurse when we get back!"

"Better get us home, Rodgers," Joe said.

"Why? Eager to get Cecilia's letter?"

Joe touched his pocket and grinned. "That and we gotta get Billy back. From what I heard, he finally got his nurse to agree to go on a date with him. Right, Billy? What's her name again?"

"Carrie," Billy muttered.

"Oooo!" Jimmy whistled. "Sounds like you're serious about this one, Knight!"

The other men laughed, until the tail gunner shouted, "Nips comin' in hard!"

The tail gunner was from California. He had a wife, a kid, and another on the way. His name was David Walker. Jimmy knew all their names.

"I don't see them!" Jimmy shouted back.

"Comin' in from behind!" Walker yelled. That's when Jimmy heard the bullets. Walker returned fire, as did the two waist gunners.

Jimmy saw them then. They flew past the front of the plane, turned, and came back.

"Just let me get one of 'em in my sights!" Honon was the

ball turret gunner. He was a Native American who'd lived on a reservation before joining up.

"Got one!" Walker yelled.

"Two!" Waist gunner Roy Wayne joined in. Wayne was the oldest of the crew but sometimes acted younger than Billy. Once, the Andrew Sisters were supposed to come to the island to put on a show but something had happened and they had canceled. The men were disappointed, so Wayne dressed up in a grass skirt and coconuts and danced around the island, singing in a high-pitched voice until the men begged him to stop.

"They're coming back!" Billy shouted. "One right-"

His voice was suddenly cut off.

"Knight!" the navigator, Norman, yelled.

Jimmy couldn't see what happened. He had his eyes fixed out the window, but he yelled back because Norman never sounded scared and never lost his cool.

"What's going on back there?"

Norman didn't answer. He kept yelling Billy's name.

"Norman! What happened?" Jimmy bellowed.

There was silence other than the shooting, then Norman's heavy Southern accent.

"They got him, Lieutenant. Billy's dead."

Jimmy looked over at Joe. He saw the same horror in Joe's eyes that he felt in his own.

"Hold on," he said through the microphone. "I'm getting us out of here."

The Japanese began to hit the B-17. They passed over and over and Jimmy could hear bullets striking his plane. They were soon followed by another shout.

"Honon!" the other waist gunner, Eddie, yelled. When he made the report his voice shook. "Lieutenant! They hit Honon! I don't know how bad he is! He ain't answering!"

Jimmy felt sick.

"Hold your position," he ordered. "Bruce! I need you to get down there and check on Honon!"

Bruce was the Flight Engineer. "On it!"

More bullets. Sometimes the smaller planes passed in front of Jimmy and his numb emotions turned cold with bitter anger. The Nips were shooting up his plane and hitting his crew.

"Walker, I want you to get them out of the sky!" he yelled.

Walker didn't answer. Jimmy repeated his order but still no answer.

"Bruce?" Jimmy was afraid to contact him, but forced himself.

"Honon's bad, Lieutenant," Bruce answered. "I made him comfortable. There was nothing I could do for Walker."

In a flash, Jimmy's thoughts went to the unborn baby who would never see his dad. He turned his head just enough to look at Joe. Joe's face was grim. Their eyes met just as a plane came in front again. A bullet pushed through the front window and struck Joe right in the head. Unable to believe what he was seeing, Jimmy watched as his copilot sagged forward in his seat, his head resting against the picture of Cecilia he had tapped up against the control panel.

Somehow Jimmy got the B-17 back. He landed and Bruce threw himself out and ran down the runway yelling for a medic. Jimmy couldn't move, though. He sat strapped in, reliving the flight back home. He thought he remembered Bruce reporting that someone else had been hit, but he couldn't be sure.

Everything else passed slowly. He was aware of men filling his plane, of Norman grunting and muttering Billy's name, of Bruce telling Honon it would be all right. He heard Billy's nurse crying and calling his name. He saw someone unstrap Joe and carry him off, and then himself being removed from the plane but nothing more. It wasn't until two days later that he was able to make sense of anything going on around him.

Eddie had been hit. A lung was punctured, and while he lived, he was so badly wounded they sent him home. Walker had died, as had Billy and Joe. Honon died a day later from his wounds. Roy Wayne had kept the Japanese back and kept the B-17 up long enough for Jimmy to get it home, but he was so devastated at so many dying that he was no longer fit to fight. He too was sent home.

With five members of his crew gone and his plane riddled with bullet holes, Jimmy could no longer fly. He was taken to his sergeant when the medic felt he was ready. The sergeant told him he couldn't blame himself but all Jimmy saw was Joe dying, over and over.

A month later Jimmy was transferred to fly reconnaissance missions over Germany. The sergeant said they needed good pilots in Germany. He said Jimmy was one of the best and should be flying. He said there was no other crew they could assign Jimmy to. But Jimmy hadn't believed a word of it.

He'd gotten four men killed. As far as he was concerned they were shipping him out before it happened again.

Thirty-Nine
Distracting Japhet

1944

The nightmares came, each and every night until Franz understood what Japhet must have been going through after his parents' deaths. It was always the same nightmare, but it never got any easier to see. For months, Franz relived the moment of himself beating Levi, breaking his hand, and then Stein shooting him in the head.

Franz had said nothing after Stein murdered Levi, which had saved his own life. At the time, he hadn't even felt anything, not until he got back to his apartment that night. When it hit him, it hit him hard, like a car slamming into his chest. He'd dropped to the couch and sobbed, unable to stop the pain tearing through his whole body and ripping his heart in half.

His promise to save Levi came back to haunt him the most. He'd failed, and Levi was dead because of it. Guilt weighed down on Franz's shoulders until he could barely eat, sleep, or function.

After Levi's death, Franz considered leaving the Nazis. When he got home the night after the whole thing, he was ready to burn his uniform and leave Berlin behind him. When morning came, he put his uniform back on and returned to headquarters.

Franz told himself he went back because he still needed to be there until his family was safe, just in case Warren needed anything else. He tried to convince himself he was staying because he couldn't leave until he found Japhet, but none of that was true.

The truth was, in his eyes the Nazis had won. They'd taken everything from him, including himself, and turned him into one of them. He was an unfeeling monster who could stand by and watch a man be shot in the head without doing anything to help him.

Franz Kappel stayed because he had nowhere else to turn. He had nowhere to go but back to the Nazis.

***

Odis was the first to learn of Levi's death. He brought word to Japhet.

"I got his body," he said though he didn't say how. "I need to take him back to his family. They have a right to know."

Japhet nodded. He couldn't speak. And Odis couldn't seem to stop.

"He didn't tell anyone but I knew. He looked older than he was. He wasn't seventeen or eighteen. He was only fifteen. He had a younger sister, Michal. She's going to be devastated."

After that it took Japhet a week to bury the pain. He didn't know what else to do with it, so he pretended it wasn't there as he'd done with all of his other heartache. He also took all the blame on himself when he went and reported Levi's death to those higher up than him.

They told him he couldn't do that to himself; that deaths, for all their horribleness, happened and nothing could change them. Japhet didn't believe them and when they offered a new mission, he sprang at it.

"We're sending Caleb out," he was told. "The Nazis' have been smuggling art and other supplies out by train...now that the Americans are getting closer. We want to blow the tracks and put a stop to the smuggling."

He liked the idea of going out to blow up things with Caleb rather than have to sit in the basement. Japhet readily accepted, told Sam and Jimmy he'd be back, and biked out of Berlin.

Japhet had been given a new cover when he'd joined the resistance. His papers now read that he was August Galland and he worked for a grocery store in town. The grocer's brother owned a farm outside of Berlin and sometimes would send Japhet out to bring back eggs and milk, things hard to come by inside of the bomb-riddled city. Japhet even managed to bring bacon once, which put him on somewhat friendly terms with the patrol guards. Only a few in the resistance knew Japhet's real name, and those who did only used it when they were alone with him. Cover names could save lives.

Outside of Berlin, Japhet met Caleb and the two traveled by bike to the section of track they were to blow. They hadn't gone far before Caleb broke the silence between them.

"I was sorry to hear about Levi."

Japhet couldn't remember Caleb ever saying something which didn't involve explosions. When he glanced at his companion, Japhet saw pain in the young man's eyes. The wall of insanity had dropped and raw sorrow lay exposed. Japhet didn't know what to say.

"He was a good man and he didn't deserve to die that way," Caleb said.

The lump came back. It lodged in Japhet's throat and tried to choke him. He nodded, swallowed, and nodded again before he found his voice.

"He didn't. I wish this war was over." Japhet hadn't meant to say so much, not to Caleb, but once the words came out Caleb slowly nodded in agreement. An instant later his eyes clouded and all his sorrow was again hidden from sight.

"Until that happens we get to blow up some tracks."

The section they'd been ordered to blow up turned out to be a bridge. They reached it an hour after sunset. A sliver of moon offered a little light but not much. Japhet pulled his bike to a stop beside Caleb, and they hid them in the bushes. Caleb unstrapped the box of bombs from the back of his bike and held them up, grinning proudly.

"Warren brought them. Every explosive imaginable. Except for mines, since they won't do us any good." As he spoke, Caleb balanced the box on one hip and pulled out a long grenade. "He even got me this!"

Japhet smiled and followed Caleb onto the bridge.

"Shouldn't we be worried about trains?" Japhet asked. He looked up and down the silent tracks.

"There's not supposed to be another train until midnight. We can set the bombs and be long gone before it shows up." Caleb tossed him an explosive and Japhet lunged to catch it before it hit the ground. He glared, but Caleb didn't notice. Instead, he started to whistle *I Didn't Raise My Boy to Be a Soldier* as he made his way down the left side of the tracks, laying bombs at intervals.

After a few minutes of work Japhet got used to Caleb's bomb tossing and whistling. He nearly joined in as they reached the middle of the long bridge but froze when a sharp whistle cut through the night air. Both he and Caleb turned and faced each other, then turned and looked behind them.

Rounding a bend farther up the tracks, lights cut through the darkness, coming right for them.

"Someone back at headquarters needs to learn how to tell time," Caleb said.

"Run!" Japhet turned in the opposite direction and took off.

Caleb didn't need urging. He set his box down right on the track and took off after Japhet, passing him.

The tracks were hard to run on. Gaping holes between the wooden beams tried to catch Japhet's feet and throw him down. He stumbled more than once, his breathing soon ragged and his legs shaking. He wished he'd taken Odis' advice and eaten some of Mrs. Schmidt's black bread before leaving on the mission.

"Faster!" Caleb yelled. He looked back and the same raw fear again showed in his eyes. He slowed down, grabbed Japhet's sleeve when they were level with each other, and tugged him along.

The train gained. The whistle screeched like a mad bird of prey descending down on them. Japhet's lungs burned and he pushed his shaking legs on faster when the light lit up the tracks in front of him. He saw the end, a sharp drop off to the left, where the grassy slope rose up to meet the tracks.

"Jump!" Caleb yelled. He threw himself forward, pulling Japhet after him just as the train hit the first of the explosives.

The bridge went up in an explosion of light, fire, wood, and metal. The blast lifted Japhet off his feet and broke the hold Caleb had on his arm. He flew into the air, was slammed to the ground, and sent rolling down the hill. Burning wood and hot metal hit the ground around him before he plunged into the river. Cold water snatched his breath away as wood beams struck the water.

Fighting to the surface, Japhet came up beside Caleb and both watched in amazement as the train crashed into the river, the cars falling on top of the engine. Water rose up into the air and crashed back down as the current carried the two saboteurs away.

Japhet came back a day later than expected. At midnight, he rolled in through the window. His clothes were rumpled, his black hair matted, and cuts crisscrossed his face. Sam was asleep when he returned but Jimmy was wide awake.

"What in blazes happened to you?" Jimmy asked. He didn't raise his voice since he didn't want to wake Sam, who had been so worried he'd worked himself exhausted and had only just fallen asleep.

"We blew up a bridge," Japhet answered. He reached up a scratched hand and plucked a sliver of wood out of his hair. Jimmy noticed burn marks on his jacket and pants.

"Sure you didn't blow yourself up, kid?"

Japhet didn't answer. He dropped to his bedroll and tugged his boots off, then he laid back and closed his eyes. Jimmy watched him. He didn't know when it had happened, but Japhet suddenly looked older. Worn and frail.

"How did it go?" Jimmy asked. He sat down next to Japhet after he'd kicked his boots out of the way.

"Would have gone better if the train hadn't come," Japhet said. He didn't open his eyes. "We got pulled down river and had to walk back to find our bikes."

"Odis came by yesterday. I think you're in for it tomorrow. He was ready to go out and find you so he could kill you himself."

The thin lips twitched and turned the hollow cheeks into the closest Japhet ever came to a smile, then a frown creased his forehead.

"You and Sam can get out," Japhet said quietly.

Jimmy stared down at him in disbelief. Japhet still had his eyes closed and couldn't see the emotions Jimmy felt play across his face.

Out. Freedom. Away from Berlin, away from Germany. Everything Jimmy had longed for over the past two years, but for some reason he wasn't as excited as he'd always imagined he would be. He realized he didn't want to leave Japhet behind – even if he did have Odis. Jimmy felt protective of him.

"How?" Jimmy asked.

"No one in the resistance was able to get you new papers, so I contacted a friend of mine – Warren. He can get you everything you need."

Jimmy frowned since Japhet couldn't see him. "Warren. How are you still in contact with him?"

"I can get messages to him," Japhet said simply, "and..." He paused, sleepily opened one eye, and gave a halfhearted sheepish smile. "I go back by the apartment after I send him messages. He sends replies there, I go in the mornings and pick them up before anyone can find them."

By anyone Jimmy knew he meant Franz. For a second he thought of saying something but instead kept silent. A few seconds later Japhet's breathing got deeper. Sometimes he wheezed and whimpered, but Jimmy knew he'd finally gone to sleep. He reached down and pulled Japhet's thin blanket up over him, then rested his chin on his knees. He closed his eyes but didn't trust himself to join his two companions in sleep.

Time passed slowly. Jimmy's body began to grow numb, and the next thing he knew he was back in the Pacific, Joe at his side. "

"We're getting married in three weeks when I go back home on leave."

Jimmy heard Joe's voice as if it were right beside him. His head snapped up, sending a sting of pain down his neck, and he took in his surroundings.

The basement. Sam snoring under the stairs. Japhet beside him, curled up on his side, mumbling Franz's name in his sleep. Joe nowhere to be found.

Rubbing his forehead, Jimmy lowered his hand and rested his chin back on his knees. The guilt came back, gnawing at his heart, and he wished he had a drink. He'd have done anything to get his hands on something to dull the ache. To dull the relief he always felt when he woke up and remembered it was Joe who had died and not Danny.

The relief had come only a week after Joe's death. Jimmy had been there, watching, as Joe's body was sent back home. That's when it hit him like a bull going full charge.

If Danny weren't black, Danny would have been beside him. Danny would have joined up in the same unit, been shipped out with him, and been made his copilot on the same plane. Danny, who followed Jimmy everywhere and helped him steal the crop duster, would have sat beside him on bombing missions.

Danny would have been in Joe's place. Danny would have taken the bullet. Jimmy knew if it had been Danny he wouldn't have been able to go on with life. He wouldn't have been able to live with himself if Danny had been the one who died.

Watching Joe's coffin leave, that realization sank in and a sense of relief followed it. Danny was still alive somewhere. He wasn't being sent back home in a box to be buried by his family. And, day after day, Jimmy's guilt over his relief grew.

Forty
A trap is laid

1944

"Mein name ist Abbey Stieg," Japhet said. He sat cross-legged on the floor, a thin stick across his knees. He'd brought the stick back with him from one of his missions.

"Say what now?" Jimmy asked. He lounged in front of Japhet, resting against an empty barrel Caleb had wanted to hide in the basement for who knew what reason.

"Mein name ist Abbey Stieg," Japhet repeated in annoyance.

He had already gone over this ten times that morning. The papers had finally arrived, bearing the names Sam and Jimmy would use for their escape. Now all they had to do was get the proper phrasing down and work on accents. And Jimmy refused to be a corroborative student.

"That's a stupid name. I refuse to say it until you get me a new one," Jimmy muttered.

Japhet had told Warren about the Americans. He'd even managed to get in a few complaints about Jimmy in his messages. He had a feeling Jimmy's name was Warren's way of extracting a small revenge on Japhet's behalf.

"It's too late," Japhet insisted. "We already have your papers

made up. It would take too long to get new ones. Be glad you
even have these, we've been trying to get them for the last two
years. My family had to wait even longer. Besides, Abbey is a
boy's name in Germany."

Sam looked up from where he was muttering, "Mein name ist
Falke Worl," over and over.

"Why did they have to wait so long?"

"Warren found a forger a few months ago. Our other one, he
was captured," Japhet explained, twisting his fingers around the
stick. He'd been using it to rap Jimmy's knuckles. "We've been
trying to find someone else, but he has to be good and someone
we can trust. That isn't an easy combination."

"I think you must have made your buddy look even harder
when we showed up. Didn't want to spend the rest of the war
sleeping in the same basement with us, right?" Jimmy grinned at
him, but Japhet didn't feel like returning it.

"I was going to tell you two," he said, intently studying the
stick as if it were the most interesting thing he'd ever seen. He'd
been putting this off, not sure what they would think of the news.

"Tell us what?" Sam asked, curious.

"I'm escaping with you."

The words left a bad taste in his mouth. Japhet liked to think
it was because he was escaping Germany, his home. Running
away from the place he had been born and raised in, running
like a coward. However, he knew that wasn't what twisted his
stomach. It was his promise to Franz.

They were supposed to get out together. They had been
planning on it when they came to Berlin. Now Japhet would be
going alone and Franz would have no idea that he'd even left. It
felt like the deepest form of betrayal he could inflict. And it also
felt like he was breaking off the tie he had held tightly to for so

long.

If he left without telling Franz, Japhet knew he'd never see his friend again as long as they both lived, and not even Jimmy's excitement over the news made that any easier to bear.

***

The pistol shot woke Franz. He fought to get out from under his blanket as the image of Levi slumped over in the chair faded in the light coming through his bedroom window. Franz shivered and pulled his blanket up over his shoulders.

Kicking his feet off the bed, Franz stomped them down on the floor then lowered his head into his hands and sighed. He had been working on turning off his emotions as he'd done before but at night there was nothing he could do to stop them. He woke to stabbing pains in his heart every morning.

When he felt that he had control over himself, Franz stood up and walked to the kitchen to get water. He had given up eating breakfast, his stomach was always too nauseated for him to keep any food in it in the mornings.

Swallowing his water in one gulp, Franz turned back to his room to get his uniform but stopped when he saw something stuck under the door. Franz recognized the envelope and had it open before he reached the couch and sat down.

Japhet, Warren had written. Franz's heart lurched when he read his friend's name but it confirmed his suspicion that Japhet was still somehow in contact with Warren. And that Warren had no idea they no longer lived together.

I wanted go over some things again to make sure you don't forget anything. Mostly about your two American friends – I still can't imagine how you found them or how you've kept them hidden for so long. I want an explanation from both you and Franz when we see each other.

I don't know how you plan to smuggle them out of Berlin but I hope you have that covered. The papers I sent with my last message look genuine enough but as I said before that is the only help I can give you until you reach the farm.

Remember, you are to meet me at the cabin where you and Franz stayed after he was shot. If you are not there on the day appointed I am going to get your family out without you, Franz, or your Americans. If that happens I will come back for the four of you, but to ensure I don't lose my temper and bash you and Franz upside your heads, just be sure you're there when you're supposed to be. I don't want to come into Berlin to drag you out myself.

I'll see you both soon, then you can all get out of this country and try and start over.

Warren.

They had a plan to get his parents, his sisters, and Japhet out. And two Americans. Japhet came up with a plan to get out of Berlin, and leave him behind.

Frustrated, Franz crumpled the letter and threw it on the floor, then dropped back into the couch and stared up at the ceiling.

He wasn't even sure what upset him more. He felt betrayed that Japhet would even consider leaving without him, but it went deeper than that. He knew if Japhet were no longer in Berlin there would be nothing to hold him back. He was already losing himself and the only thing keeping Franz Kappel still alive was the black haired boy from his childhood. If Japhet left or gave up on him, Franz would be lost, and a terrifying stranger would rise up in his place. And when that happened it would kill him.

"Japhet," Franz whispered to the ceiling, "I need you."

Forty-One
Trying to be convincing Germans

1944

"My mom is going to die of a heart attack when I write her," Sam said. He tugged a stain of hair as if he could pull it down over his eyes and look at it. "She probably thinks I'm dead since she hasn't heard from me in two years."

Jimmy looked over at him. He seemed so calm now, when only minutes before he'd been panicking and saying over and over, "I don't know how to do it, Jim! I can't get it! The Nazis will shoot me before I can even think of getting out of Berlin!"

The date of the escape was fast approaching. Mrs. Schmidt had dyed Sam's hair black, filling the basement with an overpowering stink. She had found a dye which Sam and Jimmy rubbed over their skin so they didn't look like they'd spend two years in a basement with no sunlight. Everything had been done to make them look German. Jimmy disguised his accent, mimicking Japhet's, but nothing could be done about Sam's. And every time he got nervous his accent got worse.

"We will figure it out!" Japhet had promised him. "We're all trying to think of something, but if you keep worrying, it will only make it worse. Don't you trust God?"

Sam had stared at him for a moment and then slowly nodded.

"Of course I do," he murmured, clearly hoping for something encouraging from Japhet. Jimmy realized he wanted the same.

A long time ago, during a Sunday school class, Jimmy had turned his life over to God – at least in words. Being around Sam made him question his declaration of faith and left him wondering if he did need to take it more seriously.

"Then trust Him to get you out of this. If what you keep telling me is true, you can't just trust Him through the easy times, but the hard times as well."

Sam had blushed. "You're right," he had murmured and began repeating his German name over and over again.

After that time continued to pass. Mrs. Schmidt dyed Sam's hair each time red roots showed, hoping with each dyeing it would hide all hints of blazing red.

As the time got closer for the escape, Sam would sometimes repeat things about his family likely thinking he had been dead for the past two years. Now the realization of that hit home for Jimmy.

Becky might not know anything about his disappearance. Messages and letters couldn't be sent to her in France without risk of blowing her cover. But his dad, mom, Allen, and Danny all would have heard about it by now.

After losing Joe and half his crew, Jimmy had taken it upon himself to write letters home to their loved ones and family. He had his fill of letter writing after that and had let slip his letters home. Now all he wanted was to get one to his mom, to tell her he was alive and well and would see her soon.

The week before their departure Japhet began to sleep even less. He sat up most nights, huddled beside a candle, drawing as if his life depended on it. Sam also lost sleep, pacing the basement and muttering his new German name under his breath in his best German accent. Between the two of them and their nervous habits, Jimmy felt like jumping off a cliff.

It wasn't until the night before the escape that Sam finally wore himself out so much he dropped onto his pallet and fell asleep. Jimmy ran his hands through his hair and dropped his chin to his knees.

"'Bout time," he muttered.

Japhet looked up from his sketchbook.

"Aren't you going to sleep?" he asked.

Jimmy frowned at him. "You're a fine one to ask about sleep."

"Just asking." Japhet bent back over the picture. His left hand was covered in pencil lead.

"You ready to get out of here?" Jimmy asked.

"Sure." Japhet scribbled harder.

"Me too." Carrying on a conversation with Japhet was sometimes like pulling teeth, but Jimmy kept trying. "I'm ready to get back home for a bit. Let my mom know I'm not dead."

"She will be happy to see you." The pencil snapped. Japhet looked up, stared at it, and then reached for another he kept in a little box.

"Danny won't. He's goin' to kill me." Jimmy smiled but all Japhet did was draw.

"Maybe I'll show up on his base. Shout 'Not dead!' at him and see if I can give him a heart attack. It'll serve him right for kissing Becky before she went off to France."

Finally, Japhet raised his head. Something different showed in his eyes.

"How do you know that?" he asked.

"I was spying on them."

"You were spying on them as they were saying goodbye to

each other? Your best friend and your sister?"

Jimmy heard something in Japhet's voice. He didn't think it was a smile, but it was the closest he had gotten in a long time.

"She's still my sister, even if she's in love with my best friend," Jimmy retorted. "I have to keep an eye on her. I'm her big brother."

"How did that work?" Japhet asked. He chewed on the end of his new pencil.

"Danny caught me and buried me in hay."

"I thought you lived in the city?"

"Danny and I do, but my family is still on the farm. Danny and I went back there before we joined up to tell everyone goodbye." Jimmy smiled sadly. That had been the day Becky had told him she was going into France.

"Danny has brothers and sisters?" Japhet asked.

Jimmy knew none of this was really important, at least not to someone who might have been listening in. But just then, it was what Japhet needed. Talking about family and life outside of the war as if there was no war. Just living on a farm, getting hay down his shirt because he'd been spying.

"Yeah, he has four. Kathy is older than him, Sadie is his twin sister, then there is Cliff, who is close to Allen's age, and Daisy who is about four now."

Japhet pulled a thread out of his blanket. "And since Danny loves your sister, does that mean you love his? The twin...Sadie?" he asked quietly.

Jimmy thought there was a small hint of teasing in Japhet's tone and he smiled.

"Everyone seems to think we would make a good pair...I mean Dan does, and his parents and mine and Allen, but I don't know. Truth is, I never spent much time thinking about girls and all that." Jimmy almost didn't want to say all of this out loud, but he didn't think it was fair, wanting Japhet to open up without being willing to try and talk more himself.

"Sadie is sweet, though, and she has a sense of humor." His thoughts drifted to Joe and the guilt came back, but he went on. "I flew with this man once who had a sweetheart back home. I tormented him non-stop over her. Sadie found out and she wrote me a letter, and sprayed it with perfume. She wrote 'To my darling James' on the front. My co-pilot never let me live that down, neither did Danny when he found out."

Still Japhet said nothing so Jimmy kept going.

"Sadie is really great. Not many girls like her, she works in a factory now, helping out the war by building planes. Becky has been trying to set us up for years. I was always too busy, though, getting into trouble, dreaming of killing some Nips, stealing my dad's crop duster...always too busy to pay Sadie the kind of attention she deserves. She probably has a fella by now." Jimmy shrugged, not sure if he wanted to shrug her off like he used to do when they were kids. "Some guy who knows the kind of amazing girl she is and snatched her before she got away from him."

"You do like her then," Japhet murmured.

"Guess I kind of do, maybe always have."

"When you get back, you should tell her," Japhet suggested and Jimmy smiled.

"Maybe I should," he murmured.

The next morning, they left just as dawn broke the sky.

Japhet hoped that if they left early enough the patrol guards would not feel like asking too many questions.

Sam still hadn't come close to getting down a good German accent, but he could say his forged name well enough to pass.

If he didn't have to say anything else Japhet hoped they would make it.

It had been decided that Japhet and Sam would leave together, later followed by Jimmy. Jimmy not only sounded German now he looked it. Jimmy said he looked more German than Japhet.

Sam and Japhet left on foot, sorry-looking fishing poles over their shoulders. Japhet also carried a battered tin which contained two lunches Mrs. Schmidt had made for them.

"This is for when they search you," she'd said. "They won't believe you're going fishing if you don't have a lunch. But when you stop and rest you make sure and eat it. I don't want all of you starving."

Japhet didn't think there was a chance of them starving after the huge breakfast she forced them to eat, but he didn't say anything, just took a turn to hug her goodbye, realizing he would miss her.

"Are you sure this is going to work?" Sam whispered in German.

"Yes, it will work," Japhet hissed. "Just remember to say as little as possible and not look anyone directly in the eyes or they will know something is wrong."

They'd been unable to do anything about Sam's green eyes and could only hope for the best. The half-light, Japhet hoped, would help them out.

When the guards came into sight, Japhet remembered entering the city for the first time and the fear he felt. This was the same kind of fear, but worse because Franz wasn't there with him. He glanced over his shoulder, half hoping his friend would suddenly be behind him. Japhet still wasn't sure about leaving without him. Everyone else seemed to think it was a good idea; the resistance, Mrs. Schmidt, Jimmy, and Sam. They worried about him; he knew it. They were certain he would get shot or be taken by the Nazis and wanted him out before that happened.

"Remember," Japhet whispered to Sam, "show them your papers, remember what you learned, and we will get out of this together."

Sam said nothing, only nodded, and Japhet quickly prayed to Sam's God. He still didn't know how he felt about God, but he hoped He'd listen to a prayer given on Sam's behalf.

"Fishing?" the guard asked, laughing when they came up in front of him. "It's been years since I've seen anyone with a fishing pole. Stupid war."

Japhet had never heard a German – let alone a Nazi – call the war stupid. He wasn't sure what to say about it and tried not to stare as the other guard nodded in agreement.

"Boys off fighting and dying instead of fishing. Even if we survive this the world isn't going to be the same...and for what reason?" He held out his hand as he spoke and Japhet handed him his papers as Sam stood behind and tried not to act suspiciously.

Wondering if the guards' discouragement was because the Americans were so close, Japhet stayed silent as the man hardly glanced at his papers before handing them back. The guard and his friend continued to talk, barely looking at him and Sam now. The first one waved them through with a nod and they left as quickly as they could. It wasn't until they were down the road that Japhet realized the two men hadn't even glanced at Sam. He stopped and looked at the short Irishman.

"Maybe your God is looking out for you after all," he said with a small smile.

Sam said nothing, just sat down on the side of the road and buried his head in his hands, his shoulders shaking.

Jimmy found them in the woods. Japhet was starting to worry

about him and had plans to go back for him when he showed up, strolling into the trees as if he owned the world. He grinned as he sat down beside them.

"No trouble at all," he said, kicking his feet out in front of him. "I'm a pretty good German, just for future reference. How did you two manage?" He looked from one to the other, then frowned. "Sam, you don't look so good."

Japhet wished he hadn't brought up Sam's physical appearance. Sam had been holding up fairly well considering. Japhet knew he was a brave man, but there was something unnerving about walking right between two Nazis who would have gladly have shot him in the head or worse – not that they could do so according to the Geneva Convention, but that often didn't stop such things from happening. Sam had finally stopped shaking a few minutes before Jimmy's arrival, though his eyes were still too large.

"I'm not a good German," he squeaked, his Irish accent thick.

Jimmy smiled and patted his shoulder.

"No, you're not. But you're an almost freed American, so I'd say you're doing pretty good, my friend. Just remember, in a matter of days now we will be back where we belong."

Forty-Two
Staying behind

1944

They didn't walk on the road. Even though Japhet hoped they looked like three normal German young men spending the afternoon together, he knew that wouldn't work if someone saw them. German young men didn't normally take walks through the countryside. So they stayed in the woods, shoving through branches, Sam laughing whenever Jimmy tripped over roots. They listened to the birds chirping happily over their heads and pretended they were free.

They didn't reach the little house that night, as Japhet knew they wouldn't. They didn't have the supplies they needed for a proper campsite but did the best with what they did have. Jimmy and Sam gathered pine needles for makeshift beds and Japhet put together some kind of meal with the lunch supplies Mrs. Schmidt had given them. (She'd stuffed as much as she could into Jimmy's pockets, which meant the bread was a little flat.)

Sitting on the pine needle beds, the three of them ate cheese, bread, and hard dried meat. There was even a slice of dried fruit for each of them. None of them had had such a good meal in far too long.

"Danny and I used to go camping every summer," Jimmy said as they ate. He leaned against a tree and half closed his eyes, sighing in contentment.

"Franz made me go camping in the snow once," Japhet murmured and Jimmy snorted with laughter.

"My whole family went camping," Sam joined in after they were all silent for a little while.

Japhet had never asked Sam about his family. It wasn't from lack of interest, but from lack of wanting to talk to anyone about anything. He picked up bits and pieces over the last two years but still didn't know much about them.

"We always drove two hours to get into the mountains. We had a special campsite no one else could find," Sam continued. "We'd set up our shaggy old tent. It was falling apart and had more patches on it than our original tent, but we never thought of buying a new one. We'd hike in the day, then sit out at night and watch the stars while we roasted dinner on sticks. My grandma usually always dropped hers into the fire."

"You took your grandma camping? You made her sleep on the ground?" Jimmy asked, opening his eyes and staring. "You've got a strange family, Samuel Winters."

Japhet's lips twisted, but he wasn't sure why.

"She loved camping!" Sam retorted. "She was the one who planned most of the trips, and she made sure we went every year. She could out hike us too."

"She..." Japhet hadn't meant to speak, but it came out before he realized it. Both Sam and Jimmy looked at him, waiting for him to go on, and he had no other choice but to do so.

"She sounds like a fun lady," he stammered, not sure what else to say.

"She is." Sam smiled fondly. "My grandpa died when my

dad was a kid, so after I was born my mom and he asked my grandma to move in with us. She was my teacher. Mom helped, but Grandma wanted to do most of my lessons on her own. She is smart, a brilliant lady, but she made them fun. She taught me all about the American war heroes, which is why I think I joined the war."

Sam's shoulders went up and down and he stopped talking almost as soon as he'd started. He stared off into the trees with a look Japhet was familiar with. The look of a homesick man who wished to go back to the days before the war.

"I'm sure you'll see her again soon," Japhet whispered, not sure if he was saying it to Sam or himself.

Except, if you leave now, you will never see Franz again, he reminded himself.

That night Japhet dreamed Franz was waking him up from another nightmare, the same nightmare he'd had the night the Kappel's window had been shattered. He thought he could feel Franz's hands on his shoulders, shaking him, and then the dream skipped and Franz sat beside him on the floor, talking.

In the dream, Japhet couldn't remember anything he'd said that night, but he heard Franz's words loud and clear in his head.

"You don't think I know that? I said I would die for you if I had to. That doesn't mean I plan on dying. Japhet, you need me as much as I need you. If we're going to survive this, we have to survive it together. You can rely on me, always, to be here for you. You have to trust me on that. No matter what the world tells you, I'm never going anywhere. And we will get out of this, alive and together. Do you understand? We both have to live."

There was a brief pause, then Franz continued.

"And then you and I are going to get out of Germany together. Please, Japhet. Promise me that. Promise me you will leave with me.

You have to keep fighting because I can't make it without you."

Japhet woke, covered in dew. It chilled him and his teeth chattered as he got up and leaned his back against a tree, staring up at the sky. He couldn't shake the memory of the dream, or his promise. Franz had already become a Nazi; what worse things would happen to him if Japhet left? If something happened to him, Japhet would be responsible.

Guilt ate at Japhet's heart until Sam and Jimmy woke and started walking again. Japhet had hoped that with them to distract him he would stop thinking about Franz, but it didn't work. He even tried to tell himself he had a good reason to leave; after all, Franz had betrayed him.

Japhet dropped his hand to his side and his fingers brushed against the knife he wore on his belt.

Franz had been there for him through so much and for so long. Even after everything that had happened, Japhet knew if things were reversed, Franz wouldn't leave Germany without him.

"We sound like an army crashing through here," Jimmy said. Japhet hadn't been expecting his voice and jumped.

"Well, if anyone is looking for us we can scare them off." Sam's laugh was forced as he looked over his shoulder.

"No one knows we were in Berlin to begin with, how would they know to look for us?" Jimmy snorted. "And they used to call me the dumb one."

"Who called you the dumb one?" Japhet asked. He wanted to get his mind on another subject. He was in the lead, squinting through the early morning mist.

"The fellas at base," Jimmy answered. "When Sam and I were paired up, everyone said he was going to have to be smart enough for the two of us."

"I don't think it worked." Like last night, the words came out without Japhet's permission. Even though he was leaving Germany with these two men, he wasn't sure he wanted to open up to them. They still weren't Franz and they would never be able to replace him.

"How could it have not worked?" Sam asked, coming up beside him. "After two years of being around us isn't it obvious I'm smarter than him?"

"But, even with you in the same plane with him, you were still shot down." Japhet quickly stared at the ground, expecting Jimmy to punch him.

Instead, Jimmy laughed. Not just a forced laugh to be nice, but a real loud laugh which made his shoulders shake. Even Sam joined in, his green eyes twinkling. Japhet stopped walking and turned so he stood and faced them both. Jimmy bent over to try and catch his breath while Sam kept giggling. It was an amusing sight, the two of them, disguised as Germans, laughing together in the forest. Japhet smiled as he watched them, then a faint laugh – bubbling up inside him – escaped.

The laugh surprised Japhet more than Sam and Jimmy, who both straightened and stared at him. Japhet hadn't even smiled since Levi's death and he wasn't sure what to do when he heard the laugh escaping his throat. It scared him and he stared back at the two Americans, not sure what he expected them to do.

"It's okay," Jimmy whispered and Japhet blushed.

"Really," Jimmy tried to reassure him, "it's okay, Japhet. Everything is going to be okay now."

Japhet shook his head, ready to protest, but didn't have to bother because the crack of a rifle shot did it for him. The bullet hit one of the trees near them, shattering part of the bark. All three hit the ground and Japhet searched the trees behind them.

The mist still drifted through the branches, but it wasn't so thick that Japhet was unable to make out shadowy figures moving toward them.

"Nazis!" he hissed.

"Why are they shooting at us?" Jimmy demanded, his voice rising in pitch. "They can't know about us, can they? Are they just shooting because Krauts shoot anything that moves and ask questions later?"

Not answering, Japhet ducked down even lower as another rifle fired. He'd been able to count the soldiers, the ones he could see, before he had to duck.

"I don't know why they're here," he whispered to Jimmy and Sam, "but there aren't many. You have to get out of here while you can. You have directions to get to the cabin." That had been one of the things which had been drilled into their heads, just in case they were separated.

"What are you thinking?" Jimmy snapped. He had grabbed Japhet's arm before he had a chance to even think of moving.

Japhet moved his arm, but Jimmy only held him tighter. When he looked at him, the pilot glared. It was the kind of look Franz might have given him if he found out what he was thinking. A strange lump formed in Japhet's throat and the emotions and questions he had been warring with for the last month finally had their answer.

"I'm going to lead them off," he said, his voice level, "so you and Sam can get away."

"What about you?" Sam hissed.

"They won't catch me," Japhet answered, suddenly more confident than he'd been about leaving Berlin. "I know these woods and I have escaped in them before. I can get away. Once I have them away from you, I'll disappear. All you two need to do is get to the cabin…Warren will get you out from there."

"You're coming with us!" Jimmy insisted. "You'll get yourself killed if you go back! You need someone to look out for you!"

"I have someone," Japhet whispered, knowing Jimmy would understand. "I just have to go back and talk to him. Just, keep going, please. I need you to make sure my parents and Ruth get out. Be there for them since I can't. Please."

Jimmy dropped his hand, but Japhet could still feel the pressure of it on his arm. Sorrow stabbed into his heart as he realized it would now be Jimmy he never saw again.

"I'll do it. I'll help them get out, just keep yourself alive. And when all this is over drop by Queens. I'll teach you how to fly a crop duster," Jimmy said. There were still bullets flying around them, but Japhet just smiled.

"I'll be there," Japhet said, unsure if it was a promise he could keep. He then jumped up and ran to the west, ducking under the branches which reached out to slap him in the face. He dodged and weaved, rifle shots behind him, following him. He didn't mind, though. Not this time.

Forty-Three
Death of a war hero

1944

"What's he doing?" Sam demanded when Japhet jumped up and ran off into the trees. He moved to stop him, but Jimmy held him down, clamping a hand over his mouth so he couldn't speak and give them away. When Jimmy was sure the Nazis were going after Japhet, he released Sam.

"He's going to get himself killed!" Sam hissed when he could speak. "We have to save him!"

Jimmy shook his head, hoping and praying he'd done the right thing by letting Japhet leave. Even the knowledge of why he'd done it didn't make him feel better. It was too late now, either way, to go after him.

"He's going back," Jimmy told Sam. "That brave, stupid kid is going back into Berlin."

"Why?" Sam demanded. "Jimmy, he was supposed to come out with us! He won't make it on his own!"

Instead of trying to explain it, Jimmy stood up and pulled Sam to his feet. He looked around but saw no signs of movement so he started off in the direction of the cabin. He only made it a step, though, when a shot shattered the silence which had followed in the wake of the Nazis chasing after Japhet.

Jimmy fell to the ground on instinct, twisting around to check on Sam. His stomach lurched when he spotted his copilot laying close to him, the front of his shirt red with blood.

"No," Jimmy whispered, choking. "Oh please no. Not you, Sam."

Sam touched the front of his shirt, pulled his fingers away, and stared at the blood covering them.

"I've been shot, Jim," he murmured as Jimmy crawled back to his side, forgetting about the Nazi, who was close enough to kill him if he lifted his head too high.

"Hey, you'll be okay, though," Jimmy whispered, tears burning his eyes. He forced a smile as he grabbed Sam's hand, holding it tightly. "Hear me, Sam? You'll be fine. It's just a little wound. I'll carry you out of here if I have to; we won't have to tell anyone I carried you like a baby, it'll be our secret. I'll even fly you back to America. Your parents and your grandma. They want to see you again. I'll take you back to them."

Sam's face was white, his breathing heavy and ragged and Jimmy gripped his hand as tight as he could, wishing he could bring him back from death.

"You have to come and stay with Dan and me. You already said you would, remember? Japhet is coming too. We're going to stay up late, annoy the neighbors. All that fun stuff. You can bring your grandma if you want and she can give us lessons on war heroes."

Smiling, Sam struggled to nod. "War heroes. I was going to be one," he croaked, his words garbled with blood. "Go back home; back a war hero."

The tears escaped, sliding down Jimmy's cheeks until he was the one having trouble breathing.

"You are a war hero, Sam. I'm going to make sure everyone knows it."

"Thanks. I knew I could rely on you," Sam whispered. He coughed violently and twisted to his side, then he lay still.

Jimmy carried him all the way. He waited for the Nazi to come for him and somehow – he never remembered the exact details – fought him and took the rifle from him. The Nazi was a kid, even younger than Jimmy, and ran when Jimmy told him too.

When he had left, Jimmy slipped the rifle over his shoulder and shifted it so he would be able to carry Sam the same way he'd seen other soldiers carry the wounded off the battlefield. And like that he walked through the forest until he found the cabin. When he arrived his shoulders were screaming in pain but he didn't care.

A man met him when he stepped out of the trees and Jimmy figured he was Warren.

"What happened?" he demanded as he helped lower Sam's body to the ground. He knelt beside him and felt for a pulse though Jimmy knew what he would find. He watched as Warren rocked back on his heels and shook his head.

"He's dead."

"They shot him," Jimmy explained, his voice hallow. He felt dead and empty as he stood looking down at his friend's body. "I got him into this mess and I got him killed."

Warren stood up and scowled.

"You're Lieutenant James Rodgers?"

Jimmy nodded.

"Listen, I'm sorry about your friend. I really am, but we can't stop now to mourn the dead, not right now. Where's Japhet and Franz?"

"Japhet went back," Jimmy said dully. "We were caught, so

he led the Nazis off."

Warren's hand came out of nowhere as he grabbed the front of Jimmy's shirt.

"What do you mean he led them off? And where is Franz? They were both supposed to be here. I promised to get those two boys out!"

Not bothering to try and get out of Warren's hold, Jimmy explained everything.

"Franz joined the Nazis. Japhet has been living in the basement with me and Sam for the past two years, but he went back into Berlin to talk to Franz and to give Sam and me a chance to get to you. I'm supposed to get his sister and parents out."

"Franz is a Nazi?" Warren let him go, staggered back, and cursed under his breath. "What have those two boys been up to?"

***

Losing the Nazis was easy, as easy as the other times he'd done it. When he was sure they were no longer following him, Japhet circled back around and made his way to the cabin. Once there he hid in the woods and watched everything that went on. He knew if he went out then Franz's parents and Ruth would all insist he come with them and he'd not be able to get away. So he only watched, his heart breaking when he realized Sam was dead.

It was hard to take in, seeing the Irishman laying on the ground, blood covering the front of his shirt. Japhet felt cold and numb.

While he crouched behind tree trunks, Japhet finally saw who he was looking for. Mr. and Mrs. Kappel came out of the cabin, followed by all the girls, not just Ruth. Japhet hadn't realized Leah, Bea, and Elsa had joined them at the cabin. More than anything he wanted to rush out and into their arms. It had been so long since he'd seen his sisters. They were thinner, their faces drawn with worry, but a glint of defiance was in their eyes. Leah even hugged Jimmy and Japhet smiled. She'd always been the hugger in his family.

Holding his breath for fear they'd hear them, Japhet stared and studied his sisters' faces. He listened as Warren introduced them to Jimmy.

"Where are my sons?" Mr. Kappel demanded. He frowned at Jimmy.

Jimmy opened his mouth, but Warren spoke for him.

"They couldn't get out. I'm going come back for them."

Mrs. Kappel placed a hand over her mouth while Ruth clutched Leah's hand.

"Then we are staying too," Leah calmly told Warren. "We're not leaving without our brothers."

Warren frowned at her. "I admire your persistence, Miss Buchanan," he said, "but now is not the time for it. We have a chance to get all of you out. If we don't go right now I don't know when I can get you out, it's too hard to move so many at once. When I find the boys, I can help them escape easier if it is just the two of them."

None of them liked the idea, but Warren was stubborn and argued his point until they all gave in. Crouching lower, Japhet watched as Warren led them off into the trees. He stared until they were out of sight, then he stood up and made his way back to Berlin and Mrs. Schmidt's basement.

Japhet had made a promise, and he was going to do everything in his power to keep it.

Forty-Four
A betrayal

1944

"We had them outnumbered, we knew where they would be, and they still got away!" Stein snapped. He kicked over the waste bin and Franz stared at it, waiting for Carsten to pick it up like he always did.

"Maybe it was not real information," Carsten said as he shoved the crumpled papers back into the dented bin. "Whoever sent it...who is to say we can trust them?" Once he had the bin upright, he reached into his pocket, grabbed a cigarette, and lit it. Franz was getting sick of the smell.

"But the soldiers saw someone!" Stein reminded him. "They chased him through the woods! He was there!"

Franz sat on the desk even though he knew it annoyed Stein. He only half listened to Stein's ranting and raving, not caring who got away and who outsmarted whom. He'd heard most of it before.

Someone had sent a tip that two Americans pilots were being smuggled out of Berlin with the help of a resistance leader. They'd been told the general area in the woods the three would be, but only one had been spotted and he'd bolted and vanished like a deer. Stein was certain he was the same one who kept disappearing the other times they'd been close to catching some of the leaders.

"Do you think the resistance has a traitor?" Carsten asked. He moved the bin so it wouldn't be within easy range the next time Stein got out of temper. He flicked ashes into it.

"We can only hope," Stein snapped. "I want him," he added.

"The one who keeps escaping?" Carsten asked.

Stein only partly paid attention to him. "Yes. I want him caught. I want to know who he is and what he knows. He could be very valuable to me. Let everyone know, Carsten. Tell them to keep an eye out for him, and if he's caught that I am going to interrogate him and no one else. I'm going to get everything from him, then I'm going to make sure he regrets the day he was born."

Carsten was stupid and not someone Stein could depend on, but he did what he was told and he annoyed Rupert, so Stein kept him around. Stein liked to push Rupert because, even after all of the interrogations, Stein still wasn't convinced he could trust the strange young man. Even after everything Stein had done to break him, Rupert still defied him in subtle ways.

A week had passed since the Americans had escaped and Stein sat in his office, brooding over Rupert Hoffman and aggressively drinking the coffee Carsten had brought in that morning. He'd spiked it again.

Back in the Hitler Youth days, Carsten had taken up the habit. It had been a joke between them, a last boyish act. Why he still did it, Stein couldn't begin to guess.

Carsten crashed in through the door and Stein set the coffee down. For once Carsten wasn't smoking and his old grin had returned. He slapped a folded piece of paper down on Stein's desk.

"What's this?" Stein demanded. He picked it up and turned it over in his hands.

"I think it's the resistance traitor. Also, there's a man here to see you. He has some important matters to go over with you."

Perfect, just what he didn't want today.

Stein ordered Carsten to send the man in as he unfolded the letter. He skimmed the page as Carsten left, then read it slower.

This is the address of where the next resistance meeting is to be held. There will be a man there, one who has been avoiding you for months now. His name is Japhet Buchanan and he is one of the highest ranking leaders the resistance has.

There was nothing else besides the address and Stein wasn't sure what to make of the message, but it brightened his mood enough to make him more friendly toward the soldier who was admitted into his office.

The moment Carsten left, Stein rose and saluted the man, introducing himself.

The man returned the salute with, "Gilbert Huber."

"Won't you sit?" Stein asked, motioning to a chair.

Huber shook his head. "I don't have time. I'm only here to deliver papers. However, while I was waiting, I happened to see a young man and I wished to speak to you about him."

Stein shrugged.

"Which young man and what about him?"

"I already questioned your man about him," Huber said, his tone clipped and formal. "He tells me his name is Rupert Hoffmann."

"Oh, him." Stein sighed, his partly good mood ruined. "Yes, he's one of mine. A somewhat promising young man, though he has so many rough edges, I'm not sure I'm going to be able to make anything out of him."

"I was very surprised to see him here," Huber said as if he hadn't heard a thing Stein said. "He and I used to be schoolboys together and he never struck me as someone to join the Nazis."

This at least was interesting. Stein sat on the edge of his desk, the same way Hoffmann did to annoy him.

"Why is that?" he asked.

"Because, in school, he was Franz Kappel...and he was best friends with a Jew named Japhet Buchanan."

***

Seth had always been short tempered and snappish, but he'd never been the sort to yell for no reason. Usually, he took his anger out on Japhet alone, but the week after Sam's death and Jimmy's escape he branched out. When he wasn't yelling, he was on edge and jumped at every little sound.

Japhet didn't put a lot of thought into his behavior. He had other things on his mind, finding Franz being his biggest concern. He'd gone to the apartment every night during the week, making sure no one saw him, but there were no signs of Franz ever being there. Japhet began to worry that Franz might have moved, and he wouldn't be able to find him.

On top of that, Japhet was appointed to lead one of the meetings alone. The last thing he wanted to do at the moment was to try and be a leader when all he ever seemed to do under that position was get people killed.

***

Meanwhile, Franz had troubles of his own. Stein took a sudden new interest in him and had him running all over Berlin most days. Every time he returned to headquarters Stein had a new order for him.

"Take these papers down to Karla."

"Beir can't do patrol tonight. I need you to take his place."

"Come in early tomorrow. I need someone to take inventory on supplies when they arrive at seven."

The list was endless. Franz never made it back to the apartment until after midnight. He'd then crash and sleep for a few hours before having to go back to get new orders from Stein. The only good part about the whole thing was he became so exhausted his brain couldn't torment him with nightmares.

Franz didn't put much thought into Stein's strange mood. The less time he spent thinking about his commanding officer, the better. The only thing he found even remotely interesting during the week was the letter Stein mentioned to him and Carsten.

"Carsten was right. There is a traitor in the resistance. He got word to me about one of the leaders and told us how we can catch him. I believe this is the one who keeps getting away." He glared at both of them: Carsten with his persistent smoking and Franz, who stared blearily at him. "I want him caught, and I want you to come with me, Hoffmann. I'm relying on you."

Franz nodded. Nodding was easy. He could do it even though his eyes were grainy and heavy. He could turn off all other emotions except obedience if that were what the Nazis wanted. Stein wanted him to hunt down and capture a resistance fighter and Franz could do it. He had to do something with his time now that there was no longer any point in continuing his search for Japhet. Japhet had left him behind because he too believed Franz had become an unfeeling Nazi. There was no point in trying to prove everyone wrong.

Forty-Five
Japhet's capture

1944

Odis had started up his spying again. Japhet never would have thought the big man would make a good spy, but he'd once again gathered important information and another mission was being planned. Guns were being shipped out to the soldiers fighting on the front. The plan was to get down to the tracks and switch around labels. Another band of the resistance would intercept the train farther down the tracks and relieve the Nazis of their load.

"Nothing better than confusing the Third Reich!" Odis said with glee.

He, Japhet, and five other men were in one of the cellars where they held their meetings. Seth was with them, but he was so restless it was almost like he wasn't there. He kept shifting in his seat and looking around as Japhet spoke until Japhet was certain he was going to jump up and run out of the room as fast as his legs could carry him.

"Why can't we just blow it all up?" Caleb asked. He'd kept the grenade Warren had sent him. He wore it like a pistol in his belt all the time.

"We can't blow everything up," Odis patiently explained.

"It would attract too much attention," Japhet added. He tried to keep his mind on the planning and not Seth's jitters. After all, he had been put in charge of the whole operation.

"Why?" Caleb asked.

Some of the other men smiled, but they didn't comment.

"Warren said so," Odis answered.

"Oh." Caleb sat back and pulled the grenade out, tossing it from one hand to the other. His continued bomb tossing set Japhet on edge, but since Caleb seemed to like Odis' answer Japhet decided not to order him to put the grenade up.

"When do we leave?" one of the other men asked Japhet.

"Tomorrow night. There won't be a moon then. We need to meet at the tracks at midnight, but we all need to come from different directions and leave at different times. Seth..."

When he turned to give Seth his instructions the man jumped as if someone had fired a gun.

"Are you okay?" Japhet asked him.

Seth stared at all the men who were now looking at him. He shifted around and quickly shook his head.

"No, to be honest, I'm not," he said, wiggling again. "I haven't been feeling well all week. I think I need to leave."

Japhet wasn't about to argue with Seth leaving but, sick or not, Japhet thought it strange he would go. Seth made it clear to everyone that he thought Japhet was going to mess something up and stayed with him as much as he could to make sure he wasn't going to ruin the resistance. A sudden suspicion weaseled into Japhet's thoughts, though he didn't think he had any foundation for his misgivings. The things going through his mind he didn't think Seth capable of.

Japhet had been told by the other leaders to watch for anyone acting strangely. They believed there might be a traitor among them since there would have been few other ways for the Nazis to find out about Jimmy and Sam leaving Berlin.

"We don't know if the traitor might have been after them or you but you need to be extra careful," they had warned.

Japhet didn't want to start throwing accusations around, but there were few other people he could think of who might have had reasons to turn him and the two American pilots over to the Nazis. Everyone knew Seth hated Japhet and had been angry about the resistance helping Sam and Jimmy.

"I don't think you should leave," Japhet said. He tried not to say anything that might make Seth suspicious of his intentions.

"Why not?" Seth demanded, sounding more like his old self as he stood up and inched for the door.

"Because you really don't look well. I don't think you should try and walk home just yet. Come and sit down for a bit, just until I'm sure you're not sick or anything."

Odis caught on, which Japhet was thankful for. He always felt better with the big man there to help him.

"He's right," Odis said. He stood as well. Everyone else stayed seated and stared at the exchange. "You don't look so great. I think you should rest for a while. Here," he grabbed Seth's arm and tried to force him into a chair, "sit down until you feel better."

"No!" Seth tried to pull his arm free, but Odis' grip was too strong. He stopped thrashing as quickly as he started and forced a smile. "No, I'm fine. I'd just like to go home and lie down."

Nodding, Odis still held to Seth, at the same time whispering to Japhet, "Make everyone else leave. Right now."

Turning, Japhet smiled at the other men. "We're going to get out of here early," he said, "Seth isn't feeling well so Odis and I are taking him back to his house. You know the rules about leaving, one or two at a time and make sure no one sees you. You're dismissed."

No one argued. Caleb even grinned and stuck the grenade back in his belt, a wild glint flashing through his eyes briefly. Japhet worried about him and whispered to one of the other men to make sure Caleb wasn't left alone that night. He watched as the fighters slipped out of the cellar. When they were gone, he rejoined Seth and Odis. Odis was quietly shaking and interrogating Seth.

"What have you done?" he hissed.

"Nothing!" Seth whimpered.

Japhet pulled Seth out of Odis' grasp and twisted his arm behind his back. His temper was frayed and he had trouble holding back his seething wrath.

"Are you the traitor?" he snapped, deciding Seth's behavior gave him enough reason to accuse him. "Did you tell the Nazis where Sam and Jimmy and I would be?"

"My arm," Seth complained, his face as white as a sheet. It wasn't the answer Japhet wanted to hear, but it was enough.

"They killed him!" Japhet yelled. "They shot Sam! He's dead because of what you did! Is that what you were hoping for? Out of everyone who deserved to live through this war, it was Sam!"

"I didn't want the Americans to die," Seth said. He tried to pull free but Japhet wrenched his arm even more and he stopped struggling.

"You were after Japhet?" Odis demanded, his face red with furious anger. "Is it true? Were you trying to get Japhet killed?"

Seth finally stopped whimpering and glared.

"Of course I wanted him out of the way!" he snapped. "He's done nothing but get people killed since he showed up!"

Japhet staggered as Odis yanked Seth away from him and slammed him down into a chair. He towered over him and Seth didn't move a muscle.

"You wanted the Nazis to kill Japhet? What's wrong with you? Did you tell them he'd be here tonight? Is that why you were so eager to get out of here? Leave us to the wolves while you escape?"

"No one else would get hurt...not too many others," Seth said, a glint in his eyes. "They mostly just want Japhet."

Odis slammed his fist into a wall and both Japhet and Seth jumped.

"He's just a kid!" Odis hissed, bending over Seth. "You know what the Nazis do! How could you want to do that to him or anyone?"

Japhet looked away. He tried to grasp what was happening as Odis turned and grabbed him by the shoulders.

"We have to get out of here right now!" he ordered. "You go first and I'll be right behind you!"

Before Japhet could protest, Odis shoved him toward the door and Japhet stumbled up the narrow cellar steps which led to the street instead of the house above them. It was a unique cellar, one of the best to meet in because it provided them with more than one means to escape.

"It's too late," Japhet heard Seth whisper behind him, but he didn't care. Too late or not, his feet kept carrying him out.

Opening the door, Japhet looked out into the back alley. He could see nothing but he knew that didn't mean there weren't Nazis out there. Taking a deep breath, he stepped out, the night air cool on his face.

For a moment, he stood and looked behind him, not wanting to leave until he saw Odis shoving Seth up and out into the alley behind him. He smiled but froze when something moved. It was a faint sound but enough to alert him that all was not as quiet as it seemed.

Odis heard it as well and he drew a pistol from under his jacket. He fired in the direction of the noise.

"Run!" Odis shouted, shoving Seth down as bullets filled the air. "Get out of here, Japhet!"

Japhet drew his own pistol to help return fire, but Odis glared at him so hard he ran. He heard Seth scrambling behind him but kept going until he ducked behind a building from which no gunfire came. There he stopped long enough to look back. His heart lurched when Seth hit the ground, clutching two bullet wounds in his stomach. At the same time, a bullet found Odis and he crumpled, falling to the ground while firing off two more rounds.

Angered and grieved, Japhet turned and ran, fleeing the scene as fast as his legs could carry him. He had little doubt he'd be able to get away. He knew better than to allow himself to become cocky, but he'd escaped the Nazis so many times he knew how they worked. Already there were only the faintest sounds of pursuit behind him. A few more turns and even those were lost in the darkness behind him.

When he could no longer hear anyone pursuing him, Japhet slumped against a building and worked on catching his breath around the lump in his throat. He saw, over and over again, Odis falling to the street. The lump tried to choke him but vanished when something moved behind him. Japhet set off again.

Not wanting to take unneeded risks, Japhet moved between buildings, not making a sound. For some reason, the escape reminded him of the times he and Franz had played hide and seek with the other boys in the village.

In spite of the care he took, the slight shuffle of feet continued to follow him. Japhet dodged and wove between buildings,

Franz's advice on how not to get caught filling his head.

"Never go in a straight line. Move around, circle back, anything to throw them off. Never make a sound. Even the smallest scrap of your shoe can give you away."

Franz's advice was followed by the shouts of Gilbert and Amell.

"Japhet Buchanan! Come out! You know we're going to find you."

"Always stay in the shadows. Never move if you think you can be seen. Even if you think you've been spotted stay still."

Japhet saw a shadow, so close his heart stopped. Pressing himself back against the wall behind him, Japhet froze even though all his body wanted to do was run. For a minute the shadow didn't move, just seemed to stare right at him, then finally it turned and faded and Japhet set off once again. Unfortunately, the figure stalking him started to follow.

"Get Franz! Franz can always find him!"

"It's because he's so small. He can get into all the cracks we can't!"

"And Franz trained him! It isn't fair."

Franz. A new knot formed in Japhet's stomach and something happened which had never occurred before. A wrenching feeling of panic tore through Japhet and he bolted like a scared rabbit. He tried to tell himself to calm down, but it was too late, even as Franz's voice shouted in his head.

"Most importantly never panic!"

Japhet ran as fast as his legs could carry him. He dodged and wove and headed toward one of the bigger, more populated streets, hoping to find a crowd he could disappear into. He ran until his lungs burned and his ears rang. He ran until he felt like he couldn't take another step and still he pushed himself.

It was a futile attempt. Japhet knew it the moment he bolted. He could hear pounding feet behind him, closing in on him, and in last minute desperation he pulled his knife from its sheath.

A shadow moved to his left, coming toward him like a bullet. Japhet couldn't make out details in the dark, but he saw the Nazi uniform and he slashed out with the blade. The Nazi jumped back but kept coming. Japhet thrust the knife at him, but the Nazi caught his arm, yanked him off balance, and twisted the knife from his hand. He threw Japhet to the ground, face down, and pressed the blade to his back.

Japhet closed his eyes as a voice he would never forget shouted to let the other Nazis know he'd caught the resistance fighter.

Franz knelt with his knee on the fighter's back as the other Nazis closed in. He didn't feel pleased with himself, stalking the leader like he'd stalked Japhet so many years ago, but he was glad he'd been caught so Stein would stop kicking the waste bin and the desk.

As the soldiers narrowed in on the spot where he knelt, Franz slowly eased himself off the man under him, holding the knife ready in case he thought of attacking. Grabbing the man's shoulder, Franz rolled him to his back just as Stein and Carsten emerged from the shadows in front of him. Franz wanted to get a good look at the man who had been eluding them for so long before he was dragged off, but the moment Franz glanced down an invisible force slammed into him and he almost fell over.

He wasn't looking down at some hardened resistance fighter, but instead into a face he'd been wanting to see for the past two years. The face of the boy he'd grown up with; his brother.

"Japhet," he whispered, unable to react as someone pushed him aside, then yanked Japhet up. Franz was so stunned that at first he could do nothing. He knelt on the ground and tried to stop his head from spinning.

"We've been looking for you for a long time," Stein said. Carsten held Japhet up as Stein punched him in the stomach. As Japhet gasped for air, Franz jumped to his feet and would have rushed to his aid had not the other Nazis appeared just then.

"You caught him?" one of them asked, grinning.

"Hoffmann did," Stein replied.

Through the heavy fog trying to swallow him, Franz was aware of only a few things. Japhet was in Nazi hands, even worse, Stein's hands. And both he and Japhet were outnumbered. Franz wanted to put the knife he was still clenching to good use but knew it would be foolish. He'd be shot before he could help, then Japhet would be killed. The only chance he stood of saving him was to play along, as much as he hated it.

"Good for you, Hoffmann!" the others were saying. They slapped him on the back and shook his hand.

Franz had a hard time taking his eyes off Japhet who stood with his head down. He couldn't believe how close he was to him, after two years. His friend was thinner and his face harder. Whatever he had gone through in the time they hadn't been together, Franz knew it wasn't good and it cut his heart in two – bringing back emotions he didn't think he had anymore.

"Yes, Hoffmann did well," Stein said, "but I want this one taken and locked up right now. I don't want him escaping or even getting the chance to think about it."

Nazis nodded and moved in to grab hold of Japhet. Franz did the same, reaching out for him, but Stein stopped him, pulling his arm down.

"Not you," he said. He beamed one of his annoying, fake smiles. "I'm taking you out for a drink to congratulate you on your hard work."

As he spoke the soldiers began to lead Japhet off and he finally looked up. Their eyes met for a second or two, and Franz tried to pour all his emotions into that look, even as Japhet returned it with one of complete betrayal.

Forty-Six
The Rabbi

1944

It was a nightmare, only one he couldn't wake up from. The Nazis dragged through the city and Japhet tried to walk but often his legs gave out and his feet scraped the ground as they pulled him. Sometimes they pushed him and shoved him in front of them. Japhet thought about putting up a fight but didn't see the point.

His brain refused to work. Over and over he saw Franz kneeling beside him, saying nothing as the Nazis dragged him off into the night.

Japhet had nightmares like this before. Always the same, Franz turning him over to the Nazis without any pity or regret. Japhet had never really believed the nightmares had a chance at becoming reality, but now they stared him in the face, demanding he try and make sense of what had happened to him and what was going to happen.

It was more the thought of what they were going to put him through that scared Japhet the most. It had been bad enough when Odis had been the one interrogating him and dislocating his shoulder. These men wouldn't be so kind, and would not bandage him up when they were done.

***

Franz somehow made it through a few drinks with Stein. He wasn't sure what he drank or said during that time, but he hoped he was convincing enough to make Stein believe he was happy over Japhet's capture.

When they were done, Franz staggered out into the streets, his thoughts whirring. He tried to slow them down so he would be able to sort out everything he needed to do. It was not easy, especially when images of Japhet, bruised and bloody, kept rising before his mind.

Finally, unable to take another step, Franz sat down on the edge of the street and hid his head in his hands. There was no one around this late so he had little fear of anyone stopping to check on the sobbing Nazi – even though he wasn't really sobbing. He couldn't even think of crying, his mind too muddled and his heart in too much pain.

After all his searching and his belief that Japhet was on his way to safety, to find him the way he did felt like a knife in the chest. Franz now wished that Japhet had escaped and had left him behind. It would have been better than being sent to Stein's interrogation room.

A foot scrapped the sidewalk beside him and Franz looked up at the same time a wizened, soft spoken voice asked, "Are you okay?"

A white-headed man with thick glasses stood beside Franz. He carefully lowered himself to the sidewalk so they sat side-by-side. He was frail, with busy eyebrows and a wrinkled but warm face.

"I'm okay," Franz said once the man had sat. He pulled

Japhet's knife from his belt and turned it over and over in his hands.

"You don't look okay," the old man said, the wrinkles around his eyes deepening. "Just so you know. You look like you've been crying. That's why I stopped, because it isn't common to see crying Nazis."

Franz glared at his uniform but didn't speak. He touched the cold blade, circling his fingers around the knife's handle.

"Maybe Nazis normally don't have things to cry about," Franz suggested.

"I guess. And what might you have to cry about?" The old man tipped his head to the side, trying to get a better look at Franz's face.

"We all have reasons to cry," Franz said, turning his head further away. "Sometimes we just forget them."

"I guess," the man muttered. "Why don't you tell me your reasons since you clearly remember them?"

Had it been any other time Franz would have said no. It wasn't safe, talking to strangers on the street; it was a good way to end up dead. But there was something open and honest about the man. Franz wanted to tell him, he wanted to tell someone. He felt like he had to or it would kill him.

"I did something really stupid," he murmured, resting his chin on his knees and staring down at his boots. He laid the knife down at his feet.

"We all do stupid things. What was yours?" The old man shifted his feet and sighed, almost as if he were settling back to listen to a good story.

Franz tried to pinpoint which moment was his crowning point of stupidity. It took him a while to decide, but he finally settled on it.

"I didn't tell my best friend something, something really important. Because of that he is now in a lot of trouble and I'm not sure how to save him." It hurt to talk about it, more than it hurt to think about.

"What are you going to do about it?" the man asked. The way he said the question surprised Franz. He made it sound like it was the simplest thing in the world, making a mistake and having to fix it.

"Do about it?" Franz raised his head. "You make it sound easy. It isn't going to be. I don't even know how I'm going to get him out!"

"You are going to get him out, though, aren't you?" the man asked, his head still tipped as he stared at him. "You aren't just going to leave him?"

"Of course I'm going to get him out!" Franz snapped. "He's my best friend and I..." he stopped, choking on a sob he tried to disguise. "I know what they do to prisoners. I know what they are going to do to him. I know because I've done it. I can't let that happen to him."

"It sounds like you're going to need help," the man whispered, suddenly serious.

The lump stopped trying to choke him and Franz squinted. "Who are you?" he asked.

"I shouldn't tell you," the old man said slowly, "since you are a Nazi. But I guess if you decide to kill me I've lived long enough and will just have to get over you killing me before I am ready to die."

"I..."

The old man held up a hand and cut him off. "I'm a rabbi," he explained, whispering as he looked up and down the street. "I've been living in Berlin since before the war started."

"How did you not get caught?" Franz asked, his eyes widening.

The old man smiled. "I have my ways. But I think you have more important things to worry about. I don't know your story, but I've been around long enough to understand how important friends are. And yours sounds like one who deserves to be saved."

"How do I save him, though?" Franz asked, hoping the old rabbi would have some kind of plan hidden up the sleeve of his coat.

"I'm just an old man," the rabbi said, shaking his white head. "I don't have the answers for everything, and even if I did, I think this is one you have to find out on your own. Just remember, some people are worth risking your life for."

Nodding, Franz stood up as an idea began to form in his mind. It was reckless and likely to get him shot, but he was willing to take that risk.

"Thank you," he said, turning back to the rabbi before running off like he wanted to.

The rabbi smiled and held his hand up.

"I'm glad I can help. Not sure how I did, but I am glad. Do me a favor and help me up? It's harder getting up at my age than down."

Forty-Seven
First interrogations

1944

Franz went back to headquarters the next morning. He marched in with his head held high, with his uniform neatly pressed, and with a pretend smile on his face. He put up with all the congratulations as he walked into Stein's office, trying to appear as bold as Carsten always did.

"I didn't think I'd see you today," Stein said when he walked in. "You didn't have to come. I thought you might like some sleep after all the hard work you did last night."

Franz wanted to punch him so hard he'd never be able to smile again. Instead, he shrugged and tried to act casual.

"I wanted to see the prisoner, maybe help with interrogations," Franz said, trying to sound excited about the idea of helping to torture his best friend.

Stein laughed. It wasn't even a human laugh, but Franz hadn't expected anything else from him.

"I admire your enthusiasm," Stain said, his eyes betraying some secret. "However, I have Carsten helping me this time."

Franz vowed to strangle Carsten the next time he saw him.

"Good, he needs the training. Can I see the Jew at least? It was dark last night." He tried not to rush his words. He wanted to get away from Stein and make sure Japhet was still all right as quickly as he could.

"He isn't here or I'd let you," Stein said, turning his attention to whatever he'd been working on when Franz entered. "Don't worry, though, he isn't much to look at considering the trouble he's given us. When we've killed him, I'll make sure you get to see his body or ashes or whatever we decide to do with his remains. But I do have something for you."

Reaching into a drawer, Stein pulled out the sheath Japhet always kept his knife in and threw it to Franz. Franz caught it and clutched it to his chest as Stein smiled.

"I saw you had the knife last night, I thought you might as well have this too."

Unable to speak, Franz nodded, clicked his heels and saluted, then turned and left. He marched out of the building the same way he'd marched in, only this time with no plan on ever coming back. Becoming a Nazi had gotten Japhet taken to be killed, to save him Franz was going to become someone else.

***

The room was dark and cold, without even a sliver of light to pierce the black. Japhet had lost track of how long he had been in – it could have been an hour or days, but he thought hours was more accurate.

When Japhet was first thrown in, he'd crawled around the room, feeling in all the dark corners to try and get an idea of how big it might be. Now all he could manage was to lay on the cold floor, doing his best to ignore the stabbing emptiness in his stomach.

It wouldn't have been so bad except that he knew it would

only get worse. The Nazis weren't just going to lock him in a dark room and starve him to death. He didn't think Nazis were that merciful to their prisoners. And he was with the resistance, a leader, on top of being a Jew. They were going to break him before they killed him.

Japhet knew where he was. Even though he'd been stunned and barely able to make sense of anything while they led him off, he had the sense enough to pay attention to where he was being taken. They had taken him to a closed-down ice cream shop. Japhet had passed it many times while wandering Berlin. It had gone out of business and was abandoned, at least from the outside. Inside, when he was led down, he saw it had been converted into a prison. If prison was the right word. There was a hall lined with doors and on the other side of them Japhet had heard moaning and sobs. That was before he was led to the end of the hall and thrown into the dark room. Not only could no light get into the little room, but neither could sound. He was in complete solitude.

When the door finally opened and Japhet was blinded by the sudden light, he wished they would just close the door and leave him to die by starvation. There were two Nazis in the hall and when one bent down to grab Japhet, Japhet kicked him as hard as he could. The Nazi, not surprisingly, kicked him back in the stomach.

Gasping for air, Japhet couldn't fight back as he was yanked to his feet and pulled down the hall. He wasn't able to breathe until the Nazis shoved into a room which was furnished with chairs and a small table. Japhet was pushed into one of the chairs and then left alone. Without looking back, the two Nazis closed the door and silence enveloped the room.

Realizing he was alone, Japhet stared at the door. His legs

ached from lack of food and all the running he'd done before he'd been brought in, but he still stumbled to his feet and slowly made his way to the door. He reached for the handle at the same time the door opened, shoving up against his chest. Japhet would have fallen if a hand hadn't reached out and grabbed the front of his shirt.

Stumbling back, Japhet looked up into the face of the man now standing over him. He was tall and there was a fiendish look of murder in his eyes. Japhet's empty stomach twisted as the man pushed him back into the chair and slapped him, snapping his head to the side.

"You're headstrong," the Nazi said. "I thought you might be, since you were so hard to catch." He bent forward and grabbed Japhet's face, forcing him to look up. "Don't worry, though, I can break you. I've done it to so many before you."

Japhet closed his eyes to hide his fear as the man released him and straightened up.

"I think we should be introduced, since we're going to be spending a lot of time together. My name is Gorge Stein. That one by the door is Carsten. And what can we call you?"

Opening his eyes, Japhet saw another man had entered. He stood stiff and rigged, smoking and smiling. Japhet wished he had something he could throw at him. Instead, he scowled and clamped his jaw together. If he were stubborn, they'd maybe kill him early rather than spend weeks torturing him. Not that it mattered, nothing could hurt more than Franz's betrayal.

"You aren't going to tell us?" Stein asked, his every word as cold as ice. "We told you our names. It isn't good manners to not return the gesture. How are we going to get to know one another if Carsten and I don't even know what to call you?"

Japhet looked away and Stein's fist connected with his

stomach, knocking every ounce of air from his lungs. Japhet crumpled to the floor and, for the second time that day, found it difficult to breathe. It had taken several attempts before he was able to get air back into his body.

Stein grabbed his shirt and pulled him up, shoving him back into the chair. He leaned in and this time Japhet tried to lean back.

"If you insist on being stubborn this is what you will get," Stein whispered, his voice sending shivers down Japhet's spine. "I already know who you are, Japhet Buchanan. And I have the power to take everything away from you, so just remember that the next time I ask you to answer a question. Because next time I might not be so nice."

***

They came back the same day. Japhet wasn't sure if he could safely say it was the same day, but he gave it his best guess.

This time they put him in a different room, one which only held one chair and two light bulbs dangling from the ceiling. The two Nazis who had hauled him in tossed him into the chair and moved to strap him in, using leather restraints. They pulled them around his legs, arms, and chest.

Looking around the room, Japhet saw a table pushed up against one of the walls. It was laid out with an array of needles and vials of liquid. He had no idea what was in any of the vials, but he did know he wasn't going to like it.

The straps were pulled tight, the leather digging into the flesh of Japhet's wrists. He tugged on them as the two Nazis left, but they didn't loosen. Pure, cold panic tried to seize him when the door opened and Stein walked in.

Standing in front of him, Stein smiled.

"How much do you know about these torture chambers,

Japhet Buchanan? Surely enough to know there are only two ways out of here. You can tell us what we want to know and walk free. Or don't tell us and we will carry your dead body out."

For Japhet that meant there was only one way out, because he had no intention of telling any of them anything about the resistance. Seth had been right when he said too many had died when Japhet joined the resistance. He wasn't going to be responsible for more deaths, not like he had been for Odis'.

Turning his back, Stein walked over to the one wall which was hidden in deep shadow. He bent to examine something there before he turned again and walked back over to Japhet.

"You know, I work with a friend of yours."

"What friend?" It hurt Japhet's dry throat to speak, but the question came out in spite of that.

"His name is Franz Kappel."

Japhet hated the way his stomach twisted when he heard Franz's name. He couldn't tell if it was out of anger or fear and could do nothing other than watch Stein.

"Yes," Stein smiled, "he is one of the best Nazis I have under my command. You should see him work, the interrogations he has done. I've seen him break so many people."

Japhet didn't want to believe it. It was hard enough, trying to accept his friend being a Nazi, even after two years of knowing the truth. The thought of Franz actually taking part in interrogations only made it worse.

"He even helped with the interrogation of one man whom – I believe – was under your command. Sadly, we didn't get a last name, but his first name was Levi."

Levi. Japhet's heart fell and every part of him refused to believe Franz could have had any part in his death. Japhet bit his bottom lip hard so he could feel pain somewhere other than his heart.

"Yes, I was very proud of him for how he handled Levi." Stein stopped smiling. "Of course, there is something a little strange about him. He has been going by the name of Rupert Hoffmann since the day I've met him. He came into Berlin with his cousin Stephen Achen, looking for work, according to some of the files and information we have on him."

Stephen Achen. Japhet hadn't heard that name in a long time. He'd almost forgotten about it. He wondered how different life would be now if he and Franz had avoided Berlin and gone to the farm instead. Would Warren have gotten them out at the same time he'd gotten everyone else out?

"We have all kinds of information on you and your friend," Stein said, stooping so his face was closer to Japhet's. "We know all about your families and your friends. Everything. Do you know what we can do with that kind of information?"

It wasn't easy, but Japhet still refused to speak.

"We can use it to find your families," Stein whispered.

The icy fear pricking Japhet's heart dissolved enough for him to smile.

"It won't do you any good," he said, his voice croaking. "They aren't in Germany anymore."

Now it was Stein's turn not to speak. He stood up and walked back to the dark corner. When he turned around this time, he held a thin, willow-type stick in his hand. It might have been considered a whip except it didn't have a cord dangling off one end.

Stein marched back and swung, snapping Japhet's arm. The stick left a sharp, stinging pain, which strangely enough reminded Japhet of a time years ago. He closed his eyes as Stein hit him again and again.

"Catch!" Franz threw him the thin stick he'd just fought off one of

the trees. Japhet caught it while Franz bent to pick up another one.

"What is this for?" Japhet asked, twisting the stick around in his hand.

"Sword fight, of course!" Franz explained just before he ran at Japhet, swinging his stick and grinning. He nearly hit Japhet on the head, but Japhet blocked just in time.

Back and forth, they chased each other across the field until Japhet missed a block and Franz's stick smacked into his arm. Stinging pain numbed his fingers and he dropped his wooden sword, jumping up and down, rubbing his arm.

Franz just stood back and laughed.

Stein lowered the stick and Japhet opened his eyes, calmly meeting those of the Nazi who stood over him. They stayed in that position for a while, just staring at each other, then Stein turned and ordered Japhet be taken back to his cell.

Forty-Eight
Facing consequences and going back

1944

Jimmy Rodgers escaped. It wasn't easy and many times he didn't think they would make it, but he didn't forget his promise and did everything he could to make sure the Kappels and Buchanans made it out alive. Once out, they parted ways, Warren taking the family into liberated France and Jimmy returning to his squadron. He made surprisingly good time, especially when he met up with an Allied unit who gave him a ride.

Going back without Sam was the hardest thing he'd ever had to do but he held his head high as walked into camp. When the other reconnaissance pilots saw him, they swarmed him.

"You're still kicking!" one of them shouted. He hammered Jimmy on the back. "Don't know why we should be surprised, though!"

"Just in time to help us bring the Krauts to their knees!" another said. He grinned and held a bottle out to Jimmy. "We're having an early celebration! Have a drink! It's on the Fuhrer himself."

Jimmy nearly accepted. It would have been easy, he realized. He could drink away the pain, tell everyone Sam had been shot while escaping and leave out the role he'd played in his co-pilot's death. He reached for the bottle, but before he touched it Japhet's half-starved face appeared before him and he waved it off.

"I need to see the major," he said.

Laughing, the man who had offered him the bottle led Jimmy to their commander's shabby headquarters.

Major Welsh saluted Jimmy when he was shown into the saggy old farmhouse he was staying in, and then shook his hand.

"I didn't expect to see you alive, Rodgers," he said. Major Welsh was in his late thirties, built like an ox, and had a warm smile. All the men looked up to him and would have followed him to the ends of the earth if he asked.

"Two years. We feared you were dead. It's great to have you back."

Jimmy stood at attention, unable to look Major Welsh in the eyes.

"You might think it isn't that great when you know where I was for the last two years," Jimmy said. He then quietly explained everything that had happened, not leaving out anything.

He admitted to going off course during his last reconnaissance mission and how he'd gotten himself and Sam shot down. He explained how they had been found and helped by a band of the Jewish resistance, and how it was them who helped Sam and Jimmy get out of Berlin. He then told how Sam was shot and killed while escaping.

"I know I'm responsible for Sam's death," he concluded. "If I hadn't disobeyed my orders then it wouldn't have happened. And I'm willing to take whatever punishment is seen fit to give me. However, I first have a request."

Major Welsh stayed silent through the whole story, but now he gave the smallest hint of a nod and Jimmy went on. He spoke slowly and made sure not to leave out anything he felt would be necessary for his commanding officer to know.

"While in Berlin I became friends with a Jew named Japhet Buchanan. He's the reason I escaped. He was supposed to come with me and Sam, but he stayed to lead the Nazis off. I know he has gone back into Berlin to try and get a friend of his out before he leaves."

Again Major Welsh said nothing. His usual smiling eyes had a pained look in them.

"Major, I know the kind of soldier I have been. I know I was sent to your squadron to lessen the risk of me getting more men killed. After what has happened to Sam I see no reason why should you grant my request, but I would like permission to return to Berlin and get Japhet out. I know this is unusual, but if I don't go back, Japhet will be killed."

Crossing his arms over his chest, Major Welsh squinted and Jimmy felt as if he were looking into the blackest corners of his mind.

Seconds passed without a word being spoken, then Welsh said, "What makes you think you were sent under my command because of what happened to your bombing crew?" His tone was stern but still full of compassion.

Jimmy didn't have an answer. He'd always assumed that was the reason he'd been shipped off, but he hadn't ever asked anyone. No explanation had been offered, so he'd gone with the one which made sense in his mind.

He swallowed and said, "I got them killed."

"Four of them died in war, Rodgers," Major Welsh said, "you got five back alive. You were sent out here because your captain knew you couldn't handle a new crew. He almost sent you back home, unsure you were emotionally stable to make it through the rest of the war. He figured he'd give you a chance at flying with just one co-pilot instead. I was ordered to keep an eye on you and if I didn't think you could take it, to send you back home. Your captain sent you here to keep you alive and give you a reason to keep fighting, not because he blamed you for what happened to those four men who died. Don't you ever forget that, Rodgers."

All Jimmy could do was nod. It was a lot to take in and he didn't know how to respond. He thought of Joe, of his guilt and relief, and then for the first time he thought of the men who had lived.

Major Welsh gave him a moment of silence before asking, "I have to ask, why do you wish to go back into Berlin now, when it is most dangerous, to save the life of one Jew? He's just one Jew."

"It's because of that I want to go back," Jimmy replied, finding his voice. "When I joined the war, my friend Danny told me that we are fighting for those who cannot fight for themselves, but I ignored him. I understand it better now. If we take our focus off why we are here, then there is no point in fighting at all. If I don't save Japhet, no one else is going to."

Sighing, Major Welsh rubbed his forehead. "Of course I see your point, but this is complicated. I know you are sorry for what happened to Sam, but that isn't going to bring him back or make his death any easier on his family. And it isn't going to take away the fact that he was killed because you disobeyed orders."

Jimmy heard the sorrow in the major's voice. His actions became harder to bear. Not only had they affected Sam, but now the major as well.

"I'm going to have to report your actions," Major Welsh went on.

Jimmy's stomach twisted, but he said nothing.

"However, the fact you have come and asked for permission

to go back into Berlin, instead of just running off, makes me think you have changed. I'm going to wait before I send my report in. I'll wait until you get back. When I do send it in, I'll do what I can for you, but I think you need to understand there's a strong chance you will face the firing squad."

That realization had hit Jimmy as he carried Sam's body to the farmhouse. It wasn't easier to hear the words out loud. He straightened his shoulders and saluted.

"Whatever is decided I will comply with," he said grimly, "but I thank you for allowing me the chance to go back for Japhet."

Major Welsh returned the salute and Jimmy relaxed.

"Do you have a plan to get him out?" the major asked.

"Yes, sir." This was the only part of the whole thing Jimmy felt confident about. "I have already been working on that."

***

First Lieutenant Daniel Brown never accepted that his best friend was dead. The feared letter that began with, "It is my painful duty to inform you..." had been sent to the little farm in New York to Mrs. Rodgers. She'd written Danny the day she received it.

"I don't believe it's true. Not for one minute. They said he went missing in action months ago and is presumed dead. I won't believe it until I see his body." She'd then said she was continuing to write him like she'd been doing since the day Jimmy had joined the Air Force.

Her letter was followed by one from Sadie.

"He can't be dead, Dan. Not Jimmy. He's too stubborn. I'm more willing to accept he's a Prisoner of War somewhere. You believe it too, don't you?"

Danny didn't need their reassurances and letters for him to

know Jimmy wasn't dead. There was no sense of loss, nothing he felt that told him Jimmy had been killed. Somewhere, Jimmy lived, and Danny made it his goal to find him. One way or another, he wasn't going home without James Rodgers at his side.

Nevertheless, when he got Jimmy's telegram two years later, he clutched it and didn't mind when a few tears fell on it. Folding it and sticking it in his shirt, Danny ran to speak with his captain.

"I'd like to request a week pass," he said the moment he was shown in.

"A pass?" The captain frowned. "You want a pass now? I've been trying to get you to take one since you joined up."

Danny didn't remark on that. "Can I accept it now?" he asked hopefully.

"Of course." The captain continued to frown at him, though. "I just find it strange you're coming in now for one. Did something happen back home? Your girl made it back and you need to go and propose?"

It was hard, but Danny managed not to blush as he thought of Becky. He fingered the ring hidden under his shirt as he shook his head and awkwardly cleared his throat.

"I just got a telegram from my friend. He...needs my help with something." The words of the telegram flashed in front of Danny's eyes, but he ignored them.

Something had happened to Jimmy when he'd left the Pacific. He'd stopped writing as much and seemed distant when he did write. Danny had worried about him, but not as much as he did now. Wherever he'd been during his two-year absence, he'd returned to the living world a changed man. And it had something to do with his request that Danny fly to Berlin and help him save a Jew.

"Come back in an hour and I'll have it written up for you."

Danny clicked his heels and saluted. "Thank you, sir," he said before he turned to go.

"Brown."

He turned back and the captain smiled grimly at him. "Come back in one piece."

"I'll do my best," Danny promised.

Forty-Nine
Searching for the Resistance

1944

Japhet had trouble keeping track of days. Whenever the door to his cell opened, he marked it as a new day, though he had no proof it was. He would scratch a mark on the wall with his fingernail before they hauled him out for interrogations.

The first three days were much like the first. Stein threatened Japhet, his family, and Franz. The Nazis also didn't feed him, and Stein continually beat him with his willow-like stick. Japhet's eyes began to blur, making it almost impossible to read the marks on the wall.

Bruises covered Japhet's arms and he assumed his legs even though he never got a good look at them. Every inch of his body ached day and night, but it wasn't anything compared to the mental torture.

"Your family didn't make it out of Germany!" Stein yelled at him day after day. "We caught them! Do you want to know what is happening to them right now? Your sisters are being beaten. Think of that, Japhet Buchanan! And you could end it, if you would just tell me where I can find the resistance!"

Japhet saw their faces. Leah with her warm smile. Hadi's

laughter every time their dad would tease her. Ruth's love of baking and the way she would try and torment him and Franz.

He thought of the time Leah had gotten back Franz and him for a prank they'd pulled on her, buying itching powder and putting it in their beds, and he told himself over and over that Stein was lying.

They'd escaped. All three of them. Jimmy had promised and Japhet relied on him. Jimmy wouldn't break his word. Nevertheless, the image of his sisters being tortured came close to breaking him.

On what he guessed to be the fourth day, Japhet lay in the icy cold cell, shivering and longing for even a small blanket to pull around his shoulders. When they came for him, he was almost relieved as warmth seeped into the cell from the open door.

Japhet recognized Carsten with his ever-present cigarette. The other Nazi he'd seen before but didn't know his name. Together the two Nazis hauled him to his feet since he was too weak to even think of standing. They didn't speak as they dragged him down the hall, past the closed doors and the men crying in pain behind them.

When they brought him into the room with the single chair and strapped him in, Japhet had trouble keeping his head up. Stein clicked his tongue as he stared down at him.

"You don't look like you're doing too good," he said. He motioned to someone standing beside the door. The other Nazi walked over, carrying a bowl and a spoon. "Maybe some food will help."

The thought of food made Japhet's head spin and he couldn't take his eyes off the bowl as the soldier dipped the spoon in, then feed him as if he were a baby.

The soup was revolting. Japhet had no idea what was in it,

but it turned his stomach. Nevertheless, he allowed the Nazi to feed all of it to him and forced his stomach to keep it down.

When it was gone, the soldier left and Stein smiled at him.

"Better?" Stein asked.

Japhet didn't like his smile but couldn't stop staring at him.

"You're stronger than you look," Stein said, "I was so sure you wouldn't be able to last this long. I'm not sure if I am impressed or disappointed."

Closing his eyes, Japhet did his best to ignore Stein. He allowed his thoughts to wander, to his boyhood, to the adventures he'd shared with Franz. He didn't say a word, his cracked lips helping. They bleed whenever he tried to talk.

Sighing, Stein walked over to the table where vials sat. He picked one up, held it to the light, and turned it slowly. Japhet squinted though it didn't do him any good. He had no idea what the different kinds of thick liquid in the vials might be. Whatever they were, he did know they weren't going to ease the aches in his body or help with his starvation and dehydration.

Wrapping his fingers around the vial, Stein bent to study the needles which were laid out on the front end of the table. He selected one – one which looked to be the longest out of them all – and opened the vial. Japhet couldn't look away as the liquid was pulled up into the syringe. He continued to stare as Stein set the vial down, turned and walked back to him.

For once Stein said nothing, he didn't even smile as he pulled up Japhet's shirt, exposing his shrunken and scarred stomach. He didn't look up or give any warning before sticking the needle into Japhet's stomach, injecting the liquid into his blood stream.

At first nothing happened, other than the stab of pain from the needle, but that changed in a matter of seconds. Japhet's whole body went numb, then a stinging, fiery pain doubled him over –

at least as far over as he could go with the restraints holding him
up.

Fear wrapped around Japhet's heart and squeezed. Poison; he
wouldn't have put it past Stein to poison him. He was going to
die. He closed his eyes and concentrated on breathing while he
could.

Images and memories flitted through his mind. There were
memories of him and Franz laying out under the stars in summer,
of him sick in bed and Franz sitting beside him the whole night.

Franz! Japhet lifted his head and wildly looked around the
room. He wasn't there, but Japhet was certain he should have
been.

Stein laid a hand on his shoulder as the burning tried to tear
him apart from the inside out.

"You'll live," Stein said, "but you might want to reconsider
how much about the resistance you want to keep to yourself; that
was one of the milder drugs."

When Carsten and the other Nazi dragged him back into his
cell, Japhet couldn't straighten up. The fiery pain in his stomach
kept him bent over, gasping in small amounts of air. His mind
was dazed and he couldn't pinpoint the exact moment he was
locked back in the room. He laid his cheek on the cold floor and
whimpered in pain. Closing his eyes, he fought to hold on to
memories of his family.

***

Franz left his uniform in the bedroom of his apartment, put on
everyday clothes, and left without looking back. He disappeared
into the streets and set out in search of the resistance.

The first place he started was the cellar where Japhet had been
the night he'd caught him. He hoped to find clues or some idea of

where the other fighters might have gone. Instead, all the cellar held was dust and battered chairs.

"Were they trying to build a barricade?" Franz had muttered before he left.

Franz searched until morning and then found somewhere to hide. He decided he'd only hunt at night to lessen the risk of getting caught. He wanted to avoid the Nazis at all costs, especially since Stein would likely have them out looking for him.

The second night Franz tried to follow Stein to see where he was holding Japhet. He lost him soon after he started following him and risked trailing him again that afternoon. Once again Stein somehow managed to slip away, as if he knew Franz were behind him.

With the sun still shining down on the streets, Franz returned to the cellar and crawled under some of the chairs where he tried to sleep. The moment he closed his eyes all he saw was Stein shooting Japhet in the head before Franz could get to him. He gave up on sleep.

The next morning Franz traded out the cellar for an abandoned apartment room. The walls were bare, but there were marks to show where pictures used to hang. *Jude* was written on the wall in bold, black letters. Franz sat down and faced the letters. He knew he wouldn't be able to sleep with them looming over his head. He closed his eyes and tried not to think about what might be happening to Japhet at that moment.

Exhausted, Franz started up again the next night. He found a bakery just before it closed and bought a loaf of bread. He then wandered the streets, sometimes trailing Nazis on patrol, other times combing through back streets for anything that looked out of place. Berlin had gone unnaturally quiet and the only people he ever saw were the Nazis.

When dawn painted the sky red and orange Franz stumbled back to the cellar. He was too exhausted to find somewhere new to hide and returned to his bed under the chairs. He curled up and closed his eyes, all energy drained from his body. He fell asleep instantly.

Franz didn't think he had been asleep for long when something forced him back into the waking world. He had to fight to get there and his body tried to keep him locked in the deep folds of sleep, but the prodding in his back was relentless.

Fighting his eyelids open, Franz struggled to hold them in that position. He turned his head and fought to focus on the man standing over him. He held a stick and Franz's tired mind screamed Nazi though his body was unable to react.

"Oh, you're alive," the man said, sighing. "I thought you might be dead. I was going to take your boots. How did you get here?"

Shifting his heavy arms, Franz pushed himself up and rubbed his eyes hard. He still couldn't focus.

"I was asleep," Franz murmured, his words slurred. He wasn't going to apologize, though. He was having trouble speaking and was proud of anything he could get out.

"I figured that when you woke up. What's your name and why are you here?"

"Franz Kappel." He was surprised at how easily the name slipped out, after so long hammering into his head that he was Rupert Hoffmann. Franz sleepily wondered if this meant he had left the Nazi side of him, the side which had gone numb to pain, grief, and emotion. He had been so worried he'd killed Franz Kappel, but now he hoped that he might still be there, somewhere.

"Franz..." The man's eyes widened, his face suddenly white. For the first time Franz realized the man couldn't be much older than he was.

Rubbing his eyes hard again, Franz watched as the man glanced over his shoulder, then grabbed his arm and yanked him to his feet.

"You're coming with me," he said, and Franz didn't have the energy to fight him.

***

Danny couldn't get into Berlin. H knew the moment he'd read Jimmy's message, but he flew to the edge of the city and met up with his friend in an open field. Seeing Jimmy walking and breathing made Danny's whole world suddenly better. In spite of his belief, Jimmy hadn't died. Danny felt a strong sense of relief at seeing him standing right in front of him.

The moment Jimmy saw him he walked over and pulled him into a bone-crushing hug. Danny's relief drained out of his body and he remembered his fear when he'd gotten Jimmy's telegram. Something was wrong.

"I was worried I'd never see you again," Jimmy said. He stepped back and looked Danny up and down. He tugged at the stripes on Danny's jacket.

"I always said you'd look good with a rank."

Danny just frowned. Jimmy had never hugged him before; he wasn't the type.

"You never told me that," Danny said, unable to hide his concern. "Jim, what's going on? I want the whole story."

"I have to get into Berlin..." Jimmy began, but Danny glared until he was silent.

"Then tell me quickly. I want to know where you were for those two years and what happened to you. You're different somehow."

Jimmy shrugged so Danny glared harder to get his point across.

"I got myself and Sam shot down...Sam was the one I wrote you about once."

Danny remembered. Jimmy wrote that if he got Sam riled, the Irishman would lose all traces of his American accent.

"I remember," he said, but nothing more, forcing Jimmy to continue.

"We were helped out by a band of the Jewish resistance. They kept us hidden for two years, and I became friends with one of them. A kid...he's only twenty. His name is Japhet Buchanan."

"He's the one we're getting out?" Danny asked.

"Him and his friend. That's why I needed you, Dan. Japhet won't leave without his friend, and I can't carry them both in my plane."

Danny was glad some things hadn't changed. He liked being the one Jimmy came to when he had plans which had little chance of working, but something still wasn't right about the whole thing.

"Why didn't you ask Sam?" Danny didn't want the answer, but he made himself ask.

Jimmy stared at his boots. "Sam was killed, shot while we were escaping. It was my fault because we weren't supposed to be over Berlin in the first place. I was the one who flew us in. I got him killed."

The realization of what that meant slammed into Danny like a truck going full speed. He staggered back and drew a slow, ragged breath.

"Jim." The sudden lump in Danny's throat tried to choke him. He'd been in the army long enough to know the kind of charges Jimmy was very likely going to be facing. He couldn't charm his way out of this.

"Hey, don't get sentimental on me," Jimmy said, smiling. "It's going to be okay, like always."

Danny didn't see how it could be, not this time. This was so much bigger than stealing the crop duster and going for joy rides around the farms. Bigger than jumping off the barn with homemade wings and trying to fly. This wasn't going to end with a broken leg and Danny wasn't sure he could just sit back and watch his best friend stand in front of a firing squad.

There wasn't time to talk about it, though. All Danny could do was pray.

"I'm sorry, Dan. Really. I know I've not been the kind of friend or brother you needed. If God spares us, I'm going to try and make it up to you and everyone else. Thanks for always being there for me. I hope I get to return the favor."

Then, just like that, he was gone, running off in the direction of Berlin. Danny stood by his plane and watched him go.

Fifty
Ways to survive

1944

Franz was led into a house and sat down at a table. The moment he hit the chair he leaned his head on the table and fell fast asleep. When he woke some time later, someone had thrown a blanket over his shoulder and a woman sat in front of him, knitting.

"Good morning," the woman said when Franz slowly sat up, his muscles cramped from sleeping bent over.

"It is morning?" Franz asked, looking at the dark windows.

"Well, no," the woman said, "but if I said good night I was afraid you would fall back asleep and I don't think I've ever seen a more uncomfortable sleeping position. Would you like something hot to drink?"

Franz nodded and rubbed his eyes as the woman stood up and walked over to the stove where she heated up a pot of water.

"Where am I?" Franz asked. He tried to ignore the pounding in his head.

"You're at my house," the woman answered without turning.

"Who are you?" Franz squinted.

"I'm Mrs. Schmidt," she replied.

"Why am I here?" He didn't care if he was being nosy, not anymore. "Who brought me here?"

"Caleb brought you here, and you are here because there are some men who wish to speak to you," Mrs. Schmidt finally turned, "about Japhet Buchanan."

***

Franz was in the room with him. Japhet forced his eyes opened and looked up at him even though his exhausted body told him to go back to sleep. The burning in his stomach helped to keep him awake.

Japhet's heart almost stopped beating when he focused on the blond haired man standing over him. Franz Kappel was smiling, just like when they were kids. That warm, open smile, reassuring him everything would be okay even though the world was shattering around them.

"I knew you'd come," Japhet whispered.

"I told you I'd always be here for you, little brother," Franz said as he bent, holding his hand out to him.

Stretching his arm, Japhet tried to grab Franz's hand but couldn't reach. Slowly he pushed himself to his hands and knees, his body screaming from the effort. Fire tore at his gut, doubling him over. He slowly lifted his head as the room spun around him and saw that Franz still stood there, reaching for him.

"Just take my hand, Japhet!" he begged. "Please! Let me save you!"

Japhet lifted his arm, screaming at the effort it took, and reached. His fingers fell just short of Franz's, unable to even brush them.

"Please!" Franz yelled. "Japhet, please I need you! Just take my hand!"

It was killing him to reach, Japhet could feel the life draining out of him, but he didn't want to give up. He knew if he did, he and Franz would both die.

"Please," Franz whispered, "I can't do this without you."

Japhet threw himself forward but just before he grasped Franz's hand he blacked out.

Japhet woke to stuffy, cold darkness and shearing pain. He screamed, but there was no one to hear. He knew that was wrong. Franz had to hear, Franz always heard. The nightmare would end when those strong arms shook him awake and he was told it would be okay.

It hurt to scream, but Japhet did it again. He screamed Franz's name to the darkness; yelled as loud as his sore throat allowed. All he heard was his own voice, muffled as it came back to him.

Curling up into a tight ball, Japhet buried his head in his arms and closed his eyes. His body began to shake, each shutter spiking pain through his exhausted muscles. There wasn't one part of his body which didn't hurt or burn.

With his eyes closed, Japhet begged for Franz to save him. But Franz wasn't there. He didn't open the door and make the nightmare end, and finally, Japhet drifted back into unconsciousness.

***

Franz had more questions, but Mrs. Schmidt refused to answer and said he'd just have to wait until the men arrived. She then gave him hot, but weak, coffee and led him into the basement where she had him wait until – one-by-one – men sneaked in.

None of the men spoke or acknowledged Franz in his corner until they were all there. There were five of them all together, and they turned on him at the same time. Franz gripped the handle of

Japhet's knife, ready to fight his way out if he had to.

"Caleb says your name is Franz Kappel," one of the men said. As he spoke, he motioned to the man next to him, the same one who had half-carried Franz into the house the night before.

It was intimidating, sitting in front of five frowning men. Franz swallowed and nodded.

"We've heard about you."

That he had been suspecting, from the way Caleb had reacted to his name. Franz just wished he knew what they'd heard about him. Did they know him as the cold, murdering Nazi or as the boy who used to play tag with Japhet?

"You know Japhet Buchanan, don't you?" Caleb asked.

Franz's heart fell at the mention of Japhet's name.

"Yes," he said, "he's my best friend."

"Then you're the Nazi he kept telling us about," Caleb snapped. "The one who betrayed him."

Caleb's eyes scared Franz. They were hallow yet full of anger. A slightly crazed look flickered through them, behind the wrath shimmering in their depths. Franz had to force himself to look into them as he prepared to defend himself, for Japhet's sake.

"I didn't betray him," he said.

"You joined the Nazis!" The hallow look vanished for a second, anger taking its place.

"I joined the Nazis to get information so I could help get our families out of Germany. Japhet wouldn't leave until they were out, and I knew I had to get him out of Berlin before anyone discovered he was a Jew. I did what I thought was best at the time, but I didn't tell Japhet about it and when he found out..." Franz stopped, not even sure if he should be trying to explain it. Even if he had good intentions when he first joined, he still broke in the end and became a murderer.

Unable to look longer into the glares being thrown at him, Franz stared down at his hands. "I don't care what you do to me later, but I have to find him first. I thought if I found all of you, that you could help me. I have to save him; he's like my brother."

Silence filled the room, then Caleb broke it.

"I always wondered just how much of a Nazi you could have become with Japhet as your best friend," he said. "Did you have a plan? Or are you just going to run into wherever he's being held and get yourself killed right beside him? Because I have a lot of land mines...so we can always resort to those if we have nothing else."

Franz blinked and stared, unsure what to say. Caleb was almost smiling and the anger all but vanished. The crazed look showed strongly in his eyes again.

Unsure what good mines would do in saving Japhet, Franz held his tongue. He didn't want to insult the man who carried them.

"I don't have a plan," he admitted.

One of the other men nodded. "Well, right now, I think what you need most is rest. Tomorrow morning, we can tell you the plan Caleb has."

Franz could imagine the kind of rescue Caleb might have thought up.

***

When they came for him again, Japhet tried to put up a fight but his kicks fell short and the two Nazis just laughed when they grabbed him. Carsten wasn't with them this time and Japhet didn't know what to call the two who half-carried him back into the interrogation room.

The day passed like most of the others, only this time it felt worse. Japhet kept reliving his nightmare and would often stare at the door, waiting to see Franz rush in to save him.

"I can break every bone in your body without killing you," Stein said, slapping him to get his attention. "I broke Levi's knee and he lived through it. The bullet was the only thing he wasn't able to survive. Franz broke his fingers. Did you ever suspect that your friend was capable of breaking a Jew's fingers?"

Japhet closed his eyes.

"Did you ever think of how difficult life would be if I broke your fingers? Think of all the things you wouldn't be able to do when your hand healed. If I broke your knee, you might not ever be able to walk again. Is that what you want?"

At the moment, all Japhet wanted was the bullet but he didn't say anything. Stein grunted and brought out a thicker stick than the one he had used before. He struck Japhet's arm so hard Japhet thought he might have broken it. Stein then smashed his leg but somehow managed to not shatter the bone. He hit him in the chest so many times Japhet was certain his lungs were going to be crushed. He swung the stick into Japhet's side and Japhet felt a rib crack.

"Give me answers!" Stein shouted.

Gritting his teeth, Japhet shook his head and Stein grabbed another one of the vials. Japhet wanted to cry. His stomach still burned from the last injection; he didn't want to go through it again.

"Is this what you want?" Stein demanded, holding up the needle so he could see.

Still gasping from his broken rib, Japhet dropped his head to his chest. He didn't want to have to watch again, but Stein grabbed his face and forced him to look up.

"It's only going to get worse!" he snapped. He dug his fingers into Japhet's jaw.

"I won't tell you anything." Japhet tried to ignore the needle, tried to pretend it wasn't there. Instead, he thought of the last time he'd broken a rib. He thought of Franz's scar and how proud of it he'd been.

"You should start to reconsider!"

Japhet didn't feel the needle prick, but he felt the burning liquid ripping through his body. Biting the insides of his cheeks until he tasted blood, he closed his eyes and fought back the scream wanting to tear out his throat.

"Do you think it will scar?" he heard Franz asking.

Stein stepped back and marched to the door. Japhet heard him calling the two Nazis in, ordering them to take him back and make sure he didn't eat and wasn't disturbed for two days. Japhet barely paid attention, though. All he heard was Franz bragging to everyone how Japhet had gotten a broken rib.

***

Franz didn't sleep any better in Mrs. Schmidt's basement than he'd slept in the apartment. One dream haunted him, replaying over and over. In it, he kept entering the room where he'd interrogated Levi.

As if viewing himself through the eyes of someone else, Franz watched as he beat Levi and broke his hand. He dreamed it was he and not Stein who broke his knee. Levi's shouts of pain filled the room but he never once lifted his head.

"We won't get anything out of him," Stein finally said.

Franz blinked and the next thing he knew there was a pistol in his hand. He held it up and fired as if he'd done it every day of his life.

The moment the bullet left the barrel Franz dropped the

pistol. He felt sick to his stomach as he watched Stein walk over
and shake his head at the now dead Jew.

"Stubborn people," Stein said. He lifted the Jew's head and
Franz finally came awake with a jolt.

The Jew wasn't Levi but Japhet.

***

The two days passed in a blur. Japhet slept little, nightmares
waking him up. The drug blurred past and present until he was
unsure of which was which. He wished it were the past, with
its lights and laughter and summer sunshine warming his face;
but he knew he'd had it wrong when the door opened and light
flooded the cell and blinded him.

Carsten was there this time. He yanked Japhet up, not taking
care of his broken rib. The rib wasn't the worse, though; the
movement intensified the fire in Japhet's stomach and he thought
he'd be sick except there was nothing in his stomach to expel.
Helpless, he hung limp from Carsten's hold, smoke filling his
nose.

Japhet's feet scraped the floor as he was pulled down the hall,
and he tried to prepare himself for what he knew was coming.
He searched his mind for one memory he could cling to when
Stein began to beat him, yell, and inject things into him. The pain
in his side kept him aware enough of his surroundings to be able
to think – not clearly, but enough.

He ended up remembering the time he and Franz had gone to
see The Wizard of Oz. He even managed a smile as he thought of
the flying monkeys.

The Nazis are the monkeys, Japhet closed his eyes. *All but Stein.
He's the Wicked Witch of the North. Jimmy is Dorothy.*

The idea of Jimmy with pigtails and wearing a checkered

dress was comical. Japhet would have laughed had his stomach allowed it. He could imagine what Jimmy would have to say about his casting choice.

By then they had reached the interrogation room, but it took Japhet a minute or two to realize this was not the room they normally threw him in. This was the one he had been brought into the first day he'd arrived, the one with all the chairs. It took Japhet a minute to realize Stein wasn't alone. Another Jew stood in the room.

The Jew had to have been one of the other prisoners. He was hallow and he wore no shirt so Japhet could count his ribs. His eyes were large and without any signs of life as he stared off into space, seeing nothing.

"Japhet." Stein smiled as he was placed in a chair and Carsten grabbed his shoulder to hold him upright.

The other Jews are the Scarecrow, all of them who have had their minds taken from them.

"Are you ready to talk today? I have a nice meal set out for you if you tell me what I want to know. I know you must be hungry and in pain. I can fix both those problems."

Sam would have been Glinda, the good witch who only wanted to help everyone. Japhet smiled at the idea of Sam in a billowing dress. It was almost funnier than Jimmy as Judy Garland.

Grinding his teeth, Stein walked over to him and bent down, scowling.

"Do you enjoy this?" he asked, hate glimmering in his eyes. "Because if you don't give me information soon it isn't going to be useful to me anymore. You know what that means, don't you?"

The idea of Stein in a pointed hat and dress kept the smile on Japhet's face.

"Don't you?" Stein yelled and slapped him. "It means I won't

402   Jack Lewis Baillot

need to keep you functional! I will break you, Japhet Buchanan! Even if I have to break your body to do it! You will learn to fear me and regret your stubbornness!"

Carsten moved one hand. Japhet heard a match striking and realized he'd lit another cigarette. When he clasped Japhet's shoulder again, he thought he felt Carsten's hand shaking.

Japhet was the Cowardly Lion, his courage so lost he would never find it.

"You don't believe me?" Stein shouted. He pulled his pistol out of his holster and marched back to the Jew, pointing it at his head. Carsten grabbed Japhet's face, forcing him to watch.

"Tell me what I want to know!"

Japhet panicked. He tried to pull his face out of Carsten's grip, but he didn't have the strength. He fought but only doubled the pain tearing his body apart.

"Tell me!"

The Yellow Brick Road was their way to freedom. He didn't know where the road was and if he was on it or not, but he still wanted to find it and follow it out of Germany.

The shot rang through the room and the Jew fell. Japhet closed his eyes, tears burning them. He hadn't thought he was still able to cry.

"That was your fault!" Stein yelled. "You have just killed a man, Japhet Buchanan! And there are others here, others just like him who I can shoot any time I like. Do you want to kill them too?"

Japhet kept his eyes closed even though Carsten's fingers felt like they were breaking his jaw and Stein was yelling inches from his face.

His childhood was Kansas, lost to him, leaving him with no way back. Throwing him into a world he didn't understand.

Fifty-One
Finding Japhet's files

1944

When Japhet was thrown in the cell after watching the Jew shot, he caught a glimpse of his marks on the wall right before the door was closed. As he hit the floor, he realized he had lost track of the days and wasn't sure how many he'd missed.

Crawling over, feeling his way in the dark, Japhet pushed himself up and leaned his back against the wall. He wanted to pray, but the words of his prayer got stuck on the lump in his throat.

He laid down on the cold floor, too tired to even shiver.

"I can't do this," he whispered. "I can't do this, Franz."

He couldn't watch anyone else die.

He was back in the torture room, but something was off this time. His drug induced mind tried to make sense of it, but he couldn't. Japhet turned his head from side to side even though it took more energy than he had. Nothing looked out of place, other than the fact Stein wasn't there.

It was strange, because all the times he'd been strapped to the chair Stein had never been this late showing up with his smug smile. Stein had to be there. If Stein wasn't there, then something else was coming and Japhet knew it would only be worse. He quickly closed his eyes and tried to find another memory as something moved in one of the corners.

"Remember, Japhet, you can't feel in a dream. No pain or feeling of any kind. If you're not sure if you're awake or it's a dream, just pinch yourself. If you can't feel pain, it's a dream."

Franz sat beside him on the floor of his bedroom, a year after the Buchanans had been shot. Japhet had had so many nightmares during the first year Franz had admitted to being worried he was going to die from lack of sleep. One night, after a particularly bad nightmare, he and Franz sat on the floor and said nothing for a long time. Then Franz told him what he'd recently learned.

"Really?" Japhet asked.

"Really. If it's a nightmare and you pinch yourself and feel nothing, then you will know it isn't real."

Japhet tugged at the straps holding him down and watched as a shadowy figure which looked oddly like Franz walk closer to him with one of Stein's needles. With his arms held down, Japhet wasn't able to pinch himself but he did the next best thing. He bit his lip as hard as he could. Hard enough to draw blood. It didn't hurt.

Japhet relaxed, he even went so far as to smile as Franz stepped out of the shadows and into the light. He held the needle up, but Japhet didn't stop smiling.

"A nightmare," he whispered just as it faded around him.

***

Jimmy had little trouble finding Mrs. Schmidt's house. He'd always had a good memory and sense of direction.

Re-entering Berlin had been fairly easy. He still had his papers and the clothes Japhet had given him when he escaped. Walking boldly down the street was daunting, but no one stopped to shoot him. When Jimmy finally reached Mrs. Schmidt's house, though, his knees were shaking.

Jimmy went around to the back door and knocked, not wanting to take unneeded risks. She opened the door in a matter of seconds and when she saw him standing there, her jaw dropped. She threw her arms around his neck, hugging him tightly.

"What do you think you're doing, you stupid boy?" she snapped when she released him. "I should slap you for being so senseless! What on this earth possessed you to come back?"

Jimmy hadn't realized just how much he missed her until that moment. He gave her his most charming smile.

"I had to come back," he said. "Someone had to get Japhet out."

Tears flooded Mrs. Schmidt's eyes and she yanked him inside and down into the basement which was filled with resistance fighters. They all stared when Jimmy stumbled on the bottom step.

"Jimmy Rodgers!" Caleb was the first one to stop staring and rushed over to slap him on the back. He then frowned as Jimmy gasped for air. "I thought you got out?"

"I did." Jimmy barely glanced at Caleb. He looked around the room hopefully.

"You came back?" Caleb squinted. "Who comes back after getting out of Berlin?"

"I do." Jimmy stopped scanning the room. "I came back to get Japhet. Where is he?" He'd been worried that the Nazis would catch Japhet when he led them off, now he feared it had actually happened.

"Japhet?" One of the other men stood and Jimmy looked over at him. He appeared to be around Japhet's age, with blond hair and red-rimmed blue eyes. Even though he'd never seen him, Jimmy knew who he was, if his white face and drawn cheeks were any indication. It looked like he had the same sleeping habits as Japhet.

"You're foolish to come back," Caleb muttered, suddenly serious. For the first time, Jimmy noticed a change in the insane, bomb-happy Jew. "But, we're all here because we want to do the same thing, so maybe we're all foolish. But sometimes it's okay to be foolish for someone else."

Jimmy took a step back. He laid his hand on the wall to help hold him up.

"They did take him," he whispered.

Caleb's eyes changed even more. They cleared, exposing a depth of sorrow Jimmy had never seen in anyone else.

"Yes. And we're going to save him."

***

Japhet awoke yelling in pain. It took him a moment to realize he'd been inflicting the pain on himself. He'd been pinching his arm so hard he felt blood trickled down it.

The door opened just then and Japhet looked down at his arm. A huge bruise covered it. He raised his eyes to find Carsten looking down at him and his heart sank as he thought of the other Jew. Japhet realized he didn't have the strength to face more interrogations.

Carsten bent over and grabbed his bruised arm. Japhet grabbed his hand before Carsten could haul him to his feet.

"Please," he whispered, his voice shaking and cracking, "please...kill me."

With the cigarette between his lips twitching, Carsten went as stiff as a board. Japhet could feel the Nazi's grip tightening on his arm as he dug his fingers in.

Long seconds passed. Japhet didn't move until Carsten slowly reached for his pistol. He almost closed his eyes when the other Nazi spoke.

"Don't worry, Jew! We'll kill you. That's one wish we can fulfill for you."

Carsten dropped his hand before it touched his pistol. He straightened up, jerking Japhet to his feet as he did so. Japhet fought to stand, but his legs buckled. The other Nazi grabbed his free arm and together they took him back into the room with only one light bulb.

When he was dropped into the chair, Japhet had trouble keeping upright until the restraints were in place, keeping him from falling over. There wasn't a part of his body that didn't ache and he could see no way out of the endless torture but through death. Death which would be long in coming.

By the time Stein entered Japhet was almost ready to beg the man to shoot him. Even more so when he saw Stein carried a stick thicker than the two he'd used before.

"Well, it happened," Stein snapped. He stood in front of Japhet. "Any information you could have given me will be no use to me now."

Eyes on the stick, Japhet made himself think of Jimmy as Dorothy. Stein scared him. This place scared him. Everything scared him right now but nothing more than the sight of the stick. Stein wouldn't shoot him if he begged for death; he would beat out the little life Japhet had in him. His only hope was to keep fighting. So he thought of Sam in a wide skirted dress, waving a wand, and smiled.

Stein thumped the stick against his own leg.

"Your friends have probably all moved on by now, gone off

to a new hole somewhere. And you know what that means, don't you?"

Thrusting the stick under Japhet's chin, Stein forced him to look up.

"That means I don't have to try and keep you conscious enough to get me the information I needed. That means I can make you suffer in every way possible before I allow you to die!"

For a moment Japhet looked into the cold eyes staring into his, then he remembered the bullies who had always yelled at him, who had taunted him. He remembered the times Franz limped to his house with bloodied lips and black eyes and that memory kept the smile on his face even as Stein snapped the stick across his shoulder blades.

***

The American had come back. Franz stared at him as Caleb talked to him, feeling some kind of admiration toward the man who had befriended Japhet when he'd left the apartment.

During the two days Franz had been living in the basement, Caleb told him about what had occurred during Japhet's time there – including everything he knew about Jimmy Rodgers and Sam Winters.

Franz stayed back while Caleb and Jimmy talked until Caleb turned and waved him over. Having no other choice, Franz joined them and Caleb laid a hand on his shoulder.

"Jimmy, this is Franz Kappel. Franz, this is Jimmy Rodgers."

Jimmy said nothing, but the way he looked at Franz told him that Jimmy already knew who he was.

"Glad you're here," Jimmy said after a moment. He spoke in nearly fluent German.

"You are?" Franz wasn't completely sure what he thought of

the American. He wanted to trust him but didn't think Jimmy would be willing, considering he probably had heard Franz had joined the Nazis.

"Yeah. I thought I was going to have to go all over Berlin looking for you."

Franz had always assumed Americans were strange, it was nice to have it finally confirmed.

"Why would you want to look for me?" he asked. "I thought you came back for Japhet?"

"I couldn't take him without you," Jimmy said. "Why do you think he didn't escape the first time?"

It was hard to know what to say. The idea that Japhet had remained behind and was now in Nazi hands because he refused to leave Franz behind made everything worse. If he had been in contact with Japhet, had done something more to find them, this could have been avoided altogether.

"You have a way to get him out once we find him?" Caleb asked before Franz could order his thoughts enough to think of something to say. His mind was in turmoil.

"I have my plane. And my friend Danny came with me."

"You need two pilots to save a Jew?" Caleb asked.

Jimmy sighed in exasperation. "I need two pilots and two planes to get two men out. Weren't you listening? I'm taking Japhet and Franz."

For some reason, that made Caleb laugh. "An American pilot flying back to Berlin to save the Jew and the Nazi...that's a first."

***

Japhet was awakened by screams. His cell had always been sound proof so Japhet pinched himself as hard as he could – and winced when his arm started to throb. He opened his eyes but could see nothing. He lifted his head as the screams turned into begging and pleas, some asking for their lives to be spared, others that they would just be killed.

Knives dug deep into Japhet's heart. The screams could only belong to his fellow prisoners, the other Jews he heard every time he was carried past their cells. Now they were being killed right outside his door, tortured because Stein wanted to make him suffer.

"Stop," Japhet whispered, his throat so dry it sounded more like a strangled choke. "Stop."

He wrapped his arms around himself, but it was no comfort. The screaming didn't stop and over and over Japhet saw Odis, Levi, Seth, Karl, Sam, Leb, and his parents dying. He clamped his eyes closed, but it didn't help.

Japhet buried his face in his arms and cried, dry sobs which shook his body but brought no relief to his tortured mind. He sobbed until the screaming finally stopped and silence once again swallowed him whole. Even then he couldn't stop shaking because, in many ways, the silence was worse.

***

Caleb had to explain his plan to Jimmy as he'd already done with Franz. Caleb said he knew of a back way into the Nazi headquarters and had been in often enough that he could find the papers they needed to learn where Japhet was being held. Franz wasn't sure how well it would work. He'd tried looking for files before, and it had never been as easy as walking into the file room and pulling them out.

"It's stupid," Jimmy said when he heard it. "And insane and going to get us killed. And if it's that easy, why haven't you done it before now?"

Franz continued to sit in silence. He'd been perfecting it over the last few days.

"Where's Odis? He has to have a better plan than this," Jimmy added.

"I couldn't." Caleb looked at both Jimmy and Franz. Once again his eyes flickered between grief and lifelessness.

"Odis is gone," he continued. "He was shot while trying to help Japhet escape the Nazis the night they took him. Look, I know you both consider Japhet your friend, but don't think he means any less to me. I've already lost my wife. I've seen countless friends killed right in front of me. Japhet was one of the few people who still gave me a reason to keep living. I want him safe just as much as you two and I'd have gone in for the files the day he was taken if I could have gotten them. I had to wait, though, 'till they were stored. There was no way I could get them before."

"Oh." Jimmy stared at his hands and Franz clenched the knife at his belt.

"We're going tonight. Be ready." He stood up and walked to the other end of the basement. Jimmy glanced at Franz, but Franz pulled out the knife and stared at it.

Franz jumped when Caleb appeared back in front of him and held a book out to him. It was a book Franz knew all too well.

"Japhet's sketchbook," he whispered. He took it from Caleb's hands and rested it on his legs. It fell open, the pages dropping to a sketch of Leah. Her nose was the wrong shape, but Franz recognized her features.

"I think you should hang on to it, and make sure he gets it back," Caleb said.

When Franz looked up, Caleb smiled at him before he turned and walked back to the other end of the basement. Franz slowly turned pages in the book and a small spark of hope returned to him.

When it came time to leave Franz tucked the sketchbook into the waist of his pants, pulling his shirt over it to help hide it. He then allowed Caleb to lead the way to the Nazi headquarters.

They went along single file, hugging the shadows. Caleb seemed to know where every shadow in Berlin was and stuck to it like he was part of them. They never once entered the light, a trick Franz had not picked up even during the long nights of searching for Japhet.

The headquarters building was dark, though a few lights still flickered in the windows. They didn't seem to bother Caleb, though. He stared at them as he led Franz and Jimmy around the back side of the building, then easily slipped up to a door which was hardly ever used and which – Franz knew – was always heavily locked. He was about to inform the Jew of this but didn't get the chance.

Without a word or sound, Caleb knelt down beside a low window and pulled a thin knife from his pocket. Moving with incredible speed and skill, he had the window opened before Franz had a chance to see how he did it. They next thing he knew they had all managed to wiggle down into the basement and Caleb was frowning in the darkness.

"Hate sneaking around," he muttered. "Wish I could just blow the place up."

Then, with nothing else to declare, he set off again, and Franz and Jimmy had to scramble to keep up. They ended up side-by-side as they followed Caleb down dark halls and corridors, listening for boots clipping on the tile which would alert them to the approach of Nazis.

Caleb marched through the halls as if he were a Nazi himself and had every right to be there. Franz, the only one who had been in those halls and could claim the title of Nazi, was on edge, and he tiptoed. He didn't know where Caleb found his confidence.

Franz sneaked sidelong glances at the dark-haired American as they walked. He hadn't said much to Jimmy since he'd arrived, though there had been questions he wanted to ask. Jimmy didn't act like Franz's time with the Nazis bothered him, but sometimes when Franz turned quickly, he thought he caught Jimmy glaring at him.

It wasn't that Franz blamed Jimmy for being angry with him; he was angry at himself and it was only logical that everyone would feel the same way.

When they reached the room that Caleb was evidently looking for, he quickly picked the lock and they hurried inside. Jimmy and Franz stood watch by the door while Caleb dashed around the room, muttering to himself something about grenades. Franz would occasionally glance over at him, expecting him to pull one from his jacket and blow the place up.

"Don't worry, he's a little crazy, but he isn't stupid."

Franz snapped his head around and stared at Jimmy. He expected to see anger in the American's eyes, or some kind of taunt saying at least Caleb didn't do idiotic things like getting his best friend turned over to the Nazis. Instead, Jimmy smiled.

"Japhet went on some missions with him, and Caleb would sometimes come down into the basement afterward and talked for a while. Japhet said Caleb only liked to go on missions if he could use grenades or mines."

Squinting, Franz studied Jimmy for a few seconds, but he saw no hint of anger or judgment in his eyes. There was pain, and something which reminded Franz of himself. Almost as if Jimmy had lost someone because of something he'd done. He hid it behind a smile, but Franz saw brokenness in those eyes– he almost saw himself.

"How was Japhet, when you saw him last?" Franz didn't feel very conversational, but he had to ask.

Jimmy's smile vanished.

"He's...a persistent kid," he murmured. He stared out of the crack between the door and the jamb. "He was doing the best he could, trying to be a leader and everything, but it wasn't easy on him. He...he didn't sleep well and he barely ate..."

That wasn't what Franz wanted to hear, but he was glad Jimmy was honest with him.

"But he had the will to live." Jimmy looked Franz in the eyes again. "I don't think the Krauts can break him. He has your friendship to keep him going."

If Jimmy had punched him in the stomach, it would have been less painful.

"No he doesn't," Franz whispered. "Didn't they tell you? I'm the one who caught him. I'm the reason he's in there. Japhet thinks I betrayed him."

Jimmy's eyes widened and he opened his mouth to say something, but Caleb interrupted by lifting a file over his head and hissing, "Found it!"

They left the same way they got in and made it back to the basement before dawn turned the sky light. No sooner did they enter the basement than a shadowy stepped into the middle of the room. Caleb thrust the file at Jimmy and drew his pistol. He pointed it at the figure.

"One step and you're a dead man," he warned.

Franz stared in disbelief; he didn't think Caleb had it in him to react so coldly and quickly.

"Caleb."

Franz recognized the voice but not in the same way Caleb did. The pistol fell out of his hands and clattered to the floor. Caleb sagged as if he'd fall over and Warren rushed forward and caught him by the shoulders. In the weak light coming down through the trap door, Warren smiled.

Caleb's face had gone white and his wild eyes reflected things Franz had never seen before. The young man shook head to foot and grasped Warren's arms.

"You're here," he whispered. "I've been trying to get word to you...trying to meet up with you."

Suddenly it wasn't a bomb happy man Franz saw but a young boy.

"Where's Karl?"

Warren kept silent until then. Franz briefly thought of Karl Ritter who should have been his brother-in-law but said nothing as Warren hesitated. He stared at Caleb for a second before he made up his mind.

"He didn't make it."

Caleb's shoulders sagged. "Neither did Odis."

The two stood together in shared grief for a second longer, then Warren released Caleb and turned on Franz. Franz saw his life pass in front of his eyes.

"I should punch you in the nose, Franz Kappel," he said.

Franz swallowed nervously and Jimmy positioned himself in front of him.

"We have more important things to deal with right now," he said as he grabbed the file and held it out to Warren. "I can only assume you're here to help Japhet as well?"

Warren snatched the file and opened it. He held it up to the light and scanned it while Caleb read over his shoulder. He then nodded and dropped the papers to the floor.

"Well?" Jimmy asked.

"We can get him out tonight. We need to wait for cover of darkness."

Franz hated that idea but saw the logic behind it. To try and ease his nerves he ventured to ask Warren how he'd found out about Japhet getting caught.

"I didn't know about it," Warren explained, "but Jimmy told me about you joining the Nazis. I came back to drag both your sorry hides out of here, and Mrs. Schmidt told me about how Japhet had been taken."

Every time Warren looked at him Franz could feel his anger.

"You know Mrs. Schmidt?" Jimmy asked as he sat down on one of the bed pallets.

"She's one of my inside contacts," Warren answered.

"Contacts?" Franz asked. He couldn't sit, so he stood.

"I'm with the resistance too," Warren snapped. "Me, Karl... we didn't want to tell either you or Japhet about it because we didn't want you getting mixed up in the middle of it. Looks like that worked out really well."

Franz could think of nothing to say so he kept silent. It took everything in him to remain calm though, and as Warren and Caleb sat down to talk he did something he'd not done in what he knew to be far too long. He prayed.

He wasn't sure if God would hear him or not, especially after the things he had done, but he needed some kind of assurance and peace from someone bigger than himself.

Fifty-Two
Preparing for death

1944

It didn't feel like a lot of time passed from when the screams stopped to when the door opened. As usual, pain raced through every inch of Japhet's body as Nazis got him to his feet. The cramps in his stomach were worse and Japhet figured the last drug had been stronger.

When they took him out into the hall, Japhet was met with a horrifying sight which made his legs – which he had barely been standing on – sag out from under him. He had suspected whom the screams belonged to, but he wasn't expecting the sight in front of him.

Stein hadn't removed the bodies from the hall but left them there. There were about ten, all so thin they were nothing more than bones with skin stretched over them. Most of their eyes were opened, looks of fear etched on their faces, and all of them seemed to be staring at Japhet as he was led past them.

Japhet tried to fight back. He somehow got his aching legs to work and he stood on his own. He twisted, pulled, and tried to throw himself back into his cell and away from those staring, dead faces. However, his struggles were useless against the two

Nazis holding to him and they continued to pull him along, going slowly to ensure he got a long look at the dead Jews.

They took him back into the room with only one chair and strapped him in, this time pulling the straps so tight Japhet wondered if the blood flow had been cut off from his hands and feet. Not that he cared. He would have welcomed the pain of losing them and was almost glad to see Stein since it meant pain would be inflicted on his body and not his heart.

"How did you sleep?" Stein asked, a wicked smile on his face.

Japhet felt tears — ones he thought he had shed during the long night — prick his eyes. He tried to think of Jimmy in pigtails, of Sam with a wand, but this time none of it worked. The pain was too deep and he knew Stein was winning – he had found a way to break Japhet and Japhet no longer cared. If being broken meant the pain and agony would end he was ready for it.

"You look like you were kept up all night. I hope it wasn't from all that screaming. It gave me such a headache."

Closing his eyes, Japhet tried to find a way out, but he wasn't given the chance.

"Of course, my men were tired by the end of the night and saved two Jews for today. We thought you might like to watch."

The tears refused to stay back. As the door opened and two thin and exhausted Jews were shoved in, the tears escaped and slid down Japhet's face. He looked at the two men, both only a little older than him, and saw nothing in their eyes but emptiness. At that moment, only one thought broke through Japhet's breaking mind.

He hadn't cast anyone as the Tin Man, the man with no heart.

The Nazis who had dragged Japhet into the room stepped in behind the Jews, grabbing their shoulders to hold them upright.

Franz Kappel.

His name jumped out at Japhet and he swallowed back the lump which tried to choke him as he stared at the four men in front of him.

Franz Kappel was the Tin Man. The man with no heart. The man who had sentenced Japhet to this living nightmare and left him there to die.

Stein didn't stop with the Jews. He made sure Japhet watched and listened to their screams, then he had the two Nazis drag their broken and dead bodies out the door and waved his heavy stick in front of Japhet's nose.

"I told you," he snapped, his eyes cold and heartless. "I told you this would happen. I'd ask if you've learned your lesson, but you are never going to get a chance to find out. You won't be leaving here alive, Japhet. Just like all of them. This is where you're going to die."

He stepped back, then crashed his stick into Japhet's left leg. Japhet yelled when the bone shattered. Then, before he could even register the pain completely, Stein struck his shoulder – the same one Odis had dislocated. It didn't hurt as much as his broken leg but enough to make his head spin, then he blacked out altogether.

He wasn't out long, though his sense of time was disoriented. A familiar burning, only this time intensified, woke him. Gasping, Japhet twisted in the chair and pain ripped through his leg and his shoulder.

Opening his eyes, Japhet watched as Stein pulled a needle out of his stomach and he stared down at the other red picks by the new one. Then his whole body convulsed and he closed his eyes, trying to breathe as a feeling like hot iron hands closed over his lungs.

He struggled to draw small breaths as he prayed for death.

It didn't come, though, instead another memory fought to the surface of his fading mind.

They decided to tie a rope to one of the tree branches which grew out over the river. It sounded like a good idea when they planned it, but actually getting it to work was another matter altogether.

Their first problem was they were so excited to swing out over the cool water and drop in they didn't tie the rope tight enough. Franz went first and dropped to the grass when the knot came out.

Laughing, Japhet climbed the tree and tied it again, and then Franz forced him to go first, convinced Japhet hadn't tied it tight enough because he wanted to watch Franz fall again. The rope held this time, but Japhet didn't get high enough and his feet caught the ground and pulled him off, throwing him face first into the dirt.

Franz did no better his second time, nor Japhet his. In fact, they spent nearly half an hour trying to get it just right. When they finally got it, it was worth all the cuts and scraps they had obtained hitting the dirt and rocks. However, by then they had weakened the tree branch and were only able to go once before the branch broke on Japhet's second turn and dropped him back to the grass and dirt. The branch fell into the river and went downstream with the current, pulling their rope behind it.

The burning was still there, tying his stomach into small, tight knots and trying to force out the food he didn't have in his system. Japhet's whole body burned, while, at the same time, he could almost feel the cool water closing over his head as Franz whooped in delight. He could feel the water on his face, followed by air and the sunshine as he surfaced and grinned. Japhet smiled.

"What's wrong with you?" Stein screamed. "Do you enjoy this?" He cracked the stick over Japhet's shoulder blades and he snapped upright, his cramped stomach stabbing with billions of needles.

"Why do you keep smiling?" Stein yelled. He brought the stick down on Japhet's left arm and then his right. "Do you want me to keep beating you?"

Another memory replaced the one of the river. This was a strange one that hadn't come before. It was the memory of the coldest Christmas Japhet could remember. A snow storm had knocked out the heating in the church and everyone nearly froze their toes, sitting and listening to the midnight service.

When it was over, the Buchanans and Kappels went to the Kappels' home and sat in front of the fire, wrapped in blankets while they roasted hazelnuts.

"Are you happy the others are dead?" Stein was yelling. "Is that it? Because you killed them? It was your fault! You know that, don't you?"

The drug made his mind heavy and it took everything Japhet had in him to hold onto the memory of roasting nuts and Franz trying to steal his blanket. He heard his father challenging Mr. Kappel to see who could stay up the whole night and in the end everyone joining in and not bothering going to bed. He saw his mother stand up at five in the morning and kiss everyone on top of the head, telling them Merry Christmas. He even felt her lips touching his hair as Stein brought out his thin whipping stick and beat every inch of Japhet's body. But it didn't matter, none of it. Because all Japhet saw, through the fog obstructing his mind, was his mother's face smiling at him.

***

Franz and Jimmy didn't sleep. Franz paced the floor until his legs felt like they were going to fall off, and Jimmy fiddled with chess pieces, putting them on the board and taking them off as if he were playing a game of chess all by himself.

Caleb was the only one who showed outward signs of calm. When they got back, he lay down in one corner of the basement and fell asleep holding a grenade like a child might sleep with a teddy bear. Franz scowled whenever he looked at him, not because he was mad at him but because he was angry at what the Nazis had done to him.

During all his pacing, Franz had plenty of time to think. He spent most of the day remembering some of the mishaps and adventures he and Japhet had gotten themselves into, and tried to plan things they would do once they were out of Germany. That was harder because he had no assurance Japhet would even want to be around him once he rescued him. After what he had done, Franz didn't expect forgiveness from anyone.

It wasn't just Japhet he knew he'd hurt. Even though he hadn't beaten anyone after Levi, he understood now enough of mental torture to know the Jews he had interrogated were going to spend years trying to get over what he had done to them. Even though he hadn't been tortured as they had, Franz had his brain picked apart and knew what it did to a person.

The memories he held on to only showed him how far he had fallen from the boy who kept getting black eyes because he didn't want anyone to say anything against the Jews. He knew his younger self would have been ashamed of the man he had become and his biggest fear at that moment was that he would never be able to become a better man. Stein had changed him and Franz wasn't sure how to change back. He was afraid the Franz Kappel he used to be had died, and the man he had become would always remain – cold and distant, the kind of person no one could love.

"Don't let them change you."

Those had been his father's instructions before entering Berlin and he hadn't followed them, even though he was unable to find the exact turning point of when he had been changed.

If any man is in Christ he is a new creation, old things had passed away, behold, all things have become new.

The verse hit Franz from seemingly out of nowhere. It had been one he'd heard in church once as a boy but hadn't ever memorized. He hadn't thought about it since he'd been about nine; having it come back left him with a strange feeling. Franz couldn't explain it, but it was almost like someone had whispered the verse to him. And it gave him a small spark of hope.

It was a strange kind of hope. Not the kind which tried to convince him everything would turn out fine, that he and Japhet were going to live and walk out of Berlin together that night. It wasn't the kind which gave him false promises that the things he had done would no longer affect him. It went deeper than that. A kind of hope which gave him a sort of peace. A kind which made him believe he could become a better man – not on his own, but with the help of a God he thought would never be able to love him again.

It didn't take away all his hurt and anger, his confusion and grief, but it eased it somehow. It showed him that his life wasn't over and he would be able to keep going if he allowed Someone more powerful than himself to take control. It was enough to make him realize Stein had not been able to change Franz Kappel completely.

***

Stein didn't take Japhet back to his cell. Instead, he injected him when he was done beating him and left him strapped to the chair when he left the room.

Fire pulsed through Japhet, even before the first drug had

a chance to wear off. Japhet fought and twisted against the restraints, tugging because the drug did not allow him to stay still. Sometimes Japhet was aware of himself wrenching his broken leg. Sometimes he felt pain in his shoulder and rib and he yelled, but mostly all he felt were fiery fingers racking through his chest and stomach.

The drug had a different effect on him than the others. It would ease up for a little while, then come back with sharp, needle-like pricks which made his whole body jerk. Japhet tried to bring back the memories he felt the drug taking from him but couldn't remember any other than the Christmas where everyone got so cold in church.

At first the same scenes kept playing through his mind, images of his mother kissing him and everyone roasting hazelnuts.But then he felt like someone was pulling him back to before, to when they were all still in the church and listening to the pastor's message about a Savior who came to earth to be born in a stable. A Savior, who grew up and died on earth, so that He might save sinners.

Sometimes the memory faded in and out and Japhet would see Sam instead of the pastor. He would hear Sam telling him about God and his message got mixed with the pastor's until Japhet was no longer sure who said what. One thing refused to go, however. He wasn't sure if it was from Sam, the pastor, or both. He heard over and over about Jesus coming to earth as a man and how Japhet had gotten his focus on the wrong things, keeping it on himself and his troubles and not God. And he thought about the memories, the ones that had kept him alive this long.

For the first time in years, Japhet considered his own actions in everything that had happened to him. He knew he hadn't been without fault and he remembered in detail everything that had happened the night he learned Franz had joined the Nazis. He remembered other things as well: how he had never told his friend he had joined the resistance and how he hadn't listened when Franz tried to explain what was going on. He wondered if things would have been different if he had listened.

Then, in a moment when the pain left him for a short time, everything snapped with new clarity. It was strange at first, the way it hit him, but slowly made more sense.

Japhet thought back to the night Franz had caught him and the pain he saw in his friend's eyes when no one else was watching. He'd seen the same look before, the day outside the ice cream shop, when he and Franz had been beaten up.

It had been hard, all those months with Seth, hearing him go on and on about how Franz couldn't be trusted because of what he had done.

That was when the burning gripped Japhet again, sending his body into spasms which took the breath from his lungs. He was certain he was going to die this time. Tears welled in his eyes and he dropped his head to his chest.

Japhet didn't realize he had started to pray until something stirred in the very depths of his heart. A plea beat in his chest, a longing stronger than anything he had ever felt in his life. He didn't try and fight it, but let it pour out, along with unspoken words. He prayed for repentance and forgiveness. For a healing not from his physical injuries but his spiritual ones. He acknowledged his sins – his anger toward God and the Nazis, and even the bitterness he had held against Franz for so long. And through it all he wept.

That was how Stein found him when he returned. Japhet was aware of him as he stood in front of him, watching his body convulse in agony while tears slid down his cheeks. Finally, Stein reached out and lifted Japhet's head, sighing.

"You're a fool, Japhet Buchanan, and I'm tired of this. Do you have anything you'd like to say before you die?"

Japhet wasn't filled with overwhelming courage; he wasn't given any false promise that everything would be okay and he would walk out of those doors with his head held high. Something else calmed him and he knew he could face whatever Stein had for him.

"I had it wrong," Japhet whispered, surprised his voice still worked. "Franz isn't the Tin Man. He's the Scarecrow; confused and unsure of himself because you filled his head with lies. You're the Tin Man, Stein. You're the man with no heart."

Stein ground his teeth and smacked his stick on Japhet's broken leg. Japhet yelled and Stein smiled.

"At least I'm going to walk out of this room alive," he snapped.

Fifty-Three
Final confrontation

1944

Warren took over. He went over details about their escape and how he and Caleb would create a diversion with explosions. They'd then make a run for it while the guards were distracted.

Once that had been worked out they set off down darkened streets, dodging Nazi patrols. Franz finally realized how he and the soldiers had been unable to find the resistance fighters no matter how hard they had looked.

The address in the file they'd stolen was for an abandoned ice cream shop. Franz had seen it before but never paid a lot of attention to it. He never would have guessed Jews were kept and tortured there. He wondered how many other buildings had been transformed for the same purpose.

They entered the shop with Warren in the lead, Caleb, Jimmy, and Franz behind him. When Caleb eased past the broken door, Franz saw a grenade sticking in the waist band of his pants. He hoped he wouldn't start blowing things up for no reason.

The four of them tip-toed across the floor, careful not to step on any creaking boards and alert anyone below that they were coming. They went slowly, which nearly killed Franz. He wanted to run down with pistols blazing and get his friend out while he still could.

There were stairs in the back, near the kitchen. They crept down them. At the bottom, they discovered a long hallway lined with doors. They didn't step down into the hallway, which was lit by dim lights, but instead peered down to see if it was empty. Franz stood on the step above Caleb and bent over him to look. He saw two Nazis at the end of the hall at a table, eating.

Warren turned to face the three of them.

"We have to rush them and make sure they don't have time to alert anyone," he whispered. "Move fast and as quietly as you can while they aren't watching."

Franz nodded and drew his pistol, but ended up entering the hallway last. Warren, Caleb, and Jimmy rushed the Nazis and Franz prepared to follow when he heard someone yelling in the other direction.

Nothing else mattered after that. Franz didn't hear the fight behind him. He barely saw the bodies of the dead Jews laying outside the doors in front of him. All he knew was that he had to get to Japhet while he still lived.

Franz ran down the hall and crashed through the door he heard the shouts coming from. The door flew back and slammed into the wall and Franz stumbled in just as Stein brought a heavy, metal rod smashing down on Japhet's left hand. Japhet yelled and fought against the restraints holding him in a metal chair as Franz staggered backward and hit the door behind him. The handle dug into his back as Stein turned to see who had burst in.

Letting the door hold him up, Franz stared at his best friend while he struggled to breathe. Japhet's face was deathly white, his eyes large and red-rimmed, his body thinner than it had ever been. His hallow cheeks were stretched and strained and his chest barely rose and fell as he struggled to fill his lungs with air.

"What are you doing here, Hoffmann?" Stein demanded. He lowered the stick as Japhet lifted his head and met Franz's staring gaze.

No life shown in Japhet's eyes. They were empty and lifeless, eyes that had seen so much suffering he had been forced to shut his mind down before he went insane. Franz stared into the eyes of a man who had given up. Japhet lived, but Franz feared he still hadn't made it in time.

"Japhet," he whispered, praying he could still reach him.

Those hollow eyes blinked, slowly, and Japhet stirred.

"Franz?" His voice cracked, and he smiled, though it wasn't the kind of smile Franz wanted. It was vacant, one of disbelief. Japhet thought he saw nothing more than a dream, a figment of his tortured mind.

"I came." Franz took a step closer to him, only vaguely aware of Stein still there. "It's really me. I came to get you out. I told you I'd always be here for you."

Blinking again, Japhet's body twisted and he shouted in agony. Franz tried to run to his side, but Stein got in his way. When Japhet raised his eyes again they were no longer empty.

"Franz."

"Franz?" Stein asked. He raised his eyebrows. "Interesting. I always thought your name was Rupert."

It took all his willpower to tear his eyes away from Japhet and take a step back from Stein so he could look at him. But at the same time it was easy, because Franz had been given a small spark of hope.

"Why are you here? You vanished on us, and now you come crashing through the door like a madman." Stein knocked the bar against Japhet's chair.

Anger boiled up inside Franz and he gripped his pistol tightly, though he couldn't bring himself to just shoot Stein where he stood. Instead, he held himself rigidly and refrained from punching out every one of Stein's teeth.

"I'm here for him," he said as he motioned to Japhet. "That's all. Just let me get him out of here and you never have to see me again."

"Him? You came for the Jew?" Stein glanced down at Japhet. "Have you seen him? He's half dead already. I was just about to put him out of his misery."

"Then why don't you get it over with," Japhet whispered. "You've taken everything else from me. Why not my life?"

Franz's temper blazed. "I just want this one Jew. You surely don't want to kill him, not like this."

Stein laughed coldly. "It's because he's a Jew I want to kill him this way!"

"He's just one Jew! You've killed so many others!"

Squinting, Stein studied him closely for a few seconds before he spoke. "You know, I've never trusted you, not completely. Since the day you arrived I've had my doubts. But you were always such a good Nazi, never gave me anything to accuse you of. I heard a story, though, something about you always standing up for a Jew when you were a kid. A Jew named Japhet Buchanan."

Franz had suspected he'd known for a while so he was not surprised when Stein confessed it. He didn't know how to react though and Stein used that moment to twist the pistol out of his hand. He aimed it right at Franz's head.

"Not that it matters," he said, his voice ice cold. "We can settle this once and for all. Franz Kappel, who are you really? Make your choice – either you shoot your childhood friend – or you join him."

Japhet shifted. He lifted his arms as if he hoped to break free of the restraints. Franz didn't want to look at him, but when he heard him move he did and instantly regretted it. Their eyes locked and without meaning it to happen, Franz let book-fulls pass between that look, just like when they were kids.

"Coward!" Japhet croaked. "Stein, you're a coward! Can't kill me yourself so you're going to make him do it? I didn't think you'd back out in the end, but I should have suspected it. I always knew you didn't have the courage to kill me. That's why you put it off for so long!"

Franz had feared Japhet would do something stupid when he finally recognized him as being really there and not a dream. He had been so sure Japhet would hate him after what he'd done, but that one look reassured him of the opposite. Whatever Japhet had thought of him before had vanished, replaced with the trust Franz had seen nearly his whole life. Japhet understood and would do everything to ensure Franz made it out alive, and he couldn't let that happen. Not if the price meant Japhet's life.

"Coward?" Stein shouted. He swung around and pointed the pistol at Japhet. "I should have done this a long time ago!"

He began to pull the trigger, but Franz didn't give him the chance. He threw himself at Stein and rammed him with his shoulder. The shot went wide and the bullet hit the ceiling as Stein crashed to the floor.

Stein jumped up and rushed Franz, aiming for him once again. Franz ducked and lost his balance. He stumbled as Stein crashed into him. They both hit the floor and the pistol slid across the room out of reach.

Struggling, Franz managed to pull Japhet's knife out of the sheath he wore at his side. He clutched it as he rolled, trying to get out from under Stein. They crashed into Japhet's chair once. He howled and Franz shoved Stein back so they rolled the other way.

Freeing his arm, Franz slashed blindly. He felt the knife dig into flesh, his only indication he'd struck anything besides air. Stein didn't relax his grip on Franz's other arm. If anything he just held on tighter.

Trying to stab him somewhere that would force him to relinquish his hold, Franz aimed for his chest but Stein moved and he stabbed him above the knee instead. Stein shouted and jerked and the knife tore deeper into his leg, slicing up as Franz struggled to hold onto it. He yanked it out and slashed, the same way he'd taught Japhet. This time, he brought the blade across Stein's left arm and side.

Enraged, Stein punched him on the side of the head and Franz stumbled. He fell back as Stein got to his feet and snatched up the pistol which now lay close at hand. He wavered as he balanced most of his weight on his one good leg.

"You failed, Franz Kappel!" he shouted in rage.

Franz gripped the bloody knife as he rolled to his knees.

"I failed?" he asked. He tried to sound confident, cold. The Nazi Stein had tried to make him. "Haven't you heard? Germany is failing. Your dream of Hitler's Third Reich won't last the year." Franz embellished on rumors he'd heard. "And look at you. You're bleeding to death. You failed the fatherland...you couldn't even kill one Jew."

Stein stared down the barrel at Franz. Neither of them moved, but Franz could see that his words took effect. Maybe Stein didn't believe him about Germany, but he had to believe he was bleeding to death. Already his face had gone white and his hand shook as he held the pistol.

"Give up," Franz encouraged. "Why bother fighting? It's over."

The pistol inched down and stopped close to Stein's leg. His eyes hardened and Franz coiled, ready to jump out of the way.

"Maybe I have failed," Stein said, "but at least I can die with the knowledge that you did too."

He turned and fired at Japhet. Franz threw himself forward but couldn't stop anything. He could only watch as Stein turned the pistol on himself and another explosion seemed to shake the room. Stein crumpled before Franz reached him.

"Japhet!" Franz slipped and stumbled to his friend's side. Japhet's shoulder bled and his head had dropped to his chest. Franz gently touched his arm, dropping to his knees when Japhet looked up.

"You're an idiot!" Japhet croaked weakly.

Franz used the knife to cut away the straps. His hands shook and Japhet winced every time he bumped him. The room spun around Franz until he felt nauseated.

"I'm the idiot?" Franz demanded, emotions surging through his body. Relief was the strongest. "Me? What were you doing, taunting him like that! He almost shot you in your stupid head!"

"I was trying to save you!" Japhet gasped, all of his words garbled as he struggled to talk. He slumped over again, his breathing ragged.

"You're the one strapped to a chair! I came here to save you!" By then Franz had all the straps off.

For a moment he and Japhet stared at each other, then Japhet smiled and Franz pulled him down into a bone crushing hug. Weakly, Japhet wrapped his arms around him and when Franz released him, he sagged forward. Franz caught him, easing his arm over his shoulders as he knelt down in front of him.

"Here," he whispered, "lean on me."

Franz helped him to the floor just as Japhet went limp in his arms. At the same time, Warren, Jimmy, and Caleb rushed into the room, stopping so fast Caleb ran into Jimmy.

"What happened?" Caleb demanded.

"Is he dead?" Jimmy ran over and dropped to his knees beside Japhet. He felt his neck for a pulse. Warren knelt beside him, his face drawn and white with concern.

"No." Franz shook his head. "We saved him. He needs medical help, but we have to get him out of Berlin fast and somewhere where he can be treated." As he spoke he pulled off his jacket and cut it up. Quickly he made a makeshift bandage which would stop the bleeding in Japhet's shoulder for the time being.

Jimmy filled his lungs with a deep, shuddering breath and Caleb actually cried. Warren said nothing but the look in his eyes spoke enough. All Franz could do was sit beside his best friend and pour out his thanks to God that he'd been spared. Then, without a word, he and Jimmy pulled Japhet upright. Easing his arms over their shoulders they made a sling of their free arms. Together they carried him out of the basement where he had spent two weeks of torture.

***

Japhet wasn't aware of his surroundings. The pain slamming into his body was too much to endure and he slipped in and out of blissful unconsciousness. He only woke up once, as he was being carried out of Berlin between Jimmy and Franz.

He had no idea how much happening around him was real, but he heard an explosion and the sound of running feet, and then a shout of voices. He thought he recognized Warren and

Caleb.

"Some are coming this way!" Caleb shouted.

"We'll lead them off," Warren said, as calm as Japhet had always remembered him.

"But..." Franz protested.

Warren interrupted him. "I'm staying with Caleb in Berlin until this is over. But you have to get out, get Japhet out. Now!"

"We'll meet when the war is over," Franz quietly said.

"Bring mines," Caleb said. Then he yelled and ran down the street. Japhet thought he saw Warren run after him, then Franz and Jimmy were rushing out of the city before anyone noticed them.

Outside the city, in an open field, they were met by a black man whom Japhet could only assume to be Danny. Franz and Jimmy eased him into a plane and at that moment, it became real.

Before, with his body racked with pain and his mind unable to make sense of everything going on around him, Franz had been right beside him. Now Japhet's foggy mind grasped to the realization that Franz would fly out with Danny and would no longer be at his side.

Stretching out his aching right arm, Japhet made feeble snatches for Franz's sleeve as he turned to climb off Jimmy's airplane. Japhet weakly called his name, not sure he could go through another nightmare of losing him. This nightmare felt so real, Japhet couldn't risk it fading and dropping him back in that cold, black cell.

Franz turned and grabbed his hand; he held it tightly. Japhet could feel the warmth of his hand and reminded himself this had to be real or he wouldn't be able to feel anything.

"It won't be long," Franz whispered. He squeezed his fingers. "The nightmare is over. You survived, and I'm going to be beside you until you're better. I promise, Japhet. I'm not leaving you, ever again. I'm going to be there when we land, and I'm going to be there for whatever happens next. You and me, just how it should be."

Japhet smiled and settled back into the seat of the airplane because this time, he did believe it. The nightmare was finally over and Franz had come back for him. They could make it through whatever happened next together.

Afterward

The world changed after WWII. For maybe the first time in modern history everyone saw how evil humans could be. But they also saw how brave and selfless people could rise up and fight back.

All of the wicked seen in the world left a lasting impact on those exposed to it. Some couldn't move on. They gave in to bitterness and hate. Others found hope and a chance to start over.

James Rodgers made it back to his squadron only to later face court marshaling. Thanks to a letter sent in his defense he didn't stand in front of the firing squad but was dishonorably discharged. Stripped of his rank, he returned home where the first thing he did was go to Sam Winters family and tell them that their son died a war hero.

Daniel Brown returned to finish the war. When it was over, he returned to the apartment building in Queens, where he was met by Jimmy, who had a surprise for him. Jimmy's sister, Becky, made it back from France and awaited Danny with a smile and a kiss.

Caleb Webber survived the war as did Warren Faust. The two friends were reunited and moved to France where Warren met and married a French girl. Caleb moved in with them later on and Warren kept a constant eye on him, helping him recover as best he could.

Japhet spent a week at Jimmy's base. He was put under the special care of a medic who treated enough of his wounds to keep him alive long enough to get him to a hospital. Once at the hospital Franz made sure Japhet was given the best care possible. Japhet made a slow, but steady, recovery, though there were things he was never healed completely from. His left hand had been shattered, and while he was able to gain the use of most of it again, he faced limitations. Franz became his left hand.

Once Japhet was released from the hospital both he and Franz traveled to Queens with Jimmy, where they shared his apartment with him. When Danny returned, the four of them lived together for two years.

During those two years, Japhet and Franz located their families and helped get most of them to America (Gabi decided she liked France and remained there). When they arrived in New York, Franz made sure there were apartments waiting for them. The reunions between them all were happy, though bittersweet as they were reminded of those who couldn't be with them.

After years of suffering nightmares and depression, Japhet began to recover thanks to Franz, Danny, and Jimmy. Four years after making it out of Germany, Franz met a waitress named Judith, who introduced Japhet to her best friend, Susan. Days before his twenty-fifth birthday, Japhet and Susan married. Susan insisted on the wedding being a traditional Jewish celebration, her way of showing she accepted everything about Japhet's past.

On arriving back home, Jimmy began to date Sadie, and later he and Sadie, Danny and Becky had a double wedding. It was a huge occasion, probably being the only wedding at the time where a white girl married a black boy, and a black girl married a white boy. And if that wasn't enough, Jimmy and Danny were probably the only two WWII pilots who asked a former Jewish Resistance Fighter and a former Nazi to be their best men.

Franz married Judith only a few months before Japhet and Susan's wedding. Later all four couples moved to the country, to the Rodgers' farm where they started new lives and moved past the war.

Historical Note

While writing this book I did my best to make it as historically accurate as possible. I researched everything I could get my hands on dealing with Berlin and Germany during WWII as well as the resistance.

There is one liberty I knowingly took with my story.

The Wizard of Oz came out in America in 1939. I know it is impossible the movie could have come to Germany the same year, even more so that someone would have translated it into German. In spite of this, once I got the idea to use the movie in my story I couldn't take it out. Therefore, I took my historic liberty. My only hope is that I will be forgiven this fault. (I also feel the need to point out Sir Walter Scott moved the jousts a hundred years around while writing Ivanhoe. I think my argument for my inaccuracy will be as follows... "At least I didn't pull a Sir Walter Scott.")

I hope you enjoyed the book and my little Oz connection.

Special Thanks

I have had the idea for this book for years but have always been too scared to write it. I knew it would not be easy, but I didn't realize just how hard it would be until I started.

There are three very special people I'd like to thank, because, without them, this story would not have been written.

William Knisley, who patiently took the time to answer each and every one of my war questions. No matter the problem I was having, no matter the plot troubles I ran into, I knew I could go to him and he would help me work out every little detail. He was a walking Wikipedia, only a hundred times more reliable.

Anna Dahl, my Phil. I don't know what I would do without her. If I'm ever arrested for doing something stupid or kidnapped by the mafia, Anna will be at my side. There are few people who willingly take part in all my wild schemes and I always know I can rely on her. I have come to value her friendship as something closer than a sister; as a best friend. It is thanks to her I understand the true meaning of friendship which I hoped to capture in my book. I'm sure when we became friends eight years ago she had no idea I was going to turn into the sort of friend who asked her advice on Nazi torture methods. I don't know what I would do without her and her amazing sense of humor and willingness to put up with me. And when the time comes for me to explain my web search history I'm counting on her to testify in my favor.

Bella DeLallo. My Ben, who kept me writing even during the days I threatened to give up. I knew I could count on Ben when I became discouraged over the story and felt like I was killing it. I don't know how many times I sent her messages of me screaming in agony over how the book was turning out, how I thought I was ruining it, or just sobbing over how hard it was to write. No matter what was happening, I could turn to my dear Ben and she would shove me on toward the finish line. Without her constant encouragement, this story would not have been written.

I'd also like to thank all of my blog readers who put up with me when I all but disappeared for the month I was working on the rough draft and who encouraged me by saying how much they wanted to read this book.

A special thanks to all my wonderful beta readers and editors. Every single one of you helped me so much. I don't know what I'd have done without you.

I hope the story is worth all of the insanity and craziness I put everyone through to reach the end.

The Author

Jack lives in a house because her tree house fell down when she was jumping up and down in it. She sleeps on a bed because her hammock developed a fault. She has always been known for being less than normal, but her insanity has reached new levels.

She spends most of her time writing, but when she isn't doing that she is usually trying to find ways to make her friends' fictional pain worse. She has taken to sitting in her dark room and laughing evilly while rubbing her hands together.

Between writing and trying to solve the mystery of why she even has friends, Jack is kept busy by practicing her leg breaking skills. There's a rumor she someday plans to break the leg of a famous actor or the future husbands of her friends. Depends on which she finds first.

You can learn more about her and her books at jacklewisbaillot. com